TERMINAL NEGLECT

A novel

Michael Rushnak

PublishingWorks, Inc.
Exeter, NH
2008

PublishingWorks, Inc.
60 Winter Street
Exeter, NH 03833
603-778-9883
For Sales and Orders:
1-800-738-6603 or 603-772-7200

Cover design by What! Designs.

LCCN: 2008923237
ISBN: 1-933002-69-7
ISBN-13: 978-1-933002-69-9

Printed in Canada.

Acknowledgments

Terminal Neglect began as a non-fiction story. Initially, it was to be about my personal journey after being diagnosed with cancer almost six years ago. My roller coaster ride since that awful day of being told the diagnosis has been rocky, to say the least. Three years ago, I decided to write *Terminal Neglect* as a fictional story highlighting the critical importance of living out our dreams in the brief time that we all have on this planet and to show how each of us can make a difference to make this a better world.

My special gratitude goes to Francine, my wife and best friend of thirty three years. She not only has been there every second since day one but she has been my principal sounding board in writing this novel. As an avid reader, Francine has been enormously instrumental in assisting me every step of the way in testing storylines that work, and in formulating character development through countless revisions. Our children have been a source of incredible inspiration for this story of an idealistic physician who fights the evil doers in doing what he believes is the right thing to do. Many thanks to Jennifer and Jeffrey and especially to Mark for providing ideas to keep me going when the next chapter page was blank.

Over the years, there have been so many friends, family, and experts who have provided invaluable support to me in creating this work. To start, I want to thank Michael Palmer, Tess Gerittsen, and Steve Babitsky for providing me with the critical tools to become an author. My sister, Dolores Koehler, is to be commended for her insightful comments and patience in providing valuable feedback on the dozens of drafts that she has so thoughtfully reviewed. Kate Petrella, my copy editor, Val Kraut, and Dr. Jay Blum deserve particular credit for their perceptive contributions.

On my voyage to complete *Terminal Neglect*, I was fortunate to meet a dynamic team at PublishingWorks through a referral from Judy and Dr. Frank Malinoski. My editor, Jeremy Townsend, is worthy of the highest praise in continuously stimulating me to take my writing to the next level. Carol McCarthy is a marketing wizard who has guided me through the exciting process of promoting my story. Jeremy, Carol, and I will deeply miss the late Phil Englehart who saw real life parallels in *Terminal Neglect* and who was chiefly instrumental in the four of us coming up with this title that captures so well the spirit behind this work of fiction.

For the many others who have supported my efforts to complete this first novel, you have my most sincerest appreciation.

I dedicate this book to Francine, my wife and love of my life, and to our amazing children, Jennifer, Mark, and Jeff. Your enduring support of my dreams enables the good in all of us to eternally triumph.

Prologue

Beth Murphy sped away from Mercy Hospital, her eyes blinking back tears as she headed for the airport. Sam was the only hero she had ever known, and now he was undergoing a last round of chemotherapy. She hoped that it would save him. Beth owed him everything. Her sorrow crushed her. She remembered the day her father aimed a double-barreled shotgun at her face, his finger about to squeeze the trigger. What happened next was a dark secret that she shared only with Sam. The rental car steering wheel shook in her hands. It had all seemed like yesterday.

Thirty minutes later, she pulled into the parking lot at Detroit Metro Airport. She mindlessly passed through the security checkpoints. Beth looked forward to returning to DC. It was Sam's workshop. It was where he was well known as a dedicated champion of patient rights and drug safety. A tenured member of the Board, he battled the drug companies through the oversight process at National Quality.

In recent visits to Mercy, Beth heard Sam repeat, for at least the nineteenth time, that her short stint on the Board at the drug safety review company was simply to keep his seat warm until he recovered from his recent cancer flare-up. She recalled his passionate belief that many ill-informed, underage, and desperate souls took risky experimental drugs in clinical trials just for the money, offering themselves as potential sacrificial lambs on the altar of rapacious drug companies.

Sam realized that he had become a lightning rod, attracting hostility from most members of the Board. Yet he was always more than willing to take any risk by speaking out to protect an unsuspecting population that seemed to have no other champion. Beth believed that she too was on a mission to save lives just as Sam had once saved hers. As the jet sped down the runway, the tears returned. She hoped that he would be released soon from Mercy Hospital. It was obvious to her that the country needed someone like Sam to fight against greedy drug barons. In a few hours, she would be landing at Reagan. She slowly drifted off, taking comfort that she would not be alone in their life-long quest to save innocent lives.

••••••••••

Sam had been heartened by Beth's visit. She was his future. He had painstakingly groomed her to be his replacement. Even before his own well-publicized trial for the murder of her father, and his adoption of her, he believed in his gut that she had the spunk to make things happen. He pictured her face, so alive with promise; everything about her demonstrated an unquenchable thirst for justice. After what had happened to her—how she was used by the drug companies for the testing of dangerous drugs—he could understand that hunger. But somehow she hadn't turned her hate on the man who put her in that danger—her own father. She had feared him, but still forgave him. Sam prayed that he was burning in hell. Beth just wanted to put the crooks in government, medicine, and the pharmaceutical companies in jail. Sam understood her rage.

His mind wandered as he gazed at his own emaciated body. He knew his days were numbered. It would be Beth who would have to carry his torch. His own daughter, Penny, was gone . . but that was a nightmare he couldn't revisit. The image of her lifeless body, swinging at the end of the rope . . .not now, not lying here with a needle in his arm, connecting him to the fluids that were, at least temporarily, keeping him alive.

The intravenous pole kept him from turning freely in bed. He felt restless, despite the sleeping pill he'd been given, and dreaded going to sleep. He feared that his nightly demons would once again pay their customary visit in his dreams.

Sam jerked when he heard a solitary footstep at the doorway. He smelled a fresh whiff of cigarette smoke.

"Who's there? Nurse?" But he sensed that it wasn't his nurse. There was something different, something sinister about the presence.

Sam reached for his bedside reading penlight but it rolled off the hospital tray. He lunged for it and fell out of the far side of his bed. A tumbling pillow absorbed some of the force from his plunge onto the black-and-white hospital tiles, but the fall caused the needle to pull from his arm, shearing his skin. Bewildered, he sat on the hospital floor behind his gurney barricade.

He felt something pressing into his buttocks, and found he was sitting on the penlight. He aimed the narrow beam skyward. The stream of light bounced off the face of his intruder. Sam inhaled the cigarette aroma worn by the visitor as it splashed downward.

Barely two feet away from him, the intruder whispered, "My friend, it's time." The voice was soft. Sam couldn't tell if it was from a man or woman.

"Time for what?"

"Don't go there."

The visitor wore an oversized baseball cap and a green Mardi Gras–type mask. The false-looking gray beard covered the intruder's jawline. The figure was no taller than Sam's own five-foot-seven stature, and slimly built.

"Who are you? What are you doing here?" Sam stammered.

"You don't remember me?"

Sam frantically peered up at the figure. "Wait a minute. Those eyes . . ."

"Listen, old man, this plan is bigger than us. We can't stop this from happening."

Sam spoke with a quiver in his voice. "What plan? Stop what?"

But then something connected. The pieces jelled. Sam felt his bowels turn to liquid. "No," he cried. "Not you, of all people!"

"Afraid so. You know, we don't like whistleblowers."

"But I trusted you all these years."

"Never again, my friend."

The visitor backed away from the foul odor and cursed loudly. "Damn, no matter how much time I spend in a hospital, I'll never get used to that god-awful smell."

"Where is my doctor?" Sam demanded.

"You flunked your tryout for The Health Club. And, as far as your doctor is concerned, he's not on call tonight."

"What club?" Sam felt his heart pounding so loud that he strained to hear a response.

"Sorry, membership is by invitation only."

Sam heaved himself back to bed by tugging fiercely on the sheets. Now separated from his visitor by less than a yard, the nurse call button was still a foot away. He made a quick lunge for it, but his arthritic wrists suffered a well-placed chop by the visitor.

He was stunned and exhausted. Sam barely noticed the twenty cc syringe that was being inserted into the central venous line port under his right collarbone. The nonstop flopping in his chest distressed him. He caught a quick glimpse of the visitor pushing down the plunger. An instant later, he felt his muscles twitching. All memories rapidly faded except for fleeting images of those good times that he once enjoyed with Beth. Within seconds, he closed his eyes for the last time. A brew of excessive amounts of his chemo concoction spiced with lethal doses of potassium chloride had swiftly worked its murderous magic.

••••••••••

Before reaching the hallway, the visitor discreetly pocketed the facial masquerade and cap and nonchalantly walked out of the front door of Mercy Hospital, knowing that no one would even bother to check what just happened in Room 202. One fact was clear. Sam Murphy would not be the last to fall prey to the leaders of The Health Club. The Harley sped away from the hospital that night, leaving no one the wiser.

Chapter One

"Some men see things as they are, and ask why?
I dream of things that never were, and ask why not?"
—George Bernard Shaw, as paraphrased
by Robert F. Kennedy

Damn the President. A sea of faces surrounded Dr. Jonathan Rogers as he shuffled his way down Pennsylvania Avenue toward the hotel, silently cursing. Then one familiar face popped out. He steered toward the redheaded woman, trying to shake off his foul mood. He remembered her name—Haley—and smiled. With each plodding step in her direction, his smile broadened. His early morning conversation with her while they soaked in the steamy waters of the Marriott Hotel hot tub came to mind. But then he thought of Kim, and felt a pang of guilt. He wanted to believe that Haley was just a passing fancy. His marriage was on the ropes, but he somehow believed they could work through their problems. At least Rogers hoped they could. Still, he wondered what it would be like to be with someone so young and exciting.

The young woman's stride, confident and bold in her pale blue coat, cut easily through the noontime bustle. No more than ten feet away, Roger's gaze latched onto her sensuous light green eyes, now strangely frozen in place, her silky-smooth face as tempting as it was earlier that morning.

Abruptly, Haley stopped on the snow-covered sidewalk, just opposite the Ellipse. She flipped open her cell and appeared to speak forcefully. He wondered what to say as he walked closer to her and settled on asking her to join him for a drink. That's harmless, he reasoned. And after his meeting with the President, he sure could use one. Before he could greet her, however, she rushed toward the curb. A DC taxi screeched to a halt. She spun around to face Rogers with a glint in her almond-sized eyes before she climbed into the front seat of the taxi. Rogers tracked the cab down the avenue until it disappeared from sight.

Standing still on the busy avenue, Rogers was suddenly shoved from behind, and he fell forward onto the icy sidewalk. He looked up at a couple of teenage boys roughhousing among the fast-moving lunchtime crowd. Rogers struggled to regain his footing, and winced as he looks down at his bloodied hands and the torn kneecap silk of his Armani suit. He limped over to the inside of the sidewalk, away from the crowd, and pulled out his cell phone.

A woman's voice answered, "Jonathan? How did it go?"

"It's over," he said.

"What's over?"

"I should have listened," he said as if she hadn't spoken. "You told me that it would end this way."

"No, I said I didn't think you would make the cut. You just don't fit the mold."

"But, I have all the right credentials. I'm better prepared for this job than anyone else in America."

"Please, we went through this before. So, what happened during your interview?"

"Not what I expected from the most powerful man on earth."

"Jonathan, get to the point!"

He paused for a few moments, grimacing. "Anyway, I just fell pretty hard on the ice."

"Are you hurt?"

Rogers glowered back at the White House. "No, those people can't hurt me."

"I'm talking about your fall on the ice. Stay put. I'll be there in a minute to help you. I'm walking through the hotel lobby."

He shook his head. "Kim, you know what I have always believed? When your dreams die, you die."

"At least now, you'll have more time to spend with me. We'll celebrate tonight."

"I'm in no mood. Anyway, it's only been a few months. Don't think I'm ready."

"Then why did you ask me to come here with you?"

"How about giving me some moral support for starters? You know that my interview with the President was important to me."

"You could have brought the dog if all you wanted was a friend."

He blurts out, "I can't believe you said that!"

"What do you want me to say!"

"Never mind . . . I don't know. I guess I just wonder what the hell has happened to our generation. We were supposed to change the world. Doesn't anyone care anymore about doing what's right?"

"Hey, I just know one thing." Kim's voice was calm now, gentle.

"And that would be?"

"What's right is for us to put our problems aside and focus on connecting again with one another. Let's have some fun for a change. Before we left Michigan, I thought you said you were ready. That *we* were ready."

"I was hoping to work things out, but you just don't seem to understand me anymore."

"You're obsessed with public health. But it has to be your way. Reality is not black and white, Jonathan."

"I know that. But the gray area of compromising basic principles won't give us universal health care."

"The blurring of the truth . . . the gray zone . . . is where politics thrives. Maybe you should stop thinking about becoming Surgeon General. Maybe it's not meant to be."

"I'm not going to forget it, or give up. The country needs decisive leadership, not backroom political deals between the special-interest groups."

"Then if you really want the damn job, you'll just have to follow the President's lead like everyone else. That's the way it works down here."

"I'm not his puppet. The Supreme Court crowned him, not the people."

"Listen to me. You're not in command. If you can't let go of your dream, then just follow the President's lead."

"You're fading. I think I'm losing . . ."

". . . follow the President's lead."

Rogers closed his eyes, feeling completely alone. He heard a couple of whizzing sounds zip by his right ear just as an intense stabbing pain struck him in his upper chest, followed by a sensation of damp warmth. He looked down and saw a crimson-colored spot of blood rapidly spreading across his starched white shirt. He stumbled, catching a fleeting glimpse of a young man, a jogger, dressed in sweats and sneakers. The jogger was hobbling toward a nearby stone ledge. Blood stained his pant leg.

Rogers wiped away beads of sweat from his forehead. Unable to focus, his mind whirled as though he had just climbed aboard a merry-go-round. Fuzzy-looking images were slipping away with each spin. Kim's face flashed before him. Then their daughter, Ashley. He frantically reached out to them for help, touching nothing, and fell to his knees. The avenue grew darker while he sucked each breath, fighting the mounting suffocation. His hands clawed the frozen sidewalk to steady himself against the brisk winds until he collapsed, crashing face down onto the slick pavement.

Chapter Two

Less than an hour earlier, Rogers felt as though he was floating on a magic carpet ride as he was being escorted down the red-carpeted, ornate hallway by a presidential aide. The elegant trappings of the Oval Office seemed to mesmerize him. The eastern sun, flowing through the double-hung windows, appeared to cast an ever-widening halo around the large frame of the President. As soon as his hands were enveloped in the greeting, President Will Jordan's iron-like grip caused Rogers to clench his jaw tightly. The small bones in his hand felt as if they were in a vice. He was being reeled toward the commander in chief as he tried to hold his ground. But he was off balance and felt violated by the President's aggressive handshake and piercing crystal-clear blue eyes.

"Dr. Rogers, welcome to the People's House. Your boss, Governor Peabody, assures me that you're just about the most effective Commissioner of Health in the country. He believes that your widespread popularity could help my administration if I choose you as my next Surgeon General."

"Mr. President, it's my honor and privilege to be considered," Rogers said a bit stiffly. "Providing health-care policy analysis to you and the Secretary of Health has been my dream for quite some time."

The President released his hand and grinned. "What I need are team players. But there is only one captain. I hope you know what I mean."

Rogers bit his lip, trying to ignore the President's insinuation. He remained silent.

The President's face hardened. His campaign grin vanished into a snarl. "Well, do you?"

Rogers chose his words carefully. "Yes, Mr. President. I promise you that I'll work for what's best for America."

Jordan chuckled. "That's a nice sound bite, Doc."

The commissioner replied softly, "It's the truth, sir." He wiped his moist hands on the back of his trousers.

"Well, Doc, your day of reckoning is about to begin."

"I hope to convince you that I can make things happen."

"Really?" the President replied under his breath while strolling over to his massive oak desk. He leaned over, pushing a gold button under the side ledge, just below his personal notepad, which teetered over the edge.

Dr. Rogers walked toward the couch and wondered whether the President's secret hobby was squeezing rubber balls. His hand still ached from the handshake. He remained standing until Jordan took his seat in a high-backed red-leather chair. The President gestured toward the couch. Rogers felt the knots in his neck muscles tightening with each tick of the Ben Franklin wall clock. While rubbing away the tension, he noticed Jordan picking up a vinyl-covered manila folder from the coffee table.

"Give me a moment to scan the executive summary in your file."

"Of course, Mr. President." He forced a weak smile and scanned the Oval Office, resting his eyes on the two flags behind the presidential desk.

After thumbing through a few pages, Jordan glanced up and furrowed his eyebrows. He said, "By the way, you better be ready for Ms. London. She can be a real pit bull."

"May I ask, sir, who she is?"

Jordan cast his eyes back on the report, saying nothing. A moment later, the blue desk phone rang.

"Excuse me, Doc. I've been waiting for an important call. Probably my granddaughter. Stephie promised to let me know how she made out at her softball game."

Rogers leaned back and stretched, watching the President beam as soon as he picked up. But all the while, he could not blot out the thought of a pit bull named London waiting in the wings.

"Good job, Stephie. Talk soon. Love you." Jordan hung up the phone and puffed his chest. "She threw a shutout in her first varsity game. A chip off the old block."

"Mr. President, I know how you feel. Our daughter Ashley just placed in the top ten in her first 10k race. We're so proud."

"We checked you out, Dr. Rogers. You're a family man. Your loyalty will serve you in good stead should I appoint you as my Surgeon General."

The door creaked slightly and Rogers looked up. An attendant stood in the doorway carrying a gold-plated tray bearing three coffee mugs and several enormous chocolate chip cookies. After being waved forward by the President, the young man set down the tray on the coffee table and left.

"Doctor, please," Jordan offered.

"Thank you, sir."

He chose one of the five-inch cookies and glanced up just as a smartly dressed middle-aged woman walked briskly through the open doorway. Her heels echoed off the marble floor. Jordan tossed the manila folder onto the coffee table, almost capsizing a pitcher of cream. Rogers pushed himself up from the sofa to follow. The President opened his arms toward the stern-faced new arrival.

"Doc, I've asked my Chief of Staff to join us. Tracey London, I'd like you to meet Dr. Jonathan Rogers, our Michigan Commissioner of Health."

Rogers extended his hand toward her but London took a step away from him, ignoring the invitation.

"Good morning Commissioner," she said rigidly as she walked quickly to the sofa. She sat at the end closest to the President's chair.

Rogers's hand drifted lower. "Good morning, Ms. London."

"Doc, I've been closely following your career as Commissioner," the President said, as he seated himself on what Rogers came to think of as his throne.

The President cleared his throat several times. Rogers nibbled on the cookie he was holding and locked his gaze on Jordan.

"I was very impressed with your support of the Michigan Physician Guideline Bill. Peabody informed me of your initial concerns before he convinced you. I hope your arm doesn't still hurt. The Governor can be a little pushy."

"I must admit that he made a compelling case that it was the right legislation for the people." Rogers jokingly rubbed his shoulder. "A short course of physical therapy helped as well."

Jordan slapped his thigh. "Good move on your part."

Rogers felt London repeatedly shifting her weight across the leather cushions. As the last ripple tilted his side of the couch, he turned toward her. Her mouth opened slightly and he noticed a green mint lozenge floating on her tongue.

She asked, "If you're appointed Surgeon General, would you completely align yourself with other governmental officials and all of our important constituency groups?"

"Ms. London, I'm a physician leader. I usually seek win-win solutions to pursue what is right."

"Doc, who defines what is right?" Jordan asked.

Rogers noted the lines on the President's forehead deepening. He hesitated a moment or two before replying. "I trust my own judgment as a physician."

Jordan snapped, "Not in this arena." He sprang to his feet and planted himself less than a foot away from Rogers's black wingtips. The doctor slouched back on the couch, trying to reduce the angle of his upward gaze to meet Jordan's growing scowl.

"I'll be direct," the President said. "Peabody recommended you based on your potential to work well with most of our key stakeholders. However, he promised me that you would correct your one irritating flaw."

"I'm not sure what you mean?"

Jordan growled, "You did get Peabody's message this morning, yes?"

Rogers nodded and glanced over at London. She was shaking her head in agreement with her boss. Turning back to his host, the Commissioner thought about the Governor's warning, which he had previously dismissed.

"Let's just say that I'm deeply concerned by your troublesome views on the pharmaceutical industry. You now have a chance to show us you can be flexible."

London coughed several times. Rogers noticed her yellow-stained fingers and the magenta-colored blush that seemed to be flowing down her chest. He turned back toward President Jordan.

"Sir?"

The President asked, "Do you believe that drugs should be fast-tracked through the FDA after they have been properly researched?"

"Not unless the data is compelling. There have been disasters with that approach, so I would say that it depends."

The President blinked several times. Interlocking his fingers into a semblance of a crown, he held them at chest level.

"American drug companies have poured their well-deserved earnings into devising better medicines to improve health. They are the envy of the world. We need to help them. Don't you agree?"

"Sir, I can work with anyone to achieve what's best for our country."

Jordan circled the far end of the couch. He lowered his voice almost to a whisper. "You didn't answer my question."

From the corner of his eye, Rogers saw Jordan lurking behind him, motioning like he was chopping wood with a handheld ax. He jerked his head around but only saw that the President had already dropped his hands, and was hustling back to his seat.

"Ms. London has received intelligence from those who know you best. I've been told that you want the pharmaceutical companies to produce more influenza vaccines. As you know, several of them have decided to opt out of that business citing low marginal profits."

"Mr. President, I support every American having appropriate access to vaccines in a timely manner. It's a matter of saving lives."

Jordan responded, "The majority of those lives have voted for me. They are my people. Do you understand that?"

"Of course, basic health care is a right for everyone."

Rogers spotted the Chief of Staff raising her hand. He twisted to face her.

"President Jordan and I want to know if you would pressure the pharmaceutical companies to provide free prescription medications and vaccines to those who can't afford to pay."

As she spoke, Rogers could no longer see the mint lozenge floating on top of her green-coated tongue. He rubbed the knots in his neck and glanced over at Jordan.

"It would be the right thing to do."

The President covered his eyes with his right hand. A long silence ensued. Rogers believed he had flunked the most heavily weighted question of the interview. The sunbeams showered the room with a yellow haze that contrasted with the dark gloom that deepened on Jordan's face.

"Where would you get the money to pay for your scheme?"

Rogers pointed toward the windows behind the President's desk. "Out there people are suffering. Every drug company needs to do more to help all Americans achieve better health. It can't be just about making profits."

"Sounds like you're planning on stirring up a lot of trouble for us," Ms. London commented.

"That's not my intention," he replied, glaring at her.

Her eyes took on an opaque glaze. She said, "Quite frankly, what you're saying will not reflect well on the Jordan administration."

Rogers centered his sight back on the President. "The people will always respect those who are serving their interests."

Jordan exploded. "Doc, I'll decide what's right for our country. Those people elected me, not you."

Rogers pictured Peabody cringing back in Michigan. His boss would be disappointed. The Commissioner noticed a subtle quivering around the President's pursed lips. Jordan tapped his right foot as his eyes flickered toward the Chief of Staff.

Rogers took a deep breath. Exhaling slowly, he plunged ahead. "Mr. President, I believe—"

Jordan held up his right hand in front of his face. "Look, I appreciate your idealism, but the federal government isn't your personal play toy. If I appoint you Surgeon General, would you respect my views?"

Measuring his reply, he answered in a slow cadence. "In most cases, I'm sure that we would be in agreement. If we could not agree on a major policy issue, I would resign."

The President pounded his right fist into his opposite palm. "So I would be risking my legacy on your willingness to go along? That's not the way things work around here. Do you understand why I need your complete loyalty?"

Rogers lowered his head, staring at the presidential emblem on the blue and red carpet beneath his feet. He lifted his chin and quietly met Jordan's gaze.

"Commissioner, I think I heard a 'no.'"

"Sir, you must trust me."

"It's actually the other way around. I have the power. It is you, my good doctor; yes, it is you who must trust me."

Rogers rolled back his shoulders. He felt his temples pounding; his throat parched.

He muttered, "I see."

London stood and faced Rogers. "Let's change the subject. I understand that you'll be the keynote speaker at the upcoming National Health Commissioners Forum here in DC. What's on your agenda?"

"You know about the Forum?"

Her eyes blazed brightly. "It's my job to know what's going on. I'm here to protect the President from being blindsided."

Rogers set his jaw firmly. "As the keynote speaker, I hope to provide leadership to my fellow Commissioners from the other states. I believe that there is a critical need for physician leaders to band together."

The Chief of Staff smirked. "So . . . if you're successful, we would be forced to deal with fifty Commissioners of Health blasting the drug companies. Now, we have to contend with just you."

"Perhaps not everyone will agree with me."

The President rocked back and forth several times and scratched his ruddy cheeks. "I'm confused. Peabody told me just this morning that you considered the Surgeon General position to be your dream job. Was he mistaken?"

"Becoming Surgeon General is my life's dream, yes."

"Ah, I recall the dreams of my youth. Seems so long ago."

"I hope that you'll give me a chance."

London quietly replied, "We just did." She sat down on the couch and said no more.

Rogers focused on Jordan while avoiding the Chief of Staff's angry stare.

"So, Dr. Rogers, what are your immediate plans?" the President asked, almost pleasantly.

The Commissioner took a deep breath. "I plan on calling a dozen of my fellow Commissioners of Health. It is my intent to develop a national coalition to lobby for better access to essential drugs and vaccines."

Rogers felt the cushions moving from the Chief of Staff's fidgeting. She asked, "Would you reconsider your plan and not organize all of the State Commissioners of Health? If you move forward, it would be a nightmare for me . . .for us . . . to deal with."

"I'm sorry, but I believe in what I'm doing."

"Sounds like you are about to lead a one-man crusade against the drug companies."

Rogers met her gaze and tried hard not to flinch. London stood abruptly and said curtly, "Well, we all need to do what we have to do."

The men followed suit, both rising to their feet. Jordan placed his hand on Rogers's left shoulder and the doctor felt the heavy pressure. "By the way, are you here by yourself in DC?"

"I'll be joining my wife in a few minutes. We're heading back to Michigan tomorrow after dinner and the theater tonight."

"What show are you seeing?"

Rogers could not remember. His mind was spinning. He felt the blush coming and could only shrug his shoulders.

"Please convey my best to Mrs. Rogers. Also, say hello to my good friend Bill Peabody. Thank you again for coming in today."

The inside door flung open. There was the President's secretary, presenting Rogers's London Fog overcoat with outstretched arms. Rogers looked back at Jordan, who by now was already bounding away toward his oak desk with his Chief of Staff in close tow.

The Commissioner spoke an uncomfortable farewell. "Thank you, Mr. President."

The secretary motioned for Rogers to follow him. Hastily ushered to the White House side door, he took a step outside and shivered in the frosty breeze. He could see Pennsylvania Avenue in the distance. From behind a white stone column, a Secret Service guard appeared. The Commissioner walked silently alongside the uniformed guard while being guided out of the twenty-acre complex.

Reaching the East Executive Avenue gatehouse, Rogers stared back at the temple of democracy. He pictured White House power brokers plotting to torpedo any chance of him becoming Surgeon General. He curled his fingers into a tight fist. His dream had flipped into a nightmare in less than twenty minutes. *Damn the President. Damn the President!*

Chapter Three

Kim pressed her cell phone firmly to her ear. She emerged from the Marriott lobby onto Pennsylvania Avenue, repeating her point as if Jonathan didn't hear her the first time. "Listen to me . . . follow the President's lead."

He was muttering something about the Supreme Court just before she heard him moan. She stuffed her cell in one of the pockets of her blue overcoat. Kim turned northwest in order to directly face the White House. Her first impression was that she was gazing at a still-life portrait of the Avenue leading to the presidential mansion. She saw people crouched down, not moving.

Walking carefully on the icy sidewalk, Kim stared down at her shiny black boots as they carved a steady path. She glanced up and observed random pockets of movement coming to life. Several people ran toward her. She quickened her pace after hearing screams in the distance. Now in an almost half-trot, she closed the gap on one particular spot a few hundred yards ahead. A couple of people running in her direction mumbled something about a shooting.

"What happened?" she asked, while grabbing the arm of a woman racing toward her.

"Two . . . two men were shot. One in the leg and one in the chest."

"Shot . . .?"

Kim recalled Jonathan's moan as she spoke to him over the cell. She grabbed the woman's sleeve, wanting to know more.

"Let me go," the woman screamed. "There's a sniper on the loose!"

Kim took a shaky step backward before taking off in an all-out sprint. Her heart skipped a few beats. She felt lightheaded. No more than fifty yards from the entrance to the White

House grounds, she saw Jonathan. She stopped dead in her tracks and screamed.

His white shirt was a blazing red, his chest barely moving, and his face ashen.

Kim felt the ground quake beneath her feet. She saw a young man sitting on a stone ledge leaning against the black wrought iron fence that surrounded the presidential grounds. A DC policeman was applying a tourniquet to the young man's thigh. His pant leg was ripped apart, revealing a blood-stained calf.

She spun around. A young redheaded woman was tugging on her coat. Kim slapped away her hand. She scanned the crowd that closed around them, shouting, "Please help him! He's not moving!" A local policeman quickly appeared beside her to attempt resuscitation on her motionless husband.

The redhead spoke quietly. "Miss, let the police do their job. It's going to be OK."

Kim pointed at Jonathan lying in the dirty snow. "Can't you see that he's dying? What are you saying? It's not OK!"

"He's still breathing."

"Are you a nurse? Who are you?"

"I'm just trying to help."

Kim turned away. She focused on a cop's look at the EMT workers. It seemed to telegraph what she believed. As her husband was hoisted onto a stretcher to be wheeled to the Metro ambulance, Kim felt it coming. She retched half of the plane fast food into the nearby gutter. An arctic breeze chilled every bone in her body. Ushered to the ambulance, Kim glanced back at the gawking crowd after she had climbed through the rear door. Flashes from cameras blinded her. While the ambulance raced toward the Metro Trauma Center, she stared at Jonathan. Paralyzed by the thought that just five minutes earlier he had been secure in the company of the most powerful man on the planet, a haunting feeling gripped her consciousness. Things would never again be the same.

••••••••••

Peabody fired off a series of questions. “Mrs. Rogers, how’s he doing? Did he mention to you that I spoke with him earlier this morning? Did the Commissioner tell you about my email?”

Kim felt like she was on the witness stand. “No, he didn’t mention any of that. Oh my God, he’s still in surgery. It’s been over an hour.”

“Mrs. Rogers, I spoke with his nurse while she was scrubbing for your husband’s surgery. She said his doctors felt that Jonathan would recover.”

Kim paused. Her mind focused on his earlier questions. “What email? Why is that important after what has happened?”

“I’m so sorry. I saw the news on CNN. I was shocked that such a tragedy would happen right outside the White House. You know, in a peculiar way, I feel almost responsible for what happened to your husband.”

The phone slipped from her hands and she caught it just as it was about to hit the waiting-room floor. “But why? Why do you feel that way?”

“Well, he never would have been in DC were it not for my strong recommendation to the President to consider him for the Surgeon General position.”

Holding back a sob, she replied, “It’s not your fault.”

“The police are calling it a drive-by shooting by a crazed gunman.”

She rubbed her eyes. “They decided that already?”

“Mrs. Rogers, as soon as President Jordan heard about the shooting, he ordered the Secret Service to pick up Ashley at Mercy hospital. Your daughter is currently flying down on a government jet. She should be there in about two hours.”

“Ashley.” Kim felt her jaw drop upon hearing her daughter’s name. “How did the Secret Service know . . .?”

Peabody interrupted, “Did you speak with the Commissioner after he left the President?”

“Just a few words. But, you didn’t answer me.”

“What exactly did your husband tell you?”

“You’re getting me upset by asking me so many questions.”

“I’m concerned for your husband.”

Kim's mind kept returning to her daughter. *How would anyone know where Ashley was?*

Silence.

She persisted. "How would they know the whereabouts of my daughter? Are they following her?"

This time, Peabody replied swiftly, "Your husband is being considered for an important position. Possibly, the Secret Service was doing a routine background check. Please let me know if you need anything."

The call ended. She sat down on the couch. Just before drifting off, Kim feared that she and Jonathan would never have another chance to make things right between them.

••••••••••

The ringing of her cell jarred her awake. Kim noted his name on the caller ID.

She flipped it open and murmured, "I'm sorry. I can't talk now. I told you that I would be in DC with Jonathan. This isn't a good time."

She listened, shaking her head. "I'll call you in a few days."

Kim tossed her phone back into her purse. Memories of three decades with Jonathan rolled through her mind. Their wedding song popped into her head. He had chosen the John Denver song "Follow Me." Despite her long-standing hatred of the public life he had chosen for them, she had stayed by his side until their trial separation in recent months.

A sense of hollowness gnawed away at her core. Thoughts of the emails, the phone calls, and the secret meetings all merged together. She grabbed for a tissue. *It may be too late to make it right.* For her, there was so much left unsaid; so much pain unfairly inflicted on him. As a cascade of tears tumbled down her cheeks, she stood up to pace the floor. Kim prayed for one last chance to make it right as she clenched each finger as if it were a bead in a rosary.

Soon, she heard heavy footsteps racing down the hospital

corridor. Spotting Ashley, she ran toward her.

"How's Daddy? Nobody would tell me anything except . . ."

Kim grabbed her tightly. "Honey, he's still in surgery."

"What happened? Will he be alright?"

Looking away from Ashley, Kim bit her lower lip. "Your dad will make it. He's a fighter."

"Mom, the Secret Service picked me up and flew me here. At the airport a special limo picked us up. They wouldn't tell me anything. I was so scared."

Unable to speak for the moment, Kim flashed back to the upsetting call from the Governor. She forced a crooked smile, pulling Ashley closer.

She began haltingly. "Ash . . . Ashley, Governor Peabody told me you were coming."

"Mom, you still haven't told me who shot Daddy."

"We don't know. It happened about five minutes after he met with the President. He was just walking along Pennsylvania Avenue to meet me back at the Marriott."

"Why would anyone shoot him?"

"Governor Peabody said that it might have been an accidental shooting by some lunatic who just started firing into a crowd."

"Was anyone else hurt?"

"A young jogger was shot in the leg."

Seeing Ashley's tears rim her lower eyelids, Kim's throat tightened.

"Is Daddy going to . . .?"

"No. He'll be fine. But honey, weren't you supposed to be off today from your hospital duties?"

"Yes. But my intern called me in when one of the other med students called out sick. It was a last minute change of my plans. I wonder how the Secret Service knew where I was?"

Kim spotted the OR door swinging open. Two faces appeared. She homed in on the one face in the green scrubs who was heading directly toward her.

"Mrs. Rogers, I'm Dr. Lesley Tolliver." Gesturing toward her colleague, she added, "This is the operating room nurse, Bev Campbell. I'm pleased to tell you that your husband made it through surgery. Two small-caliber bullets struck his right lung."

"Oh, my God, thank you. Thank you, doctor. Thank you."

Campbell added, "Mrs. Rogers, I spoke earlier with Governor Peabody. I told him to reassure you. Don't worry, I'll be staying with him all day."

Kim suddenly noticed the surgeon stiffening before taking a deep breath. Tolliver's eyes were now distant, seemingly distracted.

The surgeon hesitated a moment. "Mrs. Rogers, there's something else. We found a tumor in your husband's lung during the surgery. The early lab results from the frozen section we took from the tumor are encouraging, but the final pathology is pending. Dr. Rogers will be taken to the Intensive Care Unit in a few minutes after I speak with him in the recovery room. So far, so good. Now, if you'll excuse us."

••••••••••

Remembering only that she was being chased by a stranger in her nightmare that night, Kim awoke in the hospital room chair with the sun shining brightly in her eyes. Bev Campbell was tending to Jonathan. He seemed to be in a deep sleep. Kim staggered to her feet and headed toward the hospital cafeteria.

She noticed the headline in the *Washington Post* under the arm of the lady standing next to her in line. Before paying for her cup of coffee, she picked up a copy. Kim held back from looking at the newspaper until she was seated in a spot off in the rear of the cafeteria. Sipping slowly, she trembled upon reading the page one two-column story: *Commissioner Rogers Survives Shooting after Meeting with President.* Several witnesses gave detailed accounts of the shooting. A masked shooter may have been spotted in the Ellipse. There had been no arrests. Completely absorbed in the story, Kim didn't notice that Dr. Tolliver had joined her at the table.

"Mrs. Rogers, good morning."

Kim jumped slightly. "Dr. Tolliver, I'm sorry. I didn't see you. I was just reading about the shooting."

"I understand. I wanted to tell you that your husband should be discharged in a few days."

"Thank God, he's going to be OK." No sooner did Kim say those words than she saw the surgeon's face drop. Tolliver looked away, avoiding eye contact.

"He is going to be all right!"

Hearing no response, Kim reached and grabbed the surgeon's arm. "Yes?"

The doctor leaned forward and rested her chin on folded hands, propped up by elbows that rested on edge of the table.

"Mrs. Rogers, may I ask you some important questions?"

"What's wrong? There's something that you're hiding from me."

"Did your husband smoke? Did he have a chronic cough? Did he ever spit up blood?"

Kim drew her head back. "No, he never smoked. And, before today, he has been in excellent health except for high blood pressure. What are you trying to say?"

Tolliver paused a moment or two before locking into Kim's gaze. "The pathology shows the tumor we found to be malignant. For some reason we can't seem to locate the intraoperative frozen section for comparison. Unfortunately, ten percent of patients with lung cancer are nonsmokers."

Kim only heard the word *malignant*. "No. This can't be happening."

She felt Tolliver's hand on hers. The surgeon said, "I need you to keep this diagnosis from him for a day or two. I want him to recuperate further from the surgery before he has to deal with this issue."

Kim felt unable to speak. Her stomach cramped. Tolliver's image seemed fuzzier by the second. She wondered why the surgeon continued to repeat her name over and over. She tried to hold up her hand to make Tolliver stop calling her, but for some reason she couldn't raise it. All she heard was her name being said, over and over.

"Mrs. Rogers, Mrs. Rogers."

Soon, Kim heard only garbled sounds that no longer meant

anything to her. She felt as though a spell had been cast on her. Tolliver suddenly disappeared from sight. A moment later, the cafeteria lights went blank.

••••••••••

Kim handed Jonathan the letter that was hand-delivered to her by a Secret Service Agent. She knew that the presidential message would help Jonathan get through the rocky days ahead. Yet, she wished that it had never come. She hated herself for thinking about ripping up the letter, and had changed her mind at the last moment. Now, it was too late for second-guessing.

Rogers took the letter from her, looking toward Ashley and away from the bedside nightstand. He then turned toward Kim without saying a word, all the while seemingly searching for something.

She picked up his bifocals, lying in plain sight on the nightstand, and handed them to him. "Think these will help."

He smiled. "What would I do . . .?"

As he scanned the letter, she knew there would be no turning back. Nothing would stop him from what seemed to be his destiny. His face brightened as he pushed himself to a sitting position in bed.

"It's a letter from President Jordan! It's dated January nineteenth. Ashley, what's today's date?"

"It's the twenty-third. Read it to us, Daddy."

He cleared his throat. "*Dear Dr. Rogers. I'm truly sorry to hear of your recent tragedy. I'm particularly distressed to hear how soon it happened after our meeting. Please accept my best wishes for a speedy recovery. Once you're back to work in Michigan, Governor Peabody will be speaking with you. I want you to know that I need team players. I hope that you will decide to join our team. Get well soon. Sincerely, President Will Jordan.*"

"Jonathan, that's terrific," Kim said with as much sincerity as she could muster.

"Daddy, does this mean that you will be Surgeon General?" Ashley asked, grabbing the letter from him.

Before he could respond, Kim interrupted. "Let's take each day as it comes. Your dad needs to recuperate for a few weeks back home before we start thinking about anything."

Ashley nodded. "There is no one more qualified than you, Daddy. How many physicians would have the compassion to volunteer for six months in Ethiopia with Doctors Without Borders? The country needs a leader like you."

Rogers took her hand. "We've been blessed. Those children in Ethiopia needed help. It was the least that I could have done to volunteer."

Kim looked over at Ashley and smiled. She then bent over to kiss Jonathan's forehead. "We'll deal with this later."

Jonathan reached for the letter from his daughter and read it silently for a second time. "It's not like the President is actually offering me the job."

Ashley leaned over his shoulder and read one particular passage again out loud. "*I want you to know that I need team players. I hope that you will join our team*. Dad, it sounds like you got the job to me."

Kim turned her back to his bed and walked toward the window. The last thing she wanted was to live in DC. She hated the political world. Now the President's letter seemed to have put his long-sought dream back on the table. But deep down, she knew Jonathan better than anyone; she knew he could never follow the President's lead—certainly not President Jordan's. Kim felt that Jonathan's idealism was her fail-safe zone—what would keep him from being appointed Surgeon General. Yet her anxiety level ramped up. What if, through some quirky turn of events, he really did land the job? How could she deny him that chance when his life expectancy was now in question?

He turned toward her. "Are you all right?"

Kim nodded and forced a broad smile. She leaned against the radiator just below the windowsill for support.

"What's wrong?" Jonathan asked.

She stammered, "N . . . n . . . nothing. I'm just tired."

"We've all been through a lot. When I'm back on my feet, you, Ashley, and I should take a cruise."

"Daddy, I can't get away. I start my three-month surgery rotation next week."

"I remember those days. Being a med student is demanding."

"But I do have some good news. I was nominated last week by the Chief Resident at Mercy Hospital as a candidate for medical student of the year. Yesterday, the management of the hospital took a vote. Of the four finalists, I won!"

"Ashley, I'm so proud of you!" Jonathan beamed.

"I told Mom yesterday. I was planning on calling you after your interview."

"There's more," Kim said, smiling. "As medical student of the year, she won an all-expense-paid trip to Alaska for two. She wants me to go with her, but of course, I will stay here with you."

"Isn't that cool, Dad?"

"It sure is. Your mother has always wanted to see Alaska. Personally, I saw all the icebergs I ever wanted to see in that film *Titanic*. You should go, Kim. I'll be fine."

He watched Ashley's eyes dance, as she giggled. "There's still more!" she said. "Since regional Michigan charities are paying for the award, Mercy wanted the winner to represent them in a half-marathon race supporting kids with cancer."

Jonathan tried to sit up a bit. "Did you know, when I was your age, I trained for six months so I could enter the New York City Marathon? But, I hurt my back and never made it."

She hugged him tightly. "Then this is my chance to do what you were not able to do."

"I'm passing the Rogers torch to you. So when is the trip?"

"In six weeks, Mom and I need to fly out to Anchorage. But, if you're not all right then, of course, we would cancel the trip."

Kim reached out for his hand. "The doctors have told me that you'll be back to work well before then. I'll take temporary leave from the real estate office until you're back. Then we'll just see . . ."

Rogers gave a high-five to his daughter. "Promise me that you'll take lots of pictures to send back to me, OK? Keep your phone with you all of the time. For safety."

"Dad, when you were setting off on your own, were you in touch with your parents every second of the day?"

"They didn't have these types of gadgets in my day."

"Didn't you use smoke signals when you were a kid?"

"Very funny. I may be technologically challenged, young lady, but even an early boomer like me can appreciate the value of a cell phone."

"No worries. I'll carry my cell phone with me, even during the marathon."

"You know me, I'm a worrier. I just want you and your mom to be safe."

"I'll talk to no strange polar bears. We'll keep in touch the whole time."

A moment later, Kim heard the creak of the door. Spotting in the doorway the only other person who knew the terrible secret, she said nervously, "Oh, Dr. Tolliver. I'm not sure that this is a good time to talk."

Jonathan chimed in. "Nonsense, I don't see why we can't let the good doctor make her rounds." He motioned Tolliver to come toward him. "Doctor, you saved my life. You're welcome anytime."

The surgeon approached the bedside. A tall, distinguished, bearded gentleman accompanied her. Tolliver surveyed each of the unsettled faces before speaking, pausing the longest on Kim's.

"Good morning. This is Dr. Howard Lovelace. Dr. Rogers, we're sorry to intrude on your family's visit. But we would like a few moments to speak alone with you and Mrs. Rogers."

Kim felt the surgeon's penetrating stare. Taking a deep breath, she shuddered. "Ashley, can you excuse us?"

"Mom, what's wrong?"

Kim closed her eyes, feeling them well up. She turned her back to Ashley for a second or two to wipe away a tear.

"Mom, I'm staying."

Covering her mouth, Kim nodded in agreement.

Tolliver began with a half smile. "Dr. Rogers, your wound is healing nicely. I'll be discharging you tomorrow. You'll be back to work in a few weeks."

Jonathan reached for her hand and raised it as high as he could. "Great news, Doc! I can't tell you how grateful I am for your care."

With her shoulders drooping, the surgeon slipped her hand from his. "Unfortunately, I have more to tell you. Dr. Lovelace is on staff here at Metro."

Kim locked on her husband's shifting eyes. She stroked his hair, before resting her hand on his.

"What's going on?" he asked pointedly.

Rogers glanced over at Tolliver. She was biting her lip. "You told me in the recovery room that the tumor was benign."

Tolliver hesitated. "To my surprise, we found that it was malignant. Dr. Lovelace has reviewed the final pathology slides. You'll need chemotherapy to prevent the cancer from spreading."

Jonathon lay back heavily on the bed. After a series of deep breaths, he rested his bloodshot eyes on Kim.

"You knew about this?"

She sobbed, "I'm sorry."

"You know that my mom died of cancer."

"The doctors didn't diagnose your mom until her tumor had already spread. Your tumor was caught early. I already called Tom Knowton. He was optimistic."

Rogers was speechless. He turned toward his daughter.

"Daddy, you're a fighter. You never give up. I'm the same way. I learned it from you."

He smiled at Ashley, and then turned his stare to Tolliver for a full ten seconds. "Knowton's the best oncologist in Michigan."

"You'll make it, Daddy. We all will."

The surgeon added, "Dr. Lovelace will be speaking with Dr. Knowton. Your pathology slides have already been shipped to him. We hope things work out for the best."

••••••••••

Kim awoke in the chair next to Jonathan with a start. Opening her eyes, prepared to tell him about the crazy dream she experienced while they were in DC, she flinched when she looked at his face. A faraway look in his eyes appeared solidified in place as if his head was engulfed inside a square-foot ice block. She stood and touched his hand. It felt ice cold. Kim recoiled back on her heels. Jonathan blinked once. His right hand jerked away from her. She pinched herself on her left forearm, feeling pain over the reddened mark on her skin. Instantly, she knew. This was no dream. This was only the beginning.

Chapter Four

Rogers enjoyed the home-cooked pot roast dinner, but later as he looked at himself in the mirror, he had to admit the paunch around his middle was growing. He blamed his thirty-pound weight gain on his endless craving for Twizzlers. Vowing to stop, he combed his closely cropped graying hair and squirted a few drops of Visine into his eyes to counteract the redness from his chronic allergies. At six foot three, he had always prided himself on being at least a weekend athlete, excelling in golf and tennis. He pinched a few ripples of fat and promised himself to restart his lifelong habit of daily exercise now that his strength was returning after his first round of chemotherapy. A few days ago, he had bought a replica Schwinn Flyer, a blue and white retro bike with wide tires. The foot brakes were sturdy and easy to use. He had never trusted those hand brakes, that new technology. He felt lucky to be alive, and he appreciated his good fortune as a survivor.

As he walked into the living room to join Kim, she said, "I hear the front door chimes."

"I didn't hear anything."

"Ha, with your hearing, why am I not surprised?"

"Expecting anyone?" he asked her.

Kim shrugged. "No."

He rose to his feet and could now hear several voices mumbling just outside the door. As he stared through the peephole, he heard a shrill voice.

"Dr. Rogers, it's the police. We would like to have a word with you."

He opened the door barely an inch while he wedged his foot against the bottom. They flashed their shiny badges and Jonathan waved them to enter.

"Commissioner Rogers, Mrs. Rogers, we're sorry to bother

you at this time of night. I'm Detective Ryan Darden from the Oldwyck Police Department. This is Lieutenant Susan Masters and Sergeant Dave Orham from the FBI."

"My wife and I were just getting ready to go to bed."

Darden replied, "It's important. Won't take long."

Rogers pointed to the couch. He remained standing while the trio sat side by side on the couch. Hovering over his favorite chair, he rested his hands on Kim's shoulders.

His eyes darted to each of his unwelcome guests, coming to rest on the somewhat disheveled-looking detective.

"Commissioner, we're here to ask you some questions regarding your apparent drive-by shooting in DC."

Rogers took several steps toward the couch. With hands on both hips, he asked, "Have you found the shooter?"

"We've got several persons of interest under surveillance," replied Lieutenant Masters, "but we have no definite suspects."

Kim stood to join Jonathan. She asked, "So, just who are your persons of interest?"

"Sorry, this is a top-level national security matter. We're not permitted to discuss who we're tracking at this time."

Rogers raised both eyebrows. "Why is my so-called drive-by shooting now considered to be a national security matter?"

FBI Sergeant Orham spoke up. "You were shot in front of the White House just minutes after meeting with the President. I believe that is all we can say on that point."

Rogers asked, "What about the jogger who was shot? I don't think he met with the President."

Orham replied, "Please give us a chance to ask the questions."

Susan Masters stood to face the Commissioner. "We copied the hard drive on your laptop. We've analyzed every email you sent or received in the last year."

"Is that so? I don't recall you asking for my permission. Isn't that invading my privacy?"

His question was met with silence.

"I know," Rogers added, "you can't say on grounds of national security."

He smiled as each shook their head as if on cue from Darden.

"Commissioner," the detective said, "has Governor Peabody ever threatened you for not supporting any of his policy positions?"

"What kind of question is that? What has that got to do with finding your so-called drive-by shooter?"

Lieutenant Masters responded, "We can't comment on why we're asking that question."

"I see. Then, I'm sorry, but in all good conscience I can't give you an answer. Private conversations between the Governor and me are exactly that—private."

Darden parried swiftly, "Did the Governor ever tell you to cut the drug companies some slack because they made large political donations to his campaigns?"

Rogers pivoted and shot a wary look at Kim. He then narrowed his eyes on Darden. "Detective, call me old–fashioned, but I happen to believe strongly in our right of privacy."

"I respect your loyalty to your boss but we know exactly what Peabody said."

"Then why did you ask me?"

"We wanted to see if you had a different version, perhaps filling in the missing pieces. Darden persisted, "Has the Governor ever intimidated you in any way?"

"No," Rogers fired back.

Darden's face turned beet red. "Under the circumstances, I would hope that you would tell us everything you know. Remember, we've analyzed your conversations and emails."

"Tell me what you know. If you have a clue as to who may have shot me and the other young man, why can't you share that information with me? If it's a simple drive-by shooting and you have a suspect, just say so. I just don't get this national security bullshit."

FBI Sergeant Orham continued the drill. "Dr. Rogers, it's more complicated than you may think. But, you must be totally open with us."

Rogers felt stonewalled. "And, what if I refuse?"

Darden replied coldly, "Then you will receive a subpoena on grounds of possible obstruction of justice."

Rogers felt his patience ebbing away. He walked out of the living room toward the front door. "It's getting late. I would appreciate calling it a night." He yanked it open and pointed toward the street.

The visitors followed his request and filed out. Already halfway down the stone pathway, Lieutenant Masters turned back toward him. "You'll be receiving a subpoena in the morning."

He shouted, "You can find me at the Commissioner's office."

"It's our business to know where you are at all times," replied Darden.

Sergeant Orham asked, "Oh, one final question, Dr. Rogers. Do you have any known enemies?"

The Commissioner reached for Kim's hand. He saw the weariness in her eyes. In his white socks, he kicked the door. She reached out to stop it just before it slammed shut.

"Sergeant, you're not naïve enough to think that one of Jonathan's friends shot him?"

Darden stepped forward. "Under the circumstances of this case, anything is possible. Be careful, Commissioner. We'll be in touch."

"Hold on a second," Rogers said. "I just remembered what Lieutenant Masters said."

"About the probable drive-by shooting?"

"Exactly. Why would the FBI have persons of interest under surveillance if it was a simple drive-by shooting? Why wouldn't they just round up the suspects for questioning?"

"Dr. Rogers, let it go."

"What the hell does that mean?"

"We told you. It's a matter of national security."

"What about my security?"

"Good evening, Commissioner." The detective turned and quickly walked down the brick pathway toward the waiting limo.

Kim's eyes widened. "I bought a double-barreled derringer today."

He slammed the door. "Guess I won't be sleeping much anymore."

Chapter Five

Rogers enjoyed the cool breeze as he sped toward the Department of Health. Aboard his bike, he navigated the morning drive traffic along Main Street in Oldwyck. He knew the route well, having driven the 3.5-mile distance for several years. Besides getting some much needed exercise, the Commissioner had decided to do his part in reducing carbon emissions. At Oak Street, he made a hard right turn as an SUV swerved in front of him. He glanced down at his briefcase, strapped to the basket below the handlebars. Looking forward to his first day back on the job, Rogers pedaled faster and faster. On his last turn onto the avenue, he felt the front tire beginning to shimmy back and forth. Hitting the foot pedal, he pulled over onto the sidewalk. He examined the wheel where it attached to the frame. The nut on the bolt was loose. He tightened it with his hand, making a mental note to use a wrench as soon as he could. Back on the bike, he pedaled slowly toward the parking lot. While locking the bike to the rack, he thought back to the loose front tire. Could it be? Rogers laughed and dismissed the thought while bounding up the steps with his briefcase in hand.

He approached his executive assistant's desk feeling as though he had been gone much longer than his weeks of recuperation. Sally went over various messages with him. Her kind, trusted Southern drawl soothed his troubled mind.

He thanked her for keeping his appointment book blocked out and then trekked down the black-and-white marble corridor to the Statehouse to meet with his boss. He was informed by a few passing state troopers that the Governor had just left. Peabody had been summoned by the President to come immediately to DC. Rogers returned to his office to see Sally standing nervously, waiting for him.

She handed him a quarter-inch stack of papers. "This is a subpoena that I accepted for you. It just came . . . from the FBI."

"I'm not surprised."

"Is there anything I can do, Dr. Rogers?"

"Please fax the subpoena to my attorney, Brent Marshall. Hold all calls for me except if Marshall calls back. I'll be in my office most of today catching up on paperwork."

"There is one change in your calendar. You have a new appointment for this afternoon. A gentleman called just as you left to see the Governor. He insisted on seeing you today. I tried to schedule him for later in the week but he wouldn't take no for an answer."

"Who would that be?"

"Peter Chambers. He said that you know his daughter Nicki. She's the office manager at Dr. Knowton's office."

••••••••••

Around four o'clock, Rogers gazed out the large window overlooking the northwest corner of the grounds of the Michigan State Department of Health. He was unable to concentrate on his work. He watched a deer running through a heavily wooded area that surrounded the quarter-mile-long pond, and saw a murder of crows circling overhead. He cringed a bit as they swooped down for their kill on an unsuspecting lizard that had been bathing in the pond waters. His afternoon daze was broken by a sharp knock on the door and the entrance of his administrative assistant escorting the expected visitor.

"Mr. Peter Chambers, please meet Commissioner Dr. Jonathan Rogers," Sally proclaimed with her customary élan.

Rogers shook his hand firmly and motioned for his visitor to take a seat on the opposite side of his desk. "Sir, how can I help you?" The Commissioner sat up straight in his high-backed leather chair and tapped his fingers slowly on his desk.

The elderly man began. "My daughter Nicki asked me to say hello. She tells me that you have a well-deserved reputation as a fair man. I have come today to ask for your help."

"Thank you for your kind words. I just saw Tom last week. And Nicki has always impressed me with her professionalism."

Rogers noted his guest's quivering jaw and the trembling of his hands at rest. He sensed that Chambers's request for help would not be as simple as he had hoped.

"Commissioner, I believe that Dr. Knowton should be in jail for what he did to my best friend, Samuel Murphy. I grew up with Sam back in New York. Years later, we both got jobs out here in the Midwest. He became a nurse and I rose in the ranks to become a union leader. Now, he's dead at the hands of your friend."

Rogers leaned forward and raised his hands in the air. "Can we back up a little? I read about Mr. Murphy's death in the *Oldwyck Gazette*. If I remember correctly, he was an influential man in the FDA—sanctioned oversight process of drug clinical trials."

"Sam was a fierce warrior."

"I'm truly sorry for your loss. But I'm sure Dr. Knowton did everything possible to save him."

Chambers turned his face away from sight with a ninety-degree lurch to the left. Rogers waited until his visitor's moistened gaze returned to view.

"As a union man, I'm paid to make things happen. You're the Commissioner of Health. I want you to find out why Sam died so suddenly. Yesterday, I spoke with his daughter, Beth. She's outraged at what has happened."

"From what I've read in the paper, Mr. Murphy was seriously ill. Unfortunately, things like this happen."

"It's not that simple. Sam was fine when Beth left him that evening. She has proof of a crime."

"What crime?"

"Beth has the evidence."

"Can I see it?"

"When the time is right, I'll show it to you."

"Well, until you do, I can assure you that it's more than likely Mr. Murphy died from a heart attack, a stroke, or a blood clot to the lungs."

"Commissioner, down at the docks, you would be considered the top dog. In my eyes, you're the top doc around these parts. So I'm counting on you to ensure that Knowton pays for what happened to Sam."

"Sir, there are limits as to what I can do."

Chambers snapped, "Not from where I sit."

The chime of the Swiss federal railway clock over the arch of the office door interrupted the rising tension between the two men. Rogers glanced down at his wristwatch. "I promise you that I will look into the matter."

Chambers snarled, "So, you're not going to do anything?"

"Based on your story alone?"

Chambers leaped out of his chair just as Sally opened the office door.

"Dr. Rogers, if you don't do something about Knowton soon, then I will. I assure you that I'm dead serious about this matter."

The senior turned and stormed out of the office, slamming the door behind him.

Sally asked, "What happened? Mr. Chambers looked as if he was ready to kill someone."

"Apparently me. But I have no idea why."

"Since you have no further appointments, are you planning on leaving early?"

"Yes, in a few minutes. Sally, you can take off. See you tomorrow."

He was thankful that the day was finally over. He began to rise from his chair, hesitated, then sat again. He reached for the phone and dialed Tom Knowton's cell, but only got his voice mail.

••••••••••

"Kim, I'm coming home."

"Dinner won't be ready for another two hours. I just got back from meeting with some friends."

"I see. No problem. I have my jogging stuff with me. I think I'll take a slow jog around Oldwyck Pond."

"How was your first day back at work?"

"Not so good. I'll talk with you later."

Rogers parked by the pond. After a few minutes of a slow jog, he sat down on the wooden bench that bordered the woods. He took out his cell. On the first ring, Knowton picked up.

"Hello Tom. Nicki's father, Peter Chambers, just left my office. He wants me to investigate the death of your patient Sam Murphy."

"Why?"

"He thinks you did something wrong. That made no sense to me, but I can tell you that he was really upset. He said that he has evidence, but he wouldn't show me anything. Would Nicki know anything about Murphy?"

"No, I can't believe that she would have told him any of this nonsense."

"You're right. Sorry, I must need some sleep. He actually said it was Murphy's adopted daughter, Beth, who has the evidence."

"Well, thanks for the heads-up. But, there is nothing that I can tell you unless Governor Peabody recently signed a law that gives you the right to delve into a doctor-patient relationship without family consent."

"No such law, Tom."

"By the way, watch out for Chambers. His daughter Nicki tells me he has a wicked temper."

"I've seen it."

"Tread lightly, my friend. The water in Oldwyck Pond is deeper than you might think."

Chapter Six

Knowton pulled out the number from his wallet. He had dialed The Health Club only once or twice before, in the early days just after being blackmailed.

A familiar voice answered. "Yes."

"We've got a problem. Peter Chambers is causing trouble. He told the Commissioner that I somehow killed Sam Murphy."

"Who told Chambers?"

"Murphy's daughter."

"Don't worry. We'll take care of it."

"Not good enough. I want out. You promised me that I would not be implicated in any of this."

"You know that membership in The Club is forever, for as long as you live. There is only one way out. Just keep your mouth shut. We'll get everyone off your back."

"When?"

"Don't call me again."

Knowton slammed down the receiver and lowered his head to his desk. He slowly raised his head and looked up at the plaque on the wall. It was a special present from his dad when he first entered private practice. Beneath the glass-covered tablet were the words of the Hippocratic Oath. He read the well-known first four words, *first do no harm*, and abruptly spun his chair halfway around. *Primum non nocere.* Knowton hung his head and squeezed his eyes shut. *What have I done?*

Chapter Seven

Kim had marked this day for weeks. She snuffed out the ring of the six o'clock alarm and bounded out of bed. Today would be her first day back to work in months. Her therapist thought she was finally ready to face the world, and especially her boss, Taylor. She showered before getting dressed in the guest bathroom down the hallway. After gulping down a few cups of coffee, she grabbed her briefcase and left for the real estate office.

As she walked outside, she smelled the sweet aroma of the rosebuds from the front porch flowerbed. She felt as though she could run a marathon as she sprinted to the Lexus. After starting the motor, she ran her fingers through her long blond hair. Her pulse raced as the Lexus shot out of the driveway, and she turned onto Blue Falcon Drive with an ear-to-ear smile on her face.

A half hour later, settled at her desk, Kim glanced down at the silver-plated paperweight. The award for most sales in one year by a rookie associate had meant a lot to her. The desk phone rang just as she logged into the company intranet. She noted the caller ID, grinning broadly.

"Good morning, Taylor. Sorry I was so rude in DC."

"Kim, don't even think about it. I'd like to see you today so we can catch up. I'm working out of the office. I'll be on the other side of town."

"Why don't we meet for lunch? Let's do Roma's."

"See you there at noon."

Kim reviewed the real estate listings streaming across her computer screen. Home prices were falling. It was a buyer's market. She was well aware of the need to ingratiate herself more than ever to perspective buyers. It was going to be a blast.

As she skimmed through the six-inch pile of mail, a rose-colored letter caught her eye. She was thrilled to see that it was a referral. A potential buyer coming from a personal recommendation of a doctor friend of Jonathan's was asking her to show him and his wife some upscale homes in the area. She hurried back to her office to dial his number. Before calling, Kim checked her voice mail and email. Per company policy, every thirty days her inbox was deleted unless saved to a special folder and her voice mails were also deleted. If anyone had tried to reach her during that time, she wouldn't have heard from them unless they took the time to write. Given the unlikelihood of anyone doing so, she was thrilled to see the letter from this potential client. Kim called his office number as she wondered why the letter had the word "confidential" spelled out in bold red letters over her name.

"Good morning, Doctor's Choice Products, Mr. Miller's office. My name is Marissa. How can I help you?"

"Yes, good morning. My name is Kim Rogers. I'm a sales associate at DuPont Homes for Living. I just received a letter from Mr. Miller requesting me to call him."

"Mr. Miller is at a meeting right now. But I mailed that letter for him. He told me he would like you to show him some lakefront properties."

"Please let me apologize that no one in the office helped him out in my absence."

"Don't be. I called your office looking for you. A few of your colleagues called here but I turned them away. Mr. Miller wanted to speak only with you. He'll call you back soon."

••••••••••

Kim arrived at Roma's almost ten minutes late. She spotted Taylor at their usual table in the back. As she walked toward him, she felt a warm flush on her face. He always had that effect on her. Five feet from the table, her boss stood up. As his hands warmly grasped her extended hand, she noticed the softness of his skin. It was not the first time.

"Taylor, I must say that you're looking as good as ever."

"I'm so sorry for all of your troubles the last few months. How's Jonathan doing? He must be a wreck."

"He's fine. The FBI is playing it close to the vest. They're not saying much beyond 'it's a matter of national security' since he was shot just after leaving a private meeting with President Jordan. They keep saying it could be a random drive-by shooting. We just don't know."

"When the news of the shooting came out on CNN, I was worried about you . . . and Jonathan, of course."

Kim sat down. "I'm so excited to have already received a referral on my first day back."

"Who from?"

"Dr. Tom Knowton."

"The name sounds familiar."

"Knowton is Jonathan's oncologist and longtime friend."

Absently twisting her wedding ring, she asked, "So Taylor, did you finally get your divorce from Karen?"

"It came through last month."

She stared into his dark green eyes. She thought that she saw his right hand moving closer to hers. Kim picked up her hands from the table and rested her chin in both palms. His eyes were quiet, his smile inviting.

"I've been meaning to say that your yellow sundress is stunning."

"Thanks. Listen, I could use a glass of wine and a salad."

Taylor turned to the passing server and ordered two glasses of Cabernet Blanc and two Caesar salads.

"So, Kim, any regrets?"

"We had our moments. Let's stay friends for now."

"Jonathan is a lucky man to have you."

Taylor toasted to her return to work. She drained half the glass before she stuck a fork into her salad. About to down a second gulp, her cell rang. She checked the caller ID.

"Excuse me, I think this is my referral calling. Hello, this is Kim Rogers."

She gave a thumbs-up sign to her boss and walked away from the table.

"Mr. Miller, I can meet you and your wife in thirty minutes. I've several properties to show you. One is a fantastic deal. It's a gorgeous lakefront property with a private beach."

Her smile grew wider. Just before she hung up, Kim raised her right arm up, fist clenched. "See you there."

It was moments like this that she had missed the most. She was proud of her ability to convince buyers of the value of her properties. It sure beat waiting for Jonathan to achieve all of his dreams.

Kim snapped her phone shut and smiled at Taylor. "Got to run. This is a big client. Sorry I can't finish lunch with you."

She swung her handbag over her shoulder, gave Taylor a small wave, and raced out of the restaurant.

••••••••••

Kim pulled the Lexus in front of the colonial style home on Lakehurst Drive. The lake-house property occupied two acres that were heavily wooded. It sat at the end of a street lined with maple trees, running parallel to Lake Suncrest. The nearest home was at least a quarter of a mile away. She was impressed by two Ionic-styled white columns of stone on the front porch. Impatient to check out the lake view from the back of the home, she bolted from the car, forgetting her purse and the car keys.

The layout was exactly as she recalled from her computer listing. After walking around the side of the two-story brick-faced home, she heard the waves lapping up on the private sandy beach that sloped down from the patio area. Her eyes softened when she spotted the loveseat swing facing the lake. Kim found herself envious of anyone owning this home, and couldn't help wishing Jonathan had stayed in private practice so that they might have enjoyed the house themselves. There was no way that they could afford the six-million-dollar price tag on this property on the salary of a government worker. The lake water sparkled. Two powerboats raced from one end of the property to the other. A thirty-foot wooden dock marked the boundary on the right side. As she stood admiring the view, a blaring car horn coming from the street interrupted her fantasy.

She walked back to the front of the estate, and noticed a Maybach limo parked behind her Lexus. The darkly tinted windows blocked her view of any occupants. The driver's window was open several inches but she saw no one behind the wheel. Suddenly, the rear door opened. A muscular, well-dressed man in a light tan suit emerged. As she drew closer to him, the steadiness of his brown eyes and his wavy black hair caught her eye.

"Mr. Miller?" she asked.

He flashed a smile, showing teeth as white as a fresh snowfall. "Mrs. Rogers, I presume."

"Yes. I'm so glad to make your acquaintance. I just love your car. What color is it?"

"Champagne."

Trying to be as witty as possible, she offered, "Well, when you buy this terrific lake house, perhaps we can both celebrate with a toast."

"Sounds like a good idea if we can close a deal. By the way, please call me Zach. Everyone else does."

Kim liked his energy and his friendly manner. She pointed proudly toward the lake house.

"Mr. Miller . . . Zach, please let me take you inside this gorgeous home."

"Lead the way. I must say that the white columns are strikingly attractive, as are you. I'm so glad that Tom Knowton referred me to you."

"May I ask, how do you know Tom?" As she walked alongside him, she could smell his cologne.

"He's my wife's doctor. In fact, Alexis was supposed to be with me today but she wasn't feeling well."

"Tom is a good friend of my husband, Jonathan Rogers."

"The Commissioner of Health?" Zach asked quizzically.

"Yes."

After finding the key inside the lock box, she unlocked the door. From inside the front foyer, the shimmering lake came into view. Kim led her client straight back to the open French doors that were bookends for the rear glass door. Pressing the button under the picture of JFK on the wall, the glass panels opened onto a twenty-foot-square pink-tinged Belgian block patio. She stood silently alongside Zach, lingering on the patio for a few moments. His attention was drawn to the sandy beach that sloped thirty yards to the shoreline.

"This place is simply unbelievable. Come join me on the swing," Zach said.

"I've been sitting all day. I think I'll stand." Kim felt a bit awkward. Steadying herself, she swore she would resist the almost overpowering temptation to sit with him.

"Well, Mr. Miller, would you like to see the rest of the house?"

"My wife will attend to the details. Personally, I'm swayed by the charm of this view. It's stunning. As beautiful as you."

Kim felt herself blushing and she turned to face the lake. She sensed that he was taking in a visual inventory of her anatomy. She turned to face him. She was right. His eyes were focused on her cleavage.

She blurted out, "Would you like to make me an offer?"

"Yes, I would like to make you an offer. How about having dinner with me tomorrow evening?"

Kim laughed. "I meant a bid on the property."

"Not today. I would like to think about it for a few days." A moment later, he pulled out an expensive-looking cigar from his suit pocket. After biting off the end, he used his monogrammed dark blue handkerchief to dispose of the excess. He inhaled deeply after lighting up, blowing rings of smoke into the crystal-clear air. She circled in front of him.

"I'm sure Mrs. Miller would love this place. Its would be so romantic for the two of you."

"My wife is ill."

"I'm sorry to hear that. So, what type of work are you involved in at Doctor's Choice Products?"

"It's a pharmaceutical company. I'm the CEO."

"It must be exciting to be providing medicines to help so many people. You and my husband have so much in common."

"You're so right about that. I've been impressed by the Commissioner's work. By the way, I was serious about dinner. We could discuss business."

"I'm pretty booked the next couple of weeks. My husband looks forward to me staying home in the evening. In recent weeks, we've had more than our share of problems. But thank you for the invitation."

"Perhaps another time."

She paused before replying. "Perhaps."

"Kim, if you don't mind, I would like to sit here on the patio and enjoy my cigar. If you trust me staying here alone, you can lock up the house. You don't need to wait for me. I'd like to soak up some sun while I think about a possible offer. I think better in private."

"That would be fine." She reached out for his hand.

Rising, he clasped it tightly. "Kim, it was my pleasure to meet you."

She maintained a lingering contact with his soft hand. "Mr. Miller . . . oh, I'm sorry. I mean Zach. I must say that you've been an absolute gentleman. I'm sure that we'll be talking soon."

"The pleasure will be mine."

While walking back toward her car, she found herself giggling. She hadn't had this much fun in months. As she opened the door, she glanced over at the BMW, wondering why she didn't see the driver earlier. But, even with the window cracked open a few inches, there was no one behind the wheel.

Her instincts were to return to the house, but she pushed them aside and sat down on the leather-covered seat. About to turn the key, she felt a sharp prick against the side of her neck. She swatted at what she believed to be a pesky fly and the pain increased. A second or two later, she heard a muffled voice coming from the backseat.

"Don't move, or I'll slit your throat!"

Not moving her head an inch, her eyes darted to the rearview mirror. She picked up the glint of the knife against her throat. Her hands trembled on the steering wheel. Afraid to scream, she felt the muscles in her neck tightening against the cold blade indenting her skin.

"Keep your eyes closed. Don't move or speak."

As beads of perspiration bubbled up on her neck, she thought of Jonathan and their children. She prayed, fearing the worst.

"Do as I say."

Just before she raised her hands to feel the blindfold being strapped around her face, she was able to sneak one fleeting glance in the rearview mirror. Her assailant was wearing a black ski mask. She shivered. Waves of nausea crashed onto her stomach.

Kim begged, "Please don't hurt me. I'll give you anything you want."

"Shut up. I only want two things from you, Mrs. Rogers."

She felt her temples pounding upon hearing her name. *He knows who I am.* She opened her eyes under the mask, leaning her head back just enough to see the dashboard from the narrow space at the bottom of the blindfold. She calculated the number of seconds to turn on the ignition and floor the accelerator. Upon feeling further pain as the knife pressed deeper into her neck, Kim quickly lost all hope of escape.

"Number one, I want you to tell your husband something for me. Will you do that?"

She hesitated. The knife cut deeper. She felt a trickle of fluid flowing down her neck. Her skin was on fire with the burning pain.

"Anything. Please, I'll do anything."

"The next time that I ask you a question, I will expect an immediate response or I'll dig this knife in a little deeper. My request is simple. I want you to tell Dr. Rogers that he should follow his leaders and back off."

Not knowing what that meant, she was not about to ask any more questions. "I'll tell him."

"Good. You're getting much better at this game. Number two, I'll be getting out of your car in a few seconds. But I'll be watching you the whole time. You're not to move until you count to sixty. After the time has passed, you may remove your blindfold and drive away. Now, isn't that a simple plan?"

"I'll do it," she mumbled, relieved that she no longer felt the knife cutting into her skin.

She heard the rear door open. She sensed her assailant was gone but she wasn't sure. Kim remained in place. She held her breath. A moment later, she heard the door slam. With a series of short breaths, she picked up the count. She ripped off the blindfold when the time came and turned the ignition key. She hit the accelerator. As the car jerked forward, Kim could see Zach Miller out of the corner of her eye. He was walking casually toward the street from the back of the lake house. She pulled down the door to the glove compartment, spotting her derringer. She tore down Lakehurst Drive and did not look back again until she pulled into her driveway. Her husband was already standing on the walkway.

"I was stabbed after meeting a client at the lake house," she screamed, pointing to her neck.

"What? Let me see?" He examined the wound. "It's superficial. Let's go inside and I'll clean it up. Then, I'm calling the cops."

"No. He knows who we are."

"We have to. You could have been killed. And who was the client you met?"

"Jonathan, I can't think straight. All I remember is that the masked man said everything would be all right if you would only follow your leaders."

He walked her over to the living room couch. "Sit down. I'll get an antibiotic cream and a dressing for your neck."

She grabbed his hand. "Don't leave me."

"I'll be right back." A minute later he returned and began administering first aid.

"I can't stop shaking!"

He caressed her neck and then applied the cream. She pulled away.

"That stings."

"What did the assailant mean by telling me to follow my leaders?"

"Good question. Who are your leaders? Could Peabody be involved?"

"What the hell is that supposed to mean? And you still didn't tell me who you met at the lake house."

"Does it matter?"

"Yes." He sat down next to her and taped the gauze pad over the wound.

"A gentleman named Zach Miller. He was referred to me by Tom Knowton."

"I'll check him out with Tom."

"Zach said he that was impressed by your work as Commissioner. He seems to like you."

"Glad someone appreciates what I'm trying to do. So, who else knew you would be at the lake house?"

She paused. "Only Taylor."

His eyes opened widely. "When did you tell him?"

"At lunch, just before I went to the lake house."

He leaned away from her. "I thought it was over between you and Taylor."

"It is. You must believe me."

"I've heard that before."

"Jonathan, I'm afraid."

He nodded. "It's a good thing you and Ashley are getting out of town. When are you leaving for Alaska?"

"The end of the week."

"That's three days away. We'll stay in a hotel until then. Call Ashley and ask her if she can stay with us."

"She's so busy at the hospital."

He leaped to his feet. "This is ridiculous. I'm calling the police."

Kim tugged on his arm. "No. If they know my name, they know where we live."

He pulled away and headed toward the phone on the oak end table. He picked up the receiver and began dialing.

"Please don't call. I'll go with you to the hotel until I leave for Alaska."

Kim ran over and pushed the disconnect button. "Jonathan, I don't trust the police, not after what happened to you in DC."

He looked into her darting eyes and wiped away the tears with his left hand. Putting the receiver down, he hugged her. He tried to remember the last time. He struggled. But he knew one thing. It felt good to be close to her.

"Kim, promise me that you and Ashley will be careful in Alaska."

She closed her eyes and took a deep breath. "We'll be fine."

"I still think we need to call the police."

"No. Let's pack and get out of here. We need to find an out-of-the-way hotel."

"Where's your derringer?"

"In my car. Someone needs to protect us. I trust no one. No one."

Chapter Eight

At four minutes after four, Peter Chambers sat across the desk from Rogers, his eyebrows twitching, and his face crimson. The Commissioner steadied himself for an encore appearance.

"May I ask why the interest in meeting with me so soon after our last encounter?" Rogers asked.

"Last time, I didn't want to bring up your personal troubles. I'm sorry for what has happened to you. But I'm not here today to tell you things that will make you feel any better."

"Why am I not surprised?"

"Look, Dr. Rogers, all doctors take an oath to first do no harm," Chambers exclaimed. "But as you well know, it doesn't always work out that way. Not only is Dr. Tom Knowton guilty of poor medical judgment that killed my friend Sam Murphy, but I'm here to tell you today that he is also a crook. The man is a criminal."

Leaning forward, Rogers asked, "Do you have proof of these scandalous allegations? If not, these accusations are totally unfair."

The senior paused to take two sips of coffee, ignoring the Commissioner's comment.

Rogers jumped to his feet. Chambers stood slowly, pushing off the arms of the chair. "Down at the docks, we have street justice. Fairness has nothing to do with it."

The Commissioner looked away. Moments later, he refocused on his guest. His laser-beam gaze locked pupil to pupil with the troublesome witness.

"Mr. Chambers, are you on some kind of warpath against Dr. Knowton? You seem to blame him for everything under the sun."

"All right, I'll give you your damn proof."

Chambers took his seat. Rogers scrunched his face and took a few deep breaths before sitting down in his chair.

"My daughter Nicki found false Medicare billing charges. At first, she believed that there must have been a mistake by the office's billing department. But over time, she started noticing more and more checks coming in from the Centers for Medicare and Medicaid Services paying for medical care for patients that were not even being treated." Chambers stopped, took a gulp of coffee, and looked up at Rogers.

"Go on, I'm listening." Jonathan felt his heart pound.

"Nicki told me that she has been afraid to tell anybody. She was aware of these activities for almost a full year. For some reason, she could no longer keep quiet about her concerns. I suspect the fact that she is pregnant for the first time prompted her to bring it to my attention."

"For heaven's sake, show me some evidence!"

"I can also tell you that Knowton is being sued for malpractice by Beth Murphy."

"That's none of my business."

"Knowton gave Sam an overdose of a cancer medicine called Zazotene."

"Hold on, I'm not going to discuss this medical charge against Knowton with you, especially if it's already in litigation."

"Why not? Are you involved?"

"I resent your implications." Glancing down at his watch, he said sternly, "I have another meeting."

"Not so fast." Chambers pulled out an envelope from his inside suit pocket. "You'll find photocopies of a dozen Medicaid checks for patients who are not in his practice. But I want to keep Nicki out of this. I thought about going directly to the police, but I decided to go right to you. I thought you would understand."

The Commissioner took the envelope and rested it on his desk. "I'll review this later."

"When will I hear from you?"

"I need time to sort this out. Before you leave my office, please have Sally schedule you to return in the next few weeks. Until then, I would like no further mention of this issue by either you or your daughter."

Rogers rose from his seat, holding out his hand. "Well, Mr. Chambers, I can't say that our meetings are ever boring."

"Just remember, I'm not going to let this pass without justice being served."

As the door clicked shut, the Commissioner imagined what would happen the next time he would see Peter Chambers. He inspected the claims. Strangely, each of them had the same date of service stamped at the top. Gathering the copies of the signed checks, he stuffed them into a thick manila folder labeled Fraud Task Force and locked them in his file cabinet.

Rogers returned to his desk. He buzzed his assistant. "Did Mr. Chambers make a return appointment?"

"Yes, sir, he sure did. In two weeks."

"Thanks. And by the way, I need to meet with Dr. Knowton ASAP."

••••••••••

On his way home from the office, Rogers didn't see the red light until he was driving through it. A canary-yellow Mercedes sedan was no more than a second or two away from smashing into his door. Swerving instinctively, he registered a split-second snapshot of the other driver. Rogers's Hummer came to a stop in the middle of the intersection, the two cars separated by a foot or less.

Rogers powered down his side window in order to apologize to the other driver. Suddenly she sped away. Tracking her in his rearview mirror, three flash impressions struck him instantly: a DC license tag, her face, and the color of her hair.

He steered hard left to complete his U-turn to follow her. Speeding up the hill on Mulberry Avenue, the sedan was nowhere in sight. After cresting the highest point on the thoroughfare, the Mercedes came back into view. Rogers narrowed his eyes on the roadster, which was now making a left turn on Canter. He tapped the brake pad lightly, leaning into the turn as his tires screeched to hold the road.

The sedan banked a hard right turn into the Oldwyck Mall parking lot. He then steered hard right onto the service road of the Mall. The Mercedes blasted through the stop sign at the passenger crossing. The driver navigated the sharp left turn that led to Circle Drive without losing speed. An instant later, Rogers followed, but as he approached the intersection, a group of teens began to cross. He slammed on the brakes and the Hummer came to rest just a few feet from the kids, one of whom thoughtfully gave him the finger.

As he caught his breath, it came to him: The driver was the same redhead who flirted with him in DC. Deep in thought, he was jolted by the loud honks coming from behind him. In his rearview mirror he could see a string of cars stretched to the roadway. Rogers drove slowly to the stop sign. *Who is this woman, this Haley?* He needed to find out, and quickly.

Chapter Nine

Kim heard her cell ring just as she was registering at the front desk of the host hotel, the Sheraton Anchorage. It was Jonathan.

"Glad you had a safe trip. Remember what you and I discussed," he said.

Turning away from her daughter, she replied, "I won't let her get out of my sight. She's so happy."

"OK, great. Listen, I'm going to book a vacation for us in Italy. Just family. It will be a celebration for Ashley's marathon. I called the Governor to tell him I'm taking some time off."

Kim rolled her eyes. "We'll call you after the race tomorrow. I have to speak with my boss before I can commit to taking a vacation."

"Isn't your family more important?"

"Of course, but . . ."

"Put Ashley on." Kim handed the phone to her daughter and mouthed, "It's Dad."

"Hi, Daddy!"

"Hey cutie. People around town are all talking about you. The *DuPont Herald* ran a story today about your award. The *Oldwyck Gazette* even had your picture in today's paper. Front page no less. Looks like the one from your college yearbook. It seems that everyone will know that you'll be in the Anchorage race."

"Cool. I'll take lots of pictures for you with my cell. I wonder if anyone from Michigan will be at the race."

As her last words flowed so innocently, Kim's jaw tightened.

"Gotta go. Love you, Daddy."

"I love you, Ashley. Have a great race. Be careful."

••••••••••

At dinner that evening, Ashley downloaded everything she learned about Anchorage and the race. Kim tried her best to absorb every last detail that her daughter excitedly rattled off.

"Mom, there will be 3,500 runners in the Mayor's Midnight Sun Marathon. Did you know Anchorage is surrounded by the Chugach Mountains and the Cook Inlet?"

Kim nodded between bites of lobster tail, finding it nearly impossible to get in a word.

"The half marathon is 13.1 miles long. The race starts at 9:00 AM at West High School. We run down Northern Lights Boulevard, and then the Tony Knowles Coastal Trail past Earthquake Park and Point Woronzof until we turn around at mile 6.5."

Kim sipped her wine and just smiled.

"Where will you watch the race, Mom?"

"How about at the far end of Northern Lights to start?"

"The return route follows the Coastal Trail for 6 miles until we reach Westchester Lagoon. I need to finish by 12:30 in order to be counted as an official finisher."

"I'll take your picture coming back on the Trail. By the way, is the course flat?"

"We start at 220 feet elevation and finish at 490 feet. Between miles 7 and 13, I'll be running through a heavily forested section called the Oilwell Tank Trail. Apparently, there are rocks on the course the size of baseballs. Don't worry, I'll be careful. There will be the main aid stations on Northern Lights and at the Point, besides additional aid stations at the finish line and along the way."

"Let me read some of that while you finish your pasta. I'm glad there will be mobile medics patrolling the course on ATVs." Kim glanced up to see Ashley frown. "Bet you don't know how you get timed?"

Now sporting a wide grin, Ashley replied, "Could it be a timing chip issued with my official bib, attached to my shoelace?"

They both laughed.

"Of course, I know that. I need to tie the chip to my shoe. An antenna at the finish line senses the chip and assigns my gun time. Runner time results will be posted on the website starting just before noon."

Showing her daughter a picture of a sag wagon in the flier, Kim kidded, "I'm sure that I'd be hitching a ride halfway through the race."

She made a toast. "To Ashley, the marathon runner. A safe and swift race."

••••••••••

Kim was startled by the blast of the gun. Ashley ran down Northern Lights with her bib flapping in the cool breeze from Cook Inlet. Kim stared at the digital picture in her hands, snapped just minutes before the race. She already envisioned a home for the photo, on the mantel over the fireplace. She stared at the sun-kissed crystal-blue waters of the inlet in the photo, but it was her daughter's radiant, proud smile over the number 2929 on her turquoise bib that jumped out.

Hopping a shuttle, she waited at the far end of the Boulevard. When she saw 2929 in the pack passing by her, she screamed out, "Go Ashley!"

Her daughter gave her thumbs-up sign and yelled, "Mom, see you on the way back!"

••••••••••

His view of the race from Oilwell Tank Trail was ideal. Ex-FBI agent Rick Miller and his assistant were ready to join the runners. They spotted Ashley on the turn and walked out onto the track. Trotting slowly on this remote rock-strewn section of the race, they looked back to see their target closing fast. When Ashley pulled up alongside of them, Rick pretended to stumble. He wrapped his arms tightly around her. Pulling her down with him, he took the brunt of the fall with Ashley landing on top of him. At the same time, the assistant fell onto the grassy hillside.

Rick feigned being winded. He huffed, "I'm so sorry. Are you all right?"

"I guess I'm okay. What happened? Did you trip?"

"Yeah, I think I twisted my ankle on a rock. Haley, are you OK?"

The woman nodded that she was all right. Rick looked around. As the trio rose to their feet, two runners passing by slowed down and asked them if they needed help.

Rick yelled back, "We're okay. Just had a little accident. Thanks for asking."

He walked a few steps and spotted his ATV parked no more than five feet away. He could hear the motor humming. Glancing over at Haley, he winked.

Ashley said, "It looks like you're walking fine, sir."

Rick replied with a laugh, "Don't worry about me."

"Well, guys, time to get back in the race. Glad no one got hurt. See ya."

As Ashley pulled away to rejoin the race, Haley grabbed her arm. Rick opened a medical bag that he had hidden just off the trail. He pulled out a prepared syringe. Just as Ashley was about to turn to face them, he jabbed the needle into her neck. For a brief spell, their victim flailed her arms. Seconds later, runner 2929 passed out in his arms.

••••••••••

Kim paced nervously. Not having seen Ashley on the return trail, she drove to the gathering area around the finish line. It was almost noon. Even at an 18-minute-per-mile pace, she was certain that her daughter should have finished by now.

She called Jonathan. His cheery response was shocking. "Honey, I just checked Ashley's time on the web. She finished in two hours and twenty-two minutes. Not too shabby. So, how is she doing?"

Shivering in the sixty-nine-degree sunshine, Kim cried, "I can't find her."

"What are you talking about?"

"I never saw her on the return trail so I came to the finish line. I called her cell and got her voice mail. She's nowhere in sight."

"That's impossible. The time chip on the shoe for runner 2929 registered a finish time about thirty minutes ago on the web site. You must have missed her."

While Kim was running to the aid station, she heard Jonathan ask her to hold on. Pressing the cell against her right ear, she ran up the stairs to approach the marathon officials. They were sitting at a table with two computers and streams of paper listing the runners.

"Excuse me, I'm looking for runner 2929. I was told that she completed the race."

One of the volunteer staff punched up Ashley's number on his laptop. "Yes, she finished a while ago. We take a picture of all runners as they finish the race."

"Thank God! I was really worried. I wonder where she might have gone."

"Maybe she's still talking to a few of the runners. She'll show up any minute, I'm sure."

Turning the laptop toward her so she could see the screen, he added, "In fact, look. Here is her picture crossing the finish line."

Kim felt her stomach sinking. "That's not Ashley. She's not a redhead."

Just then Jonathan's shaky voice came through to her on her cell. "Oh my God, no! No! . . . I just got a call . . . they got Ashley . . ."

"Who called? Who has her?"

"A man with a heavy New York accent called me and said unless I do what they want, they will . . . oh my God, Kim, they have Ashley."

••••••••••

"Nice job, Rick. How much did you give her?" Haley asked as they boarded the twin-engine Cessna Citation X.

"Just enough that she should sleep for most of our flight back to Mexico. Take the pilot's seat. Just so you know, our fuel margin to fly back will be razor thin. I had to move fast and couldn't finish refueling."

"Hope we have enough to reach Puerto Vallarta."

"Let me know if you need a break. In the meantime, I'll go back in the cabin to keep an eye on our girl."

"She looks pretty zonked out. For a moment or so, I thought you had overdosed her. She was barely breathing." Haley paused for a moment, then asked somewhat hesitantly, "By the way, you did search her before putting her on board, right?"

"Of course."

"You never disappoint me. Just between you and me, one day we'll have to have a serious talk. You just might be ready to take over the leadership of The Health Club."

"Nothing would make me happier. You know, I was just thinking how Rogers is feeling right now," Rick said as he stood to check on Ashley.

"He has no choice but to do what we want," Haley answered. "Everyone has a price. And we have his sleeping angel right here on board with us. He'll pay that price any day."

Minutes later, Rick returned to occupy the co-pilot seat of the plane. According to the flight plan, he calculated they should be flying over Baja California before nine that evening. Seconds later, the plane began shaking violently. Haley reacted quickly to the turbulence by taking the aircraft down a few thousand feet or so. She leveled off after thirty minutes of trying to find a calm airspace. The Cessna continued to hum along at five hundred and fifty miles an hour.

••••••••••

Her fall to the floor of the plane caused by the turbulence woke Ashley from her drugged sleep. She had no idea where she was. As her senses came alive, she soon realized that she was on an airplane. She could barely hold back her desire to just scream. Her face was pressed into the floorboards. Taking deep breaths, she fought to keep her eyes open. She didn't know why, but the only thing she wanted to do to was sleep. At one point, she thought she was dreaming. Her neck felt like someone was squeezing it. She could hardly move her legs. While trying to clear the cobwebs, she began listening to strange voices just a few feet away from her. She could hear a man and a woman talking. One of them was saying that they were less than a couple of hours from landing.

Who are these people? What have they done to me? The thoughts kept coming faster and faster. Ashley craned her neck to see the cockpit. She could see through the partially open curtains and could hear their conversation. Then she spotted her cell phone just a foot from her reach in a corner of the cabin. It had apparently fallen out of her shorts pocket. She began to crawl toward it, moving as quietly as she could, but her limbs were numb. She could barely lift her fingers to reach for it. Inch by inch, she moved closer, freezing each time she heard a voice coming from the cockpit. She thought she heard her father's name mentioned, and a flood of fear nearly overwhelmed her. But she continued on across the floor until she grabbed the phone. Pressing the record button, she aimed it toward the cockpit. Her eyes widened as she listened to their conversation.

"Rick, can I ask you a couple of questions?"

"Sure."

"Can I join you in listening to Jonathan Rogers's press conference tomorrow?"

Ashley's heart pounded. *They know Daddy!*

"I can arrange that."

"What will Rogers say?"

"He'll announce a Department of Health Task Force to investigate fraudulent billing by certain doctors."

"Won't that attract attention to the leaders?"

"Actually, quite the opposite."

"What about Ashley?"

"By now, he knows what he has to do to save her. Although it won't matter anyway for his pretty little daughter. As my uncle Zach always says, never leave witnesses."

Ashley's eyes blazed. *They're talking about me.* Agitated, she remembered her yoga training. She willed herself to be fully awake despite her heavy fatigue. She searched her mind for what had happened. Something about running in the marathon. Mom would be waiting at the finish line. *Where's Mom?*

Crawling another eighteen inches closer to the cockpit door, she stretched the cell phone out as far as she could reach. She fought to slow down her breathing. Ashley began to remember being in Alaska. She recalled running on the track. And then she thought of the accident where the guy with the New York accent knocked her to the ground. That accent. *The guy in the cockpit has the same accent. What if they find me with my cell phone?* Ashley stopped the taping. She pulled herself up on the cot, shoving the cell phone deep under the soft, beige leather cushion. Resuming her former position on the cot, she pretended to be unconscious.

"Rick, our ETA is at least another twenty minutes away. We used up more fuel than I thought. We have to land at Cabo San Lucas. We'll never make Puerto Vallarta. Take over the controls. I'm going to check on our sleeping beauty."

A few moments later, Rick yelled back to the cabin, "We've got big problems. The left engine just cut out. The fuel gauge is flickering just above the line pointing to empty. We're almost running on fumes."

"What the hell? Call the control tower."

As the Cessna began its rapid descent, the tower responded that they were still five miles from the airport. Rick ordered Haley to take the co-pilot's seat.

"Buckle up." He glanced at the spinning dials on his control panel. "We just need a little luck. Come on baby. Just stay up another few minutes."

"I see the runway lights."

"Control Tower, this is Cessna 444 requesting priority landing at Cabo."

"Cessna 444. Permission granted. Runway two is clear for you to land. Emergency vehicles are being deployed."

"Rick, there's smoke coming from the right engine."

"Shit!"

"Altitude two thousand feet and falling fast."

"Wheels down."

"Now the right engine is sputtering."

"Hang on baby."

"We're coming in too steep."

Rick pulled back on the wheel. "Relax." He gripped the wheel tightly as the Cessna bounced off the tarmac.

Haley shouted, "You're drifting off the runway."

He made the adjustment. The wheels gripped the cement, down the centerline. "Dammit, that was close. I don't think we could have lasted another minute up there."

"Awesome job, Rick."

"Control Tower, I'm taxiing in to the nearest gate."

"Roger that, Cessna 444." Rick flipped off the radio to the control tower.

"Now we have to figure out where we'll stash away our priceless sleeping cargo."

"I know a small inn on the outskirts of Cabo."

"Can we trust the locals to keep quiet?"

"We'll need a lot of pesos from The Health Club coffers to buy silence."

"That won't be a problem. Go tie up little miss Ashley and blindfold her. I'll contact headquarters and update them with our plan B."

Haley liked his decisiveness. "Like I said before, I see you as our next leader."

"Hey, just don't go blabbing that around. My uncle will catch wind of that rumor and would think nothing of knocking me off."

"His only nephew?"

"Just tie up Ashley and keep your mouth shut."

"Yes, boss."

"But you know what? There's one thing that I inherited from my uncle."

"Good looks."

"A mean streak!"

Chapter Ten

Rogers did not even try to sleep. He convinced Kim to stay in Alaska, where an all points bulletin had been issued by the state police. In his mind, he replayed the haunting words from the caller over and over. The kidnapper had ordered him to call a press conference for the following afternoon. The topic was going to be Medicaid fraud. He was given specific instructions as to who should be on a Task Force to investigate certain physicians who were believed to be submitting medical claims for services not rendered. It was strange, he thought, that Peter Chambers had just privately accused Tom Knowton of this same crime. Rogers downed his third cup of coffee at three in the morning and called Kim.

"Any news?" he asked in a somber tone.

"Nothing. What are we going to do?"

"Follow the kidnappers' instructions. What else can we do?"

"No one remembers having any contact with Ashley. I think I've spoken to almost half the town of Anchorage. Who is doing this to us?"

"All I know is what I was told. If we go to the police, they will kill Ashley."

"I'll keep looking up here. A few natives gave me some leads."

"I'm starting to get a bad feeling. We've got to find our daughter!"

••••••••••

"Sally, is Dr. Carver here?"

"Yes. He's in your office. You have thirty minutes before you are scheduled to start the press conference."

Rogers opened the door and was comforted to see his colleague and friend of many years. They shook hands. Carver patted Jonathan on the shoulder. Rogers had a hard time holding in his emotions, but he couldn't betray his current desperation to his colleague. Kim had warned him against his usual inclination to share his feelings with his friends. "Victor, how are you?" he asked quietly.

Carver shrugged. "Great. You're looking a little peaked. Not sleeping well?"

"Kim and I are going through something these days." He rubbed his chin and scratched his forehead. Thinking about Ashley, he debated whether to confide in his friend. He flashed his eyes wide open after remembering Kim's strong advice.

"Well, you seem a little better than you were after Tom gave you your chemo treatment a few weeks ago."

"Our best days are ahead of all of us, my friend."

"No doubt." Carver slapped him on the back again and smiled.

"Thanks for doing this," Jonathan said. "So, are you ready for your first press conference?"

Grimacing, Carver replied, "Think so, but I'm a little nervous. I've never done anything like this before. Especially, since you just asked me a few hours ago. You're lucky today is my day off."

"Sorry for the short notice. Recently, I've received some reports of physician fraud that I believe needs to be investigated. Your name surfaced to be the chair of the Task Force to look into the matter."

"Always glad to help a friend."

"You'll do fine. Let's sit down and relax a little before we face the lions."

Jonathan took a sip of coffee, and pointed to an array of doughnuts. "Help yourself."

"No thanks. What I could use right now is a drink to settle my nerves."

"I never pictured you as being the nervous type. Since you're an oncologist, I always thought that nothing would faze you. I figure you look into the abyss every day, with your patients dying of cancer."

"It does take a definite detachment from my patients when I

know they have no chance to survive. So, I guess you're right."

Jonathan shook his head. "Remember, we're here to do the people's business. I appointed you to lead the Medicaid Fraud Task Force to take an objective look at the feedback that I have received from many citizens.

"I'll follow your lead. This is all so new for me."

Checking his watch, Rogers stood up quickly. "It's show time."

••••••••••

Rogers led Carver to the private entrance leading to the hall. He peeked through the one-way mirror and scanned the Governor Warren Winchester Press Hall. The Commissioner initially focused on the warped oak table that rested on the five-foot elevated stage. There were twenty microphones, each representing a different media outlet throughout Michigan. Though he was trying to focus on what he had been asked to do, he could not blot out thoughts of his daughter. He felt his heart beating faster in his chest, especially upon noting the absence of any of the usual security guards that patrolled the press hall and capitol building.

He led Carver onto stage. In the audience was a sea of half-asleep reporters seated in what looked like six rows of fold-up chairs. He saw a slew of laptops, notepads, and digital recorders. Everyone in the room seemed to have one characteristic in common. Whether it was the way they hung their heads or intermittently sighed, it was obvious that everyone wanted to be someplace else.

He instructed Carver to take a seat at the far side of the table. Seating himself directly in back of the podium, he pulled out his talking points from the inside pocket of his dark blue suit. He glanced up a few times while taking note that most of the reporters were still reading the Medicaid Fraud one-pager that was being distributed by Department of Health staffers. When he believed that the time was right, he walked to the podium to start the conference. He waited for silence before speaking.

"Ladies and Gentlemen, I'm Dr. Jonathan Rogers. I want to

begin by thanking you for attending this Department of Health press conference on such short notice. Seated on stage with me is Dr. Victor Carver, a trusted colleague of mine. We're here today to discuss the very important subject of Medicaid fraud."

Rogers looked over at Carver. His long-time close friend gave a barely noticeable thumbs-up sign.

"As a result of my monthly 'Meet the Commissioner' meetings with the public, I've been informed by several citizens that a number of physicians in this state may be cheating on insurance bills. Such activity is clear-cut fraud. Your state government will not tolerate such criminal behavior."

Motioning for his colleague to stand, he added, "Today, I've appointed Dr. Victor Carver to chair the Commissioner's Medicaid Task Force to evaluate the evidence that has been presented to me. As you know, the names and résumés of the nine-member Task Force were distributed to all of you just a short while ago. At this time, I would like Dr. Carver to introduce himself."

The newly appointed chairman, dressed in an inexpensive-looking blue blazer, approached the podium with steadfast strides. Rogers felt his cell vibrating. He turned it off.

"Thank you, Commissioner. For those among you who don't know me, I'm a practicing oncologist in the town of Oldwyck and a senior partner in the private practice of Knowton, Carver, and Higgins for almost twenty years. I'm making a solemn promise to you today that I will do my absolute best to lead the Medicaid Fraud Task Force to uncover the truth, wherever our investigations lead us. As Chair, I'll report back our findings to Dr. Rogers no later than ninety days from now so that he can pass on our report to Governor Peabody. Thank you for your kind attention."

The Commissioner rose. Rogers nodded approvingly to Carver while several hands in the audience shot in the air.

With his eyes drawn to the front row, the Commissioner said, "Chuck, why don't we start with you?"

"I have a two-part question. Commissioner Rogers, since payments to Medicaid come from both state and federal sources, why doesn't the Task Force have representation from the federal government? And, since Medicaid fraud is a crime, why doesn't the Task Force have law enforcement included?"

"There will be plenty of time to involve the authorities if the Task Force uncovers any definitive proof. Your other point is well taken. I'll be in contact with the offices of the Attorney General and the Surgeon General at the federal level after I review Dr. Carver's report."

While he surveyed the crowd, a young woman in the back, whom Rogers did not recognize, raised her hand but remained seated. She was dressed in a smart pink business suit and didn't look at all like the typical reporter.

He pointed directly at her. "Please state your name, media affiliation, and question."

"My name is Beth Murphy. Commissioner, is it true that some of the doctors that have been accused of fraud have also been accused of poor patient care?"

Instantly recognizing her last name from his recent conversations with Peter Chambers, he felt his antennae being pricked to a full alert level.

"Miss Murphy, all information regarding any specific doctor's patient care is strictly confidential. But thank you for your question."

Rogers turned to his left and asked for additional questions. Out of the corner of his right eye, he could see that the young woman was now standing.

She shouted, "Does the name of Sam Murphy ring a bell?"

"Miss Murphy, I would suggest that you and I speak in private after the press conference."

"Why can't you answer my questions now? Do you have something to hide?" she asked.

Stunned by dozens of flashes coming from all angles, Rogers fired back with more force than was his usual custom. "It's clearly not appropriate to be discussing private matters in this public forum."

Pushing her way through a gathering swarm of reporters, she now stood no more than ten feet away from him. Uncharacteristically, Rogers felt unnerved. Murphy held up a manila folder high above her head with both of her outstretched arms.

Her voice echoed throughout the hall. "I'm holding the medical records of my father, Samuel Murphy. These records document that your personal friend Dr. Tom Knowton gave him an overdose of Zazotene for his cancer treatment."

Rogers scanned the hall, but there still was no sign of any security guards. He gathered his notes and announced, "Thank you for your kind attention today. I'll be reporting back to all of you the conclusions of the Medicaid Fraud Task Force. This press conference is over."

As he turned from the podium, he heard a reporter yelling over the building murmur of the crowd. "Wait a minute, Commissioner. Let's hear what she has to say."

Rogers sensed that the lions in the audience were hungry. It was obvious that Murphy's story had ignited their fuses. Winchester Hall seemed to be hungering for a public climax.

Murphy shouted, "Mr. Peter Chambers came to your office several weeks ago as a friend of our family. He told you that Dr. Knowton was prescribing Zazotene for my father at doses not approved by the FDA and for a diagnosis that was inappropriate. Mr. Chambers then asked you to look into the matter in your official capacity as Commissioner of Health."

"I only promised him that I would do my best to find out what I could." Halfway through his reply, he wished he had kept his mouth shut.

"Have you gotten back to Mr. Chambers?"

"Miss Murphy, with all due respect, this conversation is completely inappropriate." Pointing her finger at him, she blasted, "You're the Commissioner of Health. Don't you care about people?"

Rogers heard the building crescendo of exclamations filling the press hall. As he watched her take a few steps closer to the podium, he wondered if Beth Murphy had anything to do with the kidnapping of Ashley.

Dramatizing each word as if she were an actor on a Broadway stage, her voice quivered. "By the fact that you did nothing, I'm holding you responsible for what happened to my father."

"I don't have the authority to tell any doctor how to practice medicine."

From the front row, a reporter well known at the Statehouse interjected herself into the conversation. Playing her customary role as devil's advocate, the veteran reporter began:

"Dr. Rogers, I know that you personally championed the Michigan Physician Guideline Bill. Doesn't that tell doctors how to practice medicine? If Dr. Knowton practiced outside the guidelines that you seem to cherish, why wouldn't you have intervened?"

He glared at the reporter. "It's not that simple. I added a clause to the legislation. Doctors now have appeal rights that may justify treatment outside the guidelines."

As he stood there, he was astonished at Murphy's singular command of the press conference. Glancing over to the Task Force Chairman, he saw his colleague approaching. Carver stepped in front of him in order to get closer to the microphone.

The oncologist spoke in a low-pitched, monotone voice. "Miss Murphy, we all feel bad for you but there was nothing that Dr. Rogers could have done. As I said earlier, I'm actually a partner of Knowton and even I cannot tell him what to do. Your father was a very gentle man who did much good for the world. I saw him once or twice myself when he came into the office to see my partner. I've also made hospital rounds, providing as much care as possible. We wish we could save everybody, but we just can't."

Rogers noticed several of the reporters approaching Beth Murphy. The Commissioner began walking toward the rear of the stage. His head pounded while imagining the headline in tomorrow's Oldwyck Gazette. There it was, right before his eyes: Commissioner Rogers Accused of Murder Cover-Up.

Moments later, he heard the clanking sounds of high heels on the hardwood floor of Winchester Hall. He turned just in time to see Beth Murphy charging at him. She came to a halt no less than four feet away from him, pointing to the sky with her right index finger, her face radiating a blazing red hue.

"This isn't over, Commissioner," Murphy ominously added.

Chapter Eleven

Onboard his flight to Anchorage, Rogers winced upon reading the Oldwyck Gazette. The headline screamed the expected news. Commissioner Rogers Accused of Murder Cover-Up. A photo of Beth Murphy angrily pointing her finger at him during the Medicaid fraud press conference dominated the front page. But with Ashley on his mind, he scanned the rest of the paper, checking to see if the national newswires had picked up the story of her kidnapping in Alaska. Seeing nothing in the local paper, he spotted a copy of the statewide paper, the Detroit Free Press, lying on an adjacent seat. Not a word about Ashley.

Even though Kim had said there was nothing he could do that wasn't already being done to search for their daughter, he felt deeply that he needed to go to Alaska. In his mind, he replayed what Kim had told him of the marathon. His plan was to walk the route searching for clues, any sign that would help to bring back Ashley.

He dozed off, remembering what his mom had once said when Ashley was born: *A son is a son until he takes a wife but a daughter is a daughter for the rest of her life.* Her birth was the happiest day of his life. It had always seemed that he and Ashley were much closer than she was to her mom. Nothing much else mattered except to find his baby girl.

••••••••••

While waiting for his luggage to plop out of the conveyor belt, Rogers saw Kim entering the terminal wearing dark sunglasses.

"Kim," he shouted, waving his hand. As she came closer, he noticed how slow she was walking, her head held low. He held out his arms, waiting for a hug, an embrace that never came.

"Why did you come up here? I told you there is nothing you can do."

"Nice to see you as well."

"She's gone. The authorities have no clue."

"Then it's up to us."

"What do you expect to find?"

He looked away, spotting the blue tag on his black piece of luggage. He grabbed it and walked back to where they were standing.

"I'll tell you what I can do—anything and everything to find Ashley. Tomorrow, I'm going to retrace every step she took in the race. Do you want to come with me?"

Kim stared at him with a blank expression. "Maybe I should stay back at the hotel, in case the police call. I had trouble today even getting out of bed. I've been waking up in the middle of the night, wide awake. My psychiatrist returned my call. She upped my dose of antidepressants."

Rogers glared at her. "Let's go." He pulled his bag along and let out a few grunts as Kim trailed behind him by a few feet. Suddenly, he stopped dead in his tracks. "Dammit, Kim. We have cell phones. If the police want to find us, they can. You don't need to hang out in your comfortable hotel room while your flesh and blood is missing."

"I'm sorry. I'm doing the best I can, Jonathan. Good luck on the trail tomorrow."

"One thing I know for sure. I'm certainly going to try. There is no excuse for not trying."

"What if they kidnap you the same way they took Ashley?"

••••••••••

Rogers looked out at the shimmering waters of Cook Inlet. The surrounding snow-capped Chugach Mountains appeared majestic. The sun blazed, with temperatures in the high 50s. He cursed that such a beautiful place would be the scene of the worst tragedy of his life.

He began where Ashley had begun. At six in the morning, the parking lot of West High School was deserted. With a water bottle in one hand and a bag of peanuts tucked into his trousers, he began his trek down Northern Lights Boulevard. With each step, he recalled that Kim had positioned herself at the end of Northern Lights to cheer on Ashley. He pictured Ashley's beaming face with her number 2929 bib flapping in the wind as she waved to her mom.

Entering the next section of the race, Rogers felt the incline on his quads as he walked up the sloping Tony Knowles Coastal Trail. By now, a few joggers were starting to pass him. Reality was setting in. He began to wonder just what he thought he was going to find on the trail that would lead him to Ashley. He focused on the dirt pathway, searching for anything that could lead him to his daughter.

Just as he got close to the forested area on the Oilwell Tank Trail, he sat down on a boulder alongside the road. He took a few sips of water to wash down a handful of peanuts. Thoughts of what Kim was doing back in the hotel room flashed into his mind. He hung his head and stared at the golf-ball-sized rocks on the trail. Hearing the footsteps of a few joggers, he blamed himself for what happened to Ashley.

He felt a lingering presence and looked up. "Are you OK?" a soft voice asked.

Rogers saw a middle-aged woman sporting a T-shirt with the word "Alaska" in large red letters written across her chest.

"I'm fine. Thanks for asking. I was just taking a break."

"Glad you're OK. I run this route every day and I've seen more than my fair share of people our age getting heart attacks running in these hills."

"Actually, I'm just walking the route."

"Training for next year's half marathon?"

"Not exactly. Our daughter just ran in the recent one."

"What time did she finish in?"

Rogers looked away, pausing to take another sip from his water bottle. "Not sure. My wife would know."

"Are you guys from Alaska?"

"It's actually a long story. We're from Michigan." He wanted to change the direction of the conversation. "So can you tell me how far it is from here to Point Woronzof?"

"A few miles." She looked at him with a quizzical expression. "It's not my business, but you don't appear to be a jogger. Did you daughter lose something on the trail that you're looking for?"

"Why would you say that?"

"Just curious . . . I guess."

He paused and presented a wide grin. "Yes, she did. Ashley fell somewhere in this area and lost a pinky ring. After the marathon, my wife and I decided to stay here to vacation. Our daughter called yesterday from back home and realized that she had lost her ring and asked me to check it out."

"Well, good luck. I'll be on my way."

Rogers watched her trot away. He blamed himself for not being more direct with the woman. After all, he needed information about Ashley. Maybe the runner had seen something if she was in the race? He wondered if she had seen the story of Ashley's disappearance in the Alaskan Herald. He began walking in her direction toward the Point, stepping carefully over a rock-strewn trail winding through the woods. Then he noticed the woman stopping thirty yards ahead. She was looking back at him, seeming to wait until he caught up.

Rogers trotted toward her. "Is it my turn to ask you if you are all right?"

"I'm fine. I was just thinking. Around the local running club, there are rumors. It seems that a young woman may have been kidnapped during the marathon."

"Really?" He recalled his orders and spoke slowly. "Thank God it wasn't our daughter."

"I'm glad for you. Ever since I read about the story of the young woman, I've thought about going to the police."

His heartbeat skipped a few. "Why? Did you see something?"

"I was in the race, and around the time when I was returning from the Point, I saw a young woman and another man and woman on the ground as I passed them. I asked them if they were OK. They said they had tripped and were fine. So I finished the race, not thinking about it again."

Rogers decided to press on. "Maybe you should tell the authorities."

"What I told you is all I know. How would that help? And I don't like getting involved in dealing with the police."

"The police are here to help us."

"Let's not go there."

"Anything that jumps out about the appearance of the joggers?"

"Why the interest?"

He could see that he was arousing suspicion. "I have a friend who suffered no end when his six-year-old son was kidnapped. This brings back memories."

"The man was slender and in his thirties. The young woman was athletic looking and wore a pony tail. The other woman was a little older and very attractive. That's about it."

"Maybe something will come to you as you're running."

"Actually there was something I recall about the older woman. She was probably about forty. Her hair was radiant red."

He turned away for a few moments, trying to hide the look on his face. "Guess it wouldn't hurt to report what you saw. Redheads make up only one to two percent of the world's population. So there can't be that many in these parts."

"Maybe you're right. I'll think about it. See you."

As she jogged off again, Rogers could only think one thing. *A redhead appeared at every mishap.*

••••••••••

On his flight back to Michigan, Rogers thought about the jogger he had met. *Why didn't I get her name?* He had told Kim the whole story. She wanted to stay in Alaska in case there was any news from the local police. He had pressing problems back home, and had to leave the search for Ashley to the authorities. Leaving Alaska behind without knowing the fate of his daughter was agony, but he had no choice.

Chapter Twelve

Zach Miller sneered at his seven-person senior management team, but their frightened stares actually amused him.

"My question," he said, pounding the conference table for emphasis, "is whether we have maximized revenues from our sales of Zazotene?"

Silence. He sighed with exasperation.

"OK, listen. All of you know that the Food and Drug Administration has limited the actual indications for our drug by regulating what we can say to our prescribers. Our official FDA label says Zazotene is to be used for only two cancers. But physicians can still prescribe off-label for any cancer. Of course, we're prohibited from promoting such off-label use. So take a few moments to think about my questions."

He drew a line down the center of the notepad in front of him. To the left side of the pad, he scribbled down the names of those who completely averted their eyes from him, as if they were still schoolchildren trying to avoid eye contact with a teacher asking a tough question. These names, assigned to column A, would be the first to be fired. To the right of the line, he recorded those executives who returned his glare as if inspired to say something brilliant, only to remain silent as they then turned toward their colleagues for support. The column B names would be the next to go. He swallowed hard, hardly believing that he had once hired these so-called leaders at Doctor's Choice Products. *At least I can control them.*

He fully credited himself with DCP's success. Zach had cultivated his widespread connections like a master. Despite his weak management team, the robust pipeline at the Michigan-based drug company always seemed to sail unscathed through the FDA approval process.

He smiled upon seeing Randy Douglas's raised hand. Zach drew a horizontal line across the bottom of both columns of names on his scorecard. He scratched Randy from the questionable column B and wrote his name on the bottom section, the keeper list.

The marketing VP stated proudly, "By next week, we'll have our first Zazotene direct-to-consumer ad on TV. It will hawk the patient benefits for both of our FDA-approved indications."

"Douglas, did I ask a question about marketing FDA-approved indications for our drug? No, I asked whether we have maximized our revenues from our first-year launch of Zazotene. As you know, DCP provides comprehensive health benefits. Maybe you need to check out your hearing. We cover that."

Surveying the team, he picked up on Douglas's visual plea for help from Elizabeth Harmon, chief legal counsel. Not at all surprised that she completely ignored him, he watched Elizabeth pretending to be jotting on her legal pad.

"Wake up!" he growled.

Samantha Andrews, director of public relations for DCP, chimed in. "I would say that we have not done enough to maximize profits."

"We appreciate your thoughtful and insightful comment."

Bored by his sycophants, Zach began watching the oversized television screen that was in the far wall of the conference room. The stock ticker at the bottom of the screen showed that the DCP stock price was down. Zach folded his arms across his chest and shut his eyes for a couple of seconds to blot out the bad news. *It's time for the lava to flow.*

"Do I have to remind all of you that after an initial pop with the FDA approval of Zazotene, our stock has been trending downward for the past two months?"

The PR director muttered, "We'll do better."

"Glad to hear the cheerleading. But I don't think our shareholders will be impressed. In fact, guess who they'll hold accountable for a failure of our stock price to go up."

"You'll be their whipping boy," Samantha agreed.

"Bingo. Drug czars get paid for rising stock prices, not for making people happy. This isn't Disneyland."

Zach next locked into the close-set pair of eyes of Dylan Matthews, senior VP of sales. He was tall and clean-cut looking. His clients seemed to be drawn to his friendly ways. But Zach was growing increasingly wary of his pin-up sales chief.

"Matthews, has there been any significant increase in off-label prescribing for Zazotene?"

"We do have a strategy to accomplish your goal."

"It's not *my* goal, it's *our* goal. Understood?"

Matthews began again. "Our sales team in the field led by Sean has been quietly educating doctors about the two case reports demonstrating that our drug may be effective in treating the endocrine gastrointestinal cancers. Of course, these are off-label indications that have not been approved by the FDA."

Liz shot up her hand. "That's illegal."

Zach held up his hand. "Continue Dylan . . ."

"By hinting, in a very subtle way, to selected oncologists, whom we trust, we have communicated that these case reports exist. So we're doing our best to increase off-label Zazotene prescribing. As Liz points out, active promotion of off-label use of any drug is strictly forbidden by the FDA. If any doctor complained to the FDA that we are doing this, we would receive a warning letter, a huge fine, and, even worse, sanctions."

"Don't worry about the FDA. That's my job. So has there been an increase in off-label prescribing, yes or no?"

"Possibly a small increase."

Zach sighed loudly. He turned his attention to Dr. Randy Phillips, chief medical officer and senior VP of research and product development.

"What do you think, Doc?"

Phillips cleared his throat. "If I may, I would like to back up a little and review the facts. First of all, the clinical trial data didn't conclusively show that Zazotene was effective for any tumors other than non-Hodgkin's lymphoma and myeloma. Those are the only cancers for which the FDA has granted us approval to openly market our drug."

Zach scowled. "Doc, you sound just like Matthews and Liz."

"Secondly, the data shows additional safety problems that we all need to remember. Unfortunately, in a subset of patients where doctors have prescribed Zazotene off-label, we have begun to see some dose-related fatal side effects. That's because higher doses are needed for these non-FDA-approved diagnoses. In so many words, when we 'unofficially' market doctors to prescribe off-label, they use higher doses that have killed patients."

Zach jumped to his feet. He paced at the head of the table. "Doctor, are those safety numbers statistically significant at this point?"

"The numbers are relatively small, but each number, of course, represents a human life lost."

"That's not what I asked."

The chief medical officer lowered his head. "Strictly speaking, the numbers are not statistically significant at this time."

"Finally, I hear an answer to my question. Listen, I just want us to stick to the facts rather than citing chance variations based on small sample numbers. People die every day for all sorts of reasons. Let's not blame Zazotene for deaths due to other causes beyond our control. God, at least you're not blaming the drug for causing global warming!"

The leader walked toward his legal counsel. "Go ahead, Elizabeth. Say your piece."

Turning to the chief doc on her left, Harmon asked, "Randy, have we gone public with that subset safety data showing that there have been fatalities?"

Seeing Phillips open his mouth, Zach boomed, "Why the hell would we do that?"

Harmon replied, "It's the law."

Zach threw his hands high in the air. "Oh, puleeze . . ."

Liz looked at Dr. Phillips. "We can do something that might be useful to drive our revenues. The FDA will allow us to respond to an unsolicited physician's request about clinical studies on off-label potential effectiveness. In that case, we are permitted by law to refer them to our chief medical officer so that Randy could accurately discuss the clinical facts. Essentially, this would be a peer-to-peer risk-benefit ratio discussion of whether it would make sense to prescribe off-label. But under no circumstances can our DCP sales reps initiate or have these types of discussions with physicians."

"Whoa, Dr. Phillips and Counselor Harmon," Zach proclaimed while he imitated a horse rider pulling back on the reins. "Let's get real. Medicine isn't an exact science. Dr. Phillips, besides your doctorate in pharmacy from Yale, you have a medical degree from Harvard. Didn't they teach you Ivy Leaguers that life is more complex than just trying to run a business based solely on experimental studies? Have you no respect for each doctor's clinical judgment?"

Zach raised his hands above his head as if he were imitating a TV evangelist. "Doctors prescribe off-label all the time. Let me be blunt. Does anyone know exactly what happens in the privacy of a doctor's office? Is it the doctor who asks the DCP sales reps about off-label Zazotene or the DCP sales rep who initiates that discussion? Who really knows for sure?"

Liz snapped, "It's only legal when a clinical person like Randy responds, not the sales force. Again, if several doctors complain to the FDA, they could shut us down."

"And will the typical doc complain to the FDA? Of course not. They're too busy. So only the doctor and the DCP sales person will know for sure what goes on behind closed doors. So as long as the docs are on our side, we can take care of our sales force. The doctors are the key to our success. Do you think the choice of our company name had nothing to do with this strategy?"

While rubbing his forehead, Zach circled the conference table, letting out an occasional grunt or two while speeding up the cadence of his strides. He knew what he needed to do. He had no choice. He would drop the blade on someone. After walking back to the head of the table, he looked back at his top doc. "About that safety data you were talking about with off-label non-FDA-approved high-dose Zazotene?"

"Yes."

"Well, how about this for an idea? What if we increased the number of paid volunteers in our clinical trials at the Southwest

International drug testing facility? By doing that, we should be able to dilute the mortality figures."

Phillips's face brightened a shade. He stroked his chin, replying, "On a statistical basis, that would make the mortality seem lower as we would be adding people to the denominator. In other words, we would be increasing the number receiving Zazotene."

"I'm glad that you're beginning to follow my logic. Lord knows I pay you enough."

"It might work, Zach," the chief medical officer replied.

"Get with the program. Of course it will work. We would just need to ensure that National Quality doesn't blow the whistle on our ploy."

Phillips replied, "Since National Quality has oversight on all clinical trials at the drug testing company, how can you be sure that they won't squawk when Southwest International arbitrarily increases the number of paid subjects?"

"It's all under our control," the boss answered with a cunning smile.

Counselor Harmon spoke up, raising her voice an octave. "What you are saying is definitely unethical and most likely illegal. National Quality is an independent oversight body to ensure the safety of participants in the drug testing trials. Their role is to make scientific recommendations to the FDA on whether a drug is safe or not, not to rubber-stamp the drug testers."

"Just find us a safe harbor. That's why we pay you. We don't care to hear about your personal ethics. And, for the record, my remarks were directed at our chief medical officer."

Phillips leaned forward. "I could not possibly have the time to speak with every doctor who wishes to discuss our data. But we do have a DCP sales force of over five hundred out in the field who are out seeing prescribers every day. At least they could share the case studies with the doctors. Of course, they would have to be discreet. The sales force would need to walk a fine line. So, in my medical opinion . . ."

Matthews interrupted. "Randy, we would be breaking the law."

Zach fired back, "Nonsense!"

Matthews paused before replying. "All I know is that I want to go on record as saying that I agree with Elizabeth. This ridiculous idea of yours would be illegal. My sales staff is simply not qualified to present clinical studies to doctors. Only a physician is qualified to say whether a drug can be used for such off-label non-FDA-approved indications."

From the end of the conference table, Zach gave the order. "Enough Matthews, let Randy finish. Don't try to browbeat him."

The sales chief roared back. "Me? What about you? Listen, I'm not going to jail over this ill-conceived fantasy of yours."

"Quiet, Matthews. Continue, doctor. Excuse the rude interruption by your colleague."

"Based on our new strategy, there should be decreased fatalities and many more patient successes with off-label use of Zazotene. Overall, I think DCP could be benefiting many patients by reaching out to physicians who may not be properly informed on off-label use. After all, can anyone really say that the FDA is always correct?"

Zach feigned a bow toward his chief medical officer. "Thank you, Dr. Phillips, for your well-thought-out medical sign-off of our new corporate strategy on off-label marketing of Zazotene. I'm taking the prerogative as your chief to name this great strategy Plan P, in your honor."

The CEO strode confidently toward his chief financial officer, Charley O'Reilly. "What are the latest off-label revenues from our blockbuster drug?"

The money man paused. After confirming the data on his sheets, he said, "For the last quarter, we have booked revenues of $624,052 from off-label use of Zazotene."

Zach quickly did the math in his head. "So, at a unit price of about $12,000 per treatment, doctors have prescribed off-label about fifty times during the first three months since launch. Correct?"

"Fifty-two prescriptions to be precise. The good news is that we had two hundred and ten million in revenues from FDA-approved uses in the first quarter. The bad news is that we had factored in at least another ten million in revenues from off-label use."

Zach resumed his march around the thirty-foot-long teakwood conference table in the board room, stopping at the chair seating the VP of sales, Sean Parker. He gently tapped his shoulder. Parker spun around to face him.

"Your boss informs us that your sales team has been quietly promoting off-label use. I assume that Mr. Matthews is accurate in his description of your efforts to date."

"Yes, Dylan is correct."

"Sean, how many years have you been with this company?"

Parker replied with a quiver in his voice, "This is my third year at Doctor's Choice. In my last two as VP of sales, I've reported directly to Dylan Matthews."

Zach walked to the opposite side of the table. He stopped behind Matthews. Pausing a moment or two to note that the DCP price had dropped another twenty cents in value on the widescreen TV, he stood silently for a half minute, pretending to be counting the gray hairs on the back of his sales chief's head.

"How many years have you been the highest-ranking leader of sales at DCP?"

"Five years," Matthews boomed as he continued to look across the table, avoiding Zach's gaze.

"That's a long time in our business. If our stock price goes down, this team must take full responsibility. Do you agree?"

"It depends."

"Really! Then I guess it depends on who I keep on this team to share the blame with me."

Zach sauntered back toward the head of the conference table and remained standing. He counted his potential allies.

"Final thoughts, anyone?"

The CFO added, "Our stock price has dropped fifteen percent in the last few weeks and it's off almost one percent since we've been sitting here. The Street is expecting that Zazotene will be accretive to our third-quarter earnings by eight cents, but right now, we will be coming in at less than six cents. And what really worries me is that we are now facing stiff competition from Loximine, just out of the pipeline at Sunview Pharmaceutical. Loximine is now taking ten percent market share from our blockbuster for the

FDA-approved diagnoses that we already had in the bag. In order to raise our profit margins, we will require a lot more help from the non-FDA-approved off-label prescribing."

Zach's eyes narrowed. "Give us the bottom line."

"We're not going to make our numbers just on doctors prescribing Zazotene for approved indications. For our stock to soar again like it did at launch, we need many more doctors using the drug for non-FDA-approved indications."

"Thanks, Charley. Team, ideas?" He scanned their faces. "Matthews, don't be shy."

The sales chief stood up and faced Zach. "This is ridiculous. Even if the doctors prescribe the Zazotene off-label, most likely the managed care companies will deny payment. Patients would be forced to shell out thousands of dollars out of pocket. It just won't work."

"Then Dr. Phillips will just have to convince his medical director colleagues in managed care to change their policies."

Phillips grinned. "I'll do my best."

"Matthews, sit down," Zach said.

O'Reilly shot his hand into the air. "I would like to bring up another issue. As long as we're talking about our company's stock price, DCP barely breaks even on our production of flu vaccine each year. I suggest we get out of that business to focus on improving our profits from our higher-margin drugs like Zazotene."

Zach beamed at Charley. "Does anyone disagree?"

After hearing no response, he pointed at his CMO and then to his chief legal counsel.

Phillips replied quickly, "As long as other drug companies can make the vaccines, I don't see why DCP has to be in that business."

"Counsel, does the law force us to make vaccines?"

"No," Harmon fired back. Her voice trailed off as she added, "It's still a free country."

Zach raised his right hand. "Enough! All I have heard today from our sales leader is that we have a so-called strategy of quiet promotion for off-label use. Well, I would have to say,

Dylan, that your efforts have been so quiet that you have put just about every prescriber to sleep. Zazotene isn't a tranquilizer! In case you forgot, it's a cancer drug!"

Matthews replied, "My plan will work if you give it a try."

"Give me a break, Dylan. For the quarter, we are millions below our needed revenues for off-label use."

Zach looked sternly at Parker. "Sean, any final recommendations to get our stock price going?"

"I will personally commit to this management team that we will improve our uptake for Zazotene by twenty percent in the next quarter for our two FDA-approved indications. Also, I fully share the DCP vision that the doctors are the key to our success. I propose that we offer a cruise to Mexico for selected doctors."

Zach cocked his head. "Keep going."

"We could target the top five to ten percent of these oncologists who have written for other DCP pharmaceuticals. We could offer Continuing Medical Education credits to these four to five hundred docs. And since they will be a captive audience for those days on the cruise, I'm sure we can influence them."

"I would agree that's a good start. But I'm not yet convinced that your plan is enough. What about Plan P, approved by Dr. Phillips?"

Parker held his hands out in front of him, meeting the gaze of each executive. "As our leaders have convincingly stated, increasing sales for FDA-approved indications will not be enough. I believe the DCP sales force can do a much better job in getting doctors to prescribe Zazotene for non-FDA-approved off-label indications."

Matthews yelled across the table. "Sean, that's not your call. I'm in charge of sales around here and what you are proposing, my friend, is illegal."

Zach said, "What matters is that we all agreed. Except for you, Dylan."

Matthews wagged his finger toward his boss. "It will take time for my strategy to pay off. If our stock price doesn't take off this year because of slower off-label use of Zazotene, then so be it."

Zach sat down, staring at the disappointing third-quarter

financials. After a few moments, he covered his face with both hands. Slowly, he spread apart his fingers. He peeked through to lock on one particular set of eyes.

"Dylan, this entire executive team signed off on our new strategy a few minutes ago. And by the way, plant your ass on your seat."

"Listen, I'm not going to jail to make you wealthy," he replied as he sat down.

Zach laughed. "We have a corporate code of ethical conduct that we all swear by."

Matthews stood up again. "You've gone over the top this time."

The boss rose slowly and buttoned his suit. "Sounds like insubordination to me." He scanned the table. No one disagreed. Standing eye to eye with his sales chief, Zach punched the intercom button on the desk.

"Yes, Mr. Miller," the security head replied.

"Come to the board room immediately and escort Mr. Matthews out the door."

Zach swaggered around the head of the table while ignoring Matthews at the far end. "One more order of business before we close today's meeting. Congratulations, Sean, on your promotion to senior VP of sales! See me in my office at five tonight."

Pleased to see Parker nodding his acceptance, he added, "The meeting is over. I promise you all that Zazotene will be a DCP mega-blockbuster drug. Now get to work."

As the door swung open, two security staff men walked swiftly toward Matthews. Zach sneered disdainfully at his former employee.

Exiting the board room door, Matthews yelled back over his shoulder. "Miller, you won't get away with this."

Zach snickered. "I think you just threatened me in public. Not that it matters."

One by one, he watched his workers filing out of the board room. He spotted Liz Harmon, who was still sitting. Zach walked toward her and stood defiantly next to her. Not looking at him, Harmon rose after a minute. She hustled toward the door and did not look back, slamming the door behind her.

From the far end of the table near the stock streaming ticker, he could see that his money man was warily approaching him. He sat down, his eyes glued on the CFO.

"Friend or foe?"

"You know where I stand. You did what needed to be done."

"Harmon's got to go. Listen, our next shareholder meeting is less than a few months away. No matter what, we need to push the prescribing of Zazotene to the limit."

"Boss, like you, I grew up poor. I don't want to go back to those days. You've been a boon to our shareholders."

"O'Reilly, inform production that we are halting flu vaccine manufacturing this year. The margins just don't cut it. And by the way, I'm sure you heard that Commissioner Jonathan Rogers was shot a couple of months ago in DC. As soon as he recovers, I'll need to meet with him. He's become a very sympathetic figure to the public ever since he was shot. Heard he is also now wearing a yellow wristband as a cancer survivor. We could certainly use his full support."

"You're right."

"Also, pass on to our brand-new senior VP of sales that I want Dr. Tom Knowton invited as one of our special guests on that cruise to Mexico. I happen to know that he is not only a top-notch cancer doc but also very influential among his physician colleagues. We need docs like that for our cause. As I said in the board room, the doctors are critical to our execution."

Chapter Thirteen

Zach passed by his executive assistant's desk with his border collie, Bootsie, on a short leash. He loved looking at the tall and athletic-looking Marissa Jones. She hadn't been hired for her administrative assistant experience, and the CEO enjoyed being around her.

Marissa flipped back her long wavy hair. "Dr. Tom Knowton returned your call. He wants to discuss your wife's treatment. Do you care to speak with him now?"

"Sure, put him through to my private number."

He walked to his executive office and sat down behind his massive maple wood desk. Zack unleashed Bootsie to roam the office. The intercom buzzed a moment later. "Dr. Knowton on line two."

The CEO pressed the flashing button. "Doctor, how is my dear Alexis doing?"

"I saw your wife this morning in my office. Unfortunately, she is no longer responding to the chemotherapy cocktail. As you know, she is complaining of increased abdominal pain over the last week. Her blood counts are extremely low so I am reluctant to try further chemo at this time."

"Doctor, have you considered using Zazotene?"

"No, I haven't. I don't think there is any value in using that drug for your wife's type of cancer. As you know, the FDA agrees with my approach. It's unproven therapy in cases such as Alexis."

"Doctor, can you hold on for a minute?"

Zach heard the sigh over the line. "Sure, Mr. Miller. My patients can wait."

After muting the phone, the drug baron walked over to his wet bar. Preparing a Scotch on the rocks, he took a swig before returning to his seat. His forty-five-pound dog hopped onto his lap. The border collie rested his head against Zach's chest. Kissing Bootsie's head, the CEO tickled his dog under his neck. "It's time to start reeling in the good doctor."

Using the swizzle stick to press the mute button, he again opened up the conversation. "Sorry. I'm back again. It was Alexis on my cell. I told her to hold on. So, Doc, have you seen the case reports showing that Zazotene has some beneficial effects on two patients where it was used for the same tumor type that Alexis has?"

"Yes, your senior VP of sales, Dylan Matthews, faxed over those case reports to me a few weeks ago. But I don't agree. The case reports demonstrated that it only helped two patients out of twenty-five. Four of the other patients died from bone marrow suppression due to the higher doses and the rest were non-responders. In my opinion, the drug would probably make her even worse."

"I'm really concerned about her. What other options do we have?"

"I would like to consult with my partners before considering other therapeutic options. I'll call you tomorrow."

"I'll be waiting for your call. Oh, and just one more thing, you'll be hearing from our new senior vice president of sales, Sean Parker."

"What happened to Matthews?"

"Good day, Dr. Knowton. I have a meeting with Mr. Bootsie." Hanging up, he saw Marissa standing in the open doorway.

"I just received a call from the highway police. It's about Liz."

"What about her?" he asked. He noticed her scrunched up face.

Marissa rubbed the right side of her temple and then hung her head. "She's dead," she mumbled.

Zach drained the last of his Scotch. "Call Human Resources and ask them to provide me with a recommendation for her replacement by this afternoon. We can't do business without a chief legal counsel. Oh, one more thing, also alert HR that we may have more executives leaving in the upcoming days."

Chapter Fourteen

Rogers strode briskly into his oncologist's office. It brought back memories. His own Mom died of cancer while under Knowton's care. He glanced down at the yellow band on his wrist, feeling fortunate to be a survivor.

After checking in with the receptionist, he entered the waiting room, where he could see through the office window. Nicki Chambers-Sanderson was talking in an animated manner with Knowton. She pointed her finger repeatedly in his face. Rogers couldn't help but notice that the doctor's face was turning redder by the moment. The Commissioner put the Knowton Medicaid file on a nearby seat.

Rogers paced the empty waiting room while pretending to be reading a magazine. He spotted Tom pulling away when Nicki grabbed his left shoulder. The Commissioner walked over to the reception window in the waiting room to get a better look. He pretended to read the insurance coverage announcements on the glass window, which was open to the inside office. Now he was within earshot. A moment later, Knowton shut the window and grabbed Nicki by the arm, ushering her out of sight.

The Commissioner sat down and thought whether he should bring up Ashley's kidnapping with Knowton. Five minutes later, he heard the door open to the patient area. Nicki Chambers appeared in the doorway, dressed in her white and blue maternity uniform.

"Dr. Rogers, I'm so happy to see you. It's been a while since the last time we really talked."

Rogers held her hand gently. She now seemed at ease, totally unlike her demeanor just a few minutes earlier with her boss.

"I'm doing fine. Looks like any day now for you."

"My OB agrees. I'm really looking forward to being a mom."

"By the way, your father came to see me yesterday.".

She leaned toward him and whispered, "Can we meet to talk about what he may have said to you? I want to make sure that you don't get the wrong impression. There are things that you should know."

"Sure, just call Sally to schedule a time."

Nicki paused before nodding. For some reason, her face became flushed and her eyes narrowed. He was about to ask her why when he felt a hearty slap on his back. Rogers spun around. It was Knowton.

"Jonathan, give me a hug. You look fantastic!"

He half-heartedly returned the hug with his left arm while tightly holding the Knowton manila folder in his right. All the while, the Commissioner was wondering why Nicki was so upset again.

"Tom, let's talk in your private office."

His physician led the way down the long hallway to his corner office. After they entered the ten-foot-square office, Rogers dropped the Knowton fraud file on the desk and took the customary patient's seat across from his doc.

"Jonathan, you look unsettled. How are you feeling?"

"Kim and I have talked many times about how unusual it was for me to be diagnosed with lung cancer. I never had symptoms, never smoked, no family history, and even the surgeon told me in the recovery room that there was no cancer found in the frozen sections. So why did cancer show up in the formal pathology report?"

"I'm sorry, but these things happen. Probably a random genetic mutation."

"What exactly did the frozen section taken during my surgery show? Before today, I've been so distressed that I've never asked you that specific question."

"Let it go!" Dr. Knowton said, his voice dropping.

"I can't let it go. The surgeon told Kim that the early results from the frozen section of part of my so-called tumor taken during the operation were encouraging. The surgeon told me in the recovery room that everything looked normal. So it's possible that there was an error in labeling the tissues that were fixed for permanent analysis and sent to pathology the following day."

Knowton fired back, "Highly unlikely!" He stood to lean against his desk, squinting his eyes, which flicked in a rapid sequence to the chart and back to the floor.

"I used the word 'possible.' Is it possible?"

"I don't want to speculate!"

"Neither do I. Let's do a DNA comparison of the lung tissues on the final pathology slides with a sample of my blood. And whatever happened to my intraoperative frozen section? Tolliver said it was missing."

Knowton's voice rose sharply. "Don't you trust me?"

"Haven't I always? With my life."

"Then you need to accept the fact that you had cancer. Don't continue to be in denial. The longer you go questioning everything about your case, the more time it will take you to get past all of this. It's time to move on."

"Easy for you to say. You don't know what I'm feeling. Listen, I've trusted you, maybe too much. We both know that mistakes are made every day in hospitals . . . by doctors." Rogers picked up the Knowton file from the desk and was ready to show the apparently fraudulent checks given to him by Nicki Chambers. But he had something to say. To demand.

"Tom, I want a DNA comparison. Don't try to talk me out of it."

"You're pretty stubborn when you're on a mission."

"I'll request the DNA comparison, but the hospital will require your signature as well."

"I'm sure that you're committed to start the process. I want to think about it. So, is that all for today?"

"Not exactly. I came here to ask you about something important." He dropped the Knowton file on his seat and for a moment covered his face with his palms. Rogers squared up to his lifelong colleague.

"About your cancer?"

"No, totally unrelated."

The oncologist frowned. "What's going on?"

Buzz. Buzz. Knowton picked up the receiver. As his doctor listened to his nurse, Rogers heard him curse under his breath.

"Please tell him that I will call him right back." The oncologist's face seemed drained of any color. "Jonathan, can this wait a few minutes? I have to call back a very demanding husband about his wife."

"Sure . . . it can wait. Go make your call. In the meantime, I'll visit with Victor Carver. Come get me when you're free." The Commissioner headed out the door. He stopped upon hearing Knowton's surprising question.

"By the way, did you know that Victor is retiring in six months?"

"News to me."

Before closing the door, his doc added, "Caught me by surprise as well. Didn't think he had enough money to sit back at his age."

••••••••••

Rogers walked toward the common area of the oncology office before making a sharp right turn down one of the hallways. As he passed the rest room, he saw Carver's name on the gold door plaque in front of him. He knocked twice and opened it after hearing a grunt from inside. His friend had his feet propped up on the desk, looking frazzled behind a foot-high mound of paperwork. Rogers noted an open pack of cigarettes lying on the desk.

The oncologist leaped to his feet, a huge smile on his freckled, diamond-shaped face. "You old geezer!" he exclaimed. "What are you doing here?" He playfully grabbed Rogers around both shoulders. "At the Medicaid press conference, I thought you would have a stroke when that woman accused you of covering up Sam Murphy's murder. Don't know why she attacked you. Lord knows you didn't kill Murphy."

"Thought you gave up smoking."

"Tried, but couldn't stop. Helps me through the tough days when our patients are dying."

"You're the only oncologist I know who still smokes."

Carver looked down at an open chart in front of him. "Listen; give me a minute or so while I finish my notes on my last patient."

"No problem." Rogers sat down and kept his eyes fixed on his friend. "So I just heard that you are retiring."

"I never thought that I would be able to afford it. You might say that I've been extremely lucky in the past year or so."

"I don't see myself retiring. There is still so much that I want to do."

"We each dance to a different drummer, my friend." Carver dropped his pen and closed the chart.

Rogers leaned forward. "What's happening with the Task Force?"

"I'll have my report back to you by next week. But let's talk about you. What's the latest on who shot you in DC?"

"The FBI won't tell me anything. They say it's a matter of national security."

"Why national security?"

Rogers shrugged.

"Anyway," Carver continued, "Tom tells me that your latest chest CT is normal. You know, in a weird way, if you had not been shot, your lung cancer would have never been detected at such an early stage. Getting shot may have saved your life."

"Next time, just spare me the bullets."

"If I ever speak with the shooter, I'll tell him. But unfortunately, you know that these drive-by shootings are uncontrollable."

"Who said anything about a drive-by shooting?"

Rogers, hearing the creak of the door, tracked Carver's eyes focusing behind him. Turning around, Rogers saw Knowton standing in the doorway with his arms crossed over his chest. "Jonathan, are you ready to talk now?"

"Sure, Tom. Hey buddy," Rogers said, pointing at Carver, "stop by my office when you get a chance. Bring your gear. We can go for a run around the pond."

Rogers walked toward Knowton and said, "OK, I'm all yours."

Carver cracked, "You guys look way too serious. Jonathan, I'll stop by your office. We'll have some fun. And, I promise you, you won't be bored."

••••••••••

Rogers noticed that his Knowton Medicaid file was wide open on the desk. Knowton brushed by Rogers and took his seat. His voice was level, but tinged with anger. "Jonathan, you need to be more careful about what you leave behind in my office."

"I presume you read the file. OK, I'll get to the point. For six months, I've been receiving complaints about the care you are providing your patients. Sam Murphy was only the latest. So before you go nuts on me, I fully understand that your medical decisions are based on many clinical details that I don't possess."

"You got that right."

"But let's talk about something that's not a matter of judgment. Your name was submitted to me as one of the docs in our state committing Medicaid fraud." Rogers watched Knowton's face tighten.

"Listen, I never gave Murphy a lethal dose of Zazotene. I can't say any more than that on orders from my lawyer. And I certainly didn't commit any fraud. Period."

Rogers found himself staring at the file, wondering if Knowton had already seen the copies of the fraudulent checks.

"Tom, I have to tell you something. Nicki's father came to see me. He said that unless I do something to stop you, he would do whatever he needed to do to put you behind bars."

Knowton's eyes flashed. "Peter Chambers said that?"

"He's deadly serious. He's prepared to turn his evidence over to the police."

"What evidence?"

Rogers picked up the Knowton file from the desk. "In the

back of this file, there are copies of fraudulent claims. I guess you didn't get to them yet. Chambers told me that Nicki came to him. In so many words, she raised suspicions that you might be submitting bills to Medicaid for patients that don't exist in your practice."

Knowton grabbed the file and flipped through the back pages. "Jonathan, there are a lot of things you don't know about Nicki."

"I'm talking about you. Don't blame this on her," he said, nearly shouting.

"I can't get into all the details at this time. You need to trust me." The oncologist dropped the file on his desk and walked toward the door.

"I'm beginning to wonder . . . if I can," Jonathan whispered.

"You've been a good friend for many years. Now's not the time for me to tell you anything more than you have a great health report."

Rogers walked toward Knowton and stood toe to toe with him. "Carver will be giving me a report of the Task Force next week. I'll be presenting an executive summary to the Governor. Can you assure me that I won't find your name on the list of doctors formally accused of fraud?"

Knowton backed up a few feet. "Let's just say that Victor and I are talking. As a full partner, he knows whatever I know about any office billing. I'll call you as soon as I can to discuss this further."

Rogers sensed that this was not the time to bring up Ashley. He shook hands with his oncologist before heading out. More questions than answers pounded his head. His trust in Knowton was heading south quickly. He hoped that he was wrong. For now, he needed to focus on the kidnapping of his daughter. As he drove away from the clinic, Rogers looked up at the cloudy skies and prayed that he would find Ashley alive.

While pulling into the parking lot of the Department of Health, he mentally slapped his head. He had forgotten the Knowton fraud file. As soon as he got to his office, he called his oncologist, but the receptionist told him the doctor had left for the day and that his private office was locked. He scribbled a note for Sally to retrieve the file.

Rogers tried to reach Kim on her cell. He was beginning to realize that he needed her more than ever now, with Ashley missing. When the call went to voice mail, he hung up, disappointed. He found Detective Darden's business card in his top drawer. He began dialing the number but then recalled the kidnapper's explicit instructions not to call the police. Slamming the phone down, he closed the office lights and headed home.

Chapter Fifteen

Ashley's eyes opened wide, but she saw only darkness. She felt a light touch on her foot, and then on her calf. Something seemed to be crawling up her right leg. She tried to scratch her chilled skin, but realized that her hands could not move. They were stretched out over her head. Her wrists ached with each tug. She picked up her head an inch and lowered it slowly. The hard, slimy surface of the cement floor did not budge. She ran her tongue around her lips. They felt gritty. Her head pounded. Soon the tickling on her leg seemed to move up to her thigh. Ashley wriggled to turn her hips, trying to flip over, but a sharp pain around her shoulders stopped her as her hands remained tethered in place. Her left leg was free, and she bent that knee and ran her toes near her upper thigh. Her toes felt a warm, hairy object. With another twist of her hips and a kick with her left foot, she could feel the outlines of whatever was creeping up her leg. An instant later, she felt the pain of a bite. She grunted and kicked the crawler off her leg. She tried to open her mouth to scream, but couldn't seem to make a noise. Instead she yawned and felt her eyes slowly close. She tried to force them open, searching for a hint of light, but there was only deep black. The dampness made her shiver, and she yawned again. A moment later, she was dreaming of winning the marathon.

••••••••••

"Morning, Miss Rogers, I hope you slept well last night." Rick slapped her face, trying to arouse her.

With her first awakening, she was blinded and scorched by what appeared to be a three-foot floodlight. The radiant heat waves seemed to burn her legs, searing her skin. She screamed. Unable to shield her face, she turned her head to the right and peeked out of the corner of her eye, squinting.

Slowly, her sight recovered to where she could make out an outline of an oval beam of light that measured four or five feet in diameter. Ashley yelled out in pain. Her back and arms ached as if she had hibernated all winter. The heat bore down on her, and she felt her skin burning.

Ashley's mouth felt like it was full of cotton balls, but she managed to plead, "Please stop. Help me. I'll do whatever you want."

"Open your mouth; I have a present for you," he commanded.

A second later, she felt a rush of liquid drenching her face and upper torso. Her tongue absorbed the flow, feeling no pain. The wetness had no odor or taste.

"Water?"

"Ding. Ding. Ding. You win the prize. Water is the correct answer."

"What are you . . .?" Before she could focus, another splash of water hit her face, as if another bucket had been emptied on her head. The light brightened.

She screamed again. "I can't see. I'm burning."

"Just wanted to warm you up this morning. It was pretty cold when I walked in here."

"Oh my God! Shut it off!"

She heard the click. The beam dimmed. Ashley squeezed her eyes shut, blinking to adjust.

"Ask and I'll help. It's that simple."

Soon she was able to make out light streaming from what looked like a door that was slightly ajar. She twisted her head up to the left, identifying an outline of her kidnapper. Her eyes strained to see around her left shoulder. Metal shackles held her wrist. The shackles were fastened to a taut chain that seemed bolted to the stone wall.

"Where am I?"

"Actually, it's a lovely place. The beaches are already filling up with tourists. Unfortunately for you, all the good rooms were taken. We forgot to make a reservation for you. So you had to stay in dungeon room 001."

Her eyes searched the room. It was no more than a twelve-foot square. Looking down at the cement floor, she saw a rat scooting through the open door.

"My legs are on fire!" She shouted, "Who are you? Why are you doing this to me?"

"It's not about you. I'm just following orders."

"Please help me. Untie me."

A moment later, she felt something pressing into her left temple. Her eyes made out the outline of a gun.

"Sure. Just don't get any ideas."

Ashley heard the keys jangling. Her left wrist was freed first and her arm plopped down on her chest. The pain in her shoulder intensified. Her hands were numb. Her right wrist was unshackled next. It fell to the floor. She began to pick up on his accent.

"Help me to sit."

She felt the barrel pressing tighter against her temple. He yanked on her arms, pulling her to a sitting position. The room spun. Ashley retched twice, but her heaves were bone dry.

"There is a bowl of oatmeal in the corner and one glass of Mexican water. And there's a toilet a few feet to your left. You have all the comforts of being the daughter of a well-known doctor. I'll check on you later."

While he walked away, he pulled the beam, which seemed to be rolling away on a cart. Looking around, she spotted her breakfast a few feet to her left. His accent echoed in her head. New York. Ashley shook as the door slammed shut. The room plunged into total blackness. Tears streamed down her face. Leaning against the damp wall, she could do nothing but sob, wondering if she'd ever see her parents again, or if she'd die alone.

Chapter Sixteen

"Local weather in southeast Michigan is expected to be cloudy for the next two days with a chance of afternoon showers," blared Central Midland WPPE weatherman Billy Leighton.

"Thanks, Billy, hopefully we'll get some sun in the metro area by the weekend," announced a soprano-like voice. The high-pitched voice of morning drive-time anchor, Nate Hudson, boomed out over the airwaves.

"Folks, please stay tuned for a new feature here at WPPE. Our very own specialty reporter, Nicole Williams, will be hosting a new program coming up in just a few seconds. Her guest today is Dr. Jonathan Rogers, the Commissioner of Health for the Great Lakes State of Michigan. Nicole."

"Good morning! I'm Nicole Williams. Welcome to our first radio show dedicated to health care. Our new half-hour show, which we call "Meet the Commissioner," will be broadcast the first Wednesday of every quarter at six-thirty during morning drive-time. We are fortunate to have our Michigan Commissioner of Health as our regular guest. Dr. Rogers, welcome to WPPE talk radio!"

"Thank you."

"I'm sorry to hear about the personal problems that you've been having. Can I ask how you are doing?"

"Thank you, but I would prefer not to discuss them."

"I understand. As a public service, we invite our callers to start dialing 1-800-444-8888. Would you like to make an opening statement on the state of health in Michigan?"

"I'm proud to tell you that the Michigan Physician Guideline Law has now been in effect for the past six months. I believe it's absolutely critical that doctors in our state use a "best practices" approach based on proven evidence on whether or not specific treatments will work. I hope that the many fine doctors of our state, through their Medical Society, will realize the value of this law to improve patient care."

"Thank you. We now have several callers waiting to speak with you. First, we have a call from Detroit. Caller, please identify yourself and then ask your question."

"Good morning. My name is Joe Sunday. I'm a manager in a local convenience store. Commissioner, why is health care so darn expensive? And why do doctors and hospitals charge more than the insurance covers? My wife and I can barely afford the insurance premiums, much less the out-of-pocket expenses. Can you help us?"

"The fact that over forty-nine million Americans do not have health-care insurance puts an extra burden on working people like you and your wife who do have insurance. Also, we need to do a better job of keeping Americans healthy instead of waiting until they become sick to treat their conditions. Preventing disease saves money for all of us. I would like you to call and set up an appointment with me so I can provide you with some detailed information."

"I'll take you up on your offer."

Rogers wished that the next caller would give a clue, any clue, about the whereabouts of Ashley. He looked over at Nicole. She seemed to read his face. She reached over and patted his hand lightly before speaking again.

"We have another caller on the line from DuPont. Please go ahead and ask your question."

"Good morning. My name is Dr. Mandy Gips. I'm the current president of the Michigan Medical Society. I'm so sorry to hear about your daughter."

"Thanks, Dr. Gips."

"Commissioner, please forgive me for asking this, but doesn't your guideline law take away the right of practicing physicians to use their own independent clinical judgment?"

"As a former practicing doctor myself, I believe that medicine cannot be completely standardized by forcing doctors to practice so-called cookbook medicine using rigid guidelines. That said, many doctors do not use any guidelines that have been proven to be effective in delivering care. In my view, there is an appropriate balance between professional clinical judgment and standardization of practice based on medical treatments that have been proven to work. Let me say . . ."

Nicole interrupted. "Excuse me, Commissioner Rogers. Doesn't the patient have a right to say what they want in health-care decisions?"

"Absolutely. For that reason, I added an appeal clause for patients and doctors. The diagnosis and treatment for individual cases should be based on a combination of physician clinical judgment and evidence-based guidelines where it makes sense. If there is a discrepancy in any one case, clinical judgment should most likely prevail. But over a period of six to twelve months, adherence to "best practice" guidelines and standards of practice should carry the day on most doctor decisions. These criteria are based on sound evidence in view of what the medical benefit allows."

"Thanks, Dr. Rogers. We've another caller on the line. This call is from Oldwyck. Please identify yourself and ask your question."

Silence.

Nicole repeated her request. "Caller, you are on the air. Please identify yourself and state your question to Dr. Rogers."

Silence.

"We have many callers waiting on the line. Are you there, Oldwyck?"

I have a statement for the Commissioner.

Rogers wrinkled his forehead as he listened. He hoped it was about Ashley.

The light in the dark shall lead you to the old judge's office.

Nicole queried, "Caller, please identify yourself and repeat what you said."

Rogers stared at the words that he copied on his notepad. A moment later, the caller spoke, this time speaking much more quickly.

The light in the dark shall lead you to the old judge's office.

Rogers held his hand over the microphone and whispered to

the hostess. "I want the tape of this caller analyzed for voice patterns."

Nicole nodded in agreement and challenged the caller. "Excuse me. What do you mean?"

Rogers wrote on his notepad, "woman's voice, high pitched."

The young woman is alive. Commissioner, I'll be in touch.

Before the line went dead, Rogers heard a dog's bark coming through the speaker.

Chapter Seventeen

Zach heard the familiar signal. He rose from his chair after the two quick knocks on his DCP office door. He was looking forward to his appointment with Commissioner Rogers, and led Marissa through the private door that led to the senior management parking garage. They walked toward his late-model Maybach limo. Zach greeted his personal driver with a roundhouse wave.

Soon after sitting back in the limo, the CEO reached out to rest his hand on Marissa's knee. Her soft powder-blue skirt was pulled up high enough to reveal most of her shapely thighs. It was time for some fun.

"Joey, slide the soundproof panel between you and the back of this limo. Don't open it again until I knock. I have some business to conduct."

After the panel slammed shut, Zach pushed a button, which changed the backseat into a semi-bed. He felt his testosterone levels pumping just like when he was a teenager making love to his latest squeeze in the backseat of his old jalopy. He cradled Marissa's head and lowered her gently. Her eyes were dancing. But he wanted more than just an admiring gaze at her beauty. Unbuttoning his trousers, he felt hard already. Marissa had yanked down her pink panties. He began kissing her pubic hairs. She let out a soft squeal. He climbed aboard and set her pelvis rocking with each thrust. Zach held out until she was moist and quivering. A minute later, he still had not moved, unwilling to break the orgasmic spell. For a moment after he'd rolled off of Marissa, he thought of Kim Rogers. He returned the seat to its usual position. After making himself presentable, he knocked on the panel door.

The panel door opened. "Yes, Mr. Miller."

"Joey, we'll be inside the department for ten minutes. Wait here."

"Yes, Sir!"

"My assistant and I were just discussing what we will say to our Commissioner of Health to improve the well-being of our citizens. Our conversation became somewhat . . . heated. Thanks for not disturbing us."

••••••••••

Zach strolled up to Sally's desk, holding Marissa's hand. "Hello, Sally. I hope that Dr. Rogers is running on time today."

"He is, Mr. Miller. But before you go, I have a message for you. About ten minutes ago, I received a phone call. A man called and asked if you had arrived. He would not provide his name but he said he worked at your company and was just checking to see if you had arrived."

Zach nodded absently. He pushed open the Commissioner's door and strolled in with Marissa.

"Good afternoon, Mr. Miller," Rogers said cordially. "Governor Peabody sent me an email this morning that you were coming."

"Commissioner, may I introduce you to my assistant, Marissa Jones?"

"Nice to meet you as well, Ms. Jones. Please, let's all take a seat."

"Commissioner, I want you to know that I've used my political contacts in DC to recommend to President Jordan that he appoint you to be the next Surgeon General."

Rogers leaned back and cast Zach a long sideways glance. "Frankly, I'm a bit surprised given what I told the President about my ideas to further regulate drug companies such as yours." He decided to hold off mentioning that Kim had spoken about meeting him at the lake house.

Zach pulled out the chair for Marissa and took his seat last. He looked sternly at the Commissioner.

"Perhaps you'll change your position. Forgive me for my bluntness in getting to the point. I'm here to discuss my wife, Alexis. Tom Knowton is her doctor. I'm not at all impressed with his care and I happen to know that you're lifelong friends. I want you to speak with him and provide some professional advice."

"I'm sure he is doing everything possible to help her."

"That's not true. So I have a favor to ask."

"What is it?"

Zach pulled out some papers from his briefcase. He laid them on the Commissioner's desk. "These are Zazotene medical case reports. I need your medical opinion."

Rogers picked up the reports and glanced at them.

"Our DCP chief medical officer believes that these reports demonstrate that Zazotene was helpful in two patients with endocrine cancer of the gastrointestinal tract. My wife has one of these types of cancer."

"I've previously seen these case reports. But I'm sorry to say that they are inconclusive. They don't prove that Zazotene is effective in her type of cancer."

Zach held back a few seconds. He hardened his face toward the Commissioner and tightly squeezed the armrests on his chair.

"My wife is dying. You have medical evidence in your hands that our drug helped some of these patients with the exact diagnosis as Alexis. How can you say the evidence is inconclusive? You sound just like Knowton."

"If you feel that strongly, why don't you get another doctor's opinion? Knowton isn't the only oncologist around."

"Alexis won't change doctors. She has complete faith in him. My wife adores him, almost as much as me."

"I see."

"No, it is Knowton who must change his treatment plan. You're the top doc in this state. I need you to persuade him to prescribe Zazotene for Alexis. I won't let my wife suffer while you doctors wait around for some hypothetical double-blind placebo-controlled study to show conclusive proof."

"It's not just the lack of evidence. I can't interfere in a doctor-patient relationship, even if I'm the Commissioner of Health."

"My God, Rogers, my wife is dying. Have you no compassion?"

"I can't get involved."

"You mean you won't."

"I understand how you feel."

"No! No, you don't! And I'm extremely disappointed in your response. I'm sure there are other physicians in your lofty position who would be more empathetic."

"Mr. Miller, I can't do what you are asking. It just wouldn't be right."

Zach rose slowly, placing his fists on his hips. "By the way, I'll be talking to Bill Peabody next week at the Annual Governors Ball. I'm sure the subject of my confidence in you as our Commissioner will be a topic of conversation."

Rogers felt his face turn red and he jumped to his feet. His temper took off like Roman candles on the Fourth of July.

"Are you threatening me?" he shouted.

"Of course not, Doctor. There's no need for that. You serve at the pleasure of the Governor. I donate plenty to Peabody's campaign. Enough said. I urge you to give my request some thought." He stood motionless for several seconds, watching Rogers take a series of deep breaths.

"OK. I'll call you as soon as I research this issue further."

"Marissa will be expecting your call."

Zach bowed deferentially to his host and walked out the door with his assistant. The CEO gave a polite nod to Sally as he passed her desk.

As they walked out of the building, Marissa asked, "Do you think he'll call, Zach?"

"It's not whether he'll call; it's only a matter of when. The ball is in his court. I don't give out many chances."

"I admire any man who goes for what he wants. I'll always stick with the winners."

"It's all about the power to get things done, my dear," he boasted while watching her opening his shirt buttons. Seconds later, in the back of the limo, he prepared for round two with Marissa. He had already forgotten all about Commissioner Rogers and Alexis Miller.

••••••••••

Dylan Matthews had been practicing in Michigan's Upper Peninsula for weeks with his AK-47 rifle. He had waited for this day ever since his DCP board room embarrassment. Well trained from his army days in Special Forces, he calmly inserted a cartridge of 7.62 X 39 shells into the sighted rifle. He positioned himself 400 yards from the planned killing zone. Dylan calculated that he was well within range, knowing that he would be able to discharge 200 rounds in the initial thirty-second spray.

A few minutes earlier, he had positioned his late-model Hummer H3 for a quick getaway. He had replayed in his mind the half-mile trip through the woods to the back road that led to a four-lane highway and from there to the Interstate. From his spot on the hill, it was less than three minutes to the Interstate.

He had predicted that it was only a matter of time before Zach paid a visit to the Commissioner. He had planted a listening device in a potted plant he sent anonymously to Marissa and knew his old boss's schedule as well as anyone.

During the past week, he had chosen this singular crossing point. To return to DCP from the Department of Health, Zach would need to take one of the two roads that intersected at this particular spot. From where Dylan stood on the two-hundred-foot-high Sampson Hill, it would be easy to get his revenge.

He had turned on the ignition in the Hummer, then jumped out, keeping the door open. After pulling on his Cabela's camouflage jacket and pinning his white metal silver cross patee marksman's medal onto the chest area just over his heart. Dylan set the rifle down on a boulder and checked his crosshairs. The AK-47 was aimed precisely at where the Maybach would appear. He waited. The countdown had begun.

Dylan fidgeted. He went over the plan in his head for the hundredth time. He would hit the tires, engine, and the windshield with a short burst of fire for ten seconds. The Maybach would then be a sitting target. Expecting the occupants to flee the car, he knew the last 140 rounds or so had each of their names written on every shell. Once the execution was complete, he would hop into the Hummer, then speed along the back roads to the Interstate.

He checked his watch. It was killing time. He stretched out on his belly while setting his sights on the cross street. Soon, the Maybach came rolling toward him. He knew that he would enjoy this kill. This would be just like it was in the Special Forces. Only then had he killed complete strangers. This time it was personal. Finger on the trigger, his eyes focused. *Payback time!* With one pull, he unleashed an initial shower of devastation. The limo skidded to a halt as the tires were ripped apart. The windshield cracking sounds caused his pulse to race.

Seconds ticked off. *Get out of the fuckin car! Dammit!!* He sprayed another fifty rounds at the windshield and the doors. No targets emerged. A black pickup truck was coming down the road. He waited for just one more shot. All he needed was one more quick pull. He prayed that the doors would open. He glanced over at the pickup truck. It was now only fifty yards away. As a well-trained soldier, he knew he needed to stick to his plan. When the Ford truck was within twenty yards of the Maybach, Dylan jumped to his feet. He threw the AK-47 into the front seat of the Hummer and sped off, cursing to himself. Tomorrow would be another day.

Chapter Eighteen

After eating dinner alone, Rogers walked into his study. Frustrated that there were no leads in Alaska, earlier today he had asked Kim to come back home. Two days ago, he had followed up with Knowton on Zach's request. His oncologist said he would leave it up to Alexis if she wanted to speak with the Commissioner. Rogers glanced down at the caller ID. He had again missed Alexis's call. Yesterday, Alexis's call had gone to his home voice mail. He had listened to her message several times. Each time, he tried to pick up any indication whether she was truly interested in his involvement. By the tone of her voice, he would decide whether she wanted to take the lead or leave it to Knowton.

Picking through a stack of mostly junk mail, he found an envelope with the radio station call letters. He ripped it apart. It contained the voice analysis of the strange caller to WPPE. The report commented on the periodic peak–and-valley patterns and the overall pitch. It concluded that the pattern most closely resembled an elderly woman's voice.

Rogers pulled Alexis Miller's private cell phone number from his wallet. It was time to ask her directly whether she was willing to take Zazotene.

"Hello."

He recognized her voice. "Hello, Mrs. Miller?"

"Dr. Rogers. I've been waiting for your call. I've tried to contact you several times. I can't be too careful myself. Zach is always hovering somewhere."

"I assume Dr. Knowton told you that I'm the Commissioner of Health."

"Of course I know who you are. Zach talks about you all the time. I think he believes that I'm too sick to understand what he's doing, but I'm much sharper than that."

"May I ask why my name is so popular in your home?"

Silence.

"Mrs. Miller, are you still there?"

"That's not something that we should be discussing on the phone."

"Perhaps we can meet at my office."

"I'm much too ill to leave my home."

"The reason that I'm calling is that your husband wants me to convince your doctor to prescribe something for you."

"Knowton doesn't believe that Zazotene would work. I trust him more than my husband. Sometimes, my mind plays tricks on me. Who knows? Maybe Zach wants to kill me with that damn drug."

Rogers was silent, not knowing where to go next. He waited, hoping she would provide direction.

"Commissioner, I'll try to help you the best I can. I have to go now. I hear Zach calling me. He was out walking his dog. He sounds very upset. Just remember, I'm not feeling very well and can only do so much."

"Mrs. Miller, when can we talk again? I'd like to ask you more about your husband."

"Please don't call me. I'll contact you again."

••••••••••

"Commissioner, Mr. Miller will see you now. Go right in."

Rogers stood just inside the doorway. The CEO was at his desk, signing some papers. Zach held up his left hand for ten seconds. The Commissioner walked forward to take a seat only after he was waved forward.

"I wanted to talk to you about how we might convince Dr. Knowton to prescribe Zazotene for your wife."

"What a pleasant surprise."

"There is one person that might get Knowton to change his mind."

"I'm hoping that it might be you."

"Why not Alexis? It's her life. Why not convince her with

the case reports you showed me that concluded Zazotene would work in her condition?"

"No, what I want is for you to persuade Dr. Knowton to prescribe it for her condition. I would also like for him to influence his colleagues to prescribe it for all other patients with her type of cancer."

"Why other patients? Isn't Alexis the issue?"

"What do you mean by that?"

"Aren't we talking about getting her the best treatment?"

"Alexis and thousands of other patients."

"Why don't you start by convincing your own wife of the value of Zazotene?"

"I'm not about to put my sick wife in the position of having to choose. Convincing Knowton is your job, not mine, and certainly not at the hands of Alexis."

"Her doctor won't listen to me. It's the way the system works."

Zach looked out the window. "Pardon me for saying something which might offend you. Why do we need you as Commissioner of Health if you can't get this done for me?"

Rogers paused. "I'll talk to Knowton. It will be his decision."

Still avoiding eye contact, the CEO's voice climbed two octaves. "I just hope you doctors do the right thing before the cancer kills Alexis. Remember my words, Commissioner. I don't play games that I don't win."

Chapter Nineteen

Ashley felt fortunate that her jailer was no longer chaining her to the wall every night. She had resigned herself to the fact that she was his prisoner. Her every thought was consumed with breaking free of this madman. She felt weak and demoralized, but at least she was getting three meals a day of rice and guacamole with a few slivers of chicken mixed in a small cereal bowl. At each of these mealtimes, her kidnapper had lit a small candle that lasted no more than thirty minutes. It was just enough time to see what she was eating and ward off the stray rat that circled the bowl. In recent days, he had spiced up her meals with a bottle of beer.

In her cell block, she paced the room, initially with her arms outstretched as a guide. Four strides to a wall, pivot to the left, and take four more strides along the adjacent wall and so on. This became her daily routine. It was a far cry from the state-of-the-art gymnasiums where she exercised on a daily basis with TV sets mounted on every treadmill and elliptical.

By her count, she had been a prisoner for at least two weeks. She agonized over how her family would ever find her in this hole. The walking helped her think. She had to come up with a plan. In midstride she was startled by the metallic sound of the door bolts being unlocked. She shielded her eyes from the sudden streaming of light from the hallway outside the steel door. Ashley could see her captor's familiar outline in the shadows. He was no more than two inches taller than her five-six stature, and was slender in build. His gruff manner seemed to be softening toward her in recent days. He was holding her bowl of food and an open bottle of wine as he approached her.

Rick placed the cereal bowl on the cement floor. "Did the blankets help you to sleep any better?"

"Yes. Thank you."

"I'm glad that my pretty little prey is holding up."

"Can you walk with me outside this building? Without any sunlight my bones will get brittle. I need the sunlight to activate the vitamin D."

"How do you know that?"

"I'm a medical student."

"Figures that you would be smart."

"Please let me out of here. Just for an hour. Please."

"Don't think so. I'm waiting for word from my leader. I'll ask. They're still deciding how we can use you."

"On the plane, I heard the redheaded lady call you Rick. May I call you that?"

"Not yet. I'm not your friend."

"We could be friends."

"Stop it! So do you have all you need to survive? I don't want you to die before we get what we want."

"A cot and pillow would be nice."

"Consider it done. I'll drop it off later tonight."

"Thank you, sir."

"What's with that sir business? Enjoy your breakfast. I'm heading for the beach."

Rick walked away and slammed the metal door behind him. Ashley heard the lock being secured. Two thoughts had preoccupied her during these endless days. She needed to keep her mind sharp and her strength up. But, most important, she needed to befriend Rick. It was her only chance.

Chapter Twenty

To clear his mind, Rogers took a drive on a pine-tree-lined country road outside of Oldwyck. Kim had recently returned to their home, but she was deeply depressed, blaming herself for what had happened. She had decided to sleep in Ashley's bedroom.

While driving the twisting, narrow road, Rogers's mind centered on Ashley. Beyond suggesting Victor Carver to head up the Medicaid Task Force, the kidnapper had not been in touch with any further instructions. Rogers's headlights outlined the winding road that led to the bridge back to town. The incoming fog seemed to be following him. Soon Exeter Bridge appeared in sight about two hundred yards up ahead. The rickety wooden river crossing was a throwback. Barely two lanes wide, with side railings no more than two feet high. Rogers recognized the bolted-down sloping-stone railings from his days back east. Called Jersey barriers, he always wondered how they made it this far west.

The road was now graded upward to meet the bridge, suspended fifteen feet above the rock-strewn, raging waters of DuPont River. From his side mirror, he noticed the dimmed headlights of a pickup truck that trailed him by twenty yards or so. He checked the time on his watch and thought of calling Kim to tell her to expect him. He glanced over at his cell phone, which was plugged into a dashboard holder just above the radio.

While his tires rolled over the decaying bridge, he could hear the rumbling sounds of the wooden planks vibrating against their metal hinges. Rogers could hear the roar of the river beneath him. It seemed to be flowing at its peak, probably from the runoff from the spring-melting snow. In the distance, he could see a large moving van just beginning to make the last turn before driving onboard the other side of the hundred-yard-long bridge. He rolled down his window to pull in his side mirror to make room for the passing van. He anticipated a tight squeeze. Checking his rearview mirror, his eyes widened. The fog-shrouded headlights of the pickup truck now seemed just a few yards behind him.

Glancing up ahead, Rogers saw the moving van swerving across the center dividing line. He slammed on his brakes and pressed down on his horn several times. He again checked his rearview mirror. The pickup truck now seemed to be right on his rear bumper. The van continued to swerve. He honked the horn repeatedly but the van didn't slow down. A second later, he heard the sound of bumpers clanging. Rogers squinted into the rearview mirror, trying to make out the face of the pickup-truck driver. But the headlights and fog blinded him. He froze upon seeing what was ahead of him.

The van was now mostly in his lane, heading straight toward him. He heard the air brakes and squealing tires. Thirty yards ahead, the van appeared to be coming to a stop, but the pickup truck steadily pushed his Hummer forward, at an angle, closer and closer to the stone side railing. He pressed as hard as he could on his brakes and grabbed his cell phone. Flinging his door open, he was ready to bail out onto the roadway, when suddenly his Hummer came to a rest. The pickup truck was no longer pushing him and had unlocked bumpers. He twisted his neck, seeing the truck back away. He tried to drive forward, but the front passenger wheel of his car was pinned against the two-foot-wide base of the stone railing. Rogers could see the rushing waters below him. He looked out his side mirror and noticed for the first time that the pickup truck was red. It had backed up forty yards or so.

He opened the car door and put his left foot down on the wooden planks. He heard them rattling, more than his partial weight would ever cause. He turned his neck so he could see the truck. *Holy Shit!* The truck was again speeding toward him. Before he could close the door, he felt the shock of the truck's heavy-duty bumper smacking into the rear of his Hummer, causing his front bumper to climb the railing. The airbag exploded in his face. Knocked back on his seat, he could feel the front of his car rising. Seconds later, he was able to push away the deflating airbag. He saw the half moon before his eyes. His Hummer seemed to be balanced against the highest point of the sloping stone Jersey barriers. He leaned out the open side window and twisted his torso around for another look. The pickup truck had backed away again. Out the window, he glanced down. The floor of the bridge was now at least four feet below him. Rogers pushed against the door; it was jammed with parts of the side airbag. He jerked his head around to see the pickup truck revving up the engine and preparing to ram him again. He trembled at what was coming next. All that he could think to do was press 911 on his cell.

He brushed the sweat beads from his eyes. "Come on! Pick up!" For an instant, he thought about diving out the open window. In the rear mirror, Rogers could see the Michigan plates hurtling toward him, no more than six seconds from impact. Too late!

"Operator 911, what is your emergency?"

He yelled into his cell, "A red pickup truck is ramming me over the Exeter . . ."

With a violent jolt, Rogers felt his neck snapping back against the headrest. Shooting pain wracked his arms. The half moon fell out of sight, replaced by the foggy horizon and a moment later, the blue waters. He took a gulp of air over the deflated airbag before being thrown against the steering wheel just as the car splashed into the river. His chest ached. The cold water quickly surrounded him. He felt the swift current sweeping him downstream. Holding his breath under water, his lungs cried out for oxygen. *I'm going to die!* While bouncing around, his head struck the roof several times. The Hummer came to rest on the floor of the riverbed.

He forced his eyes to stay wide open, spotting the rolled-down side window. He heaved himself toward the opening. Halfway through, his right hip caught the window frame. He twisted himself onto his back, breaking free. No longer able to hold his breath, he released his lungs. Using the Hummer as his springboard, he pushed against it. Kicking and swimming frantically toward the surface, he felt himself exploding out of the water. While he gasped for air, the current carried him like a floating bottle. His body felt numb. He looked up. Exeter Bridge was nowhere in sight.

Rogers filled his lungs with fresh air. The shoreline seemed to be whizzing by him. He spotted a tree stump a few yards ahead. He latched onto it, but his grip grew weaker. He kicked his legs, hurling himself toward the grassy shoreline. He felt the rocky bottom beneath his feet as he lunged forward, grazing the top of his head along the rock-strewn grass. He crawled for as long as he could, hand over hand until he collapsed.

The next thing he remembered was waking up in the backseat of an Oldwyck police cruiser. Detective Darden was staring at him in disbelief.

Chapter Twenty-One

"Dr. Rogers, Victor Carver is here to see you."

"Thanks, Sally, send him in."

He adjusted his neck collar. The pain shot down his arm.

"Shit, Jonathan, I read about your accident in the paper last week. I was so worried about you." Carver dropped his motorcycle helmet on the floor and gently patted Rogers on the shoulder. "I called Sally. She said to give you a few days to heal."

"Can you believe what's happening to me these days? Getting shot, diagnosed with cancer, and being shoved off a bridge in a few months' time is too much."

"You must have pissed off somebody."

"I do interact with a lot of powerful leaders."

"How's your neck?"

"It's coming along. As long as the collar is in proper placement, I'm fine. I actually jogged yesterday with no pain."

Carver's face brightened. "I was hoping that you would be ready. Are you up for a slow jog around Oldwyck Pond? I think you need to get out of this office and spend some time with your old buddy."

Rogers checked his watch. "It's four thirty. I've a business appointment back here at six. I'll need time to shower."

"Gives us an hour. How about it?"

"I'll meet you at the pond in five minutes."

The Commissioner changed slowly into his sweat pants and sneakers, careful not to jar his neck collar. He passed by Sally's desk before leaving for the pond.

"I need to see Beth Murphy. Please schedule her."

"Will do, Dr. Rogers. By the way, the Governor wants to see you in his office at nine sharp tomorrow."

"Our face-to-face is long overdue. I wonder what's on his agenda?"

••••••••••

The Commissioner tightly laced his sneakers. He jogged the fifty yards or so across the lighted parking lot from his office. He headed toward the tree-lined park and the twenty-foot-deep muddy pond, searching for Carver like a quarterback looking for an open receiver. He spotted his athletic-looking buddy approaching from a wooded area on the western side of the pond.

"Victor, I've been thinking. Your fraud report will probably be so well received by the Governor that maybe I should be concerned."

Carver's face hardened. "Whether it's accurate?"

"No. I'm sure that it will be truthful. I'm just thinking that Peabody will be so impressed with your leadership that he'll replace me and appoint you to be the next Commissioner of Health."

Carver shook his head vigorously. "Not interested. Doesn't pay enough. Remember, I'm retiring soon. I need as much money as I can make these days. I can't live on Social Security and my wife's government worker's pension."

"You're right about the pay working for government." Rogers stretched his legs. He felt good being with Victor. "So do you think the Michigan football team will be ranked next year?"

"Only if you are still the Commissioner," he replied with a half smile.

"Touché. Let's get going."

Rogers took off while Carver was still warming up with some stretches. After several dozen strides, he looked back over his shoulder. He had a twenty-yard lead. As he rounded the first turn, he was amazed when his buddy appeared, out of the blue, to be jogging alongside him. He had always been confident of his ability to be aware of his surroundings, but his hearing had been failing in recent years.

"You're pretty light on your feet," he said, trying to hide his surprise.

"Compared to my wife, I'm a turf pounder," Victor replied. "But, some of my patients tell me that they don't even realize when I enter their hospital room. They say that I seem to walk on air."

"Try knocking louder on the door next time."

"Good idea, old man."

After one and a half times around the half-mile-long lake, Rogers felt fatigued. He looked over at Victor, who appeared to be doing just fine. He pointed toward the wooden bench on the far side of the pond. "I hate sitting on that old bench. I get splinters every time."

"Then let's keep going."

"No, I need a break."

"You know, I'm beginning to think that maybe you are the Commissioner of Un-Health."

"Very funny!"

Rogers sat down carefully. Not wanting to touch the decaying bench, he crossed his arms across his chest to avoid getting a splinter. Dusk was quickly turning into nightfall. He looked over at Carver. The oncologist's face seemed to be strangely contorted. His mouth curled up toward a squinting left eye. His face drained of all color. The Commissioner worried that he might be having a heart attack or a stroke.

Pushing gently on his shoulder, the Commissioner said, half-kidding, "You still alive?"

Suddenly, Carver jumped to his feet. He slapped his face lightly and joked, "I must have been dreaming."

"From the way you looked, it seemed that it was a nightmare."

He winked. "Demons are after me. They're crazed killers."

"Maybe you do need to retire, my friend. Listen, we have a little more than fifteen minutes before I need to get back to my office."

Rogers led the way once more around the circumference of the pond just as a heavy spring shower began pelting them. Just before passing the wooden bench again, the rain shower stopped as quickly as it began. He looked up. The sky was clearing. A full moon was sneaking through the partial cloud cover. In the pathway twenty feet in front of them, he saw a glint of light. The brightness of the moon partially illuminated the dirt path.

He came to a dead stop after a few more paces and picked up the shiny object. It was a man's wristwatch. It read thirty-two minutes past four. The glass was cracked; neither hand was moving.

"Lord knows how long it's been out here. Toss it."

"I don't think so, Victor. Look at the date. Someone must have dropped it no more than an hour ago."

"Strange things happen all the time." He grabbed the watch from Rogers and flung it into an area of waist-high weeds.

"Why did you throw it away?"

Carver shrugged his shoulders. Resuming their run, a hundred yards up the pathway, the Commissioner saw a beam of light shining into the woods. It was flickering.

"Did you see that?"

"See what?"

"Over there about twenty yards to the right of this big oak tree."

"Not sure."

Rogers pointed to the spot as they both drew closer. "Right there."

"Maybe you're just picking up a beer can that's reflecting the moon's light." Carver snickered. "You old worrywart. Now you got me curious. Let's go check it out."

Rogers could see that in this part of the woods, there was a small clearing of trees where the light from the full moon shone onto the ground. He surveyed the landscape. A moment later, he saw a small hill up ahead. It seemed to be outlined by the flickering beam of light. As he scouted up ahead, he wasn't paying attention to where he was stepping. He pulled his sneaker from a four-inch mud hole and cursed himself for not watching where he walked.

"What's that?" Carver asked. "About thirty yards straight ahead."

Rogers squinted. Sloshing through the muddy meadow, he closed his eyes for a second or two to sensitize them to the weak light. "It looks like a flashlight pointing to the mound of dirt."

The Commissioner sprinted ahead a few yards and reached

for the flashlight first. He picked it up and fired the beam at the three-foot-high mound. He narrowed his eyes, feeling a sudden chill upon spotting his target. "Oh my God. It's a body."

As he approached the scene, he stared down at the dried blood lining a five-inch-deep gash on the back of a man's head. The victim was dressed in a white dress shirt and navy blue slacks. He was wearing black dress shoes. His body was covered with leaves, lying face down in the mud, resting on the the raised pile of dirt as if sleeping on a pillow

The Commissioner bent down on his knees to feel for a carotid pulse. "His body is still warm. But I can't feel a pulse. If there is one, it's very faint. Let's turn him over to check."

"Jonathan, we shouldn't be touching anything here. This is a crime scene."

"Maybe he tripped and it's an accident. Why do you say it's a crime scene?"

"Listen, we need to call the police. I have my cell back on my cycle."

"I say we should turn the body over to see what we can do. I thought I saw his torso moving slightly."

"I don't think so. Don't see any signs that he is breathing. His hands are blue. Let's call the damn police. They can get an ambulance. It's not like we have any medical equipment to code him out here in the woods."

Rogers stared up at Carver. He shouted, "We're doctors. We have to try!"

"We're wasting time. Be realistic. You're not thinking clearly."

The oncologist tugged on his arm. Reluctantly, Rogers stood and relented. As he ran toward the parking lot, he suddenly heard a familiar sound coming from behind them, and he froze. Carver continued on for a bit before stopping. As Rogers spun around, he recognized the sound. The low-pitched groan was something that he had heard thousands of times in his medical career. He hustled back to the victim. There was no doubt in his mind.

The Commissioner kneeled down next to the body. He pressed his ear close to the man's face. He was about to flip the body when he heard a gurgling noise. Startled, he sat back on his knees. He felt Carver's hand pulling on his jogging shirt. Rogers brushed it away.

The oncologist yelled, "Let's go! They're just agonal sounds just before his heart gives out. By all medical criteria, the man is dead. You're a doctor, my God, you know I'm right."

"Shut up. We've got to do something."

"If we left when I said, we'd be back by now. We'll come back right after we call the police."

A few seconds passed. He thought he heard noises that echoed like fast-spoken but mumbled words. He leaned toward the body to listen closely. Unsure that he could hear anything except the thumping of his own heart, he turned the body on its side. The face looked like it had been viciously smashed with a blunt object. The nose was flat, obviously badly fractured. His jet-black hair, smelling of hair dye, was caked in mud. The eye sockets were severely bruised. A moment later, he believed that he saw the blue lips quiver. He pressed his ear closer to the man's mouth and clearly heard three slurred words. "Rogers, be careful."

He lurched back on to his heels and glanced up at Carver, still pacing around and looking nervous. The Commissioner leaned forward again to wipe away the mud from the man's swollen eyes. He shined the flashlight into the pupils. They were now fixed and dilated. *Dead.*

Rogers felt Carver's hands around his chest as if his colleague was about to do a Heimlich maneuver on him. Carver pulled him to his feet. The dead man's face had turned back into the mud. *Did Carver hear the victim speak?*

"Jonathan, we're leaving. Now!"

Wiping the mud from the side of his face with the back of his hand, Rogers stared at the motionless body. "Did you hear . . .?"

"They're just gurgling sounds. The man is dead. Let's go."

Rogers picked up the flashlight. He raced back to the parking lot. His mind was in turmoil.

As they ran side by side back to the parking lot, Carver asked calmly, "What about your six o' clock appointment?"

"How the hell can you ask me about that after what just happened?"

Rogers was out of breath from the sprint to the parking lot. Carver opened the leather pack that was mounted behind the seat on his motorcycle. He pulled out his cell.

"Hurry, dial 911!"

"Commish, take it easy. It's not like we had anything to do with killing the man."

After thinking about it for a few seconds, Rogers began sprinting back on the muddy pathway. The chilling warning of the dying man sloshed around in his head.

Carver yelled out, "Come back. The police are here."

Rogers turned around and began to trot back toward the parking lot. He saw the blinking lights of the police cruiser followed by a late-model blue Corvette convertible. In the distance, it looked like a woman driving the Corvette.

Carver squared up to him. "Let's just tell the police that we found this guy when we were jogging. He was already dead."

"Don't forget the watch, the pointing flashlight, and the sounds from the body."

"Forget all that. Keep it simple."

Rogers exclaimed, "It's more than that, and you know it."

"You can do what you want, but I'm saying as little as possible."

The police car skidded to a stop just three feet from where they were standing. A middle-aged man in a dark suit hopped out of the passenger side. Rogers recognized him as Detective Darden and caught a glimpse of a local Oldwyck policewoman exiting on the driver's side.

The policewoman was Kayla Proctor. Rogers yelled out to her. "We just found a body in the woods. He's just past that big oak tree on that eastern side ridge."

His eyes darted to Carver just as Darden approached.

The detective said with a trace of sarcasm, "Good evening, Dr. Rogers. We seem to be talking to each other a lot these days. What's that in your hand?"

He stammered, "I found this flashlight close to the body."

With a chiding voice, the detective asked, "Do you normally

carry out the duties of your office with a flashlight?"

"It's not mine. I told you that I found it. Listen, someone needs to check on the victim . . . to see if he's still alive."

"Officer Proctor, check it out."

Rogers presented the flashlight to Darden. *And my fingerprints are all over it!* The detective first took out his handkerchief. He then wrapped the silken cloth around his right hand before accepting the flashlight.

Darden walked back to his car. Rogers watched him pull out a cellophane bag. The detective dropped the flashlight into the bag and threw it on the front seat of his white Ford Crown Victoria. Upon returning, he headed directly toward Carver.

"And you, sir."

"I'm Dr. Victor Carver. I'm a personal friend of the Commissioner. We were both jogging around the pond when we saw a strange light coming from the woods just beyond that big oak tree. We checked it out. Dr. Rogers found a body in the clearing by using the flashlight."

"Why didn't one of you stay at the crime scene?"

"I don't know," Rogers blurted out. "Victor didn't believe there was anything that we could do out there in the woods."

He saw the detective give a quick glance over at Carver, who merely wrinkled his brow. Darden drew closer to the duo. "Did either of you touch anything when you found the body?"

Carver glared at Rogers. The oncologist replied, "No, we ran to call the police as soon as we found the body."

The Commissioner began to stare at the blue Corvette. Preoccupied by the police until now, he had completely forgotten about the woman in the convertible. The Corvette was parked about fifty or sixty yards away. Despite being under an overhead light in the parking lot, the driver's face was a mystery. He turned back toward his buddy just as Carver's eyes widened. Looking back to the parking lot, Rogers saw a pregnant woman approaching in the shadows.

"It's Nicki Chambers-Sanderson," the oncologist exclaimed. "What the hell is she doing here?"

"Actually, she is meeting me tonight. She's my six o' clock

appointment."

Nicki sauntered up to the trio, her belly bulging as if due at any moment. She said in an off-handed manner, "Well, Dr. Rogers, it certainly doesn't look like you are dressed to take me to dinner. I was heading toward your office in the Department of Health building when I saw the police racing this way. Out of curiosity, I followed the cops."

"I should have been in my office by now," Rogers said nervously.

She stared at the mud stains covering his hands and face, chuckling, "So did you and Dr. Carver play nicely in the sandbox today?"

Stunned for the moment, Rogers said nothing. He exchanged furtive looks with the group as he wondered what they were thinking of his private evening meeting with a pregnant married woman.

Nicki asked, "What's going on here?"

"Victor and I discovered a body in the woods."

He saw her face harden. Rogers sensed that Carver wanted to change the direction of the conversation.

The oncologist pointed his chin at Nicki. "Is Mr. Sanderson joining you and Dr. Rogers tonight or is this a private dinner?"

"Oh, please," she responded.

A moment later, Rogers saw Officer Proctor running toward them.

Proctor was still twenty yards away when Darden shouted, "Kayla, what did you find?"

"I found . . . I found . . . an elderly man's . . . body."

Darden ordered, "Take a deep breath."

The policewoman put her hands on her hips. She sucked in as much air as she could. Kayla looked briefly at Nicki. "I put on my gloves to do an exam of the victim. The body was cold and lying face up. He was blue and had no pulse. When I turned the body over, I saw a large gash on the back of his head."

Both doctors looked at each other. Turning to Carver, Rogers whispered, "Face up?"

Nodding toward Rogers, the oncologist peered over at Nicki.

Carver took a few steps toward her.

Kayla continued. "I recognized the man after I cleared the mud from his face. I know him from around town."

Darden asked, "Kayla, who is it?"

Proctor turned directly to face Nicki. "I'm so sorry. It's your father. I found his wallet. It's Peter Chambers."

Carver was already in position to cradle Nicki in his arms just before she hit the ground. In shock, Rogers walked toward the woods, deep in thought. Then it came to him. "Oh my God!"

The policewoman shouted, "Let's get her to a hospital. Her water just broke."

The Commissioner barely heard her. He remembered the WPPE radio show message. "The light in the dark shall lead you to the old judge's office." The caller was not some nutty crackpot. It was a riddle that now seemed to make sense. The flashlight was the light in the dark that led the way. His mind was now sharp, focused. He remembered that a judge's office was sometimes called a chamber. He recalled the caller saying, "The young woman is alive." It has to be Ashley.

Darden commanded, "Proctor, you go with her to Mercy Medical. Officer Fairchild will drive you in his car. Drs. Rogers and Carver, come with Officer Verdon and me. We need both of you to come down to the police station."

••••••••••

Joined in the backseat of the police car by Carver, Rogers could only imagine how different the night would have been if there had been no full moon to provide a light in the darkness that reflected off the wristwatch. He glanced over at Carver and wondered why he was so quick to toss away the watch. Flashbacks to his contentious meetings with Peter Chambers rattled around in his head. He felt guilty for not doing more, somehow believing that this tragedy had something to do with the senior's charges against Knowton.

Darden turned around to face them. "Doctors, think of any details that might be important. Don't leave out any fact, no matter how unimportant it might seem to you."

Carver leaned over to the Commissioner. He whispered, "The more you say, the more they'll think we had something to do with the murder."

He replied softly, "What about the fact that he was still alive when we found him?"

Carver's eyes flashed brightly. "What are you talking about?"

"Didn't you . . ."

"Jonathan, you're on your own. Every man for himself."

The Commissioner slumped, causing a sharp pain to radiate down from his weakened neck muscles. Staring at the full moon, he wondered if the radio show caller's telling statement was somehow a warning for him. Was someone trying to provide him clues that Chambers's death was somehow connected to his own misfortunes? Chambers's dying words echoed within him. *Rogers be careful.*

Chapter Twenty-Two

The Commissioner entered one of the interrogation rooms. He asked Detective Darden, "Am I a suspect?"

"All I know is that I've got a dead man found by two doctors jogging through the woods at night. Minutes later, the victim's married and very pregnant daughter shows up all dressed to have a private dinner with you. Somehow my gut tells me you know much more than I've heard so far."

Rogers was about to respond but thought otherwise. For the time being, he shelved his inclination to call his personal attorney and motioned for Darden to continue.

"Getting back to your question, you're not what I would call a suspect. At least not at this time. Doctor, do you mind if I record our conversation?"

"I've nothing to hide."

While watching the detective flip on the digital recorder, Rogers knew that he needed to be careful. He thought back to the one time that he had been sued for malpractice. Even though it had been a frivolous lawsuit, he recalled the basic lessons of giving a deposition. Never volunteer information, and respond directly to the question, offering as little as possible.

"Dr. Rogers, you're aware that you have a right to remain silent. Would you like to consult your attorney before you provide testimony? Do you have any questions on what are your rights?"

"No."

"Glad to hear that you are going to be cooperative, Commissioner. Then can you explain why you were going to have dinner alone with Peter Chambers's pregnant and married daughter?"

"This is a very complicated situation."

"I'll just bet it is. Start wherever you would like."

The Commissioner folded his hands in front of him and rested them on the four-foot-square wooden table. "It's not what you think." Flexing his fingers, he began swinging his right leg up and down.

"How would you possibly know what I think? Take your time. I'm in no hurry."

"Over the last several weeks, I met Peter Chambers a couple of times. He came to my office to make a complaint against a local doctor. Nicki had provided her father with some information that Chambers thought would be of concern to me."

"Who was the local doctor?"

"Do I have to tell you his name?"

"Well, you could either tell me now or wait till we get in front of a judge."

Inhaling deeply, he added, "Tom Knowton."

"Go on."

"Dr. Knowton has been a friend of mine for many years. He is a great doctor. In fact, he is my personal doctor. Anyway, Mr. Chambers believed that Tom was involved in committing Medicaid fraud as well as practicing bad medicine."

"How would he know that?"

"Nicki works for Knowton. She probably told her father."

"I had a feeling that there was more than a social connection between you and Nicki Chambers-Sanderson."

"First of all, she is just an acquaintance. Nothing more. Also, detective, you need to understand that this is all privileged and highly confidential information."

"You did say that you would be cooperative."

Rogers was starting to believe that he needed to buy some time to think through the situation. He realized that each statement could be taken out of context. "Detective, may I have some coffee? It's pretty late and I'm getting tired."

Darden stopped the recorder. "I can use some myself. I'll be back in a few minutes."

••••••••••

Rogers scanned the barren walls of the interrogation room. Except for the sleek black digital recorder, the wobbly table, and four simple chairs, the small space was spartan. He could hear Darden's distant voice in the hallway. The detective was yelling for someone to get some coffee. Through the open door, he saw another detective rush out of the other interrogation room. He assumed that Carver was being questioned and worried what he had revealed. He strained his ears and believed that he heard the other detective tell Darden that they should talk privately.

Rogers rose to walk out to the corridor. There was not a soul in view. Muffled voices were coming from an adjacent room. He could hear Darden talking. The Commissioner snaked his way down the hallway. Pinning himself against the wall no more than three feet from Darden's open office door, he listened intently.

"What did Carver say?" Darden asked.

"He was invited to meet with the Commissioner earlier today to discuss State health business. A month ago, the doctor was appointed by Rogers to lead a task force to investigate potential Medicaid fraud among a group of physicians. After they met today to discuss the task force findings at the Commissioner's office, they both decided to take a jog around the pond."

"Was Carver nervous during his testimony?"

"Not in the least. Seemed credible. So around five thirty this evening, they saw a light coming from the woods on the far side of the pond. Both of their curiosities were aroused. They found a flashlight that led them to find Chambers's body face up in the mud."

"That's the position that Kayla found the body."

The other detective nodded. "So Carver claims that Nicki Sanderson is the office manager for the Knowton practice and that she is the dead man's daughter. Sometimes, she goes by Nicki Chambers-Sanderson."

"Carver remembered the Commissioner telling him this afternoon that he was meeting someone this evening on Department of Health business. When he saw that it was Nicki, he was pretty surprised. He said there was some office scuttlebutt at the oncology practice that there may be some romantic history between Mrs. Sanderson and Rogers. That's all he knows."

"Sounds pretty straightforward. I think that Rogers's story will be a little more complicated. He seems pretty anxious. Jack, send Dr. Carver on his way. Make sure we know where to find him. Meet me in the main interrogation room when you are finished."

Upon hearing the detectives' chairs screech, Rogers charged back to his interrogation room and collapsed in his seat. He took some hefty breaths to recuperate while he closed his eyes. He felt betrayed by his friend. *Chambers was face down.*

••••••••••

"Dr. Rogers, you look perplexed."

The doctor reached out for the cup and took a long sip. "Thanks for the coffee. I'm fine. Let's go."

"I'm turning on the recorder. Detective Ives will be joining us shortly."

"Isn't he still talking with Dr. Carver?"

"Let's just focus on your story. The last question I asked you was, how would Mr. Chambers know that Dr. Knowton was committing fraud and practicing bad medicine?"

"I told you. Because that's what Nicki told him."

"How's that?"

"She is Knowton's office manager, so she would know."

"How would she know anything about medical care? Is she a nurse?"

"No. Actually it was Beth Murphy who told Chambers that Knowton was using poor medical judgment. Beth is a nurse. Nicki only knew about the fraud."

"Beth Murphy was the young lady who publicly accused you of covering up the death of her father, Sam Murphy." Darden plunked his cup down on the table. "You know, you're right."

"About?"

"Your story is complicated." Darden stood to pace the floor. "So did Chambers present any evidence to you to support his charge?"

"He gave me photocopies of some of Dr. Knowton's insurance claims, which he believed to be fraudulent."

"What did you do with that evidence?"

"I filed it away in my office after my assistant retrieved it from Knowton's office."

"Why not call the police if you had evidence of fraud?"

"I wanted to ask Knowton about the allegation first before I contacted the authorities. In retrospect, it was poor judgment on my part. So much has been going on in my personal life these past few months. I'm sure you've read the local papers."

Darden's eyes seemed to soften. "Did you finally meet with Knowton?"

"Yes. I spoke to him about the fraudulent checks."

"And . . .?"

Looking up, he hadn't noticed that Detective Ives was standing in the doorway. Rogers took two gulps of coffee and swished it around. His eyes darted from Ives to Darden while swiping away the beads of sweat trickling down his forehead with the back of his hand.

"Knowton denied the charge."

"OK. Let's leave that for now. So if he was practicing bad medicine, why didn't you at least address that situation? After all, you are the Commissioner of Health!"

"Just so you understand, it's not that easy to define what is good or bad medicine."

"Really? I see. Then let me ask a much simpler question. Did you receive any specific complaints about your colleague's practice of medicine? Were you aware of any unexpected deaths in Dr. Knowton's practice?"

"Yes, but . . . a death of a patient does not mean that it was the doctor's fault. And, Detective Darden, there are reasons why I didn't report to the authorities what Mr. Chambers told me. My authority as Commissioner of Health is not to question every doctor on what happens every day."

"What if there is a pattern of poor care over a period of time by a specific doctor?"

"That would be a different story."

"Commissioner, was Peter Chambers the only one who came forth to complain to you about shoddy medical care delivered by Dr. Knowton?"

"No. I received other complaints."

"Did you do something about them?"

"Not yet," he replied defensively after taking another sip of the black coffee.

Darden asked bluntly, "Are you covering up for your colleague?"

Rogers shouted, "Of course not!"

"One last question Commissioner. What was your clinical impression upon finding Mr. Chambers's body?"

"We found his body face down in the mud. We . . ."

"Hold it doctor. Please repeat what you just said."

"We found Chambers face down in the mud."

The Detective turned his back to Rogers and punched the on-off button.

"Under the circumstances, I would strongly urge you to contact an attorney of your choice."

"Why?"

"Because I believe you will need one. You're now free to leave. We'll be speaking with you again shortly."

Rogers stood slowly. He walked between the two detectives, his eyes searching their troubled faces. Stopping on a dime, he looked back at Darden. "Next time, Detective, I'd like some answers to *my* questions."

"Like?"

"You can start by you telling me who is targeting my family."

"Excuse me. What do mean by targeting your family?"

Rogers looked down at the floor, thinking of whether to bring up Ashley's disappearance. "I mean, my family is going through a lot with what is happening to me."

"Doctor, are you hiding something?"

The Commissioner drew closer. He now stood only a foot from the detective and was ready to go on the offensive. "I think the real question is whether you and the FBI are hiding something from me."

Darden's gaze became unsettled. "No comment."

"That line is getting old."

"You must trust us."

"The track record of your local department and the FBI hasn't been so good thus far. I have a family to protect. I can't take any chances."

"I wish that I could be more reassuring. The FBI has me sworn to secrecy."

"Seems the FBI is covering up for their ultimate boss . . . the President."

"I wouldn't say that too loudly if I were you, Commissioner."

"Even if it's the truth?"

"Commissioner Rogers, do yourself a favor. Watch your back."

"Is that a threat or a friendly warning?"

Darden stared ahead, saying nothing.

Rogers grinned. "I think I just got my answer."

Chapter Twenty-Three

It had been raining heavily since dawn. It was not the kind of day to bike to work. Rogers dozed off several times in the back of the limo on the way to the Department. He had been completely zonked in bed until five minutes before his driver picked him up. Passing by the adjacent statehouse, he shook himself awake and rubbed his eyes. He tumbled out of the backseat and was blinded by the sun. He hobbled up to his office around eight fifteen.

The Commissioner shuffled a few hundred yards through the gray marble hallways, placing one foot in front of the other in the same cadence that he used to practice in ROTC back in college.

The outside door buzzed open to the administrative lobby. "Is he ready for me?"

The assistant replied, "Good morning, Commissioner. You're just a few minutes late."

"Thanks, Mary," he mumurmed.

Upon opening the huge wooden inner door to the Governor's office, Rogers saw that his boss was sitting behind his antique oak desk, rubbing his forehead. Glancing up, Peabody turned on a broad smile.

"Jonathan, it's great to see you again. You look terrific."

I look like shit. "Good morning, Governor."

"Have a seat over here at the conference table. Coffee?"

"Actually, I would love a pot; I mean a cup," he stammered before sinking deeply into a plush chair opposite the Governor.

Pressing the intercom, Peabody ordered, "Mary, Please bring in two cups of black coffee."

"Last night was rough," Jonathan said.

Peabody nodded. The Commissioner wondered if he had already heard about Peter Chambers. He decided to hold back any explanation. Sitting up straight, he just shook his head.

"Any word on Ashley?"

"Nothing at all."

"Thanks for previously sharing this tragedy with me. I wish I could help some way. She's such a lovely young lady."

"You haven't told . . ."

"No one. I'm sworn to secrecy as you requested."

"A few weeks have gone by. I can't contact the authorities or they'll ki—"

Peabody's face seemed to tighten a bit. "Have you visited the marathon site in Alaska? Have you spoken with anyone up there?"

Rogers did not respond. He wondered why Peabody wanted to know the details of what he knew about Ashley. He seemed more than curious. "Governor, I think I need a leave of absence . . . time to search for Ashley." He pulled out his handkerchief.

"I appreciate your concern for your daughter. But, what can you do that the authorities are not doing already?"

Rogers wiped away a tear. "I don't know. I wish I did."

Peabody leaned back and seemed to relax a shade. "What about your current health status?"

"Dr. Knowton feels the chemo has cleared up any loose cancer cells. I've zero aftereffects of the shooting except some superficial numbness of the chest wall where they removed the bullets and the cancer."

"Bullets? This is the first time I've heard that you were shot more than once."

"One of the few facts the FBI was willing to share with me was the weapon used in the shooting was an Uzi. I was hit twice below the right clavicle with 9mm bullets."

"You were lucky to survive."

Rogers stared at the glass-topped round conference table in front of him. "Listen, enough about me. We need to talk about our past conversations."

"What do you mean?" the Governor replied with a touch of surprise.

"After I was shot, the FBI impounded my computer. Their agents checked all the emails on my hard drive. They asked me some unusual questions."

"Such as?"

"The FBI wanted to know whether you put any pressure on me to tell the President that I would support the drug companies."

The Governor rose from his chair and began pacing. "Commissioner, what exactly did you tell them?"

"I said that our private conversations are exactly that—private."

"That was the right thing to say. When you act like this, I know that I wasn't crazy to recommend you for Surgeon General. That's why I haven't replaced you all this time as the Commissioner. Now you're thinking like a team player."

"Getting back to their demands for me to talk about our private conversations, they have no right to such information. Whether it was useful for me is a whole other question. Anyway, my good deed earned me a subpoena. My attorney is meeting with me in thirty minutes to discuss my next steps."

"I wish you well."

He watched the Governor amble slowly over to his desk and sit on the edge. Just as he was about to speak, Mary brought in the two cups of black coffee. Rogers drank the first cup in two gulps and grabbed for the second.

"What about the letter I received from President Jordan stating that he wants me on his team? Is he going to appoint me Surgeon General?"

"Actually, the President said that he needs team players. He hoped that you would join his team by being a team player."

Wrinkling his forehead, Rogers replied, "That's what I just said."

"Not exactly."

"So will I be appointed Surgeon General or not?"

"I think that depends."

"On what?"

"It depends on what you do from this point going forward."

"Just what am I supposed to do?"

"That's easy. Follow your leaders. In other words, become a team player."

As he thought about what Peabody was saying, he recalled

the same message Kim received at knifepoint at the lake house. Her life was spared when she simply agreed to convince him to follow his leaders.

"What about following my conscience?"

Peabody hopped off the desk and walked over to the door. "Has following your conscience ever gotten you into any trouble before?"

Rogers sighed. "I suppose so. But I have no regrets. I always did what I believed was right for the people we serve."

The Governor opened the door and responded crisply, "Spare me your rationalizations. I've an important appointment with a CEO of one of those drug companies that you seem to hate so much. I don't want to keep him waiting. Besides the fact that he's an excellent donor to our party, I wouldn't want to get on his bad side. I'm sorry, but we'll have to continue our conversation later."

Dr. Rogers glared back at the Governor. "I think I know who you're meeting. Can I guess his name?"

"I'm in no mood for guessing games. Listen, in case you were wondering whether I knew, I heard about your little escapade last evening in the woods. If I were you, I'd spend more of your free time trying to find Ashley than setting up evening meetings in your office with Nicki Chambers-Sanderson."

"I'm doing the best I can, and I resent your implications."

"Listen, I need you at the Department. As you know, we have important work pending with the Medicaid fraud probe. This is no time to take a leave of absence on some wild-goose chase to look for Ashley. Just stay out of trouble, my friend. Excuse me, I'm late."

••••••••••

The door to Rogers's office creaked open after a single knock, creeking, as if it was inching forward on a rusty winch. There was his roommate from college, Brent Marshall, dressed in a gray tweed suit, peeking into his office. Except for the puffy bags under his eyes, his legal confidant appeared to be aging fairly well.

"Good morning, Jonathan."

"I'm not so sure."

"Sally hinted as much."

Rogers pointed to the conference table. He remained standing while his attorney sat and opened his brown briefcase. The Commissioner suppressed a yawn.

Marshall began, "Anything about Ashley?"

"Not a damn thing."

"I'm not sure that you're doing the right thing by not going to the FBI."

"I know, but I can't take the chance. Anyway, I'm not so sure that I trust the FBI or any of the authorities."

"I understand. Heard you had a rough night."

"Who told you?"

The attorney removed a paper from his briefcase. "Your pal, Detective Darden. Here is a transcript of your recorded testimony. When the Oldwyck Police questioned you and Dr. Carver last night, they found inconsistencies in your testimony."

"Such as?"

"Policewoman Proctor and Carver both agreed that the body was found face up."

Rogers sat down across from Marshall. "That's not true. Carver and I both looked at Proctor in shock when she said the body was face up. Chambers was definitely face down."

"Possibly you misspoke. Doctors do make mistakes."

"I would certainly remember if I saw his face when we found him. Don't forget Chambers was just in this very office a few weeks ago." Pointing, Rogers continued, "He sat in that chair, just in front of my desk. As a matter of fact, he was here twice in the last month."

"So then Proctor and Carver are both wrong. But why would Proctor, an experienced cop, make such a stupid mistake? And why would Carver make the same mistake as well?"

"I don't know."

"So either Proctor was wrong or she lied. But why would she lie?"

"No reason."

"How much time elapsed from the time that you and Carver left the body in the woods until the time that Proctor found the body?"

"Ten minutes, no more."

"Tell me more about the crime scene."

"The dirt that covered his body looked like it was recently shoveled. It was muddy given the recent rain. When I turned the body on its side, Chamber's face looked like it had been pulverized with a blunt object."

"Bear with me on this. I've a theory. Could someone have been hiding in the woods? And, after you and Carver left the scene, could that person have flipped the body so that it was face up?"

"Why would anyone do that?"

"Is it possible?"

"Of course it could happen. But why?"

"Follow my thinking. Someone flips the body so Proctor would report that the body was face up. You said Carver looked surprised when she reported that position."

"Yes, we were both shocked. We were together the whole time. Chambers was definitely face down."

"Then if Proctor is correct because the body was flipped and you are right . . . then . . ."

"Carver is lying. But why would he do that?"

"I have no idea. What I do know is that you need to fully cooperate with the authorities. Tell them everything you know."

Marshall got up and walked over to the window. He pivoted to face Rogers. "Are you telling me everything?"

"There is a lot more that you need to know."

"I had a feeling."

"How much time do you have?"

"You're worrying me, Jonathan."

"Listen, this is my theory. I believe that Chambers died of an acute subdural hematoma brought about by a sharp blow to the head. People with this injury lose consciousness due to a ruptured blood vessel causing damage to brain tissue."

"I'm sure that it makes medical sense to you. But so what?"

"Whoever bashed Chambers must have been convinced that he would not survive the blow to his skull. Obviously, they would not want him alive to talk to anyone. Well, when he lost complete consciousness after being struck, a non-medical person might have believed that he died."

"Don't know where you're going with all of this."

"Bear with me a little longer. In case of a subdural, a patient often regains consciousness for a brief period before going on to further neurological deterioration just before death."

"Are you saying that you know that Chambers regained consciousness?"

"I am."

"Is this part of your medical theory?"

"It's no theory. Chambers spoke when I turned his body on his side."

Marshall pounded the table. "What? Darden didn't tell me any of this."

"I didn't tell him."

"Why not?" Marshall thundered.

"I was afraid that it would implicate me somehow."

The attorney looked out the window. "Wouldn't Carver have witnessed what you just said?"

"Carver saw everything that I did. But he may not have heard what Chambers whispered to me. I knelt down on the ground next to the victim while Carver was pacing around the body."

"Did you ever flip his body over so that his face was up?"

"No. I was about to do that but dropped the body back to a face-down position after Chambers spoke to me. I was in shock myself."

"And what did he say?"

Marshall leaned forward. The Commissioner could see the lines in his forehead deepening.

"His final words were, *Rogers, be careful.*"

••••••••••

Rogers dialed Carver's office number. His call was transferred into the oncologist's private office by the receptionist, and Dr. Carver picked up on the third ring.

"Jonathan, after last night, I'm not hanging out with you anymore. At my age, I need a quieter lifestyle. And I'm just not used to being questioned about a murder."

"Victor, I need to talk to you."

"About what?"

"I'll meet you at the Turning Point Café on Center Street at six tonight. If you don't show, then I know what I need to do."

"What are you talking about? What do you mean if I don't show? Are you threatening me?"

"Turning Point at six!"

Chapter Twenty-Four

Seated by the window at the Turning Point, Rogers watched closely as Carver pulled up on his motorcycle. He walked into the coffee shop, swinging his helmet in one hand. Rogers waved, and Carver slid into the booth across from him.

"I've got some questions for you," Rogers said, forgoing any greeting.

Carver met his frown head-on. "So what's up?"

"Certainly not Chambers's body."

"Stop the crap, Rogers," he responded angrily.

The Commissioner leaned back. Carver put his hands up in supplication. "Listen, we went through this last night. I didn't want to contradict the policewoman who said she found the body face up."

"But you know damn well that the body was face down when we found it."

"What's the difference?" Carver pleaded.

"The truth!"

"What's that supposed to mean?"

"The police believe that I've got something to do with his murder since my story didn't match Officer Proctor's or yours."

"Well, it's none of my business, but why were you having a rendezvous with the dead man's married daughter last night?" Carver persisted. "Is there something going on between you and Nicki that Chambers might have found out?"

"There's nothing going on. Do you think I killed Chambers?"

"I don't know what to think anymore. In any case, I need to get home for dinner, if we're not going to eat. I'm starving. I can't believe that I agreed to meet you here to talk about this nonsense. If I hadn't asked you to go jogging with me last evening, I wouldn't even be involved in this crazy business."

"You still didn't answer my question. Why did you say the body was face up?"

Carver climbed out of the booth and stormed out the door. Rogers rushed out behind him and caught up with him at the curbside. Carver hopped onto the bike and put on his helmet.

Grabbing his arm, Rogers said, "You need to go to the police and say you made a mistake. You need to say that you agree with me that the body was face down."

"Take your hands off me," Carver shouted.

"Not until you tell the truth. You're supposed to be my friend."

"I am. But you're acting irrational."

Rogers felt the hard karate chop on his arm, and he was caught off balance by the forceful shove that followed. Landing on his buttocks, scraping his elbows on the pavement, he yelled, "You're lying, Carver!"

"See ya."

Rogers bounded to his feet. Carver took off in traffic, but while he was looking back toward the Commissioner, his bike hit a deep pothole. The cycle tumbled on its side. Carver's leg was trapped under the back wheel. He tried to push the bike off of himself, and looked up to see a dump truck bearing down on him. Rogers began running toward Carver. The truck was no more than fifty feet away from where the oncologist was sprawled out on the street. The truck's tires screeched loudly. Rogers sprinted the last few yards into the street and yanked Carver by the arm, dragging him toward the sidewalk just as the ten-ton truck demolished the Harley.

"Holy shit, Jonathan! You saved my life." The two men sat on the sidewalk, catching their breath, as bystanders began to gather. Carver pulled up his trousers, revealing a long bruise "I don't think I broke anything."

"Now, maybe you'll start telling the truth of what really happened last night with Mr. Chambers."

"I have been honest with you. You must believe me."

••••••••••

Beth Murphy walked into Rogers's office, dressed in a V-necked beige business suit and carrying a tan attaché case.

He found it impossible not to recall the rage plastered on her face at the Medicaid fraud press conference where she publicly accused him of covering up the alleged murder of her father, Sam Murphy, at the hands of Dr. Knowton. Jonathan regretted not investigating Chambers's charge right from the start. Today, Beth Murphy's posture and face seemed relaxed, so different from the last time.

She greeted him with a half-smile. "Good morning, Commissioner."

He felt guarded from the start. "Good morning, Ms. Murphy." He motioned for her to take a seat in the chair on the other side of his desk.

"Dr. Rogers, let me start by apologizing for my behavior at your press conference."

"Your apology is accepted. I understand the emotional strain that you were under due to the unexpected death of your father."

"I've had many sleepless nights thinking of what I put you through that day."

"I'm over it. Let's move on."

Frowning, she said, "Commissioner, I have some things to say to you." She bent forward and picked up the attaché case from the floor, placing it on her lap. Beth opened her case and removed some papers.

"What's on your mind?"

She held out the papers in front of her. "This is my father's autopsy report. Would you review it for me?"

Not sure on how he should respond, he plodded ahead. "Out of respect to you, Ms. Murphy, I'm willing to take a look. But where is this going? As I told you at the press hall, I had nothing to do with the treatment of Sam Murphy."

"Commissioner, please take a look." She handed the report to him, and he reluctantly read through the three pages.

He was puzzled with the medical conclusion on the final page.

"The autopsy says that your father, Mr. Murphy, died of cardiac arrest and bone marrow suppression secondary to Zazotene. It also states that the amount of the drug in his blood at autopsy was ten times the dose that is normally used to treat cancer. Also, it mentions that the drug that Knowton prescribed is not FDA approved for his type of cancer."

"Exactly."

Rogers arched his eyebrows. "Miss Murphy, why are you showing me this?"

"Because my attorney has forbidden me from talking directly to Knowton. I have filed a malpractice lawsuit against him. What I need is a doctor's opinion."

Rogers felt that he was being used. "Then I must not say another word. It would be inappropriate for me to comment if this is a legal matter between you and Dr. Knowton. By the way, are you recording our conversation?"

"No, I'm not recording anything. And by the tone of your voice, it's obvious to me that you still don't care about protecting the health of the people of this state."

"Miss Murphy, that's simply not true. If I didn't care, I would be part of the political machine that has corrupted the health-care system. And I'm not."

She rose slowly, stuffing the papers back in her attaché. He stood and walked around the side of his desk. He could see her neck and face turning redder by the moment.

"Dr. Rogers, the nurse's notes at Mercy Hospital didn't show an order on Sam Murphy's chart for Zazotene on the day he died. In fact, the last time he received that drug from Dr. Knowton's order was at least a week before. But Sam had no reaction to it at that time."

"Then if Knowton didn't order the Zazotene, how did Sam Murphy receive it?"

"Good question. With your connections, I thought you might know."

"Why would I know?"

Murphy just stared at him. "I'm not the doctor, you are."

"Since your father received the drug the week before with no problem, I find it unusual that he would have died so quickly on the night when he received it again."

"Then what killed him?"

"I can't tell from the report. It's certainly possible that the high dose might have caused his cardiac arrest. But medically it would be a stretch to conclude that."

"In your medical opinion, could Zazotene kill within two hours?"

"I don't have a quick answer for you."

"Perhaps the truth will come out on the witness stand."

"Are you planning on deposing me?"

She checked her watch. "Commissioner, thank you for your time and medical input. I need to catch a flight back to DC. I'm late."

"Business?"

"I live in DC."

"As you probably read in the newspapers, I almost died there."

She raised her left eyebrow while the lines around her mouth tightened. "To be totally honest with you, I was jogging through the Ellipse across from the White House the day you were shot."

"Really?"

"I saw all the commotion with the Secret Service searching the Ellipse. I had no idea that you were one of the victims."

"Well, Miss Murphy, I must say that whenever our paths cross, we always find something interesting to discuss."

"Oh, and one last point. You need to know that the authorities are treating Sam's death as a homicide. Someone obviously gave him a lethal injection of Zazotene."

"If someone wanted to cover their tracks after killing your father with the drug, it would make no sense to use that enormous a dose knowing that it would be discovered at autopsy."

"I'm not only interested in what killed Sam. More importantly, I want to know who killed him. If it was Knowton, he'll pay."

Chapter Twenty-Five

Today, Ashley knew when the door would open. Her internal clock seemed to have taken over; her day was broken into three mealtimes.

She had been working for weeks digging out the large bolt from the stone wall. When she was first chained to the wall, the links had been connected to this five-inch bolt, which was screwed into the stone wall. On one of Rick's daily trips to deliver her meal in the metal bowl, he had forgotten to pick up the empty bowl when she was finished. Ashley hid it in the darkest corner of her cell, under her cot. She had used the bowl to pry the bolt loose. It was her only weapon.

She knew she had to make something happen. Her head ached as she heard the key unlocking the door bolt. Rick walked in carrying two bottles of beer and her lunch bowl in one hand and a gas lantern in the other. He kicked the door shut with his foot.

"I thought I'd join you today for lunch."

"I could use the company."

"I guess you haven't made friends yet with the rats."

She smiled. "Actually, I prefer guys."

"Let's sit on the floor and have a beer. So I bet a good-looking girl like you has a lot of boyfriends, especially coming from your well-educated family."

"I just broke up with Danny. He was boring. I like to party and dance and have a good time."

"Me too." Rick held up his bottle and made a toast. "To Ashley, the sexiest chick I have ever kidnapped." He held up his bottle of beer and tapped it against hers in a toast.

"You know, Rick, you're kind of cute. I like guys who can be tough and yet gentle with a woman. I bet that's exactly who you are."

"I do have a soft side, although I would never tell my uncle. He's a hard-assed businessman."

"And you look up to him?"

"I would say so. He's my Uncle Z."

"What's Z stand for?"

Rick looked at her suspiciously. "Why are you asking me all these questions?"

"Just trying to make small talk to get to know you," Ashley replied, taking a swig.

"So what have you been doing in this dungeon to keep that killer body of yours in shape?"

"I walk a few hours each day and dance a little. I used to be a cheerleader in college."

"Really. Can you dance for me?"

"I would love to." She stood, holding on to her beer. Trying her best, she slowly moved her hips and pulled up her shirt. She could see that he focused on her belly button. "Do you like my dancing, Rick?"

"What's there not to like?"

Ashley saw her chance.

"This is fun. Why don't you join me?"

Rich shook his head, smiling. "Nah, you keep dancing. I like to watch you."

"So, what's the redheaded woman's name?"

"Haley. Keep going, girl."

Ashley danced in ever-wider circles around him. Coming back in front of him, she took another gulp of beer. His eyes blazed as he covered up the bulge in his groin.

"You're turning me on."

"We need to get closer. If you know what I mean."

"Just keep dancing. We can fuck later." He opened a second bottle and guzzled half of it down.

Ashley pranced around him slowly. He seemed in a daze. It was now or never. She raised her bottle of beer and smashed it on top of his head. He grabbed her leg. Picking up his beer bottle from the floor, she smacked it across the same spot on his head. Blood poured from the wound. He moaned and dropped to the floor. He was out.

She reached into his pants pocket to find his keys and came across his cell phone. She didn't know if there would be a guard in the hallway, but she had to decide whether to unlock the door or just use the phone instead.

She realized she only had a few moments before Rick would awaken from the blows. She looked at the cell screen. The signal was weak. She decided to text message her father. Typing quickly, she wrote: Held in basement by Rick. Working with man named Z and redhead named Haley. My life depends on you calling a press conf on Medicaid fraud. A beach close by. Please help. Daddy, I'm scared.

She felt Rick's hands yanking on her forearms as she touched the send button. Just as she was about to press it, Rick knocked the cell from her hands and it slid across the cement floor. Ashley turned toward her assailant, just in time to be slapped across her face.

"Bitch!"

Ashley kicked him in the groin. He backed off, holding himself. She dove for the cell. A split second later, she felt him crashing onto her back. She crawled ahead, carrying his weight. She felt his hands tightening his grip around her neck. She pried away one of his fingers and bit it. He released his hold on her neck, cursing loudly. She flipped him off her back and lunged forward, grabbing the cell. Ashley pressed the send button just before his foot stepped on her hand. She dropped the cell and he pounded it with the heel of his boot, cracking the glass.

She pleaded, "Please, I was only trying to call my mom. She's not well. I panicked. Please forgive me. I never got a signal."

Rubbing his head, he looked at his bloody hand. "Shit, you split my head."

Ashley realized her safety net. She added to his anxiety. "You'll need stitches or you'll get an infection. You could die. You know, I'm a medical student. Believe me, you need to see a doctor right away."

He grabbed the gas lantern and reached into his pocket. "Where are my keys?"

Ashley saw them on the floor.

"Kick them over to me."

Rick bent over and picked up the keys, not taking his eye off his captive. "I'll be back and we'll finish this."

The door slammed shut behind him. Ashley heard the key turn the mechanism to the lock position. In complete darkness again, she sobbed. She had gambled, but had now created a monster in her captor. Shivering, she feared her father would never receive the message.

Chapter Twenty-Six

Kim was still in bed even though it was almost eleven on a sunny Saturday morning. While sitting at the kitchen table, Rogers heard the wall phone ring. He hit the speaker function by habit.

"Hello."

From the start, he recognized her voice. He had hoped that she would follow through on her promise to call him.

"This is Alexis Miller," she said in her cascading, scratchy voice.

"I'm so glad you called."

"I can now talk freely. Zach is out of town. I want to help you and Dr. Knowton. My husband will stop at nothing. Knowton does not believe that Zazotene would help me. I trust him."

"There is a rumor that the FDA might agree with your husband. I've heard that they might approve Zazotene for your type of cancer."

"Zach has tremendous influence within the FDA, with many powerful people. But he doesn't really care what drugs I get. This whole business of asking you to convince Knowton to give me the drug is only a ploy to control you so he can sell more Zazotene."

"I suspected as much."

"I've been married to him for fifteen loveless years. Make no mistake, he is interested in only three things: power, profits, and Marissa. And in that order."

"I understand. You said earlier that you wanted to help me and Knowton. What did you mean?"

"Knowton has been invited on a cruise to Mexico sponsored by my husband's company. He'll be in danger unless he plays ball with Zach."

"How do you know that?"

"It doesn't matter how I know. Ever since his Maybach was shot at, he's been on a warpath."

"So . . ."

"A young woman visited me yesterday at my home. She has good reason to believe her father was killed by someone in my husband's little band of friends."

"Would that be Beth Murphy?"

Ignoring the question, Alexis's voice trailed off. She murmured, "I'm a dying woman. I'm housebound due to my illness. I've sent you messages. I've tried to warn you before."

"How?"

Rogers strained to hear her whispers. He wanted to meet with Alexis. It was becoming more obvious. Her story was the key to the puzzle.

"Just listen to the young woman when she calls you. I must go now. I'm very tired and the room is spinning. I need to lie down before I pass out. I'll pray for you and your family. Good-bye, Dr. Rogers."

••••••••••

Rogers heard his cell phone beeping. It was a text message. He scrolled to read the words . . . and his heart began pumping faster and faster. He wiped away the streaming tears. His prayers had been answered. Ashley was alive. Taking a notepad, he wrote down her message.

Rogers's eyes were drawn to the letter Z and the redhead named Haley. It had to be the same one who was there when he was shot, who almost sideswiped his car, and the woman who the marathon jogger in Alaska remembered. Most important, *Ashley was alive.* He closed his eyes to piece together the clues, letting his mind wander. Minutes later, the voice analysis of the radio show caller came to his mind. He had thought that the voice sounded a lot like Alexis Miller's. Tomorrow, he would have Alexis's last voice mail analyzed and compared to the radio show caller.

He rushed to Ashley's bedroom to tell Kim the news. He shook her, but she was out cold. A bottle of sleeping pills was next to her bedside. He checked her pulse. It was strong. Rogers sat on Ashley's old toy box and just stared ahead, spending the rest of the afternoon watching Kim's rhythmic breathing and trying to tie together Ashley's text message.

Chapter Twenty-Seven

Zach Miller exited his new BMW. He scanned the modern eight-story façade with the floor-to-ceiling glass walls. The executive wing of Doctor's Choice Products Pharmacy was on the top floor. Set apart from the rest of the main center building, the offices of the top brass rested on four large steel beams. The manufacturing and shipping wings that flanked the main building for all DCP product lines occupied a square block of prime real estate in DuPont. Zach had defined the Pharmacy's mission as sending prescribed drugs directly by mail to both patients and physicians. However, under the managed care rules in force in Michigan, anti-cancer drugs, such as Zazotene, needed to be injected under a doctor's supervision, and so were sent by the Pharmacy directly to the physician.

Zach hung his laptop by a strap over his right shoulder. He entered the marble-floored lobby and took an elevator to the executive floor. As the door opened, he looked forward to the game he was about to play.

Strolling up to the executive administrative assistant, he introduced himself.

"Mr. Miller, Lauren Timmons is expecting you. Please go right into her office."

He swaggered toward the chief operating officer of the Pharmacy, and gave her half a hug with his left arm. "Love, thanks for clearing your schedule on such short notice to see me this morning."

"Well, I didn't think Marissa would accept a 'no.' Have a seat."

Zach laughed heartily and joined her at the conference table. Opening his computer case, he removed his laptop and placed it on the sparkling glass surface of the small conference table. He began, "So my staff tells me you are performing well. And I've a big favor to ask of you."

"I remember the last time you called me 'love.' I got screwed. So what do you really want, Zach?"

He replied sarcastically, "Can't I pay you a compliment without you pissing me off?"

"I'm sorry, Boss."

"No—you're not. But seriously, how is business?"

"We're doing well. We're certainly meeting our numbers."

"How is Adam doing?"

"He's just great. There is no doubt in my mind that my husband will be the next governor."

"Don't count on it. Peabody's got the President on his side. Just so you know upfront, DCP is officially endorsing our favorite incumbent. To the tune of two million bucks."

"I won't publicly bad-mouth your boy out of respect for DCP. But you're backing the wrong horse. Adam will slaughter Peabody in the election. For the record, my guy plays for keeps. I wouldn't want to get on his bad side."

"Lauren, my dear, you don't seriously think that I'm worried in the least. There is always plenty of time to jump on the bandwagon if the polls change. You know me well enough. I always back the winners."

A smirk rapidly grew on her face. "Yeah, just like when you and I dated in college."

"I must admit that you used to turn me on." Zach opened the laptop.

She asked, "Planning on writing a sexy email to me?"

"Not to you. Just the rest of the world."

At that moment, he felt the vibrations from his cell, which rested inside his suit pocket. He looked at the caller ID. "I need to take this call in private. Can you excuse me for a few minutes?"

"Can I say 'no'? Just because this is my office after all . . ."

"And be a dear and bring me back some coffee."

"I'll be back in ten minutes without the coffee," she fired back, closing the door behind her.

Zach flipped open the cell.

"Commissioner Rogers, I didn't think that we'd be talking again after our disappointing meeting."

"I thought long and hard on how I might be able to talk with Dr. Knowton about prescribing Zazotene for your wife. But I'm sorry. I just can't help you."

"So long, Doctor. Don't ever call me again."

"Hold on. I've got information that you may find useful. Recently, a senior citizen named Peter Chambers came to see me. And I'm not telling you anything that you couldn't find as part of the public record."

Zach's eyes widened. He lowered his voice. "Wasn't Chambers found murdered?"

"Yes. I'm sure you read about it in the papers."

"Didn't I read that you were at the crime scene? I hope you're not a serial killer, Doc."

"I can't discuss anything about the incident on advice of counsel. Anyway, we're getting off topic. Chambers was the father of Knowton's office manager, Nicki. It seemed that Chambers was aware of what was going on at the oncology practice. He asked me to investigate the death of one of Tom's patients. I can't get into the details."

"My God, Rogers, what *can* you tell me? You're wasting my time. Get to your point."

"I did learn something, and it is relevant to your concerns for your wife. There is a reason why I can't even attempt to convince him to prescribe Zazotene off-label. I researched the death certificate for one of his well-known patients who received your drug. You can check it out yourself."

"Give me something that's not public information. Tell me something new in the next five seconds or I'm hanging up."

"There was a patient of Knowton's who died, suffering from the same cancer diagnosis as your wife. In other words, Zazotene was not FDA approved for use in that case, but the autopsy found extraordinarily high blood levels of the drug."

"Why would the well-respected Dr. Tom Knowton have prescribed our blockbuster for that poor guy and not for Alexis?"

"Who said the patient was a guy?"

"Just an expression, Doc."

Rogers paused. "Well, I just can't imagine that Knowton would compound the tragic death of one patient by giving your drug to your wife no matter who tries to persuade him."

"Commissioner," Zach fired back, "who among us doesn't have a price? Don't give up on him so quickly."

Rogers recalled Ashley's text message. "Can I ask you a question?"

"I have to go."

"Hold on. Do you know anyone else named Zach or anyone whose name starts with the letter Z?"

"Don't waste my time with such nonsense. And why are you asking me that?"

"OK then. Mr. Miller, why are you so obsessed with Dr. Knowton? It seems the only thing that you want from me is to influence him to prescribe your blockbuster drug."

"For the last time, because he is Alexis's doctor and I want to help her get the best of care. He is the best oncologist around. And as I've explained to you many times before, she adores him. And I'll do anything to keep my wife happy."

"I guess I understand why you're so determined."

Miller stood up and paced about Lauren's office. "So what did Peter Chambers expect you to do about the death of this patient?"

"He was thinking of going to the police or the press if I didn't expose Knowton myself."

"Did you?"

"No." Thinking of his prior testimony to Darden, he added, "I mean, I don't think so."

"It doesn't really matter anymore. The threat has been resolved."

"What threat?"

Ignoring the question, Zach persisted. "What else did Chambers expect you to do?"

"He wanted me to personally confront Knowton."

"Did you?"

"Eventually."

"Are you satisfied that your colleague is not implicated?"

"That's really none of your business."

"Sad that you don't get it, Dr. Rogers?"

"Get what?"

"I need to go." He clicked off the call just as Lauren entered the room with a pot of freshly brewed coffee.

"I knew you couldn't say no to me. Just promise me you didn't spike the coffee."

"Don't be silly. I'm not a killer."

"Not yet at least and I'll take your response as to trying to poison me as a no."

"Zach, what's that wise crack about me not being a killer yet? You know, I'm not like you."

"My dear, I suggest we move on to the main event of today's meeting."

Pouring a cup, Lauren inquired about the phone call that caused him to displace her from her office. "It was just my stockbroker calling me about my stocks. You know how important it is to closely follow your investments. I just purchased a huge order of calls on DCP."

"Bullshit. So why are you here today?"

Zach slowly sipped his coffee. "You're so direct. It's what I always liked about you. Anyway, Lauren, we have a problem."

"We?"

"Yes, we," Zach whispered. He rose to close the door behind him. Returning to his seat, he glared at her for a few seconds before he spoke.

"Commissioner Rogers has become a real problem for the survival of Doctor's Choice Products. I can't deal with him anymore. I can't control him. As long as he sits in the influential Commissioner's chair, he's a threat to DCP. I need your help to put a scare in him. And what I'm going to ask you to do should also help me get Knowton back in line as well. I need doctors working for me, not against me."

"You want me to scare him?"

"Not exactly."

"I could dress up like Countess Dracula and sneak up on him when he is not looking," Lauren said facetiously.

"Spare me. I'm talking of leaving a lasting impression."

"Listen, I'm not interested in playing your silly games."

"What about your interest in getting your husband elected the next Governor?"

"What are you talking about?"

Resting his hand gently on hers, he mustered as much sincerity as he could. "Baby, you know I could switch my loyalty to Adam!"

"Keep talking, Zach."

He sat back. Smiling, he knew the fish would be biting today. "I want you to switch Jonathan Rogers's prescription. I happen to know a lot about his medical condition. I think it would be embarrassing to Dr. Knowton if the public would ever find out that he is giving the Commissioner of Health a potentially lethal dose of Zazotene."

"Why would he do that?"

"He wouldn't. At least he wouldn't intentionally do it. But what if the medication was modified and he was unaware of the switch? I just happen to know that DCP Pharmacy distributes the Commissioner's medications. And you run DCP Pharmacy."

"Like I said before, I'm not interested. Besides, Knowton is too good of a doctor to administer any drug without double- and even triple-checking everything."

He chuckled at her response. "Don't worry about the details. That's my job. By the way, Lauren, do you think that your aspiring husband would like to see your nude pictures from our dating years on a couple of Internet sites?"

Her eyes flashed menacingly. He caught her raised hand in midair just before it was about to descend upon him. "I hate you," she snarled.

"Calm down. Let's just call this a win-win. If you help to switch our crusading doctor's medication for me, I just might decide to help your husband become the next Governor. You see, everybody wins here. That is, everybody except poor old Jonathan Rogers. He had his chances and blew it more than once. Don't worry, he won't die. Let's just say that we're sending him a message. After he recovers, he might be more willing to understand our perspective."

Her face turned crimson. "Get out of my office!"

"Governor Adam Timmons. It sounds so, so dignified. But I wonder what your husband would say if he and the rest of Michigan just happened to discover these nude pictures. And, as you know, I have other Lauren dirt besides."

She said sharply, "You're all talk!"

"Is that so?"

He turned to his laptop and opened a file on the desktop. Photos appeared. He clicked on the preset email addresses of the major tabloids and attached the photos to an anonymous email that would be sent through his secure and untraceable server. Grinning, he turned the laptop so Lauren could see the screen. He clicked on each of the nude photos of Lauren.

"You're blackmailing me?"

"Let's call it business, my dear."

"You bastard, get out of here."

He squeezed her forearm. "You don't have much time left before I press the send button. As soon as I forward the photos, your adventurous youth will be spilled out to the biggest tabloids in the world. Every major smut-filled magazine will soon be ringing my favorite nephew's phone off the hook so he can provide additional details. And your husband's campaign headquarters should be deluged with embarrassing questions from the media."

"I'll never help you," Lauren swore through gritted teeth. "You're nothing but a slimy prick."

"Time for the countdown to begin."

Covering his bet, Zach pulled out a derringer from his laptop case and pointed it at Lauren. "Ten . . . nine . . . eight . . ."

She covered her ears. "Stop it!"

He continued slowly. "Seven . . . six . . . five. Countdown stopped at five. Before I resume, what is your decision, my dear?"

Lauren screamed, "I can't do this!"

"You can do this for your husband. Call it a trade. Do you love Adam or do you love Dr. Jonathan Rogers? It's a simple question."

Her eyes skipped fearfully around the office. Zach looked away in boredom. Staring at the ceiling, he kept up the pressure.

"Decision time, my dear. Please think of your husband's future and yours as well. I'm beginning to lose my patience."

"I need more time to think."

"Certainly. You have a little over five seconds."

"Not enough!" she pleaded.

"Sorry. You lose again. Four . . . three . . . countdown on final hold."

Placing his left index finger on the send button, he kept the small-caliber derringer in his right hand, pointed at her face.

Lauren begged, "Please don't do this."

"Countdown starting again. It's game time. Choose wisely."

Holding her clenched fist to her right temple, her voice was now reduced to a whisper.

"I can't do it. Please, Zach."

Emphasizing his touch on the send button, he began, "Two . . . and one . . . and . . ."

Shaking, she blurted out, "I'll do it. Please don't send the email."

Zach put the derringer snugly back into its laptop case compartment. "Excellent choice. But remember, if you double-cross me, I'll send out the email in a heartbeat."

Lauren stuttered, "You won. I'll do it."

He closed the laptop and put it in its case. With his evidence slung over his shoulder, he turned to face her at the door. "I'll be in touch. Thanks for the hospitality."

He flung the door wide open. It banged loudly against the wall. He smiled at the administrative assistant. "That door needs to be fixed. I'm sure you're looking forward to your three-percent merit raise this year."

"Yes, sir. I'll take care of it," she replied.

Zach climbed into the rear of his bulletproof BMW and nodded to the driver to move on. He daydreamed about how he would celebrate with Marissa. A thought struck him, and he decided to put a contingency plan into motion just in case Lauren messed up.

Chapter Twenty-Eight

Knowton stiffened. "Victor, before you go home, I want your advice."

Carver looked up from the chart he was completing. "Sure, partner."

"Jonathan Rogers wants me to compare a sample of his DNA with the pathology slide of his lung tissue from his surgery in DC."

"Why would he ask that?"

"He thinks there may have been a mistake in his lung tissue labeling by the operating room nurse."

"He's nuts. Maybe he's hoping to start a malpractice case against you. You know, the salary of a Commissioner is not enough to support his lifestyle. After all, he is sending his kid to an expensive medical school. Plus, I hear his wife has luxurious tastes."

"So what should I do?"

"Just stall him. Make up some excuse like you don't want to take a chance that someone will lose the slides if they're signed out of the hospital. Tell him that the slide tissue on file at Mercy will be critical if drug companies ever tailor a future drug to treat his specific DNA type lung cancer. Remind him that you don't want to waste any tissue in doing a comparison at this time."

"Will he buy it?"

"He trusts you, doesn't he?"

"Mostly."

"Well, make sure, and let me know. I can't afford to have our practice put into legal jeopardy just so Rogers can finance his wife's latest shopping spree."

"Let me think about it. I'm staying late to do some paperwork here in the office."

"See you tomorrow, Tom. Just don't let Rogers push you around."

••••••••••

Passing by each other in the hallway outside his private office, Knowton reached out to put his hand on her shoulder. "Nicki, we need to talk this evening after the office closes."

She moved closer to him and asked playfully, "About what?"

"We need to talk about what has been going on with our billing. We're way behind on our receivables. I know you've been leaving early to take care of your son."

"Correction, honey, *our* son."

"Can you stay late tonight? Everyone will be gone in about thirty minutes."

She ran her fingers down his arm. "I'll be ready for whatever you want. I'll need to call Hunter to tell him that I'm working late."

He fired back, "Talk, just talk. And be careful about ever mentioning me as Ben's father. Hunter would kill us both if he suspected."

"We'll see. Don't think for a second that I've been happy not having sex in months. Let's see where it goes. And I do think Hunter suspects something."

Knowton again mouthed the word "talk."

Nicki winked at him. "See you soon."

Less than a half hour later, the last nurse left the office. Tom Knowton sat down in his chair and watched Nicki come into the room. "Our little arrangement is no longer working for me," he began.

"Is there a doctor in the house? I could play nurse," Nicki said teasingly as she quietly closed his office door behind her.

"How about if you just do your job as my office manager."

She circled in back of him, placing her hands on his shoulders, kissing his neck. He did not pull away. "It would be so much more fun playing your lover."

Suddenly, he snapped a pencil in half. "I told you many times. That's not going to happen ever again. Our affair is over."

"All right, all right, you're such a tease. So what do you want, Tom?"

"We need to talk business."

"OK. I get the picture."

"I want your husband to stop taking money out of my practice."

"You also want me not to tell your wife about our new baby boy. Now let's talk about what I want."

"You and your husband can no longer blackmail me. I'll tell Veronica myself."

"Hey, doc, it's not like Hunter is stealing from you. He's just taking a little off the top."

"Rogers thinks that I'll be on Carver's list when he presents the final version of the Medicaid Fraud Task Force report next week."

"You and I know that's not going to happen."

He stood and hovered over her. "I'm tired of looking the other way while you and your husband use my practice for your own personal piggy bank."

"Why all of a sudden do you want to change the game?"

His eyes met her downward gaze. "Your father is dead. How's that for starters?"

Her eyes began welling up. "Dad was only trying to protect me."

"Yeah, by putting the blame on me for the fraud that your gang is committing."

"That would never happen. You're safe as long as you contribute to the plan. You know they need you. You're in the club as much as I am."

"I want all of this to stop."

Nicki replied angrily, "Are you nuts? The leaders will never permit that. You know that."

"Maybe I need to go to the police."

"Be serious. They killed my dad because they were worried he would expose the plan to the authorities. Get real."

"What about Rogers? Who shot him? Am I next?"

"If you want to live, keep your mouth shut. Let the leaders do whatever they damn well please."

She stormed out of his office. The outside door banged shut. Hanging his head, he knew that Nicki was right about one point. He had once been warned. Only one thing would separate him from permanent membership in The Health Club. The game was already at checkmate. Knowton knew he needed to be careful. His next move might be his last.

Chapter Twenty-Nine

Rogers awoke in Ashley's rocking chair, his neck throbbing. Something woke him, but he couldn't at first identify it, so deep was his fatigue. Then he knew. His cell phone was beeping that another text message had been received. His heart raced as he scrolled down the text message. *Go to the east parking lot of the Island Resort Casino in the Upper Peninsula. A woman will lead you to me. See you soon, Dad. Love Ashley Rogers.*

He looked over at her bed. It was empty. He saw only a note taped on the toy box. *I needed to get away. I'll call you in a day. Kim.*

Rogers crumpled up the note and threw it at the door. He picked up the phone and booked himself on a flight from DuPont Airport to Menominee-Marinette Twin County Airport. Now that he was close to finding Ashley, he believed that he could trust no one but himself.

••••••••••

Rogers checked into his hotel room and then dashed off to the east parking lot. Strangely, there were only a few cars in sight. Seconds later, a red Porsche convertible screeched around the curve and sped toward him. Rogers ran behind a stone pillar as the Porsche continued up the ramp. He felt his heart racing. Reaching into his pocket for a handkerchief, he felt a tap on his shoulder. He whirled around and did a double take. A woman wearing a short yellow toga held out a glass of what looked like bubbly champagne.

"Hey, good looking. Waiting for someone?" she asked in a seductive voice.

"Yes, I'm supposed to meet someone."

"I'm your girl. My name is Cherry."

"I'm . . ."

"I know who you are." She held out the glass. "Take a sip Jonathan . . . to celebrate your good fortune. I'll take you to Ashley."

"I'm not thirsty."

"No drink . . . no Ashley."

Rogers took a large gulp. "Where is my daughter?"

Interrupting, Cherry said, "Not so fast. Let's go inside to the blackjack tables and relax a little."

On the way, Cherry gave him instructions on what to do at the blackjack table. Inside the casino, Jonathan did a quick survey of the twenty tables and chose the one in the middle of the floor. There were two men sitting on one side of the table. He ordered a Scotch on the rocks from a passing server and sat down on a stool at the other end. Cherry sat down next to him. He stayed on seventeen as the dealer won the first five hands. He ordered another drink. His eyes roamed the casino floor. On the next hand, his luck changed.

Rogers looked over at the two young men. "Nice to win for a change."

A well-built young man in his twenties replied, "Still waiting for it to happen to me."

"I'm hoping to have a big night."

"Sure you will, I'm sure you will," his tablemate replied with a laugh.

Cherry slid her seat closer to Jonathan's.

"Maybe I can bring you some good luck or whatever."

"I'm hoping that you can."

With Cherry next to him, his luck did seem to change. He downed another Scotch and waited for some signal from her to tell him what to do. Was she just a hooker decoy, or would she be the one to actually lead him to Ashley? He figured the best thing to do would be to wait and see, although he was growing more and more impatient with this game she was playing.

"I'm up about three hundred, thanks to you," he said, half smiling. "Maybe I should quit while I'm ahead?"

"I'm glad to be of service to you. Any time. Are you here alone?"

"Yes."

"Can we go to your room?" she whispered in his ear.

"I would prefer to talk right here."

One of the men at the table stood up and walked away, tossing his cards on the table. Rogers asked for a hit. The dealer obliged with a ten, which busted him. He lost two more hands, and heard Cherry say softly, "So are you coming or not?"

"Listen, I need to make a pit stop. Can you hold my seat?"

"Sure, Jonathan, I'll be right here waiting for you. Just in case you're wondering, I'm free all night."

••••••••••

After returning from the rest room, he noticed a fresh drink in front of him. Another couple had sat down next to Cherry.

"Jonathan, you're looking a little wasted," Cherry said.

"Yeah."

Rogers's head was spinning. He checked his watch but his vision was blurry. In short order, he lost a half dozen bets in a row.

"I usually don't drink this much. I'm getting a little tipsy. I'll going to call it a night."

"I'll join you."

"Don't think so. I'm married. But what about . . .?"

"I'll see you later," she replied.

He reached into his pocket for his room key, dropping the key card on the floor. Unable to think clearly, he just wanted to sleep. He stumbled away, wishing everyone at the table a good night.

Rogers staggered down a few unfamiliar hallways, trying to find his room. In a total fog, he somehow spotted his room number and fumbled with his room key. He caught a brief glimpse of a redheaded woman passing by. "Must be dreaming," he muttered to himself. Everything seemed very blurry and strange looking.

Upon entering his room, Rogers rushed to the bathroom to relieve himself. Without turning on the light, and without disrobing, he felt his way back to the bedroom and dropped on top of the bed. He was asleep instantly.

He awakened from a nightmare sometime later. He couldn't

quite remember, but it was something about Ashley. He climbed out of the bed, groped his way to the bathroom and flicked on the light. He urinated and turned off the light again.

He headed toward the near side of the bed, closest to the bathroom. He slipped out of his clothes and climbed under the covers. He felt an ice-cold object pressed against him. He reached next to him and felt the undeniable texture of skin. His hand jerked away and he jumped out of the bed, reaching for the table lamp. He spun around and saw the naked body of a young woman.

Rogers rushed toward the bathroom, shaking, and slammed the door behind him. He called Kim, but got her voice mail. While pacing the bathroom in tighter and tighter circles, the cell rang a minute later. He felt his heart pounding as though he had just run a hundred-yard dash.

"Hello."

"I got your call. Why are you calling me at three in the morning?"

"Kim, oh my God."

"Are you all right? What happened?"

"Where have you been all day?"

"I'm staying at my mother's place. What's going on?"

"I don't know. I don't know what to do."

"Where the hell are you?"

"In my hotel room."

"Why are you in a hotel?"

"I got a message from Ashley to meet a woman at the Island Resort Casino."

"When? Is she OK?"

"I believe Ashley's fine."

"Is she there with you?"

"No. Just stop talking and listen to me. That's not why I'm calling you."

"You're confusing me. Back up. You said Ashley asked you to meet with a woman?"

"I met a woman at the blackjack table tonight. Now she's lying in my bed."

Kim's voice rang out as if she had screamed into a bullhorn. "What!"

"I don't know how she got in my room."

"Who the hell is this woman?"

"I think she's the one who sat next to me last night in the casino. I met her in the parking lot just as Ashley's text told me to do. She might have been in the hallway outside my room last night. I must have passed out. I slept until now."

"And you think I'm the only one who has been unfaithful . . ."

"No, you don't understand. She's . . ."

"Listen to me. Where the hell is Ashley?"

"I don't know."

"You're not making any sense."

Interrupting, he shouted, "I think she's dead!"

"Who's dead?"

"The woman in my bed."

"Are you drunk?"

Rubbing his eyes, he backed away from the bed. "I can't believe this."

"I said, are you drunk?"

Talking over her, he said, "Her body is ice cold. She's ice cold."

"Is she breathing?"

"I'm not sure. I don't want to touch her."

"You need to call the police. Dial 911."

"The police? What do I tell them? I've nothing to do with this woman."

"Do you know her name?"

"Cherry, I think."

"So you do know her. Dammit Jonathan, call the police now!"

"Shit. This can't be happening."

Silence.

"Kim, I didn't kill her. You must believe me."

••••••••••

Rogers sat on the edge of the bathtub until he heard several loud knocks on the door. Opening the door, he saw two cops, a man and a woman, standing in the doorway with drawn pistols. While a middle-aged cop pointed his revolver at him, the young policewoman ran toward Cherry.

Hearing her yell, "She's dead," his mind went numb.

"Sir, I am Officer Jim Jones. Put your hands above your head."

Rogers complied as the policewoman searched him.

"He's clean."

"Officer Naples, call for backup and also call the coroner's office." Turning to the Commissioner, he said, "You can lower your hands. We checked your hotel registration. Are you Dr. Jonathan Rogers? Are you the one who called us?"

With his brain still weaving through the clouds, Rogers fought to manage the out-of-control impulses stampeding through it. He stammered, "Yes . . . yes, sir."

"Dr. Rogers, I'm going to read you your rights. Then we're going down to the police station."

"I didn't touch her. I don't know how she got here."

"Dr. Rogers, I must warn you that anything you say can and will be used against you in a court of law."

Jonathan listened to the remainder of his rights being read by Officer Jones. Upon hearing the cop's order, he put his hands behind his back. He felt the tightness of the steely handcuffs around his wrists, his mind whirling. As he was marched out of the room by Jones, he asked the officer to get his cell phone from the bathroom.

"I'll dial the number for you," Jones said after returning.

"Just press number one and put it on speaker. I'm hard of hearing."

Rogers moved closer to the speaker and heard each ring as if a firecracker was exploding in his ears.

Kim's voice came blaring out. "What the fuck is going on? Is the woman all right? Did the police come?"

"The police are taking me down to the station. I need you to come here as soon as you can. You'll need to bail me out of jail."

Rogers could only imagine what she was thinking. Led out of the casino lobby in handcuffs, he tried to hide his face from the casino gamblers on the way out the front door. He felt certain his career was over. But worse, he felt helpless to find Ashley.

••••••••••

At the station, Rogers was fingerprinted and photographed, and then was told to sit down facing Officer Jones. His hands were now free but his mind felt trapped in trying to recount the events of the prior evening.

"So you are Dr. Jonathan Rogers, the Commissioner of Health."

"Right."

"Would you like to call your attorney?"

"Yes."

"What's his number?"

"Whose number?"

Seeing the cop's eyebrows shooting skyward and his brown eyes widen as he waited for a number, Rogers shook his head, trying to recall. Jones pushed the speaker phone toward him.

"What's his name?"

"I can't remember."

"If you can't remember the name or number, then I can't help you."

"Officer, what time is it?"

"Five thirty."

Squinting, he replied, "In the morning?"

"Of course. Did you think that it's nighttime?"

"I'm a little dazed. I just don't know."

"Doctor, have you taken any drugs? And how heavily have you been drinking?"

"I don't use drugs. Just a few glasses of Scotch last night at the casino. Listen, can I call my wife again?"

After Jones slid his cell phone toward him, Rogers pressed the usual number.

She answered on the first ring. "You have to call our lawyer. I can't remember his number."

"I've taken care of it. Brent Marshall and I will be flying into Harris around nine. How are you holding up?"

"I can't believe what is happening. I'm trying to focus. Can you call Detective Darden? I want him to know about what happened to me."

"Do you trust him?"

"Who knows? Maybe I was drugged. I want him to order the police up here to do a drug screen on my blood."

"I'll discuss it with Marshall to see if he agrees."

"Kim, just do it."

••••••••••

While he shivered on the sheetless mattress on his six-by-three-foot prison cell cot, Rogers felt like he was sitting on an iceberg. With nothing to do but stare through the bars at the cop reading the local Upper Peninsula newspaper, he tried focusing on what happened the previous night. But the more he tried, the less he could recall. Lying back, he began counting each of the square bricks on the ceiling. He lost track of the number of squares around twenty.

He was awakened by a tug on his arm. Rogers saw a woman with a long needle advancing toward him. He shouted, "Get away!" He leaped up and pushed the middle-aged woman clad in a white lab coat away from him. She pulled back the needle with her gloved hands.

"What the hell? Who are you?"

"Drawing blood by police order," she faltered. A few backward paces later, her back was abutting the far wall of the cell. He then realized this was what he wanted to be done.

The cop outside the cell rushed toward the cell. "Back away from her. Detective Darden from Oldwyck gave the order."

Rogers asked, "What are you checking for?" He opened his palms, trying to appear less menacing.

"Rohypnol," she stuttered.

"A date rape drug. I had a feeling I was drugged." He smiled and motioned for the tech to continue the blood draw, but she did not move. "Officer, tell the lady that it's OK to take my blood."

The cop said, "Listen, I was told not to speak with you until your attorney came. So pipe down and don't try to get me in trouble with my superiors. Ma'am, please draw his blood as ordered."

The last sound that Rogers remembered was his cell door slamming shut. He dreamed about Cherry being strangled to death. It was all so real. It almost seemed to him that he had actually watched her being murdered.

Awakening with a start, he stared at the clock. It stood out prominently on the stucco-coated wall over the police guard sitting by his desk. It was after nine. He rubbed his eyes just as he heard a familiar voice.

"Jonathan. My God."

"Kim."

As soon as the guard opened the cell door, Rogers rushed toward her. He held her tightly. Looking around, he noticed Brent Marshall.

Rogers nodded to his attorney. "They drew blood from me a while ago."

Marshall replied, "The results are positive. Somehow you were given a date rape drug."

"Darden nailed it. I know that drug can make someone incapable of thinking clearly and remembering what happened."

Kim asked, "Do you remember the woman coming into your room?"

"No."

He glanced up at his attorney, asking, "So it was that woman who drugged me?"

"Before Kim and I took off to fly here, I contacted the management of the casino. They permitted me to speak directly with the blackjack dealer who worked at your table. The dealer claims he didn't see anything but he gave me a great lead. There are cameras above each table in order for the casino to tape everything."

Rogers interrupted, "Do you know if Ashley has been found?"

"There is no word on your daughter. But when we landed in Harris, there was a message on my cell. The call was from the supervisor of the casino. He reviewed the tape of the east parking lot. It revealed that a man in his thirties sprinkled some powder into the champagne that Cherry offered you. Normally there are no cameras in the lots, but there has been a recent breakout of muggings, so they were installed only a few days ago."

"So they wouldn't suspect they'd been caught on tape."

Marshall nodded. "When you left the blackjack table, where did you go?"

"I went to the bathroom."

"The overhead casino tape confirmed that you had three drinks."

"Sounds right."

"The young man with Cherry in the parking lot tried to hide what he was doing from the overhead casino table camera. But he was a little sloppy. We caught a frame of him emptying a few more drops from a vial into your drink."

"But what about the woman? How did she get into my room?"

Marshall shrugged. Rogers noticed that Kim was trembling, her mouth tightly clenched. Putting his arm around her shoulder, he drew her nearer. He could feel the tension in her muscles. When he reached for her hand, she pulled it away.

"Jonathan, you must have let her into your room. It must have been you. Who else would have a key card to your room?"

"I don't know."

"The cops reported no damage to the door or any signs of forced entry. So someone in your room must have killed the woman."

"It certainly wasn't me. You know that I could never hurt anyone."

Kim stiffened and retreated two steps away from him. She bit into her lower lip. "Jonathan, you were drugged. Anything could have happened. Who knows what you may have done."

"I never touched her. I swear."

She closed her eyes tightly and said nothing.

"Kim, please believe me. Nothing happened."

She paused. Opening her eyes, she took one step toward him. "We have to find Ashley. Nothing else matters."

Chapter Thirty

Kim believed in her husband's innocence. She accompanied Officer Jones and Marshall back to the casino. While walking into the lobby, she noticed a crowd of gamblers clustered around a large flat-panel television set. There it was. Her husband's story was being reported by the local morning anchorman. Plastered on the plasma screen were full-face shots of both Jonathan and Cherry.

Marshall put his hand on Kim's shoulders. "I'm sorry. Until we solve this case, you'll just have to get used to this kind of garbage."

Kim turned to Officer Jones. "Why can't you let him out on bail?"

"The judge refused to set bail. He's our only suspect. He was in the room with her, slept in the same bed," the officer shot back. "This could be first-degree murder."

"He's the Commissioner of Health of this state, not a murderer. He's a good man, a loving father. He never hurt anyone."

Jones wrinkled his forehead. "I'm sure you may think so. But not everyone shares such a high opinion of him up in these parts. And right now, he's a prime murder suspect."

Marshall placed his finger across his lips. He could see that Kim got his point, as she did not continue the argument. As the three walked toward the casino floor, the clinking of the coins in the slot machines became background music. With each step, the echo of the coins dropping into their metal bins grew louder. Kim's head began to pound with each winning pull of the lever. She threw her arm out in front of Jones to restrain him from walking any further and pivoted to face him squarely.

"Excuse me, Officer Jones, but what do you mean people don't like him in this area?"

Jones did not back down. "I stand by my statement. My own doctor is very upset with your husband for passing that bill that tells my doc to follow some rule to care for folks. I think you call it medical guidelines or something like that. Doc Smith says it's like a cookbook, and he's no chef. The Commissioner is forcing doctors to practice medicine a certain way. That's just not right. Your husband is meddling in our business."

Kim wanted to smack him on the spot. Taking a deep breath, she said tersely, "My husband's responsibility is to protect citizens like you against doctors violating well-recognized care treatments supported by medical evidence of what works best. The Guideline Bill that he supported was passed by our elected legislature and signed by Governor Peabody. He was only doing his job."

Jones seemed to gawk back at her like she was an alien. "Don't know about that. Up in these parts, we go by what our doctors say. And my doc isn't happy. That's good enough for me."

"All of this has nothing to do with what happened last night," she fired back.

Jones shrugged his shoulders. "Maybe so . . . maybe so . . . All I know is right now your husband is in serious trouble and I'm not about to let him skip away on bail."

Marshall grabbed her hand. She turned to face him directly. She searched his face for answers that weren't there. Feeling exhausted, she just wanted to scream.

The attorney said softly, "Please, Kim. This is not helping."

She pointed for Marshall to walk toward a more quiet section in the lobby. After finding a seating area in an isolated corner, she sat alongside their attorney on a plush red velvety couch. Jones pulled up a high-backed slot machine chair. Kim forced herself to take slow breaths while avoiding the icy stare of the local sheriff. As she alternated her view between Marshall and the murals on the casino ceiling, her mind raced with thoughts of Jonathan lying all alone in his cell.

The attorney gazed at Officer Jones and smiled as if they were all lifelong friends. "Let's review the facts that we know so far."

Jones held up his arms. "What we know, Mr. Marshall, is that your client was found in his hotel room earlier this morning with a dead woman."

Maintaining his cool demeanor, Marshall added, "We also know that an unidentified young man was captured on tape in two locations slipping something into Dr. Rogers's drink. The drug that was put into his drink was a powerful hypnotic. It showed up in the Commissioner's blood. Furthermore, we know that this young man was speaking to Cherry while my client was in the restroom."

Jones replied quickly, "How do we know that Rogers wasn't in the restroom taking the hypnotic himself? Maybe he's an addict."

Kim spoke softly with her eyes glued to the floor. "He's no addict. He's the most decent man that I've ever met."

The attorney continued in an almost inaudible pitch, "With all due respect, Officer Jones, I'm talking about facts, not speculation."

The sheriff glared back at both of them. Kim asked Marshall to step away with her. While walking away from the officer, she looked back several times to make sure they were out of earshot.

"Brent, we're wasting time talking with Jones. He is totally convinced that Jonathan killed her."

"I hear you, but I need you to understand that it doesn't help to rile up the local law enforcement."

She replied with certitude in her voice, "I'm calling Darden." She paused. "We need to find Ashley. Jonathan said that she contacted him to come here and that a woman would lead us to her."

"I hope that woman was not Cherry."

Kim begged, "Do something, Brent. Get us out of this nightmare."

Marshall looked back at Jones. The officer was now circling around the area where they had their recent chat. She caught an annoyed look from Jones. Kim dialed the private line at the Oldwyck Police Station using her speaker cell function so Marshall could also hear. Darden picked up on the third ring.

"Mrs. Rogers, I'm glad you called. After I got verification of my hunch that the Commissioner was drugged, I called the coroner up there in Harris. I asked that a drug screen be done on the dead woman. And I was right."

Kim took a huge gulp.

"She was positive for the same drug that they slipped in your husband's drink. But the drug didn't kill her. The coroner said that she was strangled to death."

She could feel her stomach churning. "Detective, did they find any fingerprints on the body? On her neck?"

"None."

"So how was she strangled without a trace of prints?"

"Officer Jones has a blowup print of the casino tape from the blackjack table."

"He didn't tell us that."

"I don't think he likes you folks very much."

"Not surprised to hear that."

Darden added, "The guy at the blackjack table was wearing the skintight gloves that professional football receivers wear. No one wears gloves like that in the spring."

Kim felt her heart skip a beat. Seeing Jones approaching them with a strange look on his face, she noted that he was just closing his cell phone.

"Hold on, Detective Darden," she said.

Jones walked up to Marshall, completely ignoring her. He said, "I just spoke with a witness who called headquarters with important information. He was staying at the hotel last night on the same floor where the murder took place. It seems he is willing to testify that he saw a man and woman knocking on Dr. Rogers's door."

Marshall said, "This changes everything."

"Not so fast. The witness saw Dr. Rogers letting both of them into his room. And one more thing. The doc seemed barely able to stand up."

Kim spoke into her cell, not forgetting it was on speaker. "Detective Darden. We just found out . . ."

"Mrs. Rogers, I heard most of the conversation. We need to find the young man on the tape. Put Officer Jones on the line."

Kim closely studied the face of the local officer. She could tell that he did not agree with everything Darden was saying.

"OK, I'll take care of his release," Jones said just before he flipped his cell shut.

"Detective Darden asked me to release your husband on bail until we can locate the man on the tape. He said he would go to the local judge up here in Harris if I didn't agree to go along with him. I'm not convinced of his innocence. But I don't want any more trouble. I'll call the judge myself. I hope you folks can make bail. It won't be cheap."

"Just do it," she replied.

Marshall turned to Kim. "I can't believe it. We screwed up. We forgot to ask about Ashley when you were talking to the police."

"No, that was intentional."

"I'm not following you."

"Brent, the police don't know she's missing. Jonathan received a call saying that if we told the authorities, they would kill her. I've been a wreck ever since."

"A call from whom?"

"We don't know."

"This is nonsense. We're going to call the FBI as soon as we get Jonathan."

As they walked out of the casino, a young redheaded woman appeared out of nowhere to snap their picture. The photographer quickly slipped away behind a panel of slot machines.

Kim checked her voice mail and listened to a message from Zach Miller asking her for a business dinner date. She slammed the cell shut and went to bail out her husband, trailing Marshall and thinking of calling her charming real estate client. *Maybe he'll know what we should do.*

Chapter Thirty-One

Rogers dropped off his home answering machine tape at the radio station. The hostess of the "Meet the Commissioner" radio show promised to have it analyzed by the same lab that checked the caller making the strange statements.

After leaving WPPE, he headed toward police headquarters. Darden had told Marshall that he would drop the subpoena demanding that Rogers talk about his past conversations with his boss, Governor Peabody, in exchange for full cooperation.

"Do you have any objections with my taping our conversation?" Darden asked, once they'd settled down in their seats across the table in the interrogation room.

"No."

"Good. Let's start with my last question on Governor Peabody. Has he ever threatened you for not supporting his political health-care policy positions?"

"Define 'threaten.'"

"Commissioner, I don't have the time to parse words. I thought you said you would cooperate."

"The Governor has never physically threatened me. But, of course, as a political figure, he exerts substantial influence to sway me to public health-care policy positions that he supports."

"What type of influence?"

"The power of persuasion. But this is a normal process between employer and employee. I work for him just as I try to help millions of citizens in Michigan. I would never do anything illegal or unethical. That's where I draw the line. What are you getting at, Detective?"

"As we told you at your home weeks ago, we went through your hard drive. We have an email from Peabody requesting that you tell the President of the United States that you would do anything the drug companies want in exchange for becoming the next Surgeon General."

"And you saw my response?"

"Yes, you told him that you would never do anything like that."

"Precisely. So where is this conversation going?"

"The Governor's email back to you said that you were messing up the plan. Exactly what is the plan?"

"I don't know. It sounds like you should be asking Peabody . . . Wait, I just remembered something: Governor Peabody called the President just before my meeting with Jordan at the White House. The President told me that at my interview."

Darden mumbled something. Rogers spotted him kicking the electric plug to the recorder from the wall. "Hold on." The recorder stopped working. "We know about that phone call."

"So what did Peabody say to the President?" Rogers asked.

"That's strictly confidential. We'll be calling you in a few days to follow up on the Chambers murder. And before you ask, we still have not found the red pickup truck that pushed you off Exeter Bridge."

"So is there anything you can you tell me?"

"I'm in close touch with Officer Jones regarding the murder in the Upper Peninsula. No news as yet. And one more thing, Dr. Rogers."

"Yes?"

"The flashlight that you carried from the crime scene showed only your prints. And there was no trace of the victim's DNA on the flashlight."

"How did it get there without anyone else's prints? Did it drop from the sky, battery intact?"

"Good question. Perhaps if you get kicked out of the medical profession, you might want to consider law enforcement."

Rogers closed his eyes tightly, praying that he was about to make the right decision. Marshall and Kim had convinced him that there was no other way to proceed. "Detective, I have something important to tell you."

The Detective frowned. "I knew you were hiding something."

"Our daughter has been kidnapped. I was told by the kidnappers to keep my mouth shut."

Darden spun his chair away from Rogers. He said nothing for

a minute and then whirled back to face the Commissioner. Raising his voice, he asked, "When did this happen?"

"Weeks ago."

Darden hung his head. "I can't believe you would hide this from me all that time. Why did you trust the kidnapper more than me? Your daughter could have been killed by now."

"She's alive. Ashley contacted me by text message and told me to go to the casino. She said a woman would contact me there and lead me to her."

"We can try to trace the origin of that text message."

"I didn't think that could be done."

"Commissioner, I know you've had more than your share of problems, but you must trust me to help you."

Rogers pointed his finger at Darden's chest. "Don't let anything happen to Ashley."

"Tell you what, doc, don't ever hold back anything from me again. You either tell me everything or stop wasting my time. Understood, Commissioner?"

"I don't see any photos of children onyour desk."

"Don't have any."

"If you did, you would understand my perspective." Rogers grimaced and pulled out the note he had taken from Ashley's text message. He handed it to Darden, who rolled his eyes before reading Rogers's scribbling.

Held in basement by Rick. Working with man named Z and redhead named Haley. My life depends on you calling a press conf on Medicaid fraud. A beach close by. Please help. Daddy, I'm scared.

"Does any of this ring any bells for you?"

"Haley was a redhead I met in DC the morning of my interview with the President."

"We're well aware of her whereabouts."

"She almost broadsided me when I was driving back to my office."

"Was that the last time you saw her?"

"Yes."

"Who is Rick and this guy named Z?"

Rogers paused. He had no proof of what he was thinking. He replied softly, "I don't know."

"Somehow, I think you're still holding back. Call me if you think of anything . . . Anything."

••••••••••

Rogers stood at Sally's desk. "Governor Peabody called late yesterday afternoon demanding to speak with you. I told him that you took a sick day at home. I told him you had a sinus infection and a migraine."

"And what was his response?"

"He hung up on me."

"Please schedule the meeting for tomorrow. I could use another day to clear my head. I also need you to make an appointment with Dr. Carver. I want him to present the Task Force report to me. Also, please call Nicki Sanderson. Ask her if she could come to my office."

"Since we're talking about your upcoming schedule, don't forget the National Commissioners of Health Conference in DC. Last week you asked me to remind you to start preparing for your keynote address at the conference."

"It's only a couple of weeks from now."

"Commissioner, may I ask the topic?"

"Big pharma must provide timely access to flu shots for all Americans."

••••••••••

"I've a special-delivery letter for Dr. Jonathan Rogers," the non-uniformed courier said when Rogers opened his front door.

The Commissioner scribbled his signature on the electronic pad while he examined the outside of the envelope. Strange, he thought, that his name was spelled with block letters of different colors. There was no return address.

Rogers went inside to sit on his sofa. He slit open the letter and saw a sea of colored block letters in a complete circle glued to a piece of plain white paper. Halfway around the circle, he read out loud, "The old Chambers is dead and we got Sam too." He rotated the page to read the last sentence: "Be nice to Fred or we won't be to you."

The circle of words led to the bottom right of the page, where he saw the words *Turn the page*. Rogers flipped over the letter. On the backside, he saw a photo of Kim, Ashley, and himself on their last vacation together to Aspen. Plastered across the top of the picture in half-inch red block letters were the words *It's not too late.* At the bottom of the photo, in one-inch block letters, was a warning: *You do not know when your time will come.*

Chapter Thirty-Two

Rogers opened his right top desk drawer and pulled out an OraDose tablet. He placed it under his tongue for a minute before swishing it down with some lukewarm black coffee. His feet anchored his swivel chair in place to avoid any movement that would make his migraine worse. He shut his eyes for a moment and didn't see the visitor walk into his office. But the condescending tone of voice was unmistakable.

"Commissioner, are you all right?" the Governor boomed.

Dr. Rogers staggered to his feet with his eyes still half shut.

"Yes, Governor. I'm fine."

"Dr. Rogers, what's going on here? I heard about your wild escapade at the casino. By golly, can't you ever stay out of trouble?"

"Governor, I was drugged. I didn't do anything wrong."

"We'll see. If they formally charge you for murder, you'll need to resign. I can't have a possible felon working for me."

"Don't worry. I was set up."

"You look like you're still sick."

Collecting his thoughts despite the anvil pounding away at his head, he replied, "A wicked migraine."

Peabody had already taken a seat at the conference table. Shielding his eyes to block out the sunlight, Rogers sat down directly opposite the Governor.

"Before we start, do you mind if we shut off the overhead lights and close the blinds?"

Peabody nodded. "Stay put." He got up and took care of both the lights and blinds, much to Jonathan's relief.

"Thanks."

The Governor returned to his seat. "Doc, I've some bad news for you."

Is there ever good news anymore?

"The President is no longer considering you for Surgeon General."

Rogers gawked at the Governor. "Why not?"

"The President doesn't have to give a reason. But let's just say there were concerns."

Rogers was not about to let go of his dream without an explanation. "Concerns about what?"

The Governor shifted uncomfortably in his seat and stared at the marble floor. "Have you thought about taking a vacation? I seriously think you could use one."

Rogers persisted. "Concerns about what?"

The Governor said nothing. He smiled for a few seconds before rising to walk toward the door. The Commissioner slumped in his seat.

"I think we should talk again when you're feeling better," Peabody said.

Rogers tightly closed his eyes for several seconds. It was time to face reality. The prize that he had dreamed about for years was gone forever.

"Commissioner, one last question. When are you going to give me the Medicaid fraud report?"

Still seated, Rogers replied, "The chairman of the Task Force is due here any minute. After I review it, I'll pass it on to you."

"Good. Get some rest." The door creaked open.

"I'm sorry to interrupt, but Dr. Carver is here. Shall I ask him to wait?" Sally asked.

Peabody spoke up quickly. "Please have him come in. I would like to meet the chairman."

Seconds later, Carver walked through the door dressed in a three-piece gray Hugo Boss suit, an immaculate white button-down-collar shirt, and a muted dark red silk tie. Shocked to see his friend in such expensive attire, Rogers almost forgot about his migraine.

Rising to his feet, the Commissioner spoke. "Governor

Peabody, I'd like you to meet Dr. Carver."

The Governor looked positively jovial as he proclaimed, "Dr. Carver, I have heard so much about you. Let's all sit to talk."

Carver walked toward Rogers and tossed a manila folder on the table, then turned back to the Governor.

"It's truly an honor to meet you, sir. I hope that you will be satisfied with the Task Force report. I'm here to present it to the Commissioner."

Peabody said, "I'd like to take a look."

Attempting to take the lead, Rogers said awkwardly, "The Governor and I were just finishing."

Peabody's eyes blazed. "Are you kicking me out of your office?"

"No, what I meant is that Dr. Carver and I should review the report before I present it to you."

"I don't think so. Forgive me, but in your medical condition, I suggest that we cut out the middleman."

"But I haven't even seen the report yet. It's my responsibility as Commissioner."

His boss replied curtly, "I don't think that will be necessary."

Peabody reached for the manila folder. Removing the papers, the Governor appeared to be merely skimming through the document.

"Interesting report, Dr. Carver. Thank you for your leadership on the Task Force. Perhaps you can join me at my press conference next week when I present these findings to the legislature at the annual State of the State."

Carver looked over to Rogers and seemed to be telegraphing an innocent look that said, *don't blame me!*

The oncologist replied, "Sure, I'll do whatever I can."

"I've some work to do. Dr. Carver, I'll be in touch with you. Maybe you might be interested in the Surgeon General position one day. Of course, the acting Surgeon General, Dr. Fresca Gomez, should sail through her confirmation hearings."

Peabody glanced at Rogers before adding, "And I hear she is working out quite nicely." The Governor handed the report back to Carver and turned toward Rogers.

"I hope you'll be feeling better soon. Good day, gentlemen."

The Governor promptly exited the commissioner's office, not even bothering to shut the door behind him. Rogers remained seated. Carver tossed the report on the table and remained standing, saying nothing.

Rogers said with a trace of sarcasm, "Well, Victor, your timing was impeccable."

"Listen, my friend, Peabody invited me into your office. It's not my fault. I'm sorry that the Governor intercepted your report."

"It's actually the people's report. By the way, where did you get those pricey shoes?"

"Like them? They're Barker Blacks."

"So did you win the lottery since I saved your life on the Harley?"

Carver ignored him and just smiled.

"Victor, I've a few questions for you. Was Tom Knowton's name on the Fraud Task Force list?"

"Of course not. Tom and I are partners. Neither one of us would ever cheat."

"Then why did Peter Chambers tell me Tom was guilty of fraud?"

"Because Nicki told him so. Why wouldn't he believe his own daughter? But since dead men don't talk, I guess we'll never know."

The Commissioner raised his eyebrows. "Chambers gave me evidence."

"What evidence?"

"It's in the Tom Knowton file. Sally retrieved it after I left it in Tom's office by mistake." Standing up slowly, Rogers walked over to the eye-level cabinet. He reached into his pants pocket, pulling out the key to open the cabinet drawer. After spotting the target file, he held on to it tightly, as if it were a priceless object, and returned to the conference table. He sat down and thumbed through a few dozen papers in the manila folder, searching for the envelope containing the fraudulent checks that Chambers gave him.

"They're gone." Rogers delivered a suspicious look at Carver.

"Why are you looking at me that way?"

"They were there when I was in Tom's office. But then I came to visit you."

"So I guess I'm off your suspect list for once."

"Tom must have removed the fraudulent checks while I was talking with you."

"Who knows?" Carver shrugged. "What can I do to help you?"

"How about starting with telling the truth about what happened when we found the Chambers body?"

"Are you going to start in on that again? For the last time, I didn't remember if the body was face up or face down."

"Any ideas who might have killed Chambers?"

"How the hell would I know anything about that?" Carver barked. "What I do know is that I did my job as chairman of the Task Force. Listen, we've been best friends for a long time. I'll call you in a week or so. We can play tennis or something. I hope you feel better."

The oncologist walked toward the door. He stopped in his tracks. "By the way, I didn't want to mention it, but I heard about your arrest in the Upper Peninsula. But I'm sure you didn't do anything wrong. Things are not always what they appear to be. I trust you."

Rogers reached out to shake his hand. "You're right. I'm not sure what's happening these days. Let's talk when I feel better. Thanks again for chairing the Task Force for me."

Extending the handshake into a hug, Carver added, "Correction my friend, I chaired the Task Force for the people of Michigan. Someone once told me, we all work for them."

"Touché."

••••••••••

"Mrs. Sanderson is here to see you, Dr. Rogers."

His second dose of the migraine medicine had helped. He was starting to feel better. The door opened and Nicki walked through as if she were a high-priced fashion model. He was struck by the keyhole surplice on the front of the burgundy-colored body-hugging dress.

"Nicki, you look terrific. I can't believe you just had a baby."

Rogers enjoyed the warm hug that the new mom initiated. Venturing to give her a brief kiss on her cheek, she appeared pleased that he had made the effort.

"Commissioner, we have so much to catch up on."

"The last time we spoke was at your dad's funeral. I felt so bad for him."

"It wasn't your fault. My dad had faith in you. But there was nothing that you could have done to stop what happened to him."

He pointed to the conference table. She chose a seat with her back to the window overlooking the pond. Rogers took the chair to her immediate left, just after opening the blinds.

"Nicki, I just can't believe that it was just a few months ago that your dad was in this office. He sat right over there in front of my desk. His main concern was you. I want you to know that." He gently reached over to touch her hand, lingering for a few seconds.

"Thank you. You know that the night I was supposed to meet you here for dinner is all a blur to me. So what exactly did my dad tell you?"

"He said that you told him about Medicaid fraud in Knowton's practice. He claimed that Tom was the ringleader. Also, both your dad and Beth Murphy directly blamed Knowton and indirectly blamed me for the death of Sam Murphy."

"Is that all he told you?"

"Basically that's it."

"Did he mention my husband, Hunter?"

"Not a word."

"Hunter does the books for Knowton's practice."

"Now I remember. Carver recommended your husband to serve on the Task Force. I agreed."

"He's a good CPA."

"So your husband would have been involved had there been

such a crime in Knowton's office?"

Leaning back in her seat, Nicki asked, "What do you mean, Commissioner?"

"Well, since the Medicaid Task Force chaired by Dr. Carver found no fraud in Tom's practice, this may be a moot issue."

"It didn't?" Nicki couldn't hide the astonishment in her voice.

"Why are you so surprised?"

"My father was an honest man. I never should have told him what was happening in the office. It's so complicated. Whoever killed him probably did not want him going to the police to implicate Tom."

"Tom?"

Nicki blushed. "Dr. Rogers, can I ask you to keep something confidential?"

"Of course."

"Tom and I have been having an affair for the past two years. He is the father of our baby boy."

Rogers held his stare but said nothing. He thought back to what Victor Carver had said about Peter Chambers wanting to get even with Knowton.

"Hunter found out about the affair and blackmailed Tom. But my husband doesn't know that Knowton is actually the father of our son. Anyway, the deal was that Hunter would not tell Tom's wife about our affair if he would let my husband skim money out of the practice by submitting fraudulent claims."

"Tom's too smart to have done that."

Nicki merely smiled.

"So the Task Force is covering up the truth," Rogers added indignantly.

"Don't forget, Commissioner, you appointed Hunter as a member of the Task Force. I'm sure that he has covered his tracks."

"So Carver might not have known about the fraud?"

Nicki paused. "Anything is possible."

Changing the subject, Rogers asked, "What do you know about Samuel Murphy?"

"Only that he was a good friend of my father."

"That's it?"

"Yes."

"The way I see things is that you need to go to the police to tell them what you know about the blackmail and the fraud."

"I can't. Hunter would kill me."

"Not if he is arrested and put in prison."

"As soon as he would make parole, he would kill me. Or have someone else kill me."

"Do you realize that you are aiding and abetting the federal crime of Medicaid fraud?"

"At least I'm alive for my baby."

"I'm under subpoena forcing me to talk to the authorities about many things. If asked, I will not lie about what you just told me."

Nicki stood up. "But you promised that you would keep our conversation private. I thought I could trust you."

"I never promised to cover up a federal crime."

"So, I guess that I . . ."

He put his hand on her shoulder. She flinched. Her eyes grew moist.

"Commissioner, my baby needs me."

"I want to help you," he replied. "I feel guilty about what happened to your dad."

"Don't be. It's not your fault. Just be careful."

"What do you mean?"

"Look, I have to get home. See ya." She turned and strolled out the door.

Rogers stood quietly with his hands in his pockets. The door closed without a sound. He couldn't help but feel that there was a lot that Nicki wasn't telling him. Recalling Knowton's warning that there was much more about Nicki than he knew, he mentally added her name to his growing list of suspects.

Chapter Thirty-Three

"Nicole Williams from WWPE is on the line."

"Thanks, Sally. I'll pick up."

"Dr. Rogers, I wanted to get back to you on the analysis of your home voice mail."

"What did your lab find?"

"They are certain. It's a complete voice pattern match between our radio station caller and the person who left you a message on your home voice mail."

"This is making sense. I spoke with that woman after she left her private phone number. She said she was giving me messages all along."

"May I ask, who is this person?"

"I can't reveal her name, but thank you so much for your help. I'll call you after this is all settled. If you still want me as a guest on your show, I'd love to return."

"Anytime, Commissioner."

••••••••••

"Hello, Detective, this is Jonathan Rogers."

"Glad you called. I was just about to call you. I have some news for you. The government traced Ashley's text message to a particular cell. They checked phone company records under national security protocol."

Rogers's hands shook as he held the receiver. "So where did Ashley use her cell?"

"The cell wasn't your daughter's. It belongs to an ex-FBI agent named Rick Miller. The FBI called the number. They traced it to somewhere around Baja, California, in Mexico. That's where the beach reference fits."

"But I received two text messages from Ashley."

"The one telling you to go to the casino to find her was

obviously bogus. The first one makes sense. We now know who Rick is. He lives in Michigan. The FBI raided his house, but no one was there."

"So the first message was real. I already told you about the redhead named Haley," Rogers added.

"What about this Z-something person?

Rogers thought back to the WWPE voice match. It was Alexis Miller. The Z had to be Zach Miller. But he needed to be sure. Ashley's life was hanging in the balance.

The Commissioner rubbed his chin and turned his back to the detective. "Don't know what that could mean. What about telephone records of this Rick Miller?"

"Dr. Rogers, I'm impressed. The FBI is impounding them now and analyzing all calls he made in the last six months."

The Commissioner turned abruptly, shooting a passing glance at Darden. "Let me know what you find. I'll be in touch if I think of anything."

••••••••••

Rogers needed time to think. If Zach Miller was involved in the kidnapping of Ashley, how could he prove it? Miller would just deny it. And as long as Ashley was missing, and Zach was involved, something bad could happen to her. If he called Alexis, her husband could answer the phone and his hand might be tipped. He wanted to talk this through with someone he could trust. Kim had left their house again. She said her psychiatrist recommended that she needed to get away. Rogers had no idea where she went. Brent Marshall was in Europe and left no contact number.

Rogers could feel his blood pressure rising. He didn't want to make the wrong move and possibly jeopardize Ashley's well-being. He needed to clear his mind somehow, and decided to go for a swim at the local fitness club.

••••••••••

The air in the spa smelled of chlorine. Except for a shapely woman standing between a pair of hot tubs at the far end of the Olympic-sized pool, this section of the DuPont Fitness Club appeared to be vacant. But with each step closer to the woman in his sights, his eyes widened. It was Haley. Wanting a few minutes to think, he dove into the deep end of the heated pool while swimming in her direction. After a few dozen strokes, he floated on his back, watching her perform a series of yoga exercises.

He pulled himself up the ladder, facing her. Her body was taut and well tanned for such a fair-skinned woman. Her brilliant red hair flowed, reaching the middle of her back. Rogers's senses were wary, even as he admired her beauty. She gave him a quick once-over, presented a half smile, and jumped into one of the hot tubs.

He wiped water from his eyes while walking past her to the unoccupied hot tub. He avoided looking at her; he needed more time to think of how to approach her. As he slowly sank into the steaming water up to his neck, he caught a scent of perfume.

"Mind if I join you?" she asked. "The water in my tub seems to have cooled. Your tub is still hot. I always like my water hot." She stepped down into his tub.

Rogers realized it was time. "We've met before."

"Ah, I see that you remember me."

Rogers scoffed. "The point is, how could I not remember you?"

"I'm flattered."

"I want to ask you some questions."

Opening her mouth, she ran her moist tongue slowly around her bright red painted lips. "I don't see why not. No one is around to hear us anyway."

"Are you stalking me?"

She giggled. "Now, why would you ask that silly question?"

He pushed himself backwards against the side of the tub as she moved closer to him.

"Why did you almost run into my car last month?"

The redhead broke the silence. "I don't even own a Mercedes." She laughed.

"I didn't mention any model of car."

She smiled seductively and pursed her lips.

Rogers demanded, "Who the hell are you?"

He watched her drop down into the bubbling waters. She was now at eye level with him. She drew closer to him and he felt her light touch on his chest from beneath the surface. "What the fuck are you doing?" Rogers shoved her away.

She shook the water from her hair. "Having fun, what else?"

"Stop following me or . . ." he snapped.

"Or what?" she chuckled. "I'm only doing my job."

It was time to counterpunch. "I forgot your name. What is it again?"

She said coolly, "Sorry, can't tell you."

Rogers looked deeply into her eyes. "I saw you on Pennsylvania Avenue just before I was shot. Did you have anything to do with it?"

"That would be a very bad thing to do. And I'm a good girl, except at party time."

"I'll just bet you are. Who are you working for?"

"Just call me your guardian. I know your name though. Dr. Jonathan Rogers."

Rogers knew she was playing him, and decided it would be best to continue playing dumb. He was determined to find out about Ashley.

"I'm furious about what has happened in the last few weeks. Maybe you can help."

"Tell me how," she purred.

"Only if you promise not to repeat this to anyone."

"You can trust me, darling."

"My daughter has been kidnapped."

Haley's eyes widened. "How awful. What happened?"

"She was running in a marathon but never finished the race. My wife couldn't find her."

"Did you call the FBI or something?"

"No, the kidnapper told me they would kill Ashley if I went to the authorities."

Haley drew closer, putting her hand on his shoulder, as if she were comforting him. "What are you going to do?"

"I don't know. I just wish I could talk with her to know she is all right. I haven't heard from her since she left to go to Alaska. I would do anything to know she is alive."

"Do you have any idea what the kidnappers want?"

"I wish they would contact me. I'll do anything."

Haley stood in the hot tub. "Listen, I need to be on my way. I come here on Thursday afternoons if you ever want to talk again. I'm sure the kidnappers will call you. Maybe they're just testing you to see if you'll run to the FBI."

"No way. I want to see my daughter alive again. I'll not going to tell anyone."

Haley walked up the steps of the hot tub. "I'll pray that things work out."

Rogers watched her every step until she disappeared into the woman's locker area. He had wanted to wring her neck. He hoped she would take the bait. At least, she would report to Rick Miller that Ashley's message never got through. Believing that he bought Ashley some time, he plotted his next move.

Chapter Thirty-Four

Ashley awoke. Her legs felt on fire. It was just like a really bad sunburn. She tried to rub them, but her arms wouldn't budge. Her shoulders ached. There was no light in the room. Remembering the last time she felt this way, she knew that Rick had punished her. The pain in her legs grew fierce. She tried to divert her attention from her legs and shoulders by thinking of her parents. Moments later, she could no longer stand the pain. Ashley screamed until she heard his New York accent.

"Wake up, Miss Sunshine."

Ashley felt a hand on her breasts. She opened her eyes. The pain was gone. She saw Rick holding an empty syringe.

"It seems as though you got bad sunburn on your legs. I just gave you a shot of Demerol. And before that, I put some cream on your legs."

"I haven't been out of this room in weeks. How did I get a sunburn?"

"Tit for tat, you could say. The pain I went through getting my scalp stitched back together after you bopped me with the beer bottles in exchange for me giving you another painful sunburn with the sunlamp."

Ashley moaned, looking up at her captor. "I needed your cell phone. I had to call my mom. I told you she was sick."

"Well, I have bad news for you. Your message was never received. And stop this mom bullshit. I saw the text. It was addressed to your father."

"Please untie my hands."

She watched Rick pick up a jug. He poured it into her mouth. She swallowed hard. Gasping, she tried to swallow as fast as she could. She shook her head from side to side.

"Stop. Stop!"

"All right. I'll see you tomorrow. If I'm in a good mood, I'll let you walk around like you did before you became a bad girl. If I'm in a bad mood . . . well, let's hold that thought. I don't want you to have nightmares tonight about what I might do to you next."

Ashley watched him swagger toward the door. The light from the hallway was streaming in. She saw his shadow vanish against the wall and a moment later reappear when he blocked the light. It had to be the sun. It appeared to be shining brightly, as if the hallway just beyond the door led directly to the outside world.

"Please don't leave me here another night."

"Good afternoon.. See you in the morning."

Just before the door closed shut, Ashley spotted the resident rat crawling toward her beet-red legs.

Chapter Thirty-Five

"Marissa, the new Surgeon General is speaking at a local medical conference in Detroit. Get her on the line for me."

"Will do, Zach."

Miller scrutinized the internally released financials. He began to hum. In his imagination, the jangling sound of hard cash pouring through the DCP coffers was playing his favorite tune, Up, Up, and Away. He tossed the quarterlies on his desk. His attention shifted to his fantasy of making even sweeter music with Marissa later that night.

Marissa buzzed. "The Surgeon General is on your private line."

"Dr. Gomez, thanks for taking my call. I hope you're doing well in your new position."

"I am indeed. Thank you so much for your support. I wouldn't be here without your strong recommendation."

"Your modesty becomes you. Your credentials are impeccable."

"What can I do for you?"

"I'm glad you asked. Listen, our researchers have been working with the FDA trying to get additional indications approved for our blockbuster cancer drug, Zazotene. You also need to know that ever since we convinced the management of National Quality to take a harder look at the data from our human drug testing company, the FDA is finally starting to pay attention."

"What company does your drug testing?"

"Southwest International. And the Institutional Review Board that oversees them is National Quality in Bethesda, Maryland."

"Mr. Miller, I've heard that National Quality has a reputation of being tough on the drug testing companies."

"That was true until a while ago. Now they are playing fair. Months earlier, a board member at National Quality unexpectedly passed away. Unfortunately, while this nurse was still alive, he led the National Quality board to question most of the research we had outsourced to Southwest. Since his death, the oversight company has given us a reasonable shake in their reviews of the data."

"It always amazes me, Mr. Miller, how one person can do so much damage to so many people. It's truly a shame that he would criticize the excellent work being done by well-run drug testing companies like Southwest."

"I never met the nurse, but apparently he was a real dynamo. His name was Sam Murphy. It's hard to believe, but he almost single-handedly torpedoed Zazotene. It was regrettable that such an influential clinical board member was so biased against Southwest and DCP. But let me change the subject and get to the reason why I called you."

"Of course. I'm here to serve your needs."

Zach beamed."The FDA is now taking a fresh look at new data on Zazotene coming out of Southwest International and a recommendation from National Quality."

"So . . ."

"Someone in the FDA is stalling the Zazotene expanded-use approval process ever since my company ceased manufacturing the influenza vaccine this past winter."

"Sounds like politics."

Zach deadpanned, "Don't you just hate those political types with a personal agenda?"

"Mr. Miller, I've been working with the FDA in order to achieve the goals of President Jordan and his Secretary of Health. I've built some excellent relationships at the regulatory agency. I would like to work with you on this matter."

"I suggest we have dinner so we can discuss the details. I'll have Marissa set it up. She will have a limo take you to DuPont, where we can meet at the best restaurant in town."

"I'll be looking forward to receiving the invitation."

"Doctor Gomez, one more thing. Please say a fond hello to President Jordan for me."

"You know him personally?"

Miller replied smartly, "Doctor, once you get to know me, you'll never ask that kind of question again."

"I'll make sure the President knows we're working together."

"Actually, he already does."

Zach slapped the intercom before barking out his order. "Marissa, schedule a dinner for me and the new Surgeon General. Call Lauriol Plaza. Dr. Gomez will feel right at home. And have Sean Parker come to my office as soon as possible."

"Will do."

Playing back his voice mail, he listened to a hurried message from Knowton. He pictured the oncologist fidgeting as he seemed to be making up one excuse after another as to why he would not give Zazotene to Alexis. Less than a minute later, he looked up to see his senior vice president in charge of DCP sales walking through the doorway carrying a file in his right hand.

"Sean, you're really smoking these days. I've seen your plan for the Mexican cruise. It's awesome, but have you reeled in the big tuna?"

"You mean . . ."

"Knowton. He's our key to the rest of the docs. He has their professional respect. Once he publicly recommends Zazotene to his colleagues, Sunview will self-destruct in our wake turbulence. We'll knock our chief competitor on their ass."

"Is he finally willing to prescribe it for Alexis?"

Zach shook his head impatiently. "I need to teach you something. Alexis is just the hook. Not only is Knowton shivering about Sam Murphy, but once Jonathan Rogers goes down under his medical care, we'll reel in the good oncologist. So far, we have left Knowton's wife alone and have kept the good doctor off the Medicaid fraud list. He owes us big time. On the cruise, I predict that he'll be giving out samples of Zazotene to every doc on board."

"Sounds like a winning game plan."

"So how many docs have we landed so far?"

"We've racked up five hundred and eighty doctor acceptances for our Continuing Medical Education cruise to Cabo San Lucas."

"Just imagine that many pigeons eating out of Knowton's hand. I think I'll have Marissa hire an artist to paint that image for our boardroom. It will be DCP's version of the *Mona Lisa*."

"Our cruise leaves in two weeks. I'll keep you up to date," Parker added. "When you get a chance, please take a look at my recommendation to cut our sales force. Mirroring docs with their personalized sales representative has marginal value, but having physician leaders like Knowton working for us will quadruple our profits compared to the old-school methods we used under Dylan Mathews."

Zach patted Parker on his shoulder and grinned. "Move forward on your suggestion to eliminate fifteen percent of the sales reps to start. For the survivors, just make sure they know their job security is tied to selling more Zazotene. Plus, any new hires must be former college cheerleaders. We need their perky personalities to attract the attention of the horny docs. Just make sure you match up opposite sexes."

"Will do, Boss."

Zach rose to exchange a hearty high-five with Parker before the VP of sales left the room. He imagined the layout in the DCP boardroom. He asked himself where he would hang the caricature of Knowton feeding the hundreds of pigeons. *Behind my own seat in the boardroom, the portrait would work nicely.*

•••••••••

"A toast, Dr. Gomez, to the fine job you're doing as Surgeon General."

"Mr. Miller, thank you. This is a terrific restaurant."

"I believe in nothing but the best for the 'top doc' in America."

"There was a time when I would have been lucky to be a server in a restaurant as fine as this one."

Zach sniffed the wine. "I also started working at similar jobs while I was in school. My father picked cotton for a living. You and I should be proud that we have worked ourselves up the line to where we are today. Dr. Gomez, the leaders tell me you are a team player."

"I am," she replied proudly.

"I need you to work some magic for me and the team. May I be blunt?"

She nodded. But before he could start, the server appeared alongside them to take their order.

"May I recommend the filet mignon?" Zach suggested. "Perhaps a Caesar salad?"

"Sounds like a perfect choice. I like my meat rare."

Addressing the server, he commanded, "Me too. Two drenched pieces of your finest filets. And my usual wine selection. I'm sure you'll enjoy this particular wine, Doctor. It has a distinct flavor."

Once the server departed, Zach began. "Dr. Gomez, I need you to motivate some of our friends at the FDA to fast-track additional indications for Zazotene based on the new data from Southwest."

"I can do that."

"I'll leave the details to you."

The server returned to open another bottle of cabernet sauvignon and filled both their glasses for the fourth time. As the two drank their wine, Zack relayed the background information of Zazotene and his battle with the FDA while Dr. Gomez sat and nodded.

"I'm glad you understand my predicament."

When the waiter returned, Zach sat back to relax as the main course was served. "Does everything meet your expectations, Doctor?"

"I'm ready for any challenge thrown my way."

He skipped his salad and deftly cut off a hefty slice of rare meat. Wiping a few droplets of blood from his mouth, he studied her face intently.

"I assume that the quality review board will not interfere?" she inquired.

"With Sam Murphy no longer walking their hallways, you have my word. National Quality will support whatever we want. Just take care of the FDA. And be aware that it may not be so easy as I'm saying to you. Mr. Murphy's daughter will be joining the board at National Quality."

"No problem. Count on me to make it happen."

"One last thing. You will be getting a call from Dr. Tom Knowton. Your job will be to convince him to give Zazotene to his favorite physician patient."

The Surgeon General nodded. "I'm here to serve my leaders."

"Dr. Gomez, welcome to the team."

Chapter Thirty-Six

Beth felt as though Sam was watching her every move. His dream had become her life. She felt dedicated to the mission. *His mission*. She lay in her bed, gazing at the ceiling and waiting for the alarm to go off. Ecstatic that she was going to take Sam's seat on the board, she flipped the alarm switch and leaped out of bed, stretching her muscles. She felt as though she was floating on air as she began her big day.

After a quick shower and a cup of coffee, she dressed quickly. Beth scanned her studio apartment one last time before placing a small can of red-pepper spray in her purse, picking up her beige attaché case, and unlocking the four deadbolt locks on her door. With the door three inches ajar and held by the door chain, she carefully surveyed the hallway. Seeing no one, she proceeded down the stairs of her three-story walkup in the southeast section of DC.

She checked the Metro map at the station before boarding the train at Southern Avenue. She then counted the number of stops to Bethesda, taking special note that she would need to change cars at Metro Center. She pulled out a one-page letter from her attaché case. It was the original document, signed by Sam Murphy. Beth reviewed the language one more time while shielding it from those around her. Not at all surprised that he seemed to have thought of everything, she remembered him telling her that this letter would serve as her ticket to ensure that his work would continue in case anything ever happened to him. Beth filed away the letter and locked her case. The board meeting was due to start in an hour. As the Metro sped past Friendship Heights, she stood to await her stop.

Beth stepped out onto the Bethesda station platform in her low-heeled Angel suede shoes. Checking her bearings, she walked one flight up from the subterranean station. Wisconsin Avenue was a block away. She emerged at street level a half block from the office building of the National Quality Institute. With each step, she was reminded that this was the identical path that her hero and father had walked for so many years.

The modern two-towered structure had an enormous amount of glass in the middle foyer. *Well, at least some things at the company are transparent,* Beth thought. At the ground-level front desk, she flashed her photo ID and presented her signed letter for admittance.

Beth wondered why the receptionist frowned. "Ms. Murphy, per our policy at National Quality, we need a notarized letter. I can admit you today but you will need this letter to be legally certified for you to return to the board. I'm sorry for any inconvenience."

"That's odd. No one ever told Sam or me of this policy before."

"Dr. Ulrich, the chairman of the board, just announced this policy yesterday. So there was no way you could have known."

She sighed deeply. "Then I better ensure that this letter does not get lost. I'll have it notarized. I'll bring it with me for next time."

Beth was provided with a temporary badge and an individualized gold-plated key to the twenty-eighth floor. In the elevator, she inserted the National Quality key. She punched the button to the right floor and fastened the badge to her business suit. As the door opened, the magnificence of the silver-plated company insignia of National Quality struck her. Beth walked up to the reception desk.

"Ms. Murphy, welcome to the National Quality Institute. The board meeting will be starting in about twenty minutes in the Gold Room, which is at the end of the corridor on your left. I notice that you have a temporary badge."

"Yes, the front desk . . ."

Interrupting her, the receptionist said, "I know the whole story. Next time, I'm sure you'll have a permanent badge. Please don't lose your original signed letter, which will need to be notarized. Without that letter, you'll not be able to sit on the board."

"I'll guard it with my life."

"Can I get you anything?"

She smiled. "No. But can you tell me if any of the board members have arrived?"

"Actually, Ms. Lindsay Mason and Dr. Peter Ulrich arrived just a few minutes ago. I believe they are in the Gold Room."

"Then I think I'll just head down to meet my new colleagues."

As she passed a couple of men in Armani business suits, she made solid eye contact with them, but they seemed to focus on the temporary bright yellow badge on her lapel. Beth slowed the pace of her steps so that the clanking sound of her heels on the gray marble floor would be less noticeable to the pair of board members chatting just outside the Gold Room.

As she neared the duo, she held out her right hand, introducing herself. "Good morning. I'm Beth Murphy."

The trim, gray-bearded man in his late fifties merely nodded at her presence. Beth's hand was still extended as she turned toward the woman. Dropping her hand to her side after it remained untouched, she waited for a response.

The woman spoke in a low-pitched but hurried manner. "I'm Lindsay Mason. Both Dr. Ulrich and I have served on this board with Samuel Murphy for at least six years. You must be his daughter."

"Yes. I'm not sure you know that Sam died suddenly."

"We know," Lindsay replied.

"It was about three weeks after our quarterly winter meeting. As his replacement, I was planning on making the spring meeting but I was ill with the flu. But now, I'm committed to serve."

"I'm sorry for your troubles," Lindsay Mason continued. "Good luck. By the way, you'll need a permanent badge to continue working with the board."

"So I hear."

Lindsay and Ulrich turned away. Beth lingered a few moments in the general area while her board colleagues resumed their private conversation.

"Well, please excuse me. I'll see you inside."

"Sure, we start in ten minutes," Lindsay replied while keeping her gaze firmly fixed on Dr. Ulrich.

Beth walked into the Gold Room. The panoramic view of the National Institutes of Health campus in the distance was awe-inspiring. It was easy for Beth to imagine the inspiration that Sam must have felt each time he looked out the huge plate glass windows. She walked around the forty-foot-long ultra-modern glass conference table, reading each of the thirteen nameplates before returning to her assigned seat. She checked her watch.

Beth walked toward the corridor outside the Gold Room. She saw a dozen or so well-dressed men and women huddled around Lindsay Mason and Dr. Ulrich. Since she had left the pair several minutes earlier, both of them had repositioned themselves another thirty feet down the hallway. As she walked toward them, it appeared obvious that Ulrich was holding court. Just before Beth arrived at the pack, Lindsay whispered something to the group. Beth strained to hear what was being said, but the group disbanded when she was no more than five feet away from them. The suits filed away down the hallway, most of them keeping their heads down. Suddenly, Lindsay turned to face her. She wore a grim-looking expression.

"Ms. Murphy, the meeting will be starting in a few minutes. We're all heading into the Gold Room."

Beth felt like a lost penguin at the South Pole. "Then I guess I'll join the group inside."

Upon entering the boardroom for the second time, her eyes focused on the bearded man sitting at the head of the glass conference table. Ulrich glanced up at her for only a second, just enough time to shoot an uncomfortable dagger her way. After taking her seat, Beth turned to the member who was the last to enter the room. He sat next to her on her right.

With an Irish brogue, he whispered, "Ms. Murphy, I'm Michael O'Kane. I knew your father quite well. Around here, he was known as "the Whistleblower."

He winked at her just as she heard Ulrich gavel the meeting to order. The chairman glared at Beth before he began.

"Good morning. I'm calling this summer board meeting of

National Quality to order. May I have a motion to approve the spring minutes?"

Beth was not surprised to see Lindsay, who was seated next to Chairman Ulrich, make a motion to approve without correction. Ulrich promptly asked for a second.

A familiar voice bellowed out. "Point of order, Mr. Chairman. I've some important changes."

Ulrich replied, "Michael, you are out of order. There is a pending motion on the floor to approve without correction."

"Mr. Chairman, as you know, a point of order supersedes a motion according to the rules."

Scanning the conference table, Ulrich persisted. "Is there a second to Ms. Mason's motion?"

Seated alongside him, Beth could hear O'Kane's chair sliding back on the hardwood floor. She turned to see him standing. With his arms folded, his dark brown eyes seemed to be shooting bullets of disdain at the chairman.

Ulrich looked around the room for several seconds before declaring, "Hearing no second, the motion dies. May I have another motion?"

Still standing, O'Kane roared, "Motion to approve with changes."

Beth looked around the table. No one budged. She made her move. "I second the motion. And by the way, since I have not been formally introduced to the board, my name is Beth Murphy."

Ulrich dropped his head and softly acknowledged the motion. "What are your changes Mr. O'Kane?."

The tall Irishman began, "At the spring meeting, there was barely a quorum. If you recall, I made a comment that Mr. Samuel Murphy had passed away since our winter meeting. I asked that the board recognize him posthumously for his contributions to National Quality. I believe my motion for this recognition received six votes in support and five votes opposed."

Ulrich nodded several times. "That is correct. But your motion was ultimately defeated. So what's you point?"

"Mr. Chairman, after the six-to-five votes in favor of my

motion, you then voted to oppose. According to rules, the chair can only vote in cases of a tie. The chair cannot vote to create a tie. So I believe the minutes need to be changed to reflect that my motion carried. I don't know why I didn't object at the time, but I'm doing so today."

Ulrich narrowed his eyes upon O'Kane. "Is there an objection to the motion to amend the spring minutes?"

Silence.

"Hearing none, the minutes will be amended to reflect that Mr. Sam Murphy is hereby recognized for his contributions to National Quality."

O'Kane smiled. "Thank you, Dr. Ulrich. Since Mr. Murphy's daughter is now a full-fledged member of this board, I motion that at the fall meeting we present her with his certificate of recognition."

Beth shot up her hand. She screamed out, "Present." Seeing the strange looks coming her way, she rebounded. "Second . . . I mean I second Mr. O'Kane's motion."

The chairman asked, "Opposed? Hearing none, the motion is carried. Well, now that we've spent fifteen minutes getting the minutes approved and granting awards, I would like to get down to business."

"Lindsay, please read the list of the drugs recently approved by the FDA and their indications as pertinent to our agenda. We'll need to review the clinical trial research for them."

She replied, "Since our last meeting, Mr. Chairman, there is only one drug to which National Quality provided oversight to the FDA. We reviewed the supplemental clinical data from Southwest. That company did the drug testing clinical trials on Zazotene. Recently, the FDA has approved the drug for the treatment of all cancers that stem from endocrine glands. This supplements the previous indications, which included only non-Hodgkin's lymphoma and myeloma."

Beth noticed O'Kane's raised hand. He seemed to be a tiger, just like Sam.

After being recognized, O'Kane spoke forcefully. "At the

spring meeting of this board, by majority vote, we specifically asked for further data from Southwest on Zazotene. We also recommended to the FDA that they not approve the drug for any additional indications until it was proven to be safe. Also, you assured us that Southwest was taking another look at the twenty patients they intentionally excluded from the clinical trials. Thirty percent of those excluded patients died as a result of the higher doses used to treat these endocrine cancers."

Ulrich reached for his gavel but held it in midair. The chairman stared at O'Kane.

The Irishman's face had turned beet red. "With all due respect to the FDA, what's going on here?"

"Mr. O'Kane, the FDA does not have to abide by our recommendation. As you well know, we only serve as an advisory board for them."

Beth asked, "How many times in the last five years has the FDA approved a drug without our recommendation?"

The chairman replied, "Ms. Murphy, we don't have time to rehash the past half decade."

O'Kane chimed in. "We all know the answer to Ms. Murphy's question. It's been zero times."

Beth replied, "Well, in that case, Dr. Ulrich, I would ask that you conduct an official inquiry into why the FDA acted against the majority of this board."

Ulrich leaned back in his seat. "I'll follow up with the FDA. To be clear to everyone today, this board submitted a minority and a majority report to the FDA on the safety issues around additional indications for Zazotene. One report was in favor of approval and one was opposed to additional indications. The FDA made their decision. Their conclusion agreed with the minority report from this board."

Under his breath, O'Kane whispered, "How odd."

Beth looked at the chairman. "When can we expect your findings?"

"Within four weeks. I'll have the secretary mail out to each of you a summary of my findings."

O'Kane smirked. "I'll be counting the days. I would have

thought that the majority report would have carried more weight than the minority report."

Ulrich looked over at Lindsay but said nothing.

Beth tapped O'Kane on his elbow. She passed him a note. *Thank you!* With these early victories tucked away, she enjoyed the remainder of the board meeting. She found herself actually bonding with a few of her fellow board members. Their review of summary data on a series of new compounds that Southwest was planning to use in upcoming clinical trials brought back bad memories when she was forced by her own father to participate in similar testing. The meeting concluded around three in the afternoon without any new recommendations to the FDA by the quality assurance oversight board at National Quality.

••••••••••

Her mind fixated on the day's events, Beth stood in the middle of the train platform, her attaché case held loosely in her right hand. Suddenly, she was pushed from behind by an elderly man with a cane. She accepted his quick apology and walked over to the station wall. Now out of the mainstream pedestrian traffic on the platform, she waited for the Metro back to DC. For a moment, she wondered why perhaps a dozen people seemed to be mulling around her. She felt a gentle tap on her left shoulder and whirled around. It was the same elderly man who had just bumped into her.

He pointed his cane at the Metro schedule posted on the wall and asked for help in reading it. Beth turned toward the schedule but she was unable to understand his stuttering speech pattern. When she asked him to repeat what he was saying, he cursed loudly, spun around with his cane and appeared to lose his balance. She tried to catch him before he struck the ground, but she was too late. Beth lifted him to his feet. Focused on ensuring that the old man was all right, she barely noticed a young woman running away from both of them. The woman was carrying an attaché case that looked just like hers. Beth looked down to the spot where she dropped her case when she reached for the old man. She saw only pavement.

She took off in the direction of the running woman, who was now about thirty yards ahead of her. It soon became apparent to Beth that she was losing ground. She memorized the runner's description: Athletic looking, tall at around five-ten, red hair, and wearing bright red Nike sneakers.

Beth watched the redhead turn the corner and disappear. She slowed down to a trot to catch her breath. Reaching the spot where the redhead made a sharp right turn, Beth began to walk. Twenty yards ahead of her, she saw her attaché case in the middle of the pathway. She sprinted forward, rushing to open the case. She searched for the original letter signed by Sam Murphy. It was gone.

Chapter Thirty-Seven

The Commissioner pulled up in front of the ranch-style home shortly before six thirty in the evening. A balding middle-aged man answered his light knock on the screen door.

"Good evening. I'm Dr. Rogers. Is this the home of Nicki Sanderson?

The man responded gruffly, "How do you know her?"

Rogers smiled. "I know her from Dr. Knowton's office. Is she home?"

"Sir, that's none of your business."

"I'm sorry to be bothering you at home. I need to speak with her. It's important."

"Hold on." The heavyset man let the spring-loaded door slam in Rogers's face.

Minutes later, he reappeared. "She's not interested in speaking with you."

"Are you Hunter Sanderson?"

His eyes flickered. "Why do you ask?"

"I just want to speak with Nicki for a minute."

Sanderson shouted, "Don't mess with my wife. Do you get that, Doc?"

At that moment, Rogers's cell phone rang. "Excuse me for a second. Hello?"

A woman's voice on the phone whispered for Rogers to be at the cement bench by the pond. She would be there at nine o'clock.

Rogers looked up at Sanderson. "Wrong number. So I hear from Dr. Carver that you were very helpful on the Medicaid Fraud Task Force."

"I just want to serve my state," the burly-looking man said with a guffaw.

••••••••••

Rogers parked his Lexus on the other side of the Department of Health parking lot. To avoid being caught on the security cameras, he hugged the side of the building as he made his way to the pond. The cement bench could be seen in the distance. That area was showered by the same Department security beacon lights that illuminated the parking lot. He walked carefully, out of the perimeter reaches of the high-powered beams. Twenty yards from the bench, he squatted down and checked his watch. Eight fifty-five.

As the moments passed, he heard a rustling sound coming from where the woods met the grassy knoll. His nerves were stretched like an accordion stuck in a fully expanded position. Rogers listened closely. He thought he heard the sound of branches cracking in the woods. The sound seemed to be getting closer. He scanned the horizon, but could not see anything in the darkness beyond his lighted wristwatch and cell. Nine o'clock. *What am I doing here?*

Soon, it was ten minutes past nine. He checked his cell phone to make sure that it had been switched to vibrate. The animal-like sounds of the evening seemed to be coming from all directions. His heart was pounding. Though the night air was a balmy sixty-five degrees, he shivered.

He stood up to stretch just when he felt a light tap on his shoulder. He whirled around, his fist cocked, but he pulled his punch when he saw her face. "Nicki, you scared me to death."

"Just follow me. We don't have much time."

"What are we doing here?"

I wanted to talk with you. To help you. But things have changed."

"What does that mean?"

Nicki turned to take off toward the woods. Rogers reached out and grabbed her arm. "I'm not going in there with you. In fact, I'm heading back to the parking lot to get the hell out of here. I must be crazy to be out here with you."

"Commissioner, I wouldn't go back to your car tonight."

"Why not?"

"After you left our doorstep tonight, I convinced Hunter that I needed to pick up some cereal and milk for breakfast. A short while later when I didn't return, he called me on my cell. He was screaming like a wild man. He said he figured it all out after you stopped by our house earlier tonight. Hunter believes that I was probably sneaking out to meet you. He's a very jealous man. He watched you hop into your Lexus back at our house. He'll be looking for it. I'm sure the first place he would check out tonight is the Department of Health. So unless you want a shotgun or .345 magnum pointed at your temple, forget your car tonight."

Conceding her point, he reluctantly began following her into the woods. "Nicki, what do you want to talk about?"

"In due time. We've got to get out of here. Who knows where Hunter is right now. Let's go!"

Rogers began huffing after fifty yards and soon trailed her by twenty. They leaped over a small stream and had begun climbing a ten-foot grassy hill when they heard a gunshot.

"Get down!" Nicki screamed.

"Shit! What's going on?"

"It's got to be Hunter. He has a telescopic sight on his rifle. That sounded like a rifle shot."

A second later, Rogers heard a bullet whizzing a few inches above his head. Clawing his way up the final five feet of the hill, he scrambled furiously to reach the top. He picked up his head for a second, seeing Nicki waving him on. She was already in a clearing about thirty yards ahead, seated behind the wheel of a convertible with the top down. It then dawned on him. It was the same car that had brought Nicki to the Department of Health on the night they found her father's body in the woods. Rogers slid down the far side of the hill a few feet and jumped up. He heard Nicki yelling.

"Hunter will be over the hill in a few seconds. Run! He'll kill both of us."

Rogers tripped over a branch, sliding on both knees on a weed-covered area before pushing himself to his feet. He sprinted the last twenty yards to the convertible. As he was opening the passenger door, he heard a shot ricochet off the front bumper.

Nicki yelled, "Duck!"

Rogers dove to the floor, banging his head on the dashboard. Nicki gunned the gas pedal, spinning the car onto the dirt path. Rogers crouched on the floor as she violently spun the car around, then he heard another shot ring out.

A hundred yards up the path, he crawled up from the floor to strap himself into the seat. Once she navigated the Corvette onto a side street that led to Main in DuPont, he took his first deep breath in what seemed like an eternity. The air never seemed to taste so good. He looked down at his bloodied hands and knees. He glanced over at Nicki. Every few seconds, she took quick looks back over her shoulder.

"We need to go to the police," Rogers told her while rubbing his forehead.

"Are you crazy? I can't go to jail. I have a baby to protect."

"I promise that I'll do everything I can to get you out of whatever trouble you're facing. You have no choice. You can't go back to Hunter ever again. He'll kill you."

In her panic, Nicki sped down Main Street while her eyes darted in all directions. Her blouse was drenched in sweat. Rogers reached out for her shoulder and patted it gently.

"Nicki, I came to help you tonight. I put my life in danger for you."

She said nothing. Five minutes later, she pulled up in front of the Oldwyck Police Station.

••••••••••

Rogers flung the door open and yelled out to the cop manning the main desk, "Call Detective Darden. Tell him Dr. Rogers and Nicki Sanderson need to speak with him right away."

The cop looked like he would rather be enjoying a Tigers–White Sox game. He needed two shoves off the arms of his swivel chair to struggle to his feet before accompanying them into the same back interrogation room where Rogers was questioned the night of the Chambers death. The cop asked them to wait. Darden would be coming in five minutes. Rogers sat directly opposite to where Nicki was sitting.

"Dr. Rogers, do you think this room is bugged?"

He shrugged his shoulders. "What will you tell Darden?"

"I've been thinking of what I can and what I can't tell him."

"Why not tell him everything?"

"You know why. Don't you get it? Knowton is safe. They need him. I'm the one who is expendable. Hunter is not my worst nightmare. I'm afraid of those who control us."

"What do you mean?"

"I hope you are not so naïve that you thought someone killed my father simply to silence what he heard from me about Medicaid fraud. If it was that simple, they would have eliminated me as well."

"Who are 'they'?"

Nicki stood up and faced the two-way mirror. She turned toward Rogers. "Do you think the cops are watching us? I bet they're listening to our every word."

Rogers rose to grab her hand. He pulled her to the opposite wall, away from the mirror. "I think I know who controls you. I've figured it all out."

"No you haven't. You're just guessing. They're too smart to ever let you pinpoint their plan—their leaders."

"Nicki, it's—," he began, but stopped when he heard the door open.

Darden walked up to them. "Well, you two look like you're getting ready to make out. Pillow talk?"

Rogers said nothing and motioned for Nicki to sit down beside him. The cop placed his cup of coffee on the table and sat down on a chair across from them.

"Normally, we would separate each of you for your statements, but since I have already spoken with the Commissioner several times, we can make this a threesome. So which one of you is going to tell me something that I don't already know?"

Rogers pointed at Nicki to start the conversation. As she was opening her mouth to speak, the cop pressed the digital recorder button.

"Hold on! Detective, before I say anything to you, I want a

guarantee from you, on record, that I will be given immunity from any prosecution," Nicki said.

Darden stopped the recorder. "No way."

"Then I want police protection for me and my baby in exchange for my testimony."

"I can do that." Darden then hit the recorder's start button once more.

"OK. I told my father that I thought the office was billing Medicaid for patients that we didn't have in the practice. And now Dad's dead."

"Excuse me, you're the office manager. Aren't you in charge of the billing?"

Rogers watched her stare at the digital recorder while she held her tongue.

"I repeat. Aren't you in charge of the office billing to Medicaid, Mrs. Sanderson?"

Nicki rose to walk over to the recorder. She paused a moment before pushing the off button, then resumed her seat and stared at Darden.

"Mrs. Sanderson, I must tell you that if you are covering up a crime, we'll prosecute you."

"Detective, why do you think I shut off the recorder? I'm not going to implicate myself in a federal crime on record. Anyway, you promised me police protection."

"Not immunity," he snapped back.

Nicki lowered her head and nervously tapped her fingers on the table. "Then this meeting is over. I have an innocent baby boy to protect."

Darden said angrily, "Then you're both going to jail for obstruction of justice. I think you're playing me."

The Commissioner leaped to his feet. "Nicki, please tell the detective everything you know," Rogers pleaded.

Darden said, "You're both hiding something. I'll be back in a couple of minutes. If you don't tell me the truth when I return, I'm booking you both." He turned and walked out, leaving the door open.

The Commissioner sat down next to Nicki, shaking his head.

"I'm not going to jail for your cover-up."

"I'm sorry, Dr. Rogers. I'm sorry for everything."

"Nicki, I don't believe you anymore. I have a family to protect as well."

"Trust me, I know. You're on their list."

"What list?"

Nicki stood and paced the room. "Why can't you just let things be the way they want them? You could have been Surgeon General if you'd just played along."

"Because it's wrong."

Rogers heard the footsteps approaching the door. "You have to tell Darden what you know."

Nicki sat down and dropped her head onto the interrogation table.

Darden appeared in the doorway, arms folded and jaw firmly set. "Well, should I call for help to book you both, or do either of you want to sing?"

Rogers took a deep breath, thinking of Ashley. He needed Darden's help to save her. "Sit down, Detective. I have a story to tell."

Nicki raised her head and mouthed the words, shut up.

Rogers said, "I think I know who Z is."

He looked over at Nicki. She said, "Commissioner, think before you speak. Remember, we both have families."

"It's time to say it like it is."

She shouted, "Shut up, Dr. Rogers! Remember what I just told you."

"Detective, I've reason to believe that Zach Miller, CEO of Doctor's Choice Products, is involved."

"Now we're getting somewhere. I'll put on a trace of Mr. Z. You're both free to go."

Rogers walked out of the room with Nicki. Halfway down the hall, she stopped. "You're a dead man and a fool."

She ran out of the police station, just as Darden walked up to Rogers.

"You and Mrs. Sanderson seem to see a lot of each other. Isn't she married?"

"We've been acquaintances for years."

"Lovers?"

"Absolutely not.

"Go on."

"Nicki's husband is the accountant for the Knowton practice. She claims that he is solely responsible for submitting false Medicaid claims on behalf of the practice."

"What's his name?"

"Hunter Sanderson."

"Why won't she cooperate with me?"

"She's afraid that her husband will kill her if she does. She has a newborn baby."

"Is your physician friend part of the fraud?"

"Nicki implied that he seemed to look the other way when Sanderson submitted the fraudulent bills."

"Why would he do that?"

"He was being threatened by her husband. Sanderson said that if Knowton didn't cooperate, he would tell Knowton's wife that her husband was having an affair with Nicki."

"Was he?"

"According to Nicki, Knowton is the baby's father."

"You doctors seem to be involved in a lot of activities besides taking care of people's health. But how does this all relate to Nicki's father?"

"She believes that someone killed her father so he would not go to the police and expose the Medicaid fraud and get Knowton in trouble."

"Who?"

"Don't know."

"Do you think Sanderson killed Chambers?"

Responding indignantly, Rogers said, "How would I know that?"

"Calm down. I'll bet that Nicki knows a lot more than I'm hearing from you."

Rogers nodded.

"Is there anything else that you haven't told me that might be relevant?"

"Yes. I need to show you something."

Rogers pulled out the special-delivery mailing from the inner pocket of his tweed sports jacket. The detective's eyes glistened at his first view of the colored block letters.

"Now I think I know why you're being so cooperative."

"I'm afraid for the safety of my family."

"Commissioner, I'm bringing in Nicki Sanderson."

Rogers held up his hand "No, please give me a chance to speak with her first. I'll try to convince her to become a witness for the State."

"Why do you want to help her?"

"Because I feel so guilty that I didn't help her father. If I had gone to Knowton right away to check out the accusations more vigorously, maybe Chambers might still be alive. More important, I think she knows Zach Miller is behind all of this and that if you arrest her and Zach is involved in what happened to Ashley, they could kill my daughter."

"All right. I'll call you with any trace of Z. Miller."

"Now that I've done what you wanted, tell me something I don't know. So who shot me, and who pushed me off the bridge?"

Darden ignored him. "You have forty-eight hours to get Nicki to voluntarily come here before I start booking both Mr. and Mrs. Sanderson. Maybe I'll book Knowton as well."

"Guess I'll have to find out on my own."

"You'd best just stay out of trouble."

"Please, I've been dealing with this shit ever since I met the President."

Rogers turned away from Darden and stormed out of the station. "Good night, Detective," he said quietly, without as much as a look back.

Chapter Thirty-Eight

"I was thrilled that you agreed to have dinner with me, Kim."

"It gives us time to follow up on our conversation at the lake house."

"After we order, we can take care of business. For now, let's just enjoy ourselves."

"The lobster is delicious."

"Great choice. It goes well with the Champagne."

"Cheers, Mr. Miller." She took a small sip and lowered the glass, averting his locked-in gaze.

Feeling his hand gently resting on hers, Kim hesitated a second before pulling it back. Earlier that evening, she had convinced herself that this dinner was all business. Now in the moment, she was starting to doubt if she believed that anymore.

"Who is this 'Mr. Miller'? Unless you believe you're having dinner with my father, I insist that you call me Zach."

"Sorry, I'm not used to addressing clients by their first names."

He laughed. "Then let's pretend I'm a long-lost friend."

She hesitated. "I'm not sure that would be right." Kim thought for a moment about what it had been like having the six-year-long affair with Taylor. She had felt so alive. She couldn't wait to meet each day. Now, with Zach, she felt that same, wonderful arousal.

"Let's pretend that you are my former girlfriend. We broke up years ago over some silly argument. Today, we bumped into each other in the mall, and on the spur of the moment we decided to come to this restaurant . . . just as friends."

She held her glass high and made a toast.

"Zach, to old times."

"And to even better times ahead."

Kim sipped her wine, gazing at Zach's rugged features and

coal black hair. Realizing that she was staring at him, she looked away at the painting on the wall. "So what do you think of the lake house? Are you ready to make me an offer?" she asked.

"I am. But I would like to see the place one more time before deciding on a figure."

"When?" She wiped away the dripping butter from her chin with her napkin.

"How about after dinner?"

She gave him a coy look. "I guess I can trust my former boyfriend."

"By the way, how is your husband doing these days? He seems to be snakebitten."

"It's been rocky. We haven't spoken much to each other these days. The stress has been unbearable."

"Can I help?"

"Not unless you work with the police."

"I have my connections."

"I'll keep it in mind. Thanks for the offer. You're so kind."

"Have they found who tried to push him off the bridge?"

Kim shook her head.

"I have an idea," Zach said. "I have a friend who is a private detective. She's really smart."

Kim watched Zach reach inside his wallet. He pulled out a business card and handed it to her. "Call her. Her name is Haley Tyler. Just mention my name. I'll take care of the fee as a personal favor to you."

"I can't accept that," Kim protested, raising her hand. "It wouldn't be right."

"You can lower your commission on the lake house. We can call it even."

Kim looked at the card for a moment before dropping it into her handbag. "Thank you, Zach. I'll call her tomorrow. Dinner was terrific."

"Kim, let's take a ride out to the lake house. We'll discuss business. I can drive."

She checked her watch. By now Zach was already behind

her chair. He held out his hand. She stood and grasped it. As they walked toward the door, he offered her his left arm. Kim clutched it while he handed a couple of hundred-dollar bills to the maître d'.

••••••••••

Kim brushed her hair from her face as Zach drove the BMW down the road to the lake house. She saw the quarter moon rising. Looking over at him, she thought he seemed ready for his next deal. And, she believed she was one kiss away from sealing the deal. As the BMW broke the local speed limits, she thought hard and long. She needed to decide now before things went too far. She wanted to promise herself that nothing more would happen between her and Zach Miller, except for business. But deep down inside, she realized the power of his charm, and knew that it could be too much for her to resist. Sighing, she knew what needed to be done. She was committed, at least for now. When she returned home that night, Kim would tell Jonathan everything about the evening.

"So I read about the dead man your husband found in the woods around Oldwyck Pond," Zach abruptly said.

"What about it?"

He looked at her quickly. "What happened?"

"It looked like someone killed the poor man and left his battered body face down in the mud."

"How horrible!"

Kim squirmed in her seat. "Please, let's change the subject."

"Of course. About my offer on the house."

As he pulled up in front of the lake house, she said nervously, "The seller will come down."

Her heart started to pound when she realized where they were parked. It was exactly where she had been attacked, just minutes after she had previously shown Zach the property. She thought back to that day. Kim recalled the sense of calmness on his face while she sped away after the attack.

"Let's check out the beach." Zach opened his door, assuming

no objection would be forthcoming.

Looking at the deep forest outside her passenger window, she said, "I've changed my mind. Please drive me back to my car."

Zach slammed his door shut. "Did I say something to offend you?"

"No, its not you. It's me."

"I don't understand."

She met his sympathetic gaze. "That day I met you here, I was attacked by a man wearing a mask. Right at this spot. It's making me very anxious just being here. Please, let's go."

"Kim, I wish you had told me earlier. I could have helped you find the creep."

She rubbed her neck, stopping at the spot where the attacker's blade had nicked her. "I still have nightmares."

"I completely understand how you must feel. I'll take you back to your car."

Kim began to feel better as he accelerated down the street. She smiled at him, feeling her breathing slowing with each passing mile.

Zach leaned toward her. "Can I ask a question? What did the attacker want?"

"I know you want to help, but I don't want to talk about it."

He seized the wheel tightly. He pushed down hard on the brakes. The BMW came to a screeching halt. Reaching for her hand, he kissed it. Kim did not pull away. She felt herself slipping. He began caressing her shoulders before lightly moving his hand up her neck.

"Such a beautiful neck. Is that a scar from the knife?"

She pulled his hand away. Her pulse quickened. "Who said there was a knife?"

He shrugged his shoulders. "I don't know. It was just a guess."

Kim's hands shook in her lap. "Zach, let's just get my car. I want to go home."

"Of course. I'll call you again."

She nodded, but kept her gaze on the road ahead.

"Just don't forget to call Haley, my friend the P.I."

Kim and Jonathan laid side by side, looking up at the whirling ceiling fan. "Jonathan, face it! Someone is out to get you and our whole family."

"I just told Darden everything."

"Why? That wasn't our plan. The police better not compromise Ashley's safety."

"I had no choice. We have to trust someone."

"How about trusting me for a change?"

"Meaning?"

"I think you should resign as Commissioner and go back into practice. We could relocate. You were a wonderful doctor. Your patients loved you."

"You know that my dream has been to help my country. I promised that to my mom on her deathbed."

"Enough already. How about making a promise to your family? I need you. We need to find Ashley."

He rolled over to face her. She was still staring at the overhead fan. "You need me? That's news to me. You barely talk to me these days."

"Think of how I feel. It's like being married to the public health champion of America."

"What's so bad about that?"

She rolled over and looked at him. "Listen, I married Jonathan, a loving husband and father of our child. Where the hell is he?"

"Working my ass off to get health care improved."

"What about me?"

"I've been here all along. You're the one who strayed."

"Your dream to save the world is killing us," she said.

"When you and I were young, we agreed that we would do whatever it took to make a difference. To make the world a better place."

She pushed on his chest. "Stop it! You're trying to be a hero in a world that has moved way past any idealism, Jonathan."

"I'm no hero. Far from it. I'm just doing what I believe needs to be done."

Kim shut her eyes and rolled onto her back again.

"I have something important to say. Tonight I had dinner with Zach Miller."

"What?" Jonathan shouted. "Why did you hook up with him again?"

"He called me. You know that Zach is my client. It was business."

"Come on... do you expect me to..."

"Nothing happened."

"I have good reason not to trust him."

"Why not? He's been a perfect gentleman."

"Tell me the truth. Are you having ...?"

She yelled, "How can you ask me that?"

Jonathan turned on his back. "Can't you call or meet him during business hours?"

"I met him to discuss his offer for the lake house property."

"That's all that happened?"

"Not exactly. He said he wanted to help us find the person who pushed you and your Hummer off the bridge."

"Why would he care a damn about me?" He wondered whether he should tell Kim about Ashley's text message mentioning a person named Z-something. He decided to keep it to himself, for now.

"He gave me the business card of a private investigator. She's a friend of his. I think we should call her."

He lowered his voice. "I don't like this one bit."

Kim hesitated before speaking again. "One thing that he said really bothered me. It was after I told him that I was attacked at the lake house. When he touched my neck ..."

Rogers leapt out of bed and bellowed, "What? Why the hell was he touching your neck? Was that part of the deal to sell the lake house?"

"It didn't mean anything. He was trying to show that he cared."

"And you wonder why I don't always trust you?"

Kim covered her face with her pillow and said nothing.

He shouted, "What the hell were you thinking? What did you

tell him about being attacked?"

She peeked out from the pillow. "Nothing, that's just it. He mentioned a knife, but I hadn't told him about the knife. How would he know that?"

"You tell me. He's your friend."

Kim threw the pillow at him. "Stop it! Jonathan, I'm scared . . . All I know is that I can't take this anymore. If you really care about me and Ashley, you'll find another medical job and get us away from all of this crap."

"First, we have to find our daughter," Rogers said. "In a week, I'll be the keynote speaker at a national conference of state commissioners. We'll talk again about what I'm going to do after my speech."

He saw the fire build in her eyes. It was obvious that they were at a crossroads. He sat down beside her on the bed and began stroking her hair. He could not recall the last time he had done that.

"Kim, I'll try to make things better."

"Remember the message you received in the special-delivery mailing. It's not too late."

"How did you know about the letter?"

"I found it in your study drawer."

"I had hidden it there to keep it from you."

Rogers took his wife's hand. "Kim, we both need each other more than ever. Let's stop arguing."

Kim leaned her head on his shoulder. "I'm just so frightened of what's happening."

"We'll get help. What's the name of Zach's P.I.?"

"Haley Tyler."

Rogers felt his stomach cramp. It was time to reveal what he suspected. "I have news for you. Zach's friend is probably the one who kidnapped Ashley."

Kim sat up. "Why would you say that? Why would Zach give me her card if she's involved? He cares about me . . . about us."

He saw her face tighten, her eyes wildly darting. "Let's go down to the kitchen. I'll make some coffee. We've got a lot of catching up to do."

Chapter Thirty-Nine

Rogers felt uneasy going to the Commissioner's Forum without Kim, but she had an appointment with her therapist. The day before Jonathan left home, he gave Haley Tyler's business card to Darden, who told him to hold off confronting anyone while they were following Zach Miller. Before leaving Michigan, Rogers told Kim to have no further interactions with Zach and certainly not to contact his P.I.

Back at the same Marriott for the first time since the day he met with the President, the Commissioner peered warily into the lobby before he approached the front desk. Ever superstitious, he requested any floor but the sixth. The reception clerk changed his room to 510 upon his second request.

He tossed his suitcase on the bed. He opened one side to remove his black tuxedo and dressed quickly, deciding to take a stroll on Pennsylvania Avenue for some fresh air. He checked his watch, noting that he was free for thirty-five minutes before he had to give the keynote address. With each step down the Avenue, he felt his head clearing. So much had happened since the past winter. But one fact stood out. He had survived it all.

Rogers crossed the Avenue well before the spot where he was shot. Sidestepping the pigeons that were congregating in a feeding frenzy in the Ellipse, he triangulated his position. He gazed north to the White House before pinpointing the area of the so-called drive-by shooting. For the first time since that day, he recalled seeing the young man who faltered after being shot in the leg. He remembered seeing the redhead approaching him and then being whisked away in a cab just seconds before he was shot.

As Rogers made his way back to the Marriott, he could not help but observe the passersby gawking at him. *With my black-tie outfit, all I need is a stovepipe hat.* He took the elevator to the third floor, where the Capitol Ballroom was located, and ran into a former classmate from Dartmouth Medical School.

"Hank Kettering, good to see you."

"Jonathan, how are you doing these days? I read about all your troubles."

"Kim and I have both survived quite a few challenges this past year. But I'm still trying to serve my country the best I can."

"That's the understatement of the year. You're by far the highest-profile state commissioner of health at the forum."

"Is that because I was the only commissioner who was shot and shoved off a bridge?"

"No doubt those events made you a household name. But rumor has it that you were being considered for Surgeon General until they heard your ideas on mandating pharmaceutical companies to do more to manufacture preventive vaccines like influenza. I'm sure the drug company leaders are throwing darts at your face as we speak."

Rogers cringed. *Zach Miller.*

"Have you spoken with the new Surgeon General?" Hank asked.

"No, I haven't." Rogers changed the subject, "Hank, are you here with your wife?"

"Yes. Is Kim here with you?"

"No, she stayed back in Michigan. Listen, it was great chatting with you. I need to review my notes for my talk. Please excuse me. I'll see you later."

"I'm really looking forward to your presentation. Knowing you, I'm sure you won't pull any punches. Give 'em hell!"

••••••••••

Halfway to the speaker's staging room, Rogers realized he had left his prepared remarks back in his room. He raced up the five flights of stairs, figuring that was faster than waiting for an elevator. He turned the corner of the hallway leading to his room just as a thin person wearing a dark brown hood similar to that worn by monks was leaving his room. Rogers was not sure whether it was a man or woman, since the loose-fitting wool sweater covered up any obvious physical signs of gender. He stopped and retreated back around the corner of the hallway juncture. A few seconds later he sneaked another look. The intruder was gone.

He looked down at his watch. He was due on stage in about five minutes. One thing was clear; he would have to give the speech without his notes. Rogers raced down the two flights, dashing breathlessly into the speaker's room. The forum's greeter for speakers looked at him oddly. He wiped the beads of sweat from his face with his handkerchief and asked for a cold drink.

"How much time do I have before I speak?" he asked nervously.

"I hope you don't mind me saying this, but, Commissioner Rogers, you don't look well."

"I'm fine. Is the current speaker finished yet?"

"She will be in a few minutes."

"I'll be ready. Give me the sign when I'm on."

Rogers sat down on a leather chair in the corner of the speaker's meeting room. The greeter handed him a Diet Coke. He pulled out his cell phone. Kim answered on the fourth ring.

"I don't have much time to talk. There's a small problem. I'll be speaking to the Forum in a couple of minutes."

"You'll do fine. Just go over your notes one final time."

"I don't have my notes, but I don't have time to explain. Please call Detective Darden right now. Tell him I'm speaking at the Marriott on Pennsylvania Avenue. Ask him to contact the DC police. They need to come over immediately to the Capitol Ballroom."

"You're scaring me. What's going on?"

"Someone was in my hotel room."

"Not again! It wasn't a woman, was it?"

"I've got to go. Call Darden immediately. Listen, I love you."

"Hold on, I don't like what I'm hearing. Don't give the talk, Jonathan. Do you hear me? Jonathan?"

He flipped the phone shut.

•••••••••

Random thoughts raced through his mind upon getting the sign from the greeter that he was on in one minute. He thought back to the riddle that he received in the mail. *The old Chambers is dead and we got Sam too. Be nice to Fred or we will get you too.* His daydream was broken by the announcement of his name over the loudspeaker in the Capitol Ballroom. He tugged on his yellow cancer survivor wristband before trotting onto the stage. Standing at the podium, Rogers scanned the audience while adjusting the microphone height.

To his surprise, his fellow health commissioners gave him a standing ovation. Rogers wondered when the DC police would arrive. He drank from the water glass on the podium, nearly draining it before realizing that it might have been spiked. He tried to focus on what he would say, but he kept thinking about the special-delivery letter. *It's not too late. You do not know when the time will come.* The clapping stopped, and the commissioners took their seats. Rogers squinted and rubbed both eyes. The audience seemed like a blur to him. The moderator, seated at the far corner of the stage, cleared her throat as a signal for him to begin.

Rogers fiddled again with the microphone while his vision seemed to sharpen. Most of the attendees were dressed in business suits. He knew most of the commissioners from previous conventions. There were a few attendees in short sleeves. Probably reporters, he guessed, not recognizing any of them. No ski masks or monk outfits. *Where are the police?* He picked up the glass to take a swig but came up dry. His buddy, Hank Kettering, seated in the front row, was making a motion of rolling his index finger in a circular manner.

He cleared his throat. "Thank you, ladies and gentlemen, for your support. As most of you know, it's been a difficult few months for both my family and me."

Rogers motioned to the moderator for a refill on his water. Collecting his thoughts as fast as he could, he took a sip from his refilled glass. He looked down again at his yellow wristband. It had carried special significance to him ever since his cancer diagnosis. Suddenly, his fears dissipated. He felt his passion rising. Rogers felt totally in the moment, almost invincible.

"Every American is entitled to basic health care. It's everyone's right to receive timely vaccines. We should never again hear about shortages of supply. In return for the opportunity for the drug companies to serve every American, there is no question that they are entitled to make a fair profit."

He paused as the audience provided a round of moderate applause. Judging from Kettering's thumbs-up signal from the front row, the Commissioner could tell his words were resonating.

"When I return to Michigan, I intend to propose to Governor Peabody and the state legislature a plan that I hope becomes the law." He heard his own voice soaring over the loudspeakers. It felt good. He knew his mom would be proud. "Fellow commissioners, I ask that you work with me to organize ourselves to lobby for a federal law to guarantee our demands to improve the health of our patients. Shamefully, only one of the two Michigan-based drug manufacturers currently provides an influenza vaccine at this time. I will not publicly cite the name of the company that has ceased production, but they know who they are. In my opinion, they're avoiding public health responsibilities borders on criminal-like behavior. My hat is off to Sunview Pharmaceutical, which understands its moral and ethical duty to the citizens of the great state of Michigan."

He paused for another sip. The audience applauded again.

"It's time that we as physicians stood up for our citizens . . . for our patients. We should be relentless in our pursuit of what is right."

While waiting for another round of applause to die down, Rogers noticed a man and woman entering the ballroom simultaneously from the rear door. The man was middle-aged and wearing a blue blazer over a yellow golf shirt. The woman was younger and wearing a khaki business suit. As they began to approach the center aisle, they split apart. Each took the nearest seat on either side of the center aisle. He recognized the woman. Out of the corner of his eye, he saw the moderator approaching the podium. The Commissioner nodded in agreement to her request that he take a few questions.

The moderator called on Kettering. The Commissioner hoped that his Boston friend would serve up a softball.

Kettering said, "I applaud your initiative. Dr. Rogers, would you be willing to come to Massachusetts to work with me on crafting a state law to ensure the patient rights that you have cited today?"

"I'll be there anytime you invite me. Furthermore, let me say to all the commissioners who believe in what I'm saying, I'll stand shoulder to shoulder with you in our fight to take back the power from those drug companies and the political leaders who do not put the people's interests ahead of their own."

The moderator selected another questioner from the audience. She chose the young woman in the khaki suit. As the woman approached the microphone in the center aisle, Rogers took a deep breath and mentally prepared himself.

"Dr. Rogers, I greatly respect your views on public health. My question is whether you would support a federal law tightening FDA regulations over the drug testing companies. And would you support federal legislation to strengthen the influence of the Institutional Review Boards over the drug testers? As you know, these boards, such as National Quality, ensure that human drug testing is done in an ethical and scientifically sound manner."

"The short answer to your questions is an absolute and resounding 'yes.' And, I would suggest that you also ask that question of the new Surgeon General, Dr. Fresca Gomez."

The moderator stepped up to the podium to announce a twenty-minute break before the next speaker. The Commissioner ventured to descend the stairs that led to the Capitol Ballroom floor, stopping to shake hands with his fellow commissioners. Breaking away after spotting Beth Murphy, he tapped her on her shoulder. As she spun around, he frowned.

"Ms. Murphy, I guess that I shouldn't be surprised to see you here. You seem to show up whenever there's trouble."

"Trouble for whom?"

"Never mind."

"Dr. Rogers, when I visited your office I told you that I work in DC. If you recall, Samuel Murphy used to work for the National Quality Institute."

"I'm not familiar with the Institute."

"National Quality is an IRB. As an independent review board, it supervises drug testing companies doing clinical trials for major pharmaceutical companies. My father was a nurse all his life before he retired to join the board at National Quality. Sam was an ardent advocate of the rights of human participants in drug testing centers. He felt the FDA was not supervising the drug testing companies as carefully as they should have. While he was alive, he was a one-man show at National Quality."

"Sounds like he was quite a man."

"Some called him a whistleblower. Someday maybe I'll tell you the whole story of how great a man he really was. I miss him dearly. And thank you for your comments today. I do intend to follow up with the new Surgeon General. I'll be in touch."

As he watched her leave, the man wearing the blue blazer and yellow golf shirt approached him. Still distracted by the appearance of Beth, Rogers saw him reach into the blazer's inner breast pocket.

"Please come with me, sir."

"What? Who are you?"

The man pulled gently on Jonathan's right forearm while flashing his FBI badge. Rogers complied. Walking with the middle-aged man in silence up the center aisle and out of the ballroom, the Commissioner came to a halt, and held his arm in front of the man."Where are we going?"

"Sir, we have reason to believe you may be in danger if you linger any longer at this hotel."

"What is your name, and where are you taking me?"

"Agent Jeff German. Any additional information will be provided on a need-to-know basis only."

The Commissioner studied German's face. "Did the FBI find out who broke into my room today?"

German replied, "We picked up several clues in examining your room."

"Is that a yes or a no?"

"No comment, sir. We need to get you out of here before you get shot again."

"Again? Why don't you just give me a bulletproof vest?"

Rogers was pulled toward the waiting black sedan at the curbside. The Commissioner climbed into the backseat. Hands in the pockets of his tux, he began to collect his thoughts. He looked over at the agent sitting silently alongside him, and noticed he was holding out a ski mask to him.

"Dr. Rogers, you are a lucky man. Pull down this specially made ski cap over your face. You'll notice there is no way for you to see. We covered the eye holes."

"I don't think so . . ."

Then he saw the standard issue revolver. He sensed his choices were a bare notch over zero. The Commissioner pulled down the ski mask to neck level as ordered just after he noted that the driver seemed to be following signs to Georgetown.

"Thank you, Commissioner, for your cooperation. I'm sorry but this is standard protocol these days in matters such as this."

Tired of his long roller-coaster ride, Rogers laughed. "Don't you just love those protocols?"

"We have our orders," German sternly responded.

"From whom?"

German remained silent.

"I'm sure it must have something to do with national security. It seems as though everything does."

The agent remained quiet the rest of the trip. Blinded by the ski mask, Rogers forced his eyes to remain open, alert for any signs as to what was happening to him.

Chapter Forty

Rogers heard only the usual sounds of traffic and was clueless as to where he was headed. After about ten minutes, the sedan came to a slow stop. Helped out of the car by the agent, Rogers walked alongside, fully masked. After scaling a short step, he believed that he was being led down a long hallway. He felt cool breezes hitting him. Suddenly, their walk came to a halt. German tugged his arm forward. Rogers took two steps and heard the door close just before he felt a sensation of gradual falling. A few seconds later, no longer feeling a descent, he was guided forward. Keeping quick pace with the agent, he picked up mumbled conversation coming from straight ahead. Soon, his guided journey came to an abrupt standstill.

The ski mask was stripped from his face. Rogers blinked away the bright lights as he was asked to sit down. His first image was of three women and two men standing in front of him. Each had a shoulder holster with a revolver and wore a cheerless expression.

Rogers deadpanned, "Did you find my notes? I certainly could have used them during my speech." He rubbed his eyes, gradually focusing.

A woman in her late fifties wearing a simple white blouse and brown slacks took charge. "Commissioner, while you were giving your speech back at the Marriott, a few of our FBI agents searched your room."

He recognized her as Lieutenant Susan Masters. She had once come to visit him at his home along with Detective Darden to question him about Governor Peabody and his own shooting.

"Did you find my notes? I certainly could have used them during my speech."

Masters asked in a stern voice, "Can you describe who you saw leaving your room?"

"Short, no more than five-six, slender build, wearing baggy brown sweat pants. Both the face and head were covered by the hood."

"Man or woman?" German asked.

"Can't say for sure. Only got a fleeting glimpse. I ducked expecting a bullet at any moment. You can just imagine. It wouldn't be the first time."

"Do you know anyone who might fit that description?"

He grinned widely. "Approximately twenty percent of America."

Rogers saw Agent German deposit a dossier an inch thick on the small metal desk in front of them. It was cluttered with a desktop computer, phone, and tape recorder. After glancing at the black leather dossier, Rogers's eye wandered to one of the balding male agents, who moved forward to open the file.

"Take a look, Dr. Rogers. Have you seen this dossier before?"

The Commissioner saw a mostly familiar name in large font across the first page. Not previously ever knowing his boss's full name, his mind focused on the name "Alfred."

"No, this is the first time. I never knew the Governor's full name before, as he always used just a middle initial."

"The intruder must have left this dossier in your room for you to find."

"How do you know?"

"We found it on your bed with a note attached. The note said, The old Chambers is dead and we got Sam too. Be nice to Fred or else.

Rogers began to connect the dots as he stared at the name on the first page of the dossier: Governor William Alfred Peabody. He reached forward to turn the first page, but Agent German swiftly pulled his hand away. Glaring at the agent, the Commissioner remembered the Governor's early morning call before his meeting with President Jordan.

Doc, I want you to be careful with what you say to the President at your interview. Remember to follow your leaders. I put my credibility on the line for you. Don't let the prize slip away. Remember our talks. Be care—

German spoke up. "Sorry, the contents are confidential. Do you have any idea why the intruder would want you to see this?"

"My guardian angel was on duty."

A well-built agent in his early thirties added, "We thought so, too."

"Agent German, back at the Marriott ballroom, you told me that I might be in danger if I stayed at the hotel. Why?"

"All we can say is that the contents of the dossier spell out a plan that involves you," German said.

Rogers looked around the room. "A plan to kill me?"

"Let's just say that we have a plan of our own to protect you. You'll be informed on a need-to-know basis only," added Masters. "Oh, there is also a tape that we want you to hear before we take you to the airport. We obtained it from WPPE radio."

Ignoring Masters, he turned back toward German. "If that dossier was meant for me to find in my hotel room, then why can't I see what's in it?"

"We would have had a real mess on our hands if you had found it. There are names listed that could cause us some real heartburn. The good news is that we got the message meant for you so that we can do what we need to do."

"Sounds like you expect me to trust you to save my life. Based on your track record so far, I don't."

Masters responded sharply, "We do. But let's get back to the radio show tape."

Rogers growled, "Thank God that I requested it. Perhaps the FBI should put me on payroll for all of my work to help you guys to do your job."

Agent German leaned over to start the tape. Rogers scanned the half dozen agents staring at the spinning reels of the old-style RCA recorder. He chimed in, "Is this technology the best the FBI can do?"

Ignoring his comment, Masters said, "See if you can detect an accent on the tape."

The Commissioner listened to a few sentences. "It's obvious. It's a New Yorker."

The Lieutenant nodded. "Let me play the tape at a slower speed. Concentrate on all the sounds you hear."

He listened intently. With the first shrieking whistle sound heard on the tape, Rogers said, "The sound is familiar. It could be coming from the defense factory whistle in DuPont. I hear it every time I visit Tom Knowton."

Masters stopped the recorder and pulled up a chair next to Rogers. She asked, "Do you know any ex–New Yorkers who live in that area?"

He paused before answering. "Not offhand."

Agent German stepped forward. "We'll do our best to protect you. I'll drive you to the airport and accompany you back to Michigan."

"Hold on! I've got to get this off my chest. I'm getting tired of all this secrecy. I'm sick of hearing that everything is a matter of national security. If anything happens to my family, I will hold each of you responsible."

German pulled on his arm. "We have our orders. Doc, we have a plane to catch."

"Orders from whom?"

"Commissioner, put the ski mask on and do as we say."

"And what if I don't?"

"We'll have to force you to . . ."

". . . And protect me?"

"Glad you understand our game plan."

Chapter Forty-One

Appearing in Lauren Timmons's doorway, Zach said mockingly, "I'll bet you missed me."

"What do you want?" she asked while inviting him to join her at the conference table.

"I'll be there just after I lock the door," Zach said. "This meeting is private . . . very private."

"Did you bring a gun?"

"That was last time. Now, we're friends again. But it's time for you to do a good deed for your husband."

"What do I get?"

I'm ready to switch my allegiance to support Adam's run for governor." He noted her eyes lighting up as a subtle grin broke out.

Lauren put her hand on Zach's shoulder. "You're serious?'

"Do as I say and your pictures won't be spread over the Internet. I threw in the Adam thing as a bonus."

"What exactly do you want me to do?"

"You'll prepare a dose of Zazotene based on the Commissioner's weight and age. You'll add the ingredients that our DCP researchers found to increase the chance of side effects occurring. No one would ever suspect to test for these substances. Also, they have a short half-life, so his system will metabolize them while the chemo drug is still present."

"Since when is Zazotene indicated for his lung cancer?"

"You've got to pay more attention to the FDA's recently approved changes for Zazotene."

"Give me a break. Ever since you threatened to expose my pictures the last time we met, I've been a wreck."

"Get over it. Marissa or I will call you for a delivery date to Dr. Knowton's office. Make it happen."

He left her speechless, and slammed the door behind him. Once on the street, he spotted her standing at her office window, looking down at him. He smirked. Zach understood her hot button—her fantasy about being a governor's wife. He stood there a few minutes, watching her shut her eyes as if by doing so, his demand would go away. He kept his sight on her grim-looking face. When he saw her open her eyes, he waved at her. She waved back at him. He was not surprised. He pivoted on his heels and laughed all the way back to his limo.

Chapter Forty-Two

Rogers and Agent German drove off from the Commissioner's home in a rented black Crown Victoria. They headed toward Tom Knowton's office. Arriving for an early-morning Monday chemo session, Rogers ordered German to stay in his car. It was time, he felt, to start breaking loose from the grip the FBI was trying to exert on him. Rogers walked up the oncologist's pathway for what he hoped would be his last treatment. The receptionist informed him that Knowton had been called away on a last-minute emergency. He was told that he could reschedule his session or see Dr. Carver. Rogers elected to get the treatment done, once and for all.

He waited impatiently in the chemo chair for a private Saturday session. The remaining three chemo chairs were unoccupied. Rogers flipped mindlessly through some sports magazines before he looked up to see a familiar face.

"Nicki, " he muttered. "Have you heard from Detective Darden?"

She whispered, "Why?"

"Because if you don't tell him everything you know, he's going to arrest you and your husband. Maybe even Knowton."

"You're stirring up a lot of trouble for yourself if Knowton gets arrested."

"My advice is for you to come clean with the police."

After Nicki came closer to whisper something in his ear, he recalled her warning that he was on the list and that he was in danger. She pressed her mouth against his ear. "I know that you've made progress in figuring things out. It's all up to you. Don't involve the FBI. You know that."

He looked at her blankly. "What exactly are you saying?"

She winked. "Tom was called away to the hospital. Wouldn't you feel better to reschedule your chemo treatment? Call it my advice to you."

"Listen, call Darden. As for me, Victor Carver will give me my chemo. He's as qualified as Tom."

Nicki frowned just as Carver entered the room. The oncologist appeared to be in his typical jovial mood. Rogers believed that his upbeat attitude would make the chemotherapy seem more palatable.

"Jonathan, how are you today? You heard Tom was called away."

"No problem. Let's get started. I'm looking forward to a nice dinner tonight. Kim invited some close friends to celebrate my last chemo session. Since I had no bad effects with the last round of chemo, I plan on devouring a big plate of mashed potatoes, gravy, and turkey."

"Terrific. That's the difference between preventive chemo, like you've been getting, and the kind of chemo we have to use to treat existing cancers, or those likely to spread. There are fewer side effects with the kind of treatment you've had, and the patients generally feel better—more normal—through the whole process. I'll go wash my hands. I'll be back in a minute."

Nicki drew close. She whispered, "Did you get my note?"

"What note?"

"The one you found in the hotel. And what about the letter I sent to your house?"

"I never got a letter or note with your name on it."

She folded her arms across her chest. "Did you expect me to sign it?"

A moment later, the oncologist walked into the room pushing a medical tray table. Carver motioned for Nicki to leave. She hesitated a few moments and stared back at Rogers.

"Nicki, please excuse us. It's time for his chemo." She walked toward the door and turned around to face the Commissioner. She waited until Carver was not looking at her, and then shook her head back and forth.

Rogers ignored her and took the paper Carver was presenting to him. "I'm ready."

"Please sign this informed consent form."

"Sure. No problem." Rogers glanced up to see Nicki's latest

reaction. She had already left the chemo room.

"Just to be clear, my friend, this medicine is a little different than the last time."

"Why is that?"

"Knowton ordered it for you after getting a call from the new Surgeon General."

"Dr. Gomez? Why is Tom talking with her about my medication?"

He called her when our drug representative from DCP recently told him that this chemo treatment had been approved by the FDA for lung cancer based on new data from the clinical trials. He was so shocked that he called Gomez to get her medical opinion. Apparently, she convinced him that the new data was compelling."

"Did you say DCP?"

"Yes. Knowton ordered you to have Zazotene."

Rogers suddenly wished that his oncologist was there. "I want to talk with Tom."

"No can do. He gave me instructions not to bother him."

"Medical emergency?"

"No, personal problems."

Rogers sighed. He wondered if Nicki was involved, and Lord knows who else.

"Is there a problem?"

The Commissioner paused and studied Carver's angelic-looking face for a few seconds. "Can I see the label on the chemo bottle?"

"Of course."

Carver handed over the prescription signed by Knowton specifying the exact dose of Zazotene, which appeared to match the label on the chemo bottle. Rogers did the calculations in his head. The dose was accurate for his body mass index. No chance of an overdose here. His doctor's name was on the label as the prescribing doctor. Looking back to Carver, he saw that his colleague was reading a financial magazine. Rogers went through his mental gymnastics. Logic told him to wait to speak with Knowton.

Tossing Fortune on the floor, Carver yawned as he asked, "Just let me know what you want to do. I do need to get to my next patient."

"Victor, do you agree with Tom's decision to give me Zazotene?"

"Based on the new data from Southwest International that Tom learned about from Gomez, it does make scientific sense. Zazotene destroys any remaining cancer cells by a different mechanism than the chemo you received last time. Tom felt that this would be the icing on the cake. National Quality reviewed the data from the drug testing company and recommended approval by the FDA. It was then fast-tracked through them. Sounds like all bases were covered. But if you're not comfortable with proceeding, we can cancel. It's totally your call, Commissioner. If you're concerned, let's pull up the FDA Web site."

"Let's do that."

Rogers walked down the hall to the nearest computer. Carver signed on and pulled up the official FDA Web site. He did a search on Zazotene.

"There it is," Carver said pointing to the reference. "The new list of FDA-approved indications with doses. You'll note that Tom prescribed the right amount, and according to the FDA, Zazotene is appropriate for your diagnosis."

"I understand. It certainly seems like the right course to pursue."

"Would you like to call the Surgeon General yourself? If you want, I'll get her on the line."

"That won't be necessary. Let's get this over with."

"Commish, are you sure? If you want to wait, that's fine with me."

"Actually, I have read a few medical case reports that did show some promise that the drug works on my type of cancer." Rogers grabbed the consent form and scribbled his name.

Thirty minutes into the Zazotene intravenous drip, Rogers felt extremely nauseous. He dismissed the symptom as a minor side effect while watching each drop empty the chemo bottle. He tried to focus his mind on Kim and Ashley, but he continued to feel increasingly ill.

Soon the Commissioner felt as though his head was about to explode. He yelled out for a nurse. He saw her blurry image appear in the doorway. She placed a plastic eight-inch bucket in front of his mouth. A second later, he felt the rumblings in his gut. With one violent heave, he nearly filled the bucket.

Grabbing another bucket, she yelled, "Dr. Carver, come in here right away."

Rogers caught glimpses of Carver and Nicki running into the room. The nurse shouted out that she just got a blood pressure of eighty palpable. The room was spinning. He thought he saw Agent German wandering around the room. He could not see the blotches popping out on both palms, but wondered why his hands suddenly felt on fire. The room was getting brighter by the second. Everything appeared to be in motion as if he was riding a Tilt-A-Whirl. His last recollection was Carver screaming at Nicki to call for an ambulance.

••••••••••

Rogers awoke in his Mercy Hospital room with a shaking chill. His nurse had just covered him with two extra blankets, making a total of five. Kim was sitting nearby. She told him he had been in a coma for almost two days. Then, piece by piece she filled him in on what he had missed while unconscious. Multiple antibiotics and treatment in the Intensive Care Unit had worked wonders. His white count was finally stabilizing. Normal therapeutic levels of Zazotene had been found in his blood. Knowton and Carver had both been apologetic, explaining that he probably had an allergic reaction. Kim told Rogers how angry she was at Knowton for changing the chemo without speaking first with them.

As the Commissioner lifted his head, he could see a slender woman. He blinked his eyes, trying to focus.

The woman walked toward the bedside. "Dr. Rogers, I'm so

glad you're awake."

He recognized the voice, but her face was still hazy.

"I need your help." Her features now came into focus. Beth Murphy.

"You always seem to show up when there's a problem."

"It's the story of my life."

"What do you mean?"

"One day, at the right time, maybe I'll tell you why my father meant so much to me. Sam was the only one who could solve my problems."

"Why did you come here today?" Kim asked.

Murphy smiled at Kim but spoke to Rogers. "Did you know that Samuel Murphy died in the same bed you are in?"

"Is that why you came, to tell me that?"

Murphy's face hardened. "It's ironic. Both of you had a reaction to Zazotene. Yet, he died and you lived. You seem to have the luck of the Irish with you. Sam obviously didn't."

He demanded, "Stop this. Why are you here?"

"I came here to ask you to join forces with me against Doctor's Choice Products."

"DCP?"

"Do you remember what I told you back at the Marriott after your speech to the health commissioners?"

"Go on."

"Let me paint you a picture. My father was a great man. In many ways, Dr. Rogers, you and Sam Murphy are very similar."

"What has this to do with fighting DCP?"

"Everything! You may not want to hear this, but I believe that you are living life on the edge. Just like my father, you're ruffling a lot of feathers."

He rolled over to face the window. He was in no mood for this kind of talk. Kim then asked, "Can this wait until he gets out of the hospital?'

Beth placed her hands on both hips. "Dr. Rogers, it's your life."

"Hear me out," Rogers said. "My life is a mess. It's been one thing after another since I walked into the White House. The shooting, the diagnosis that never made sense. Kim doesn't

even believe that I ever had cancer. Sometimes I wonder, too."
"Why would you think that?"

"Nothing about the diagnosis made sense. It was a total shock."

"What about a second opinion?"

"I asked my oncologist to compare my DNA to the pathology slide tissue that was read as cancer when they removed a piece of my lung along with the bullets."

"Sounds like an easy thing to do."

"You would think."

"Why don't you just sign it out yourself?"

"God knows I've been trying. Knowton is putting bureaucratic barriers in my way. He claims that he doesn't want the slide signed out of the hospital for fear that it will get lost."

"It's your body. It's your right to know if that tissue on the slide came from you. My father knew that medical errors happened all the time. A nurse could have mislabeled your name on the pathology jar containing someone else's tissue. A few friends of mine at the hospital have told me of similar cases."

"I've been so preoccupied with all that's happened to all of us that I haven't had time to fight the system. I wish you knew someone on the inside at Mercy Hospital. I need someone who can 'borrow' the slide so I can get a DNA comparison without having to hire a thief to steal the damn thing."

"Maybe I can help. I have connections at the hospital's path lab. I have a friend there, Aletha."

"I just want to get out of the hospital. I have other problems that I'm fighting right now."

"I'll be in touch. We need to get DCP."

Rogers cast his eyes downward. He felt like an empty soda bottle, bobbing aimlessly down a river headed for the rapids and the waterfall.

....

Kim walked up the steps to the private investigator's office. She had thought long and hard about what she was doing. She knew that Jonathan would be furious if he knew she was about to meet Haley Tyler. But she was desperate to do anything to find Ashley and find out why such horrible things had been happening to her and Jonathan. She knocked on the door.

A soft voice replied, "It's open."

Kim turned the knob and entered the small twenty-by-twenty office. It was cluttered with stacks of papers in neat piles spread across the floor around her desk. Sitting behind a six-inch pile of folders was a redheaded young woman. "Are you Kim Rogers?"

"Yes. Haley Tyler?"

"That's me."

"I need your help."

"Just take away the papers from the chair and have a seat."

Kim studied her face; she looked familiar. "Zach Miller highly recommended you. By the way, have we met before?"

"Don't think so. How can I help you?"

"It's hard to know where to begin. The bottom line is that someone is trying to hurt my husband and daughter. The police and the FBI have been of no help."

"What's your husband's name?"

"Dr. Jonathan Rogers."

Haley leaned forward. A blush appeared on her neck. "I've been reading about him in the papers."

"I don't know what else to do. Can you help?"

"I believe so. But, you have to promise that you'll tell me everything."

Kim nodded. "I'll tell you every last detail."

"Let's get started." Haley grabbed a notepad and a pencil.

Chapter Forty-Three

Beth checked her watch. She dialed the number of the phone booth on Main and Oak at precisely the time that Aletha promised to be there so that there would be no record of the conversation.

On the sixth ring, she heard a soft response. "Hello."

"My friend, I can always count on you to be on time."

"My job requires precision."

"I received your fax. I was standing at the machine just as it was coming through. The map you drew for me is excellent. I'll dig up the copy of the original keys right after you bury them at midnight tonight."

"Good luck."

"I'll call you the same time tomorrow. If I'm successful, your keys will spend the rest of eternity at the bottom of the Potomac."

••••••••••

Coming off the afternoon flight, Beth felt charged. She had eaten a brief snack on board shortly before arriving at Detroit's Metro Airport at five o'clock. She took off her Red Wings cap during the cab ride to the Holiday Inn just outside of DuPont. Paying cash and checking in as Joan Smith, she carried only her tan attaché. Beth opened the door to room 142 and sat down on the bed to review her plan. She pulled her return ticket from her attaché. She would have at least one hour at Mercy Hospital to collect the confidential information. Holding a six a.m. return ticket to Reagan National, she would be back in DC with plenty of time to call Aletha. Even though she didn't expect to fall asleep, Beth set an alarm for twelve thirty in the morning before lying back in bed to watch some old Western movies on TV.

It seemed as though only minutes had passed when the alarm

startled her awake. She hopped out of bed, quickly brushed her teeth, picked up her attaché, and marched down the stairs to the lobby, smoothing her hair as she went.

Beth paced nervously, waiting for her taxi pickup to the Oldwyck Bus Terminal. Judging by the map, the terminal was less than a block from Stony Brook Park. She paid her fare to the cabbie just as the bus was powering to depart. She ran to jump on board. Except for the driver, she was alone. At the third stop, she got off the bus and walked a few hundred feet in the darkness. She spotted the sign under the last lamppost. Stony Brook Park. An arrow pointed to the right. Beth searched the street. The town seemed almost abandoned; not one car had passed her since she hopped off the bus. The shattered lamppost light at the entrance to Stony Brook Park gave her plenty of reasons for pause, but she was committed to continue, to help him. She walked down the main pathway, surrounded by five-foot-high shrubbery. From her memory of Aletha's map, the boulder on the hill before the playground was up ahead about a hundred feet or so on the left. She broke into a run.

Beth caught a glimpse of the car-sized boulder and ran toward it. Aletha would have buried the key only an hour earlier. The dirt behind the boulder would be freshly turned. She dug as fast as she could while keeping a wary eye on her surroundings. Her senses throttling on edge, she came upon a metal object. Beth felt the sharp edges. She picked it up. It was key number one. After another few seconds of digging, she found the second key. She grabbed both of them and ran as fast as she could toward the entrance of the park. She did not stop until the streetlights surrounding Mercy Hospital came into view.

Under the bright lights outside the main entrance to the medical center, she checked the second map one last time. Beth calculated that she would need to enter the hospital through a side entrance near the morgue. Noting the swamp behind the hospital, she navigated the perimeter. A barred owl flew silently overhead. It was almost two in the morning when she spotted the side door next to the pine tree. She took a bottle of water from her attaché and doused the keys and her hands to remove the dirt, then dried her hands and the keys in the grass. She inserted one of the keys. The lock turned easily as the door opened.

She put the water bottle back in her case, pulled out a penlight, and beamed it straight ahead. The long corridor reminded Beth of her high school. Closing the outside door behind her, she walked slowly forward while checking off in her mind each of the names on the offices that she passed. Up ahead, she could hear distant voices. She was ready to sprint back to the outside door just as the voices appeared to fade. She took a series of deep breaths. From behind her she heard loud, barking calls. Hoo-hoo-too-hoo. Hoo-hoo-too-hoo. Damn owl. In the distance, she heard a gurney rolling over the tiles. Think. Every second she just stood there in the middle of the corridor would be one second closer to a tap on the shoulder by a security guard. Turning on her tiny beacon, Beth searched quickly for the room where Aletha worked.

As each step drew her further away from the only exit, every muscle tensed. Her jaw throbbed in pain. Out of the blue, she hit pay dirt. Next to the number on the door, she saw the word printed on the glass that made up the top half of the door. Pathology.

She inserted one of the keys. It didn't fit. The key felt gritty, so she spit on it, wiping it against her faded blue jeans. Beth heard footsteps. Locked on the sound of shoes striking the tiled floor, the approaching echoes became louder with each passing second. The exit door to the parking lot was a full fifty feet away. She inserted the cleaned-up version of the key, holding her attaché case between her knees. It still didn't fit. Shit! Craning her neck, she could now see that she was ten feet from a perpendicular hallway to the corridor from where she had entered. Half-crazed that she didn't notice the other passageway earlier, she noticed the hallway lighting up, brighter by the moment. From the increasing cadence of the footsteps, it seemed that someone was just about to make the turn into her corridor.

She frantically looked down at the keys and tried the second one. The door opened immediately. She scurried inside, with her attaché case in her left hand. She pushed the door slowly until the latch caught with the barest of a click. Beth looked up from her hiding perch, her butt pressed against the door. The light was now shining brightly through the opaque glass of the door. The footsteps stopped. She could hear a man mumbling to himself about whether he had heard a sound by the door. A terrifying thought came to her: *The door is unlocked.* One turn of the knob by the security guard and she would be discovered. But the knob never moved.

She snaked along the floor as if in combat. Six feet from the door, she bumped her head into a lab bench. Beth held back a cry of pain. Holding the attaché case close to her body with one arm, she removed her sneakers and stood. As she tiptoed behind the file cabinet, she heard the turning of the pathology lab doorknob. The security guard's flashlight highlighted most of the room. A second later, Beth heard two or three more footsteps. Another few feet to the left and he would find her. Suddenly, there was complete silence.

She held her breath, the top of her head beginning to ache from her recent bump on the bench. Beth could smell the guard's body odor. She again heard his footsteps, but this time they sounded different, fainter. The room grew darker by the moment. Not moving a muscle, she heard the door close with a bang.

Her chest pounded. She heard the central air conditioning cycle on. No footsteps. A minute passed. She then peeked out from the level of the cabinet drawer second from the floor. She saw nothing ahead of her. Beth sensed that no one remained. She tiptoed toward the lab bench. The silence was total except for the hum of the AC. If he was still there, he would be around the last bend by the bench. She peeked carefully. He was gone.

Beth turned the doorknob and found that it was unlocked. The guard probably didn't have the right key. But she was sure that he would be returning soon with the right set of keys to lock the door. And there was no inside lock.

Beth stood there for a moment, not knowing how long she

had to accomplish her mission.

She pulled Aletha's map from her pocket and pointed her penlight at the crumpled paper. Her target was the file cabinet by the lab bench. Looking up, she realized that she was already there. She opened the bottom drawer and glanced over the file names. Raymond, Reynolds, Ripin, Rizakowski, Rugers. No Rogers. She continued to flip the manila folders. The Commissioner's file was missing. Her eyes widened, and she frantically searched one more time. Then she found it misfiled under the next letter in the alphabet. Rogers. Thank God! Turning toward the door, she heard the owl hoot once more.

She opened the Rogers and Rugers files, and found the pathology slides tightly tucked into their compartments. She took one slide from each folder and inserted them into a compartment box strapped inside her attaché case.

She ran for the pathology room door, then turned the knob quickly. She was in the corridor a second or two later. Quietly closing the pathology room door, she picked up the approaching footsteps. The guard's light beam grew brighter. The sound from the footsteps grew louder. With her sneakers in her left hand and her priceless cargo in the other, she raced toward the exit door. *Don't look back. Don't stop running*!

Reaching the exit, she flung herself against the bar that opened the door. The night breeze touched her sweaty face. The owl called once again. Hoo-hoo-too-hoo. Hoo-hoo-too-hoo. She ran across the parking lot, her bare feet aching with every strike on the pavement. Beth ran for another forty yards before putting on her sneakers. No one was in sight. She ran as fast as she could to the Oldwyck Bus Terminal with her attaché case swinging wildly at her side. Hopping on the bus, she allowed herself at last to close her eyes.

••••••••••

Nearing a phone booth in DC, Beth approached a deep-water tributary leading to the Potomac. She heaved both keys as far as she could into the river, then walked to the streetside phone booth and dialed Aletha. The hospital lab insider picked up on the second ring.

"Mission completed. Don't forget to report that someone left the outside and inside door unlocked."

"Will do."

"I owe you."

"We're even."

Chapter Forty-Four

"Jonathan, glad you stopped by the office. I want to apologize again for changing your chemo cocktail to Zazotene without telling you beforehand. It was an allergic reaction. There was no way that it could have been predicted. According to the FDA studies, it was administered under the latest standard of care."

Rogers snarled, then threw down his DNA report on the desk. "Explain this!"

Knowton's hand trembled as he picked up the DNA comparison analysis. Reading the report, he nervously glanced between Rogers and the executive summary.

"Well, Tom, it looks as though you need some help in interpreting the results. The conclusion is that there is a 99.9 percent probability that my DNA doesn't match the DNA on the lung biopsy taken in DC."

Knowton kept on his eyes on the report. "This doesn't absolutely prove that you didn't have cancer. It's still possible."

"I would have had some last ounce of respect for you if you had just admitted a mistake was made." Rogers threw down another report. "It's the DNA from Mickey Rugers. He's the man who had lung surgery in the operating room next to mine, on the same day as mine. I located him. He still lives in town. He agreed to have his DNA checked. After all, he's a three-pack-a-day smoker. Rugers was finding it hard to believe that his lung biopsy was normal. He was losing weight and spitting up blood."

"How did you find him? That's a HIPAA violation of his privacy rights."

"Rugers waived those rights. He is now getting proper treatment for the cancer that he was told he never had. As a specialist, you will know whether the delay in the correct diagnosis caused by the hospital mix of specimens will adversely affect his prognosis."

Knowton remained silent and opened the Rugers report.

"Tom, I've never seen you so quiet. I'll help you out again. There is a 100 percent match of Rugers's DNA with the DNA from the lung biopsy that was supposedly removed from my lung."

The oncologist's hands trembled. "Accidents happen, Jonathan. Labs mix up biopsies. It wouldn't be the first time that this has happened."

"Then why didn't you just admit a mistake was possible?"

Knowton replied quickly, "I was afraid you would sue me and Mercy Hospital for malpractice."

"Why would I or Mickey Rugers sue you? We would only have a claim against anyone who did mix up the samples. If it was a lab accident, it wouldn't have been your fault."

Knowton turned his head away. "I . . . I don't know what to say to you."

"Just say the words I want to hear. Say them to me. It's the least that you can do." Knowton's jaw clenched several times. Biting his lower lip, he locked on Rogers's gaze.

"My God, Tom, you took the Hippocratic Oath. What has happened to you?"

Knowton leaned back in his chair. His chest was heaving, his eyes darting around the room.

"God forgive me." His voice dropped. "You never had cancer."

"God will forgive you, Tom . . . unless you knew the tissue samples of Rugers and me were intentionally switched."

Knowton covered his face with both hands. Perspiration beads gathered on his forehead.

"Jonathan, please forgive me."

"I think you need to talk with Mickey Rugers. This lab mix-up could have cost him his life."

"I can't. They would kill me."

Rogers sucked in a full breath, reflecting on what his oncologist just said. This was no simple lab error. Others were involved.

"Tom, we've been friends for decades. You've been one of the best oncologists in the country. How could you have gotten involved in something like this?"

Knowton put his head on his desk and began to sob. Rogers felt no sympathy for his friend. His daughter was missing, likely as a result of the same conspiracy that had sucked in Tom Knowton.

The oncologist lifted his head. Tears streamed down his reddened face. He mumbled, "I'm a dead man, Jonathan . . . a dead man."

Chapter Forty-Five

Zach woke up early. He had tossed uneasily most of the night. He had asked Victor Carver to meet him at the baseball field at the county park. While driving to the park, he finalized his plan. He believed that this latest ploy would shift attention away from him. After his dinner with Kim, he realized he had made a serious blunder when he mentioned that her scar was made by a knife. Something had to be done to remove the bulls-eye from his chest.

He waited in the dugout for his mark to arrive. The oncologist wandered about the outskirts of the baseball diamond.

"Victor, over here."

Zach sat patiently on the bench. He felt like a manager summoning the closer to save the game. Yet he never believed that Carver was a game saver. Victor playfully kicked the bag as he crossed first base. Zach knew what happened when teams lose. The relievers became free agents and the manager got fired. He had figured out a way to change that scenario. While Carver was crossing the coach's box, Zach prepared to throw his best knuckleball.

The oncologist shouted, "What's up, Boss?"

Now standing, Zach gave Carver a high-five just after he jumped down the last step into the dugout. "I just thought we would play a little pitch and catch, in a manner of speaking."

"You've been the pitcher so far. I've been catching your fastball for years. But to be honest, you're capable of a few wild pitches. You should have given the Uzi to a real man, not to your nephew."

Ignoring his crack, Zach replied, "You're right. I've been sort of the unelected leader of The Health Club. Well, maybe it's time for me to take a rest and let the brainy guys like you take the lead for a change. Unlike you, I never got into med school."

He could see that he had struck a chord by the way Carver's face brightened. This was exactly the reaction that he wanted. It was so predictable. Zach pressed on with his game plan.

"You know, I wasn't too pleased that they found such high doses of Zazotene in Murphy's body."

"I got the job done, didn't I?"

"Don't insult me. You know damn well that DCP doesn't need any bad publicity. Why would you use Zazotene? The potassium chloride killed him, not our chemo."

"I had my reasons."

"Don't be stupid. I'm talking about the press. I'm talking about Rogers and Knowton. They're always ready to pick a fight with DCP."

"Fear not, Zach."

"Well, as long as I'm the boss, we'll do it my way. Is that clear? I think you screwed up by mixing in the Zazotene. Next time, I want all things cleared through me."

Carver grinned. "Mixing the drug was no accident. You might say it was my ace in the hole."

Zach had already figured that Carver mixed in the Zazotene with the real killer drug just to keep Zach and DCP in the mix. Just to give him an out, if the authorities got too close. It was time for a countermove.

He patted Carver's shoulder. "And stop pushing Rogers over bridges."

"Please . . . I'm so sick of his smugness all these years. He wants to save the world. So I did it on impulse. I was riding along in my pickup truck and there he was, right in front of me. To be honest, I never had more fun. I can't believe he survived the fall."

"Listen, my friend, this is business. Next time, clear it with me or else."

He saw a gleam appearing in Carver's eyes. "So, what if I take over as the leader?"

"Then you can make the rules. Until then, you check with me. OK, Doc?"

Zach watched Carver pace the dugout, kicking up some loose dirt. Noticing a few nervous twitches, he believed that he had his man on the ropes.

Zach lay down on the dugout bench. As he let the silence permeate the spring air, he realized that deep down, he no longer wanted to drive from the pole position. *Everyone is gunning for you!* He wanted to drop back a notch or two. All that mattered was who finished first in the end. He had cast his hook. It was only a matter of time before he would get a nibble.

Carver pulled out a pack of Lucky Strikes. Zach shook his head. It was time to go for the jugular.

"You know, I changed my mind. I don't think you're ready to lead us."

Taking a long drag, Victor shot back angrily, "Why not?"

"Well for starters, you don't even have enough willpower to keep off those cancer sticks. You should know better. You need to be disciplined to lead our team."

"I'd love to see if you have the guts to take accountability for day-to-day life and death decisions. I've made them for decades. Do you think it's easy for physicians to see patients dying under our care?"

Playing along, Zach asked sarcastically, "So how did you do it for all these years?"

"I learned my lesson. I survived by not getting emotionally involved with any of them. In my early days in practice, I would beat myself up every time someone died. But I knew it couldn't last. Half of my patients died every five years. It happened so often, I became numb to death. I did what I needed to do to get through each day."

"Was it tough handling Sam Murphy?"

"No, he was just another cancer death at Mercy Hospital. When the nurses called me on my cell ten minutes after I left the hospital, they knew that I had just visited him a short while before. I feigned being upset. They bought it right away. I told them to call his daughter about the bad news."

"Just like that?"

"Just like that. It was just another day in my life."

"Is Knowton like that, too?"

"No. He tortures himself with every decision. He agonizes over every single death."

"Then maybe you are strong enough to lead the group. It's yours for the asking.".

Carver stared back at him. The CEO stroked his chin.

"So, do you want to be the leader? Yes or no?"

Smiling as Carver paused, Zach was prepared to reel in his fish.

"If you can't make up your mind, then I'll give it to my nephew, Rick. Just to keep it in the family."

"That young prick. He's just a kid. Listen pal, I'll take the lead for The Health Club. I want the ball. You'll now catch what I throw. I'm in charge and you can tell your nephew to jump off a bridge before I push him off as well."

Zach grinned as he sealed the deal with a firm handshake. "Whatever you say, Boss. Whatever you say."

••••••••••

Zach counted up the scores after watching Marissa three-putt into the cup. They were only two strokes down to their opponents. There was still time to win. *Four holes to go.* He predicted that Marissa would win strokes for their team by distracting Carver, knowing that the oncologist would be rushing his putts to get back on the golf cart with her.

While watching Carver drive off with Marissa huddled so close that the doctor was halfway off the seat of the cart, Zach drove his cart and kicked off his conversation with the Governor.

"Fred, how's the fundraising going for your re-election campaign?"

"Great. My war chest has over six million. And I'm ahead by six points in the early polls against Adam Timmons."

"DCP donated plenty, you know."

"It's much appreciated, Zach."

"That's the good news."

Peabody frowned. "And, the bad is . . ."

"To be honest, I'm now publicly supporting Adam Timmons. It was payback. Business, nothing personal."

Peabody gulped. "Did the President sign off on your decision?"

"What do you think?" Zach laughed. "Let's change the subject. Fill me in on the details of the Rogers shooting. We never had a chance to discuss them."

"Give me a minute to get over not being re-elected." Peabody wiped his forehead.

Zach pretended to place a karate chop on the Governor's wrist. "Drop it. We've got more important things to discuss."

"The President believed that he could have used the Commissioner on his team. Rogers's excellent reputation among the public would have been a real political asset in a second Jordan term. He could have been a silent show horse—our figurehead for The Health Club. But at his interview with the President and his Chief of Staff, Tracey London, our boy would not back off on his radical ideas to pressure drug companies."

"I think I heard this part."

"The Chief of Staff mostly worried about Rogers's keynote address to the National Commissioners of Health Conference in DC. She wanted to stop him before he infected every state commissioner with his silly idealism. She was right to pull the trigger. Because he survived our attacks, Rogers gave that speech. My God, from what I've heard, it sounded like he was leading a one-man jihad against the drug companies."

"Yes. It was just as London predicted; he did rile up the Commissioners at the Forum. They're putting a lot of pressure on Congress to pass laws that will hurt our profitability."

"And for us politicos as well. The President and I don't get elected based on our policies. Cold hard cash creates the wins. And certain companies in big pharma are some of our best cash cows. Too bad your nephew missed. An inch to the left or right and we wouldn't still be talking about him."

"I think my nephew needs a little more practice for the next time. I'll have to come down on him a little."

Peabody added, "Maybe Rogers will start backing off. Don't know how much more he can take. His missing daughter has stopped him in his tracks."

"For me, taking that chance isn't good enough. Sooner or later, he'll stumble upon The Health Club. He's got to go."

"He seems to have the luck of the Irish."

Zach pulled up to bump Carver's cart. The huddled occupants hardly noticed the intentional shove. Zach cackled. Carver had been so far off his seat that he landed on his backside after the mild collision.

Zach pointed to the fallen oncologist. "Victor, why don't you tee off?"

"After I get off my ass."

"Carver, maybe you could use a seatbelt."

Victor's eyes roamed to Marissa. "I'd rather try a condom instead."

Zach picked up on the vibes Marissa was sending Carver's way. The CEO yelled out, "Hey Carver, keep your eyes on the golf ball."

As Carver's ball sliced deep into the woods, Zach laughed. "Looks like we now have a match."

Marissa smiled sensuously. "Actually, I like playing with Victor. I like winners."

Zach glared at Marissa and then drove his ball into the woods. "Never bet against me, my dear. I always find a way to win."

Chapter Forty-Six

Zach walked up the gangplank of the Prince America cruise ship. He marveled at the beautifully crafted ship. Made of teakwood, it carried just over nine hundred passengers. He looked back at the Los Angeles port and the smog in the distance. He soon realized that the DCP party alone comprised over two-thirds of the ship's manifest. Scattered throughout the six hundred oncologists on board were another hundred or so tourists eager to leave the smog for sunny Baja California. A staff of another hundred and fifty completed the ship's load.

On the way over to the harbor, the drug baron had calculated the cost of the trip. Driving Zazotene sales just two percent higher for the next quarter alone would more than pay for the expenses of the six hundred doctors. All of them would soon be prescribers. The real value of this elite group of oncologists was in leading the way for the thousands of their peers around the country who looked to them for clinical leadership.

Zach checked on the whereabouts of key people. He confirmed with the bursar that eighty-five percent of his doctor guests were already on board, but most important, Tom Knowton was one of them.

In the master suite, Zach admired his reflection in the windows before sitting down to jot a few notes. He planned to meet with his business partners at noon the next day to announce the leadership change of The Health Club. Afterward, he would host a private meeting with Knowton. He stretched his muscles, envisioning the following day's meeting with the rank-and-file doctors. At that time, the well-respected Tom Knowton would tell six hundred of his peers that Zazotene was better than sex. Zach could then relax.

••••••••••

His cell phone, set up for international use, delivered the news from the bursar's office. All the invited doctors were on board. Zach showered and headed off to mingle before dinner. Dressed in a Brooks Brothers blue blazer, white slacks, and white Topsider boat shoes, he was pleased to see women turning their heads as he walked about the deck. He spotted Nicki walking all alone in her spaghetti-strap white sundress and Givenchy navy suede stingray heels. An idea struck him. Grabbing a couple of Kangaroo cocktails off a passing waiter's tray, he called out her name.

She stopped as he caught up to her. He passed her a martini. "Good evening, Mrs. Sanderson. Is Mr. Sanderson getting ready for dinner?"

Accepting the drink without gratitude, Nicki drained the glass in just a few gulps. "He's on board, but I have a restraining order forbidding him to come within twenty yards of me."

"Sleeping alone tonight, Nicki? Or is it possible that you hit the jackpot? I don't believe I saw Veronica Knowton's name on the manifest."

She turned away from him. "That's none of your damn business."

"Spare me. In any case, I would appreciate anything you can do to help tomorrow's meeting with the good doctor go smoothly. And, my dear, in case you forgot, anything concerning Dr. Knowton is my business."

"We're just friends."

"Then maybe you can be lovers again."

"He's moved on. He says he loves his wife. I've resigned myself to that."

"We'll talk soon."

Zach surveyed the deck. He began to stroll in order to mingle with as many guests as he could. Glancing back at Nicki, he added, "I'll see you at dinner. Have fun."

He chuckled upon seeing Victor Carver and his wife walking hand in hand and heading in his direction. Zach couldn't remember the last time that he had held hands with Alexis. For the next hour, he counted up the faces of some thirty doctors that he greeted, all the while enjoying the sight of the physician pigeons walking around in their ship-deck leisure wear.

As the sun set, he headed for the main dining room. He ran into Marissa. She was wearing a casual black crisscross dress with low back exposure. He was not surprised at her cold demeanor toward him. Giving her a peck on her cheek, he vowed to get her back for her comment on the golf course.

Zach checked out the seating arrangements. He had mixed the pigeons he wanted to capture tonight with the feeders that were already on the payroll. He expected a lot from Carver and Sean Parker. They were high-priced DCP pigeon-feeders.

He circled his table, strategically placed in the center of the ballroom, to view the name cards. He chose Knowton to be seated to his right. As his physician guests began filing in to find their pre-arranged seating, he welcomed as many as he could. He shook hands with the five physicians who sat down at his table, all the while searching for Knowton.

He made mental note of the names of the oncologists at his table. Each had been carefully chosen based on leadership ability and geographic influence. In his mind, they would be the early disciples of Knowton. Learning their backgrounds prior to the cruise, he believed each of them was a mini-Knowton in many ways. However, the only oncologist who was widely known nationally was the doc who would soon be seated to his right. As he scanned the ballroom, he felt a tap on his shoulder from behind. It was Marissa, with Knowton in tow.

Zach noticed that the ballroom was nearly full. He stood while watching his staff trying to quiet the room so the boss could speak. He turned his gaze to every corner of the room while holding his champagne glass at his side. He was pleased to see that with a conductor's swift upward move of his left hand, everyone stood.

"Good evening, ladies and gentlemen. Welcome to the cruise to Cabo San Lucas sponsored by Doctor's Choice Products. We hope that you thoroughly enjoy your stay with us. We're pleased that you'll have the opportunity to earn Continuing Medical Education credits by attending our seminar on cancer drugs.

In particular, we believe you'll be impressed by the latest data around our Zazotene. Our main speaker, Dr. Tom Knowton, is an acknowledged expert on chemotherapeutic agents. As the CEO of Doctor's Choice Products, I'm extremely grateful that he was able to squeeze this cruise into his extremely busy schedule."

Grinning, he bowed slightly toward Knowton. "Two days from now, we'll dock in Cabo around eight in the morning. The tenders will ferry you in so you can enjoy the town until noon. We'll start heading back to L.A. later that day. Our seminar will begin that afternoon at three sharp while we're sailing back to California."

Zach then raised his champagne glass high in the air. He watched the entire ballroom following suit. "But tonight I would like everyone to enjoy a great dinner and a relaxing night at sea."

He took a long sip. A second or two later, he covered his heart with his right hand while raising his champagne glass a second time with the left. "A toast to the health of the American people through better pharmaceuticals."

In unison, most of those in the room, prompted and led by DCP staff, loudly responded, "To the health of the American people."

Zach sat down to feast on roast duck, jumbo shrimp, and lobster tails. After the physicians at the table polished off the champagne, he leaned over to whisper in Knowton's ear. "I'm looking forward to our talk tomorrow afternoon in my cabin. By the way, what's the latest on how Alexis is doing?"

Knowton asked, in an annoyed tone of voice, "Don't you know?"

"We haven't had a chance to talk. I've been so busy at work. I hope she has not taken a turn for the worse. I would miss her dearly."

Knowton smirked. "Alexis has stabilized on my current treatment. I'm hopeful for her prognosis. As for our meeting tomorrow, be aware that I continue to have strong feelings on the appropriate uses of Zazotene."

"Doctor, let's just enjoy the evening. There will be plenty of time to talk tomorrow about your prescribing the same drug to Dr. Rogers and Sam Murphy."

Zach saw Knowton's eyes light up. He had set the fuse. He turned away from his main attraction and gave Marissa a hug. With all eyes on him, he said to his dinner mates, "I am so proud to be having dinner with the finest oncologists in America. Please let me know if there is ever anything that DCP can do for you."

••••••••••

Zach sent the email to The Health Club members early the next morning. They were ordered to appear at the private meeting room, just off the Swordfish Lounge.

Zach sat at the head of the table. Rick Miller, arriving by tender from town, was posted at the door to greet each of the team members. Hunter Sanderson was the next to arrive. Nicki arrived shortly afterward and sat opposite Hunter around the ten-foot oval table. Neither of them spoke a word. A minute later, Haley Tyler and Victor Carver arrived.

Zach opened the meeting, "First item on the agenda is the announcement of the new leader of The Health Club. Victor and I have talked. He'll step up as our leader once we all get back to Michigan. Any questions?"

Sanderson grunted and stood up. "What's the reason for the change? We're doing just fine with you as our leader."

"Hunter, thanks for your support. Victor and I thought it was time for a change. We're a team. Change is good."

Zach saw Rick's face growing red. "Something to say, Rick?"

"Uncle Zach, I thought you and I would talk before you offered the lead to anyone else."

"Well, our DC members were not too happy when you didn't kill Rogers with your Uzi."

"So, that's why I was passed up?"

"That and a few other things, like landing in Cabo instead of Puerto Vallarta."

Watching Hunter nod, Zach continued the meeting. "I will be meeting with Dr. Knowton this afternoon. I hope our meeting goes well. Victor, any recon?"

"Tom was not in any mood to discuss anything last night. He seemed upset about something. As far as I can tell, he went directly to his room after dinner and no one has seen him since."

"What if he balks?" Hunter queried.

"We've worked out a contingency plan." Zach's eyes rested on Nicki.

Hunter gave Nicki a hostile look. With an edge to his voice, he asked, "What exactly is the contingency plan?"

"Zach was talking to me," Carver replied.

"Okay boys, let's move on. Hunter, don't worry. We have a plan."

Sanderson responded, "I trust you Zach. That's about it."

"No problem. Listen, I want each of you to circulate as much as possible before our meeting with the doctors tomorrow at three. I want you to report anything you hear, see, smell, or even think might be relevant to our business. At the meeting, you will take down the name of any oncologist who seems to be unsure of the value of Zazotene. Marissa and I will meet personally with those fence-sitters."

Each member of The Health Club nodded in approval.

"Marissa has a way with smart people, especially the men."

Carver added, "She and I will work together. She seems to like me."

Zach surveyed the team. All eyes were upon him. "Any final questions?"

Carver stood up. "No, but you won't believe who is on this ship."

"The ghost of Christmas Future," he wryly shot back.

The soon-to-be leader seemed pleased to share the news. "Dylan Mathews. I saw him sneaking around the ship earlier today."

"He's so incompetent that he couldn't shoot his way out of a paper bag."

"Then maybe he'll try to throw you overboard."

Zach picked up on the oncologist's cockiness, his fatal flaw, which the CEO knew one day might come in handy. He turned toward the redhead. "Haley, keep an eye out for Mathews."

Zach turned to his nephew, who looked more pissed than ever. "Rick, I hope you paid off the guard well to watch Ashley. She'd better be there, or there'll be serious consequences for you."

His face still a bold crimson, Rick replied, "I guess I'm still good enough for the crap jobs."

Zach turned his back on Rick. "Oh, and one last point before you all leave. I don't want to see any of you hanging around together."

Zach puffed his chest, thinking of how he would miss being in charge of The Health Club. But for now, he had more work to do to shield himself from the spotlight. It was the only way to survive. And survival was all that counted.

Chapter Forty-Seven

"Well, if it isn't Lieutenant Masters and Agent German. Please come in."

Rogers motioned for them to sit on the living room couch directly opposite his wife.

The Commissioner paced the floor. He said, "Let's start out with what you know about Governor Peabody. It seemed that things turned south just after he emailed me in DC. That was just before my meeting with President Jordan."

Susan Masters responded, "We've permission to tell you more than you currently know. However, we are not permitted to discuss anything related to President Jordan in any way."

"I'm listening."

"We've good news for you. The Harris police force today picked up the man who was taped in the casino with you and the deceased hooker."

"And . . .?"

"The police cut a deal with him. He was a two-time loser, wanted for armed robbery. Spent five years in state prison. Police got him to confess to killing the woman on a plea down on a lesser charge of manslaughter. He claimed all of you were taking drugs that night and having one big party."

"That's a lie!"

"Doesn't matter. The Harris police dropped all charges on you after we spoke with them."

Kim said, "Jonathan, let it go. It's one less worry. We still have more than our share."

"All right, so who shot me? And where is our daughter?"

Masters began calmly, "Let's start with what we know for sure. We have the computer records showing that Governor Peabody emailed you to request that you cooperate with the pharmaceutical companies. By tying in the threatening note phrase that you need to be nice to Fred with the fact that Governor William

Alfred Peabody has an eight percent stake in DCP stock, the Governor is most likely the Fred in your letter."

"We already figured that out. So do you think the Governor shot me?"

"Of course not."

"Then who?"

The FBI lieutenant took a quick glance at German and changed the subject. "Dr. Rogers, we have learned through our sources that DCP has hired a cruise ship that is presently on its way to Cabo San Lucas. Detective Darden and our team had discussed Zach Miller and his company after you thought he might be the man named Z-something in the text message from your daughter."

"Where's Ashley?"

"We don't know."

"I don't believe you." Rogers pointed to the front door. "Answer my questions or get out of our home."

Masters leaned forward. "We now have reason to believe that your shooting was not a simple drive-by. Whoever shot you also shot the other young man in the leg, most likely to make it appear as though you weren't their target. We now believe whoever sent you the letter was an insider to this conspiracy to get you. It was an attempt to warn you of the danger you are facing."

Kim spoke up. "But you still haven't solved the case, have you?"

"We're doing our best. First of all, Tom Knowton is the featured speaker on the DCP cruise to Mexico. He's expected to be lecturing to over six hundred cancer specialists. The FBI already has undercover agents on board. We believe you must join the cruise in order to help us determine if there is a connection to your attempted murder."

Rogers could feel the anger building in Kim. Her face became increasingly contorted. "My husband is not on the federal payroll. He's not bait for your hooks to catch the bad guys."

Masters stood and said, "Mrs. Rogers, your husband has seriously upset many important political and well-connected business power brokers. I hate to say this, but unless we crack the case, it's only a matter of time before they will succeed in eliminating him. We need to find them before they get to him. We've been playing defense. It's just not working. We have to go after them."

Kim turned toward her husband. "Don't listen to them."

Rogers walked over to the front door and flung it open. "Get out of our home immediately. Don't contact me again until you can tell me exactly who shot me and what you're going to do to stop these attacks on my family."

German walked toward his hosts with both palms facing upward. "Dr. Rogers, we . . ."

The Commissioner pulled his own hands back from his initial instinct to shove the agent through the door. Lowering his voice, he said, "Out."

"I'm calling Brent Marshall. He should be back from Europe by now. Maybe he'll have some ideas."

As he was walking toward the phone, it rang. He hit the speaker function by habit.

"Hello?" From the start, he recognized her voice.

"This is Alexis Miller," she said in her usual cascading, scratchy voice.

"I've been hoping that you would contact me. Do you have any news?"

"A young woman visited me yesterday at my home. She has good reason to believe her father was killed by someone in my husband's little band of friends."

"Yes, I know. It's Beth Murphy."

"Just listen to the young woman when she calls you."

"Mrs. Miller, you've said this before. What about Zach? Is he involved?"

"My husband is a dangerous man. But I must go now. I'll pray for you and your family. Good-bye, Dr. Rogers."

••••••••••

Rogers hung up the phone and sat down on the couch. He looked at Kim. "What if the FBI is right? Maybe I should go on the cruise."

"Are you crazy? The FBI has been no help. And Mrs. Miller sounds as though she is on her deathbed. Maybe she has Alzheimer's. Who knows if she understands what she is saying?"

"Why shouldn't we believe her?"

"Why is she calling us all the time? I don't know her. I just don't trust her. And, I just can't believe that Zach Miller could ever be like she says."

Rogers threw a sofa pillow across the room. "I think you're in love with him or something."

"I'm not. But I did something when you were in DC at the Commissioners Forum."

"I'm afraid to ask."

"I met with Zach's P.I., Haley Tyler."

Rogers kicked the coffee table. It flipped on its side, causing the vase of roses to topple onto the floor. He thundered, "Shit, don't you ever listen to me? She kidnapped our daughter!"

"We have no proof of that."

He raised his hands to the ceiling. "Kim, connect the dots!"

The front door chimes rang out several times. Rogers walked over and yanked the door open.

"Beth Murphy, somehow I had a feeling it would be you."

"May I come in?"

"I believe Kim and I were sort of expecting you."

Ushering Beth into the kitchen, he asked Kim to make some coffee. He noticed that Beth was dressed in faded blue denims and a Stanford sweatshirt. She kept rubbing her neck. Her eyelids twitched. She looked as worn out as he felt.

"By the way, thanks for helping me with my DNA. But Knowton still maintains that it was just an accidental medical error by the lab."

Beth said, "He's covering up the truth."

Kim looked at her husband. "So, Miss Murphy, what the hell is going on?"

"It's a long story."

"Take all the time you need," Rogers said. Kim walked over to the coffeemaker.

"Ten years ago, my parents—my real parents—were bankrupt. They forced me to be a human volunteer for clinical drug testing at Southwest International. My father took charge of all the money that they paid me for being a drug tester. It paid the family bills. But I became very ill taking so many experimental drugs. I wanted to stop, but my father wouldn't let me. My mother tried to help me. But my father beat me with a leather strap until I agreed to continue to participate in the trials. He told me that he would kill Mom if I ever ran away or went to the police."

Kim set the cups down in front of each of them, along with a pitcher of cream. She reached over to gently touch Murphy's shoulder.

Rogers said, "I'm so sorry to hear this. How old were you when this was happening?"

"Sixteen."

"That's horrible."

"Well, one day at the drug testing company while I was waiting for them to inject me with a new experimental drug for hepatitis, I saw a group of well-dressed people walking through the center. I discovered that they were auditing the quality controls at Southwest. They were from the IRB oversight company, National Quality. One older man in the group walked over to me. He asked me my name and how old I was. Of course, to protect my mom, I lied and said that I was twenty-one. He didn't seem to believe me, but he rejoined the rest of his group."

Rogers sat back. He recalled his conversation with her after his speech at the Marriott. "You once told me that Sam Murphy worked for National Quality. Was that the man who approached you?"

"Good memory, Commissioner. In any case, one day while I was confined to my drug testing room after being injected, Sam received permission from Southwest to visit me. Somehow he found out that I was underage. Of course, I denied what he was saying. My father would have beaten me twice as hard if he had found out that I told someone the truth."

Beth sipped her coffee. Rogers could see that Kim was completely unnerved.

"To get to the point, Southwest threw me out of the program rather than risking any chance of getting their quality control license revoked. My father thought that I had told my correct age to Southwest. He threw a plate at me for what he believed I had done and then viciously beat my mom. She ended up in the hospital with pancreatitis after he kicked her in the stomach over and over again."

"Oh my God," Kim said, cringing.

"My father was so cruel that he made me watch the entire beating. He threatened me with the same punishment if I didn't cooperate. Of course, I felt I had to do it. So he simply enrolled me at another drug testing company, where they didn't know that I was underage."

"What a bastard," Rogers countered.

"One day, Sam Murphy came to our house. He had apparently tracked me down. It seems that his own daughter committed suicide years before back in Ireland. So, as he told me later, he singled me out from that first day when he met me at Southwest as someone who needed to be saved. He had felt so guilty that he had ignored his daughter's warning signs that he made saving me his new mission in life."

Kim provided her with a box of tissues, and then wiped away a tear of her own.

"My father roared a few choice words when he found out that Sam admitted turning me in at Southwest. He ran from the living room. He pulled out a shotgun from the hallway closet, came back, and pointed it at my head."

Barely able to speak, Beth muttered, "I was so angry with my father. I prayed to God that he would just die. Then while he was shoving Sam with the butt of the shotgun, I hit my father on the back of his head with a large silver clock that was on the end table. Somehow, I wrestled the shotgun from him. He charged at me and I pulled the trigger. My father fell to the floor."

Kim gasped.

"I looked at him, lying on the floor. His face was gone. There was blood everywhere. Oh my God, what did I do?"

Rogers took a deep breath, letting it out forcefuly, "You did it in self-defense. You had no choice."

"Sam covered up for me. He wiped off my prints from the shotgun and called the police. He told the authorities that he had shot my father when he tried to kill me. The case went to court and Sam was found not guilty."

"What happened to your mom?"

"She died two months later due to complications from her pancreatitis. Six months later Sam adopted me."

Rogers reached out for Beth's hand. "Kim and I wish that there was something we could do for you. You've been through so much pain. You're so young."

Beth blinked away a tear. "Anyway, that was the turning point in both of our lives. Sam was my hero. That's why I must find out who killed him. I believe he was killed by people involved in making profits in drugs through illegal and unethical behavior."

Rogers asked, "What can we do to help?"

"I need you to come with me."

"Where?"

"I want you to fly to Cabo so we can join up with the DCP cruise ship."

Kim interrupted. "Beth, I'm so sorry for your troubles, but I'm not letting you go to Mexico alone with my husband . . ." She paused as Jonathan began to protest, and then continued, ". . . because someone needs to watch your backs. I'm going with you."

Chapter Forty-Eight

Zach simply felt that he could not lose. He already planned two moves ahead to guarantee a checkmate. He took a quick shower after a thirty-minute nap. Dressed in tan shorts and a green golf shirt, he was tying his black Nikes when he heard the knock on his cabin door. Grinning, he made his way to open it. Ironic, he thought, that he was so casually dressed for a meeting that had the potential to drive DCP stock up millions of dollars.

"Good afternoon, Dr. Knowton. I admire a man who is punctual. Come in."

The oncologist seemed preoccupied from the start. He responded coldly, "How long will this take? I have a massage scheduled in one hour."

"Ah. Is the masseuse a man or woman?"

"A woman, of course."

"A woman's touch is so soothing. Alexis has been such a joy to me over the years," Zach said.

"Cut the crap. Let's get back to why I'm here."

"Do you think Alexis now qualifies for Zazotene since the FDA has expanded the indications for use to include her diagnosis?" Zach said.

"No, I don't. I still question the data. How many times are you going to ask me that question?"

"Then why did you order the same drug for Dr. Rogers?"

Snapping back, Knowton said, "Each case is different."

Zach knew he needed to establish common ground to agree on some minor point, something to break the rising tension. He nodded in agreement. "Of course, you are right," he conceded. Then he decided to cut to the chase.

"When Sean Parker invited you on this cruise, did he tell you that we hoped you would present Zazotene in an unbiased light?"

"Yes. And I told him that I would present the facts."

"Facts can be interpreted differently."

"Only a physician is qualified to make these judgments."

Getting nowhere, Zach sensed that it was time to change the subject. "Doctor, have a seat. Can I get you a drink?"

"Water would be fine."

Zach poured himself a Scotch on the rocks and filled another glass from the tap, which he handed to the oncologist.

"To health and happiness," the host toasted with flair.

Knowton sipped from his glass, keeping his eyes fixed on the floor.

"I have some questions for you."

Knowton raised his voice. "About what?"

"Doctor, it's just you and me. I don't bite. Are there any questions that you would consider to be off limits?"

"Frankly speaking, I'd rather not talk about anything except maybe when this meeting will be over . . . that and the real facts about Zazotene."

Zach counterpunched. "Excuse me, doctor. National Quality Institute has reviewed all the data coming out of our human drug testing at Southwest International. The Institute recommended to the FDA that the data was compelling. The FDA approved further indications for the use of Zazotene. Those are the facts."

Knowton shifted in his chair. "That's not exactly the whole truth. As you know, my patient Sam Murphy used to sit on the board at the National Quality Institute. After he died, the Institute seemed to forget that they're not in the rubber-stamping business. The human trial data coming out of Southwest International is flawed. The FDA accepted the Institute's minority report. The majority report co-authored by Sam had asked for more data. The majority of board members at National Quality did not recommend approval for these new indications, including lung cancer or your wife's type of cancer."

Zach replied, "I see that you have done your homework."

Knowton's fist clenched tighter. "Reporting to the Secretary of Health and Human Services, the new FDA commissioner has become a political puppet. Those are the facts!"

"Doctor, maybe you should have had the Scotch, instead of me. Calm down. It's such a nice day, I'm sure we can discuss this professionally."

Knowton stirred in his seat a few seconds before launching himself toward the exit.

Zach rose and reached out for the oncologist's shoulder. "Isn't it a fact that you prescribed Zazotene for Sam Murphy?"

"That's none of your business. And take your hands off of me."

Releasing his grip, Zach said, "I've a copy of Murphy's autopsy report showing excessive blood levels of the chemo drug. So how do you explain that, Doc?"

"I did prescribe it for Murphy a week before he died, but in normal doses, given for tumors such as his type of cancer. Those doses were previously approved by the FDA. I had always agreed with that data."

"So if that's true, why did the pathologists find excessive blood levels at autopsy? Don't you know how much you're giving?"

"I just told you that I gave Zazotene a week before. It would have been out of his system by the night he died. And there is no indication in the hospital chart of me ordering excessive doses. So I ask you, Mr. Miller, who really gave my patient the high doses?"

"I'm no doctor."

"Then how did the high levels of the drug get into Murphy's system?"

Zach squirmed. "How would I know?"

"I think you do."

Zach looked away for a few seconds. "The bottom line is that the FDA has recently approved the drug at higher doses for expanded uses such as lung cancer. True or not?"

Knowton nodded reluctantly.

"Thank you."

"But," Knowton protested, "it was not approved by the FDA at higher doses at the time of Sam's death."

"Oh, one more question. Since you were treating Dr. Rogers for his lung cancer, why did you prescribe the medication if you don't agree with the new FDA ruling that National Quality recommended?"

"I prescribed a low dose of Zazotene for Rogers, just as I did for Murphy. I thought it would help both of them. Surgeon General Gomez convinced me of the safety at those levels. The different mechanism of action seemed to be worth the risk at the dose I prescribed. The issue is not whether I prescribed the damn drug; the point is that I used low doses well within the safety range."

"But Rogers almost died from a reaction to the chemo?"

"It can happen to anyone. It was almost like a higher dose was used. But, as you know, the levels of Zazotene in his blood were not excessive."

Zach smiled. "Medicine can be so complicated."

"The National Quality majority opinion did not vote to recommend Zazotene for the expanded indications. Somehow, the FDA was influenced by someone."

"What are you saying, Doctor?"

"I'm late for my massage."

"Before you go . . . have you seen Nicki Sanderson on board?"

"We passed by each other last night when I was walking on deck."

"Cruises are a perfect time for friends to get together."

"It's time for me to go," Knowton said, reaching for the door.

"I hope that you will be fair in your presentation tomorrow. I don't think acting belligerently helps anyone. Especially since you have prescribed our blockbuster for two influential men. One died and one almost died. I know you claimed to use a low dose, but the coroner will testify that Sam's blood contained excessively high doses. I would hate to publicly ask you a question about those facts at tomorrow's oncology seminar."

Knowton began to look pale and chastened. He released his grip on the doorknob and turned to face the CEO.

"I'm sorry I blew up. I'll be civil tomorrow. In my opinion, the drug has its place for specific indications at the right doses. Nothing more."

"Then why are you a bundle of nerves?"

"The Health Club promised me they would get Rogers off my back. Well, guess what? The Commissioner found out that his biopsy was mixed up with another patient's."

"Simple lab error. Happens all the time."

"Rogers now believes someone switched the biopsies."

"Do you?"

Knowton turned, walked out the door, and did not look back.

••••••••••

The drug company baron checked the manifest. Nicki was in cabin 410. He headed out believing that he could no longer trust Knowton.

Zach knocked lightly. He found the door unlocked. He entered her cabin and heard the shower running. He took a seat on the couch to wait. Minutes after the shower flow stopped, Nicki emerged into the cabin. He was amused by the stunned look on her freshly scrubbed face. She was even too startled to scream. Zach enjoyed the view.

"You look amazing," he said, watching her shapely bottom shimmy out of the room. Soon, she returned in her pale pink bathrobe and sat down next to him.

"Zach, you surprised me."

Putting his hand on her knee, he said, "Sorry, but it was worth it, my dear."

"So, how did your meeting with Knowton go?"

He looked her square in her blue eyes. "He's on the fence. I need your help. I need you to reel him in as only you can. Try to have some fun with the good doctor, Nicki. After all, as your father found out, life can be all too short."

Chapter Forty-Nine

Zach monitored his plan from the stairwell. He had approved of her choice of a hot pink dress that barely reached mid-thigh. The miniature microphone he planted in her pocket would allow him to listen to every detail of their encounter. After Nicki knocked, Zach caught a glimpse of Knowton opening cabin door 432 dressed in baggy blue shorts and a white T-shirt. The CEO could hardly wait for the show to begin.

"Nicki, what are you doing here?"

"I thought since we're both on board you would like to hear how Ben is doing. You do remember that you're his father."

"Come in."

Zach was so proud of this plan. He adjusted his earphone and listened intently while reveling in his cunning ploy.

Nicki asked, "So are you enjoying the cruise?"

"Very much so. I just came back from another great massage."

"Do you remember the rubs that I used to give you?"

"That was then. It's over, Nicki. Can I get you something?"

"A beer would hit the spot, but only if you join me."

Zach heard the bottle caps coming off. *Perfect.*

"Come sit next to me," she said seductively.

"To the future and a long life for all of us," he replied, sitting down at her side.

"Cheers. It's good to see you. Ben looks so much like you."

"Nicki, actually I'm glad you stopped by to talk. I've been meaning to discuss what I can do to support him."

"Hunter has many faults, but he's been supportive of my care for Ben. I have enough money for now. Possibly when he goes to college, I could use some help."

"Just let me know. Whatever I can do, I will."

"What I could use right now is a hug from the man who used to make love to me."

•••••••••

Zach saw Sanderson approaching from his hiding spot beyond the stairwell. Hunter's face was crimson, his step determined. The CEO had sent Sanderson an email just five minutes earlier. Now he checked his watch as his programmed missile opened the door to Knowton's cabin.

"Knowton, get your fuckin' arm off my wife," Sanderson bellowed. Zach listened attentively, enjoying the brawl he had created.

"She came to see me. Nothing happened."

Zach peered in through the half-open door. He took care that he was not noticed. He saw the empty beer bottles on the couch and how close Knowton and Nicki were sitting next to each other. *Sanderson will go berserk!*

Just then Sanderson pulled a .38 caliber derringer out of his navy sport jacket pocket, released the safety latch, and ran toward the couple with the gun pointed at their chests. He pulled the trigger twice. Nicki dove to the floor. Zach saw blood spurting from Knowton's neck. It splashed onto Nicki like a shower of red rain. She got to her feet and tried to stem the flow with a pillow from the couch. The oncologist's eyes rolled back just before his head dropped. His chest appeared frozen.

"Hunter, you asshole! You killed him!" Nicki kicked Sanderson in the groin just as he was reloading the double chamber.

"You're next, you whore," he roared just before she kicked his right leg out from under him. He fell backwards, the back of his head bouncing off the cabin floor. The gun flew from his hand and Nicki dove for it. She latched onto it tightly just as her head was yanked backwards by a powerful pull on her long blond hair. Falling back onto his torso, she was somehow able to pin his left arm to the floor with her free hand. His arms were flailing wildly. Nicki sank back on her heels to get her face out of his range. Holding the derringer behind her head, she screamed as her thighs and pelvis were pelted with his rapid blows. She lowered the gun and aimed below his left rib cage.

Zach saw Hunter's hips moving, seemingly ready for a mighty

thrust. Just as she was about to be catapulted off of him, Nicki squeezed off a single shot. Sanderson went limp. Bright red blood began to gurgle from his mouth. He gasped repeatedly. She rolled off of him onto the floor and sat up alongside his motionless body. The gun slipped from her hand.

Zach banged on the open door. Nicki spotted him and jumped up to run toward him, her mouth open in a silent scream. Struggling mightily, Sanderson rolled over and grabbed the derringer, firing at her head just before he collapsed. Nicki landed at Zach's feet in the doorway, blood gushing from what remained of the back of her head.

••••••••••

Zach hid behind the lifeboat. He saw the security guards and men dressed in plainclothes galloping to Knowton's cabin. He thought it was curious that a ship of this size had so many security guards. About a half dozen of them piled into the cabin. He looked around and saw no one else rushing toward the scene. He casually walked up the stairway to the next deck, waving to a few unsuspecting guests before reaching cabin 515. He found the door unlocked. Five minutes later, Carver arrived.

"Have a seat," Zach told him. "There's been an unfortunate accident. You will present in place of Knowton tomorrow at the conference."

"Why?"

"Unfortunately, Dr. Knowton couldn't resist Nicki's charms. Now they're both dead."

Unfazed, Carver asked, "What about Hunter?"

"Dead."

Carver did not blink. "I never liked him anyway. I'm sad for Tom, but as Rogers always says, the show must go on."

"Are you OK with presenting in place of Knowton?"

"What do you think?"

Tossing him a manila folder, Zach said, "Familiarize yourself with what Dr. Gomez has written about our blockbuster. You will express your shock and sincere condolences about the tragedy that just occurred. You will tell some pithy anecdotes about what a great man your partner was. But, most important of all, you'll convince six hundred oncologists that your pro-Zazotene speech is the exact presentation that Knowton was prepared to deliver before his unfortunate death at the hands of a jealous husband."

"Good to know that our backup plan worked."

"Like a charm. Listen, I'll be getting off the ship tomorrow morning. I'll be flying out of Cabo San Lucas. I need to be in DC by tomorrow afternoon to prepare the political leaders for the next steps. We need to plan what to do with Peabody. He's become a liability. I'll be meeting with Tracey London."

"Understood. You know, I'm actually looking forward to feeding the pigeons with our crap about Zazotene. Tom had his chance. He blew it."

"One more thing. Rogers had his DNA checked against the lung biopsy. He told Knowton."

"Then he knows."

"He knows crap. All he knows is that there was a lab mix-up, nothing more."

"What if he finds . . .?"

"Enough already. Once we are all back home, you can take charge as the leader of our group. Good luck on your presentation to the docs. Just remember that everyone has a boss."

"I'll make sure the security guards don't try to cancel my meeting with the docs. After all, we're paying them. They work for us."

"Victor, you're going to make a terrific leader of The Health Club!"

Chapter Fifty

Sailing back to Cabo on the tender, Rick cursed Zach. He pounded the sides of the boat as he thought of Carver being given the leader's job over him. He was furious and resented the way his uncle was treating him. While making his way back to the inn to find Ashley, he thought of ways to get even.

When he arrived, he walked up to the armed Mexican guard standing outside the metal door. He gave him one thousand pesos for watching Ashley and told him to never return. Rick opened the lock and pushed open the door.

Ashley pleaded in a weakened voice, "Help me. I'm in agony. The rat has bitten my leg. My arms are killing me. They feel frozen in place. Please, Rick. Please. I'll do anything you want. Anything at all."

She watched as he unlocked her from the wristbands, which were tethered to the stone wall behind her head. Her arms felt like dead weights and plopped to the cement floor. Feeling as though they were detached from her body, her limbs were numb.

"I'm ready to explode," Rick fumed.

Ashley shrank back. "Why? I didn't do anything."

"Not you, bitch. My Uncle Zach. He really got on my nerves today."

She studied his eyes. They appeared as blazing red globes trying to pop out of his sockets. She ventured ahead cautiously. Calmly, she said, "What happened? I'm sure he trusts you."

"No he doesn't. He treats me like a kid."

Ashley knew she had to win him over, not wanting to be the final victim of the rage he was expressing. "You're no kid. You're a strong, good-looking man."

"Don't bullshit me." Rick's breathing began to slow. His eyes appeared less jumpy, less threatening.

"Listen, you've done your job. I'm still here, and you prevented me from sending out that text message. What more does your uncle want from you?"

Rick turned from Ashley, looking at the steel door. "I don't know, but I'm going to find out."

She began to feel some sensation in her arms. Ashley squirmed to stretch her stiffened muscles. She was able to turn onto her side facing Rick. He sat down on the floor facing her. She saw the revolver in his left hand.

Ashley reached for his hand. "Can I help you?"

"No, I've got to confront him and that damn doctor he picked over me."

"When?" Ashley's mind was centered on every twitch on Rick's face. She felt like she was connecting, helping him to shift his anger away from her.

"Soon. I'll never be able to look at myself in the mirror if I don't do it today."

"Where are these people?"

"On a ship off the coast."

Ashley sensed that she was pushing it too far. She decided to back off, for the moment.

"Rick, can you get something for me to eat? I'm starved."

"Tell you what. I'm going to take you outside to a street vendor. Just remember, I'll think nothing of shooting you if you try anything."

"I'll do whatever you want."

Ashley put out her hands. Rick helped her to her feet with his right hand, still wielding the revolver in his left.

"Walk in front of me. Remember, I'm in no mood for any shit from you. I'll shoot you in a heartbeat."

Ashley walked out the door for the first time in weeks. She shielded her eyes from the light. Rick led her up a flight of stone stairs and out to a garden.

"Sit down on this bench."

The sun blinded her. Gradually, she was able to make out shapes by blocking the sun with her hand. "I can see the harbor from here."

"Just keep your mouth shut. I'll get us a tortilla and a Coke at the vendor over there. Don't move or else."

Ashley surveyed the harbor. With the clarity of her vision improving, she saw the tenders sailing from the dock to ships out in the harbor. She knew it had to be a shallow-water port. Besides the large, well-known cruise lines anchored in the harbor, there was a smaller ship, closer to shore. By now, Rick was walking toward her with lunch.

"This should tide us over," he said, giving her a small plate with one tortilla and a scoop of rice. "Here's a Coke."

"Thank you. I'm starving. Where were you last evening? I missed you at dinner and also at breakfast this morning."

"Taking care of business."

Ashley watched his eyes. They appeared to be focused on the smaller ship in the harbor. His face seemed to tighten with each mouthful he consumed.

"Nice ship."

"Which one?"

"The smaller one," she said, pointing to it.

"What about it?"

"I wonder what it's like to be on it. It seems so cute compared to those big monstrosities."

"I've been on it. No big deal. Just a lot of rich folks. Listen, finish your lunch. I've got some thinking to do."

Ashley sensed him getting upset. She finished her meal in silence. If ever she could escape her basement cell, she knew where she would go. A moment later, Rick ordered her to start walking back. The fresh air felt so great after weeks of captivity. She would focus on her next opportunity to escape. It was her only chance.

Ashley sat on her cot in the dark. The dampness was especially uncomfortable after feeling the fresh air. At least Rick was no longer chaining or beating her. She bent down and pulled out the sharp-edged bolt that originally bound her to the stone wall. She felt her way. The stone wall would be a few steps away from her cot. Her hands felt the slimy cold surface. Ashley inched her hands to the right. Feeling for the door, her fingers outlined the perimeter. She moved her hands across the metal. She sensed a protrusion of the metal.

A hinge?

Ashley stood there with the bolt in her right hand. She had an idea. It was worth a try. She wedged the bolt into the small crevice where the door was hinged. Pushing hard, it seemed to fit snugly, at least a couple of inches into the gap.

She felt her way back to her cot and waited. Her hunger pangs began to increase. It had to be dinner time. Either Rick was returning soon or not until the morning. A few moments later, the door swung open.

"Brought you dinner and a bottle of water."

"Thank you."

"Listen, I've got some work to do. I'll see you tomorrow."

Ashley stood and followed him as he neared the door. She spotted the sharp bolt that she had wedged into the crevice between the door and the wall. The door began to close. It made a grating sound for the first time. Her bolt was still snugly in place. She heard him trying to bang the door shut several times. It wasn't closing completely. Rick jangled the keys. Ashley heard the deadbolt move a little. A second later, there was silence.

In the pitch black, she could feel a flap of metal that was not flush with the wall. She pulled. At first, nothing budged. Feeling her way to the hinge side of the door, she felt for her sharp-edged bolt. She found it and shoved it deeper into the gap. Sidestepping back to the other side of the door, she grabbed the metal flap. She pulled as hard as she could. A ray of light appeared in her cell. She yanked the flap. It moved. She strained to pull harder. A moment later, the door opened and she fell on her butt.

Ashley leaped to her feet. She turned to her left and saw the light bouncing off the staircase. No one was in sight. She saw the stone steps. Though her legs felt like they would collapse, she scaled the steps until she was in the garden. She looked around. The street vendor was closing up for the night. The harbor lights caught her eye. She headed toward the port. A tender was just arriving from one of the ships.

A middle-aged couple got off the tender and was walking toward Ashley. She noticed the sign on the wall. *Port Cabo San Lucas.*

"Excuse me, my name is Ashley Rogers. I seem to have lost my cell phone and my wallet. Could I borrow your cell just a minute to send a text message?"

The athletic-looking man replied, "Sure, no problem."

Ashley addressed the message to her father. *Daddy, I'm free on a dock in Cabo, Mexico. Please come for me. I'll hide under the dock. Love Ashley.*

"Hope you find your wallet, young lady. Listen, are you OK? You look hurt."

She hesitated a moment, but decided it would be too dangerous to tell him the truth. "I'm fine. Thanks again."

Chapter Fifty-One

Zach and Carver sat on cushioned lounge chairs and hung their legs over the side of the railing. Tomorrow, the newly chosen leader would act in Knowton's stead. The nighttime breeze soothed Zach's face.

The harbor lights had taken over the horizon. The deck was barren. Most of the guests appeared to have retired to their staterooms for the night. Zach was lighting up a cigar when Rick appeared.

Zach blew a ring of smoke. "What are you doing here? You're supposed to be watching the Rogers girl."

Rick pointed a finger at his uncle. "Zach, I'm tired of you treating me like a kid."

His uncle rose from his lounge. "I'm sorry you feel that way." He noticed Carver steadily moving alongside of Rick.

Rick persisted. "Why can't I be the new leader?"

Zach replied from his gut. "You're not ready."

Rick quickly pulled out his revolver and pointed it at Zach.

Zach backed away. He took a deep breath and said softly, "Rick, please put that away."

"Not until I get what I want."

Zach could see Carver getting into position, ready to pounce. "Let's sit down and talk about it."

By now, Carver had moved slightly in back of the CEO's nephew. Rick's eyes focused only on his uncle. Zach nodded, almost imperceptibly. Carver pulled out his own pistol and struck it on the back of Rick's head. Zach's nephew hit the deck with a thud.

Carver said without a trace of emotion, "We've got to kill him, Zach. I don't care who he is. I'm the leader."

Zach hesitated for only a moment. "You're right. We don't have time for this nonsense."

But Zach turned away. He could not bring himself to watch as the pistol crashed down on Rick's head again and again. The blood poured onto the deck.

"Help me throw him overboard, Zach."

Zach grabbed Rick's legs and with Carver at the head, tossed his nephew to the waiting sharks below.

"Victor, what about the girl?"

"She's locked up in the basement at the inn. Rick had told Haley where he kept her. She's not going anywhere. Tomorrow, we'll take care of her."

••••••••••

Zach and Haley took the first tender off the ship the following morning. He wore a large Mexican sombrero and dark Versace sunglasses. They were the only occupants taking the water shuttle from the ship to the shallow-water dock in town.

As they approached the dock, he noticed a young woman hiding underneath.

"Haley, do you see that girl? Under the dock."

"That's Ashley Rogers!"

"Pretend like you didn't notice. Give me a kiss." Zach grabbed Haley and planted one on her lips as if they were honeymooners.

Still holding Haley, Zach said, "When we get off the tender, I want you to circle in back of her. Put on this sombrero so she doesn't recognize you. She doesn't know me."

Zach climbed onto the dock and walked down the side toward the beach. He then dropped himself down onto the sand. He noticed Ashley warily looking at him. Around the other side, he spotted Haley closing in fast.

"Miss, can I help you?" Zach asked.

Ashley replied, "No, I'm just admiring the harbor."

Zach walked toward her, drawing her full attention. A moment later, Haley had her in a headlock.

••••••••••

A private car took the trio to Los Cabos International Airport. His private jet would be waiting. Ashley would come along under gunpoint. After landing, she would stay on the plane with Haley. He was anxious to meet with President Jordan's Chief of Staff. In his mind, events were beginning to spin out of control more than he would have preferred. He sensed that it was time to distance himself from the fallout of the killings on the cruise ship. Soon, Carver would be the new leader, the new Caesar. Grinning, Zach was pleased to be Brutus.

Chapter Fifty-Two

The Commissioner searched around the dock for Ashley before boarding the private tender shuttle pre-arranged by the FBI to take Rogers, Kim, and Beth to the Prince America, anchored a quarter mile out in the Cabo harbor. She was nowhere in sight. While the tender navigated the rough waters, Rogers wondered whether the last text message about her location was another false clue. As the shuttle neared the cruise ship, Rogers scanned the deck. There was no sign of either Zach or Knowton.

Following the women up the gangplank, the Commissioner noticed Lieutenant Masters and Agent German waiting for them. "You need to come with us," Masters said as soon as the group stepped aboard.

Once inside the cabin, Rogers demanded, "Now what?"

German spoke up. In a subdued tone, he said, "Yesterday, there were several shootings on board."

Rogers felt his stomach flipping over. "Shootings? Who was shot?"

Masters stood up to approach the trio.

"You must keep this strictly confidential. The passengers haven't yet been notified."

Rogers roared, "Dammit! Just tell us!"

"I'm sorry to have to tell you this. Tom Knowton, Nicki Sanderson, and Hunter Sanderson are all dead."

Rogers slipped off his stool, parroting what the FBI chief said. "They're all dead? How could this happen?"

"Jonathan, we're leaving," Kim shouted.

"No, we've got to find out who is doing this to us . . . to Ashley."

Rogers looked into his wife's tearful eyes. Their world no longer made any sense. He closed his eyes and prayed for Tom and Nicki. One thing was sure. Deep down, he believed that he would be the next victim. Through FBI intelligence, he learned that he had just missed running into Zach earlier that morning. He was also told that Carver was going to take the deceased oncologist's place at the seminar coming up in less than two hours.

••••••••••

Rogers entered the Sunset Ballroom only a few minutes before the scheduled start of the main event. He wore dark sunglasses and a tan sport jacket. Pleased that no one had recognized him, he sat in the last row of the ballroom. About three-fourths of the room was already full. He surveyed the rows of seats, searching for backs of heads that looked familiar. The Commissioner spotted Carver sitting in the first row. He was seated next to a tall, good-looking gentleman who kept turning around to do a head count. Moments later, he saw that same man approach the podium.

"Good afternoon, ladies and gentlemen. My name is Sean Parker. I'm senior vice president of sales at Doctor's Choice Products. I'll be your moderator for today's seminar. I'm sure by now you have all heard about our recent tragedy. Before we start our conference, I would like all of you to rise for a moment of silence in memory of the people who passed away yesterday."

Rogers stood in with the crowd. *Passed away? They were slaughtered!* As the silence approached one minute, the Commissioner thought of Kim back in their cabin. He hoped she was being protected by Agent German.

Parker asked the audience to take their seats and then introduced Dr. Victor Carver as a twenty-year partner and close friend of Dr. Tom Knowton. As the doctor approached the podium, Rogers thought back to a similar scene at Winchester Press Hall back in Oldwyck when he had so proudly introduced Carver to the press. Looking over at Beth, his brazen accuser on that day, he realized that the Medicaid fraud press conference now seemed so long ago.

Carver began in a somber voice. "I'm Victor Carver. I'm deeply saddened by the passing of my friend and partner. I've just extended our deepest sympathies to Tom's wife and two daughters."

Rogers scanned the audience of practicing physicians. As a former beeper-carrying doctor himself, he knew what it was like to walk in the shoes of a physician. If anyone faced the abyss every day, it was each of these oncologists, who dealt with death around the clock. He watched them bow their heads. He heard an occasional sniffle. Clearly, they were moved by the circumstances.

Carver wiped his reddened eyes with his index finger. "It's my high honor to present to you today the personal notes of the late Dr. Knowton. Tom and I started to prepare our findings on Zazotene and other life-saving cancer therapies approximately two months ago. Weeks ago, Tom had actually asked me if we could co-present at this conference, but I declined. As we all know, he was the nationally known expert."

He's lying through his teeth! Rogers shifted uncomfortably in his seat.

With his eyes downcast, Carver continued. "I'm extremely saddened that Dr. Knowton is not here to present the information to you."

Rogers felt his gut tightening. He knew that Tom was a procrastinator by nature, and wouldn't have worked on his speech any sooner than on the actual day he would deliver it. Oftentimes, Tom would discuss his views on the theory of chaos in the universe. Knowton would always argue that the randomness of the world should motivate one to wait for the last possible moment to act. To do something too soon was folly, because something would always change that would necessitate rework.

The oncologist walked in front of the podium, standing a foot or so from the front row. "Dr. Knowton believed that pharmaceutical companies were to be respected for their excellent research and discovery of newer and better compounds. He told me many times about his belief that American drug companies are to be praised for their unrelenting efforts to prolong life and to improve the quality of life in those patients suffering from cancer."

Rogers scoffed silently at Carver's gratuitous introduction. Unfortunately, it seemed to be working on the unsuspecting audience.

"Tom Knowton has reviewed the research data religiously. He was pleased when the National Quality Institute finally stopped playing politics and approved the solid data on Zazotene. The FDA then acted in the best interest of the American people."

Rogers could feel his blood pressure rising. Carver was clearly misrepresenting his ex-partner's beliefs. Though the tone of his presentation was professional, the Commissioner knew that Carver was stating half-truths at best.

Carver was now claiming to be quoting directly from Knowton's remarks. "Phase three data on expanded use of Zazotene for several cancers is scientifically compelling. The safety margin even at higher doses is outstanding. Of those finishing the clinical trials at Southwest, there were only minor side effects."

Rogers squirmed in his seat. Carver paused to ask for questions. Seeing no hands being raised, he said assuredly, "Based on Dr. Knowton's own analysis of the cost-benefit ratio of our popular chemo treatment, he believed we could be saving thousands of lives if we would prescribe Zazotene for additional uses. Dr. Knowton states that he has personally used this drug for several types of cancers including lung cancer and tumors of the endocrine glands. He concludes that all of his patients have had their life significantly improved with the use of both low and high doses."

Carver stopped to gaze out into the ballroom. He asked again for questions. Seeing no hands being raised, he lowered his head to continue to his reading of the false gospel according to Knowton.

A solitary voice rang out. "That's a lie. You are a liar, Dr. Carver. Zazotene is a killer drug and you know it."

Rogers craned his neck quickly toward the familiar voice. Even though her small frame was enveloped among the many oncologists, he pinpointed her immediately.

Carver shot back, "Excuse me, young lady. Please stand and identify yourself."

Rogers saw her rise with both hands on her hips. She proceeded to stride down the side aisle toward the podium with her head held high. Stopping five feet before she reached the podium, she turned and faced the murmuring audience.

"My name is Beth Murphy."

Carver walked toward her. He held up his right hand. "Hold on, Ms. Murphy. Are you a doctor? And if so, what are your oncology credentials to be flinging about such absurd and libelous statements?"

Undaunted, Beth persisted. "My father was a patient of Dr. Knowton. He died under his care. The autopsy report revealed an enormous overdose of Zazotene in his body. The pathologist concluded he died of an overwhelming infection secondary to bone marrow suppression by the DCP chemo treatment."

Carver's face seemed almost contorted. "Ladies and gentlemen, I'm sorry for this rude interruption of our seminar. Sean, please call security."

Beth glared at him. Walking slowly toward Carver, she looked like a tiger stalking its prey. She emphasized every word with each step that she took. "So, Dr. Carver, though you say that Dr. Knowton never had a death with that killer drug, the chief pathologist at Mercy Hospital in Michigan certainly believed that my father was killed by that damn poison. That makes you a liar."

Rogers could see Sean Parker closing his cell phone as he approached the podium. The Commissioner stood and watched the side door flip open.

Carver said sarcastically, "Ms. Murphy, you are quite the actress. I recall that you pulled this same stunt at Commissioner Rogers's press conference not too long ago."

Two cruise ship security police ran in from the side entrance. With one security officer on each arm, they began escorting her out of the ballroom.

Somehow Beth broke away from them, shouting, "Sam Murphy was a board member of National Quality. As a quality assurance company, we didn't accept the flawed data from the DCP drug testing company called Southwest International. He was murdered by DCP to silence him."

Rogers stayed to the rear of the ballroom, hearing the gasps now spreading throughout the ballroom. An oncologist five rows up stood to ask Carver for permission to speak.

The leader of The Health Club granted his request. "You have the floor, Doctor."

"I've read all the data from the Southwest International testing reports, and twenty of the subjects were asked to leave the clinical trial. All of them were eventually hospitalized with severe reactions to the drug, with several subsequent deaths. With such a serious mortality and overdose rate, why did your chief medical officer omit these patients from his summary of the data to the *New England Journal of Medicine*? Surely this warrants mentioning, especially given how the drug was fast-tracked through the FDA."

Carver replied, "Doctor, let's talk after the seminar. I'll get the CMO from DCP on the line to discuss your questions. I'm sure there is a logical explanation."

As she was being dragged from the ballroom, Beth continued to blast away. "I'm now a board member of National Quality, and our chairman has been charged with finding out why the FDA overruled our majority report of not recommending expanded use of *Zazotene*."

Rogers had never witnessed anything like this at a professional seminar. Clinical arguments were breaking out among the clinicians in the audience. Carver tried desperately to gavel the meeting to order. Scanning the crowd, Rogers identified the whereabouts of FBI agent Masters. He wondered why she did not budge an inch during the whole disruptive scene.

Sean Parker put an end to the turmoil by pleading, "Doctors, please come to order. Thank you for your attention and participation in the first annual DCP pharmaceutical cruise. Scientific papers summarizing the key data on the effectiveness and the safety of Zazotene are available at the table just in front of this podium. We hope you have learned that this miracle drug can save lives. We are looking forward to working with you in the future. Enjoy your stay with us. The conference is now formally adjourned."

The doctors continued to argue with each other as they left the ballroom. Rogers stood in the aisle leading to the rear exit. Carver made his way toward him.

Carver spoke in a monotone voice. "Jonathan, I'm so happy to see you. Can you believe this Murphy woman? She's a fruitcake."

Rogers walked up to Carver, standing a foot away from him. "You're a disgrace. I pity you. You'll burn in hell!"

"Does this mean you won't be asking me to jog with you again?" Carver chided.

"You're worse than any of them. Beth Murphy was right. When we get back to Michigan, you'd better have a damn good attorney."

Carver shouted, "No problem, we already own all the good ones."

Rogers shook his head in disgust. "What a fool I was to trust you."

"Whatever. Listen, my friend, you had a shot to go to the top. You were that close before you blew it by being so self-righteous in front of the President."

"We're doctors. We took an oath to help people."

"We'll be talking again. For your own good, you better wise up a little."

"I've given up hanging out with assholes like you."

Carver replied, "I'll see you back in Michigan."

The Commissioner exploded. "Don't ever try to threaten me again."

Carver grinned. Calmly, he added, "I think I just did."

••••••••••

Still a day out of their home port in L.A., Carver emailed Zach a message to initiate their contingency plan. Then he ordered room service until the docks were in sight.

Permitted to be the first to disembark, along with Sean Parker, Victor was picked up by a private limo. The senior vice president of sales waited alone for a cab to the airport.

After boarding the DCP Cessna, Carver went into a private soundproof cabin. He called Zach on the secure line that linked him to the Chief of Staff's office in DC, knowing the CEO would be there in accordance with their plan. "Tracey London here."

Carver roared, "Zach, you won't believe what happened! An hour after you left the ship, Dylan Mathews broke into your cabin. The security police on board discovered him leaving your cabin carrying a small machete. They arrested him on the spot."

Zach replied with bravado, "Well, Boss, as you know, timing is everything."

"It's interesting that you took the tender off the ship just before Mathews broke into your room to cut you to shreds. You're one lucky SOB."

"Some would call it good surveillance. In any case, Haley and I have Ashley Rogers. We found her hiding under a dock at Cabo. That was another of Rick's screwups. Glad he's gone."

"He's in the belly of several happy sharks today. So what are you and Tracey up to?"

"We both just called our boy Fred from the Chief of Staff office. The Governor has already put out a press release decrying the deaths of our fellow cruisers. Peabody stated that each of them was dedicated toward better health care for state residents. He left an impression that their deaths were a private matter among married folks. The public will believe it was just a love triangle that ended badly."

Carver interrupted, "By the way, Beth Murphy tried to torpedo our seminar by calling me a liar. But don't worry; I think she discredited herself with the docs. Security dragged her away while she continued to rant like a lunatic."

London spoke up. "Sounds like you handled the situation just fine. Now, besides neutralizing Rogers, we need to add Beth Murphy to our list. They both need to go. And soon."

Carver said arrogantly, "I'll decide when and where. We still have our lovely bargaining chip."

Zach cut into the conversation. "Victor, per our agreement,

the team will await further instructions from you. The necessary pieces are already in place. Haley and I will bring Ashley back to Michigan on a flight due to take off at one o'clock this afternoon. We will pull the triggers whenever you want."

"After Rogers and Murphy, we have to dispose of Peabody. He knows too much. And Tracey, please pass on all my best to President Jordan."

The Chief of Staff closed the conversation. "Dr. Carver, thank you for your leadership on your first day as our new boss. Don't worry. We'll execute your plan flawlessly."

Chapter Fifty-Three

Rogers convinced Kim to let Beth sit between them on the flight back to Michigan.

"Beth, I must say you have spunk. Were you always like this?" he asked.

"Not until Sam adopted me."

The wheels began to turn in Roger's brain. Embarrassed that he had not thought about this earlier, he asked Beth, "When was the last time you saw Sam alive?"

"About two hours before Dr. Carver called me to say that he had passed away."

"Did Sam look sicker than usual that night?"

"No. He was chronically short of breath from his forty-year two-pack-a-day smoking habit. But I believe that his cancer was in remission after his chemotherapy. He was supposed to have been released from Mercy within a day or so."

"Based on what you have told me, I don't believe that Sam died of bone marrow suppression from Zazotene. That condition would not have occurred that quickly. Sam Murphy was killed. But it wasn't due to the chemo."

"But they found twenty times the normal dose in his blood at autopsy."

"I'm not saying that he didn't get an overdose of Zazotene. I'm saying that something else killed him. He died much too suddenly for his death to be caused by any drug. The bone marrow suppression that the pathologist found at autopsy could have been from his previous dose of the drug a week earlier."

Rogers watched her reach for her briefcase. She handed him a folder marked *National Quality Review of Zazotene: An analysis of both majority and minority reports.*

"Sam wrote this executive summary before he went into the hospital. He told me to keep it safe. He was about to release it at the next board meeting and then go to the press."

The Commissioner rifled through the papers. He concentrated on the highlighted summary paragraphs. Reading it carefully, he looked up several times at both Beth and Kim. He knew the implications of Southwest excluding data that revealed a safety problem. They were the same facts that the balding oncologist presented at the seminar on the cruise. It seemed as though everyone had concerns about Zazotene except the FDA.

"Beth, when we get back to Oldwyck, you and I will call Surgeon General Gomez. We will also need to meet with Governor Peabody."

"Why not the FBI?"

"Because that is what they will expect us to do," he whispered into her ear.

"They?"

"Trust me on this. Trust me and trust no one else."

Rogers peered out the window down at the thousands of homes below them. He believed that the story he held in his hands needed to be delivered to every driveway and front porch across America. It symbolized everything that was wrong with the drug safety process.

In an hour, the plane would be crossing into Michigan airspace. Recalling the day he had taken his oath to promote the public health, he was ready to do whatever it took to make things right. He thought about his boyhood days, when he used to leap across the rooftops. But this time would be different from the carefree days of his childhood. He could no longer ignore the reality that a fatal free fall was always just a mere slip away. He remembered how he used to line up his toy soldiers to face the enemy. The difference was that now his foe was firing real bullets and playing for keeps.

••••••••••

"Sally, please get Surgeon General Gomez on the line."

As they waited in his office for his call to be connected, Rogers spun around in his chair. He looked over at Beth. He was ready to throw caution to the wind. About to speak with the doctor President Jordan had chosen over him to fill the "top doc in America" slot, he felt his heart racing. He would test her resolve to protect the health of all Americans. She would have to prove her mettle to him now that she was sitting on the prize he felt he deserved.

The door opened and Sally mouthed the words they wanted to hear. Pressing the speaker button, Rogers opened cheerfully.

"Good morning, Dr. Gomez. It's so nice to finally be able to speak with you."

"Dr. Rogers, I've heard a lot about you."

"I'll bet you have. Probably more than an earful."

"Are we on speakerphone?" she asked with a slight tone of suspicion.

Hitting the mute button, the Commissioner said to Beth, "We need to make her nervous. Maybe she'll slip up and tell us something."

Pressing the button to open up the line, he said, "You know how busy we commissioners can be. I'm multi-tasking as we speak. Actually, I'm reviewing the clinical trial data on Zazotene. I'm also a little hard of hearing, so being on speaker makes it easier for me to hear."

"I understand. How may I help you today?" Her tone was even and professional.

"Have you studied the clinical trial research that enabled Zazotene to be fast-tracked through the FDA with approvals for additional indications such as lung cancer?"

Silence.

"Are you still there? Hello, Dr. Gomez?"

"Yes. I'm here," the Surgeon General replied in a hushed voice.

"So did you see the research?"

"I believe that I may have seen the reports."

Hitting the mute button again, he said to Beth, "We'll surprise her with your executive summary. When the time is right, I'll point to you."

On speaker again, he asked, "Dr. Gomez, which reports have you seen?"

"The fast-track research."

"Did you ever see the original research done by Southwest International?"

She hesitated a moment before responding. "Of course. Their research was approved by National Quality and subsequently by the FDA."

Rogers pointed to Beth, who muted the phone while she cleared her throat and scanned her notes. When she was ready, she unlocked the mute.

"Good morning, Dr. Gomez. I'm Beth Murphy. I am a board member of the National Quality IRB. I'm working with Commissioner Rogers."

The Surgeon General lashed out. "Dr. Rogers, it is very unprofessional not to inform me that you had someone listening to our conversation. I will not tolerate such behavior."

Silence.

Beth continued. "Dr. Gomez, my father was a key board member of National Quality. I've since taken his seat on the board. I have the conclusion of the majority IRB report in my hands as we speak."

"Put Dr. Rogers back on the phone or I'll hang up."

"Are you afraid to speak with me? Maybe I'll call the *Washington Post*. I know that they'll talk with me after I introduce myself as the adopted daughter of Sam Murphy."

Gomez replied coldly, "I've been told that he was a real troublemaker."

Beth cocked her fist, wishing that the Surgeon General was within her sight. "Doctor, the only trouble Sam Murphy ever caused was for evil people like . . ."

Gomez angrily interrupted. "Dr. Rogers, please take me off speaker immediately."

Beth replied calmly, "The Commissioner will be back in a minute. He apologizes, but nature called. As I was saying, the National Quality IRB was close to being deadlocked on the issue. There were two reports, a majority and a minority report.

By their rules, more data should have been requested from Southwest International, but the FDA intervened to approve without formal IRB approval. I'm sure you were aware, as was the National Quality Advisory Board, of the high complication rates in the clinical trials when Zazotene was used at higher doses for other cancers, including lung cancer."

"Ms. Murphy, I have another appointment at this time."

"Let me finish, Dr. Gomez. I hope you didn't use your power to unduly influence the FDA to approve this dangerous drug for any additional cancer indications."

After a pause of several seconds, Gomez added quietly, "I'm going to hang up."

"Hold on. How do you know that a reporter from the *Post* is not here with me? I can just see the reporter becoming upset by your unwillingness to speak about an important health subject that you signed off on."

Beth could hear the prolonged sigh coming through loud and clear. She gave Rogers a high-five.

Gomez said softly, "Ms. Murphy, I'll speak only with Dr. Rogers."

Enjoying the desperation in her voice, the Commissioner replied, "I'm back and fully refreshed. I heard your last comment. You sound upset, Madam General."

"I don't know what you're talking about."

Rogers could hardly contain himself. "The summary that Beth Murphy just read to you will be shared with Governor Peabody as well as with the Michigan and national press. It seems the FDA has some explaining to do as to why they overruled the majority vote of the National Quality Advisory Board. And Dr. Gomez, I'm looking forward to seeing your explanation on CNN tonight."

Waiting for a reaction, they heard only the dial tone. The Governor's office was next. Rogers found himself almost skipping along the marble floor.

••••••••••

Waving to the state trooper guarding the door, Rogers let Beth precede him into the outer office. Not stopping at Mary's desk for permission or pleasantries, he knocked once before flinging the Governor's office door open. He smiled mischievously upon seeing his startled-looking boss talking on the phone.

"Excuse me, Governor, I would like you to meet a friend of mine," Rogers said as he and Beth walked over to sit down before the elected head of state.

Peabody slammed down the phone without saying another word. He glanced over to Beth. She was leaning forward, elbows on the Governor's desk, seemingly enjoying the moment.

"Please meet Beth Murphy. She once accused me of covering up the killing of her father. She now knows better."

Peabody roared, "Commissioner, what the hell is going on here?"

Rogers pointed to Beth.

"Governor, I understand you are a major shareholder in Doctor's Choice Products."

"With all due respect, Miss Murphy, my personal investments are not on the table to discuss. So before I call the state troopers to remove you from my office, I will give you one last chance to leave on your own accord."

She stood for a moment, glaring down at him. She then walked over to his bookcase on the side wall. Beth pulled out one of the books and chuckled.

"Well, Governor William Alfred Peabody, I see one of your favorite reads is *Why Americans Hate Politics.* Could it be because many of the politicians are pure scum?"

The Governor blasted, "Rogers, I've had enough of you. Effective immediately, you are relieved of all of your duties as Commissioner." Peabody picked up the phone. "Mary, please ask the state . . ."

Interrupting, the Commissioner shot back, "I called the *Oldwyck Gazette*. The reporter should be here any minute. I have a story to tell about government corruption and kidnapping. Does any of this sound familiar, Fred?"

Peabody hung up the phone and stood up abruptly. "No need to involve the press."

"I'm not so sure. I bet they would love to hear what I know about a man named Fred and a certain riddle linking Sam Murphy and Peter Chambers."

The Governor was speechless. He looked at the intercom for a second or two before locking sight with the ex-Commissioner.

Rogers asked, "I wonder who they will choose as the next Commissioner of Health."

"As Governor, it's my choice. What do you mean by saying who 'they' will choose?"

"Spare me, please, of your parsing of words. I would predict 'they' will choose Dr. Victor Carver. I'll go one step further. I don't think they'll nominate you for re-election. I've heard the scuttlebutt. Adam Timmons looks like the power brokers' latest candidate du jour."

Seeing Peabody squirm only added to his suspicions.

Peabody shouted, "We can talk, but not with her in the room."

"She stays or I leave to talk with the press. Your choice, Governor Fred."

Pushing himself up from his seat, Peabody began to pace. His face was drawn, and a river of perspiration cascaded down his face and neck. "What do you want me to do?"

"Do what's right. Stop asking who wants what. Governor, I'll bet the Surgeon General was talking with you when Beth and I barged in here a few minutes ago. Face it. Sooner or later, this scandal will hit the papers. But what will you do about the mess you and your buddies have created?"

Circling the room, Peabody wiped his forehead with his handkerchief. The Governor replaced the book that Beth had removed from bookcase. A minute later, he returned to his seat.

"Dr. Rogers, I acted in haste to fire you. I would like you to stay on as Commissioner."

Casting a suspicious eye toward Beth, Rogers thought quickly. "I accept your offer on one condition. I want you to promise that you'll work with Beth and me to uncover the truth about

Doctor's Choice Products, Southwest International, and the FDA."

The Governor sat down and swiveled his chair slowly in a circle. Stopping for a moment or two with his back to his visitors, he returned to face them fully. He leaned forward and held out his right hand to Rogers.

Peabody's perspiring handshake was weak. The Commissioner knew it was all a lie. He motioned for Beth to rise. While walking toward the door, Rogers craned his neck back toward his boss. "It's good to be back on the team, Governor. See you on the local news."

••••••••••

Approaching his office, he could see the troubled look on Sally's face. He knew it all too well.

"Lieutenant Masters from the FBI is waiting in your office to speak privately with you. I've accepted a federal subpoena on your behalf."

Rogers quickly scanned the document. Tossing the papers on Sally's desk, he turned toward Murphy. "Beth, I'll need to meet with the FBI alone."

"What's going on?"

"I'll call you later."

Walking past Masters without acknowledging her, he sat down and drummed his fingers on his desktop. He then spun his chair toward the window, freezing his gaze on Oldwyck Pond. Rogers spoke with his back facing the Lieutenant, having lost all respect for what she had done.

"So the FBI is giving me a subpoena to cease and desist from all investigative activities related to Doctor's Choice Products and anything connected to the pharmaceutical industry?"

He turned his chair slowly to face the FBI chief. She nodded.

"And the subpoena wrapped itself around the axle of national security and the Patriot Act."

"Dr. Rogers, we have our orders from the top."

"Isn't that what the Nazi generals claimed at Nuremberg?"

Masters rose. "That was an entirely different story."

"Maybe. But let me ask you . . . what do your orders say about the deaths of Samuel Murphy, Peter Chambers, Nicki Sanderson, and Tom Knowton? What do your orders say about the thousands of innocent lives that will be lost taking a killer drug that their government sanctioned as safe?"

Masters dropped her head. "I understand your feelings. But I'm in no position to answer your questions."

He shook his head. "That's where you're wrong. If everyone felt they were powerless to do what they believed was right, nothing would ever change."

"With all due respect, I would recommend that you just return to your duties as Commissioner. We'll handle the rest."

Rogers pounded his fist into his desk so hard that the receiver fell off the phone. "Get out of my office with your damn orders. Don't you ever try to tell me again what I should or should not be doing! I'll do what I think is right!"

"I'm sorry that you feel—"

"Get out of my sight!"

Chapter Fifty-Four

It was 7:30 in the morning. Rogers's cell phone rang. When he picked up the text message, he saw that it had been sent the previous evening.

Be in your office at eight tomorrow morning. You will read a prepared statement. Someone will show up and give it to you. If you call the FBI or fail to show, we'll slit Ashley's pretty little throat. THC.

Rogers called Alexis's private cell. It was time to break his promise not to call her. She picked up on the first ring.

"Mrs. Miller, I know that you've been completely truthful with me."

"You have the wrong number."

Rogers tried a different tack. "Is Zach in the house?"

"Yes, of course. Wrong number."

"Alexis, someone kidnapped my daughter. Is it Zach?"

"Yes." She paused. "I'm hanging up. I'm not feeling well. Sir, please call information."

••••••••••

Rogers told Kim what happened. He asked her to stay at home in case he needed her. He raced to the Department of Health. Once inside, he hurried to his office. It was empty. Slamming the door behind him, he sat down at his desk just as his intercom rang out. He pressed the button and heard Sally's voice.

"Beth Murphy is here to see you."

He checked his watch. It was eight o clock. *She's the mole.* How he could have been so gullible as to trust her? "Send her in."

As Beth came in the door, Rogers thundered, "So it's you. You're the one who will give me the speech I need to deliver? You set me up! Anything to get me to trust you." He felt tears sting his eyes. "My daughter was just a device to get what you wanted. You're in bed with these monsters."

Beth's jaw dropped. "What speech? What are you talking about, Commissioner?"

Rogers stared at her. She looked as shocked as he was. He faltered, sitting back down. "Aren't you working for Zach Miller? I got a text message . . ."

"Of course not! I'm here to play a recording for you from Alexis Miller." Beth pointed to the digital recorder on his desk.

"I just spoke to Alexis," Rogers countered. "She didn't mention any recording."

"She called me after she hung up with you. Alexis could no longer ignore Zach's activities. Ashley's kidnapping was too much for her. She wants to end this nightmare before she dies."

"So where did you go after we both returned from the Governor's office the other day? You disappeared while I was still talking to the FBI," Jonathan said, feeling his pulse finally slow.

"I took a call from Alexis."

"This better be good. I'm in no mood for any games."

Beth placed a memory disk into the digital recorder. Alexis's distinctive but barely audible voice told the story. *One day, when my husband didn't think I was lucid, I overheard Zach speaking to Hunter Sanderson about his fight with Peter Chambers. During a brief scuffle, Chambers had fallen back and struck his head on the kitchen counter, suffering a fatal head wound. Sanderson then planted the body in the woods after smashing Chambers's face with a large rock.*

Rogers was speechless.

Alexis continued. *Zach instructed Hunter to flip Chambers's body to be face up after Carver and the Commissioner found it in the woods. Then Rogers's story would be in conflict with the police findings. According to what Zach said, Governor Peabody, the President's Chief of Staff, and the FBI each played a role in covering up for the drug companies and ordering the murders of Sam Murphy and Peter Chambers.*

Rogers put his hand on Beth's shoulder. "When I walked in, I thought you were somehow involved with these bastards. I'm so sorry." Rogers pressed number one on his speed dial. Kim picked up on the first ring.

"Beth just played a recording of Alexis Miller incriminating all of them. They have Ashley."

Kim's words were delivered slowly and deliberately. "Erase it."

"Are you crazy? This recording will put all of them behind bars for life. I'm calling a reporter from the *Gazette*."

Her voice rose to a near shout. "Erase it now! Don't you get it, Jonathan? Whoever these people are, they still have Ashley. If you publicly release the recording from Alexis, they'll kill our little girl."

Rogers's mind was spinning. "This is our opportunity to put these bastards away for good."

Kim screamed through the receiver, "Are you crazy? You're not thinking. If you release this before we safely get our daughter back, I'll kill you myself."

At that moment, the door opened slowly. Rogers watched Victor Carver stroll into his office.

"I have a visitor. Call me later on my private line." He closed his cell.

The oncologist walked over to Rogers and Beth, still huddled over the digital recorder. "Well, what have we here? Listening to Bon Jovi?"

"Carver, you bastard."

"Calm down, old man. So what's the deal?"

Rogers removed the memory disk from the recorder. He dropped it in his shirt pocket. He glared at Carver, wanting to tear him apart and rip his heart out.

"Jonathan, my tennis friend, I think we have some trading to do. I have your speech and you seem to have an interesting recording."

"Not exactly a fair trade."

"Then I'll sweeten the pot. I seem to have something else you want. Your lovely daughter."

"I'll tear you to shreds with my own hands if anything happens to her."

Pulling out a typed page from his inside pocket, Carver shoved it in Rogers's face. "Listen Commish, hand me that recording or else."

"Or else what? I've taken your best shots and survived."

"Stop trying to save the world. You can't win. Save your family. Save Ashley."

"Carver, you asshole. If anything happens to any of my family, I'll hunt you down and stick a knife down your throat."

"Save the silverware for the filet mignon. You wouldn't last that long. Next time, we'll aim for a head shot by a professional shooter."

"How do I know you have Ashley? How do I know you will deliver her safely to me?"

"Trust me; I'm your lifelong friend and colleague."

"Dammit, I want proof that you have my daughter."

"For the last time, hand me the fucking recording and start practicing your speech. In a few minutes, if you're not on TV gushing about the greatness of Zazotene, DCP, and the FDA, I'll give the order to slit her throat. Don't push me any more. Another death won't matter one bit to me."

Carver swaggered around the office, stopping to look out at Oldwyck Pond. He pivoted sharply to face the Commissioner. "It's over, my friend. For you and your petty little idealism. If you had it your way, we'd be curing cancer with tribal herbs and pagan rituals."

"Who's the leader of your group?"

"Stop stalling."

"You're not smart enough to pull this off."

"Jonathan, give me the fucking recording. Now! I'm in charge. Not Zach. Not Peabody. Not the President."

"Come and get it from me."

Carver pulled out his cell. "Ashley will die within the next minute," he said sharply. He paused and lowered his voice. "Come on, it's an easy decision. A few lies to save your daughter's life."

Seconds later, the Commissioner heard a loud knock on the door. A pair of TV technicians bolted through the door for final preparations for the airing.

Rogers's private office line rang. He grabbed for it and shoved it to his ear. It was Kim.

Her voice was clear and measured. "Listen to me carefully. Do not react to what I am about to tell you. Do you understand? Just say yes."

"Yes."

Seeing Carver speaking into his cell at the other end of the room, Rogers yelled out to him. "OK, just hold on. You win."

The oncologist hung up. "You're not as dumb as I thought you were. I'll be right back. I want to make a private call. Then we'll be ready to broadcast.

Rogers turned his back and whispered into the phone. "Alright, Carver can have the recording."

"Jonathan, listen to me. Ashley is safe. She's on her way over to your office under the protection of Detective Darden and half of the Oldwyck Police Department. In a couple of minutes, she'll come into your office. We have much better evidence than the Alexis's recording."

"How do you . . .?"

"The FBI bugged your office. We've been listening to you and Carver the whole time. The maniac is on record. The FBI rescued Ashley after Zach landed in Michigan. He had taken off and left her on his private plane with that redheaded P.I. You were right about Haley. I'm sorry I didn't listen to you."

"Gotta go before Carver returns." He quietly cradled the phone. He took a deep breath just as Carver re-entered.

"Get ready to sell the remarks I wrote for you. And, hand over the disk."

Rogers reached into his shirt pocket and handed over the Alexis memory disk to Carver. As if following a script, the Commissioner donned his suit jacket. Practicing the speech as the cameras focused on his face, he could not help but notice the sarcastic smile that Carver now wore.

"You know, you could have been Surgeon General if you started to play ball sooner."

Rogers asked with a sneer, "I'm curious. Where is Zach? Isn't he the real leader of all of this?"

"My friend, you're looking at the only leader of The Health Club. At this moment, Jordan, London, Peabody, Gomez, and Zach are all huddling around their closed-circuit sets. Your face will be broadcast to a hundred or so oncologists and health departments across America. You're our best salesman. People believe in you."

Where are the police? Where is Ashley? Was Kim under duress to tell him that Ashley was safe? Rogers listened to the customary countdown from ten. At the count of zero, the tech pointed to him.

The Commissioner sat upright. "Good morning, ladies and gentlemen. I'm Dr. Jonathan Rogers, Commissioner of Health for the Great State of Michigan. Welcome to this live broadcast from my office. I'll be addressing you on some important subjects related to the pharmaceutical industry."

Rogers looked over at Carver, who gave him a two-thumbs-up sign. He had no choice but to read the speech. He began, "I'm here to discuss the benefits of . . ."

A split second later, the office door flung open. There was Ashley with a huge smile on her face. She was followed by four Oldwyck detectives with guns pointed at Carver. The Commissioner leaped up from his chair.

"Daddy, it's over!" Ashley ran to him, and he hugged her as she held up her cell phone high in the air. "The evidence is on my cell," she exclaimed proudly.

As the camera rolled, Ashley played back the recorded cell phone conversation of Rick and Haley bragging about their deadly games while they held Ashley hostage on the Cessna.

"Rick, can I join you in listening to Jonathan Rogers's press conference tomorrow?"

"I can arrange that."

"What will Rogers say?"

"He'll announce a Department of Health Task Force to investigate fraudulent billing by certain doctors."

"Won't that attract attention to the leaders?"

"Actually, quite the opposite, Haley."

"What about his daughter?"

"By now, he knows what he has to do to save her. But it won't matter. We can't let either one survive. My uncle Zach always said, never leave witnesses."

Rogers shut off the phone recorder and cast a sideways glance at the handcuffed oncologist.

Carver shouted at Rogers as he was being led out of the room by the police. "You idiot, you just crossed the most powerful people in this country! Don't you know what they'll do to you?"

With one arm around his daughter, the Commissioner just nodded at his former friend and replied, "Good-bye, Victor."

Rogers looked directly into the camera. "I'll be issuing a statement in a few hours about the promotion of unsafe drugs in America. I want to emphasize that most pharmaceutical companies don't behave in such an unethical manner. Doctor's Choice Products is a company run by the worst among us. But without the consent of government at the highest levels of power and the willingness of crooked physician prescribers, The Health Club could never exist."

Rogers paused briefly. "Government has much more . . ." he swallowed hard before continuing, "Government has much more to do to ensure safety in drug development and distribution. But going beyond that, I believe this is a wake-up call for every citizen in America. We all must become more involved in what is happening in our government to ensure that only ethical leaders are appointed to these powerful positions. Our very lives are at stake. Thank you again for your attention."

His desk phone rang just as the cameraman stopped filming. A reporter from the *DuPont Herald* called to ask about a story breaking across CNN. The report stated that President Jordan's press secretary had just issued a public statement saying that the FBI had arrested Zach Miller, Victor Carver, Haley Tyler, Tracey London, and Governor Peabody for murder, kidnapping, extortion, and racketeering. Rick Miller had not yet been found. Federal investigators were also looking at possible criminal charges against the senior management team at Doctor's Choice Products. Prominently mentioned in the investigation was Dr. Randy Phillips, chief medical officer at DCP, who had just announced his resignation. Also on the wire was an announcement that Surgeon General Gomez had recommended that the FDA immediately recall Zazotene from the market until safety concerns could be addressed. Highlighted in the story was Dr. Gomez's promise to do whatever was necessary to uphold the health of all of our citizens. The statement went on with the Surgeon General of the United States of America vowing to work with President Jordan to ensure the safety of all pharmaceuticals. The Surgeon General thanked Mr. Sam Murphy posthumously, on behalf of a grateful America, for blowing the whistle.

Chapter Fifty-Five

Rogers told Kim he needed to go to the Department for an emergency meeting with Acting Governor Holmes. As he drove to the airport, he felt guilty about not telling her the truth. He knew what he had to do. There was no turning back.

••••••••••

"Marissa, I want you to charter a Cessna with the money I wired you. Meet me at Bakers Field Airport."

"Zach, where are we going?"

"We're getting out of the country, my dear. I told the prosecutors plenty. I was lucky to make bail, but I'm certainly not sticking around for any bullshit trial. And the hell with The Health Club. Let them rot in their prison cells."

"But they were your friends."

"I have no friends."

"What about Alexis?"

"It's just you and me, baby. Heading to South America. We have millions."

"Won't they find us? I don't want to spend my life constantly worrying about where the cops will show up next."

"Have I ever let you down?"

Marissa paused. She said, "There's always a first time."

"See you at eight tonight at the airport. Watch for me. I'll be driving my blue Ferrari. Since I can't take the sports car with me, I want to experience the thrill of driving it one last time."

"I'm sure you will," Marissa said as she slammed her cell shut.

••••••••••

Pulling out of his driveway with the top down on the Ferrari, Zach couldn't believe how easy it had been to convince Rogers to meet him at the airport. He laughed out loud so hard that his ribs ached. He took the mountain turns with his usual bravado, the squeals of the screeching tires turning him on. It reminded him of being in bed with Marissa. With one hand on the sawed-off shotgun on the front passenger seat, Zach savored the thought of finishing off the troublesome Commissioner. This time the shot wouldn't miss. As he rounded a series of hairpin curves, he could see the airport a half mile away. Downshifting with glee, he just could not believe his good fortune.

Just then his cell phone rang, demanding his attention.

"Zach, I'm getting nervous out here. I don't want to get arrested."

"Marissa, I'm pushing the limits already."

"The plane is ready to take off. Can't you speed it up?"

Zach hit the pedal and the Ferrari shot forward as if launched out of a giant rubber band. He relished making his sadistic vision come true. Seeing the blood pour out of his nemesis would be a fitting payback for the disruption that Rogers had caused to his power game. Zach fantasized about executing Rogers. He would order the Commissioner to his knees and smack his face with the butt of the shotgun, hoping to fracture his nose, then taunt him with the times he spent with Kim. Anticipating that Rogers would try to fight back, Zach would kick him in the groin, forcing him to beg for his life. Zach laughed so hard at this point in his daydream that he crossed lanes, nearly losing control of his car. He slowed down and focused on his drive. But the final chapter of the Commissioner's execution returned quickly to his mind. He felt his heart racing as he imagined aiming the shotgun to Rogers's face and squeezing off two head shots.

A hundred feet away, he saw the last hairpin left turn. It snaked sharply around the side of Midland Hill before the downhill straightaway to the airport. Zach entered the final turn at sixty-two miles an hour. He slammed the brakes hard. A second later, the pedal hit the floorboard. As he was veering over the line between the road and the side of the hill, he desperately leaned into the curve. Struggling to steer clear of the edge, he yelled, *Hold the line, baby.*

He spun the steering wheel toward the right, trying to regain control. With a screech, it came off its brackets. Panicking, he tried pulling the emergency brake. It failed with a loud boom. With its driver-side tires in midair, the Ferrari was rapidly running out of real estate. Zach popped his seat belt. Standing up, he was about to make a desperation jump out onto the roadway when he caught his foot on the belt. Zach screamed as the Ferrari careened down the embankment. Flipping over once, the Ferrari exploded into a million pieces.

••••••••••

Already at the airport, Rogers heard the explosion. Realizing that it came from somewhere along the road that led to the airport, Rogers jumped back in his car and retraced the route he had taken only a short time before. He saw a huge fireball rising to the heavens. When he arrived at the spot where the Ferrari had left the road, he saw the shotgun lying on the pavement. He picked it up and tossed it into the weeds. It didn't take long to register. His nightmare was over.

••••••••••

"Dylan, it's Marissa. The bastard is burning in hell. I'll see you in DC with the rest of our group, as planned."

"We'll need to pick a new leader of The Health Club."

"Why not you? You were the only one who tried to take Zach out. That means you're our leader."

Epilogue

"The only thing necessary for the triumph of evil is for good men to do nothing."—attributed to Edmund Burke

Rogers and Kim sat for over an hour in the front seat of their Lexus while admiring the majestic view. Parked on the side of Desert View Drive, they gazed down the steep canyon walls that corralled the cascading Colorado River. They climbed out of the car and headed for Hermit's Rest, carefully snaking along the narrow two-foot dirt pathway on the white granite side of the canyon.

Jonathan's cell phone rang, shattering his concentration. He stumbled a bit, one foot sliding on the dusty path near the edge of the walk. Kim reached out and pulled him back. As they leaned against the safety of the canyon wall, Rogers chuckled. He took a quick series of breaths and responded on the sixth ring. Mostly listening, he offered an occasional "thank you" before hanging up.

"Kim, do you remember what I said to you when Jane Williams was elected president?

"That we needed to go back to DC, since we never did get to enjoy ourselves? And also," she added, "that you were happy to stay in Michigan as Commissioner."

"Well, I just took a call from the Chief of Staff for our new President. They want me to interview next week for Surgeon General."

"Jonathan, are you certain that we're ready for that again?"

The thought made Jonathan rub his hands over his chest, feeling the marks of the bullets that almost killed him a year ago.

"Yeah, I'm sure," he replied, smiling.

"I bet you don't know what I'm going to get you for your birthday."

Peeking over his shoulder at the sun setting behind him, Rogers playfully ducked down before replying. "A bulletproof vest!"

"No. What you really want is the prize that you've wanted ever since your mom died."

Smiling, he said, "Being the top doc of the whole country."

He strained to read Kim's expression in the dimming light streaming from the overhead lamps along the West Rim. For tonight, however, nothing else much mattered to Jonathan. He and Kim had been through the worst of times, but they had survived. Gazing out at the magnificence, he squeezed the hand of his lifelong best friend, feeling as happy as he had ever been.